Pauline

A New Beginning on Whidbey Island

Avis Rector

DENVER, COLORADO

Pauline
A New Beginning on Whidbey Island
All Rights Reserved.
Copyright © 2015 Avis Rector
v3.0

Karen Ashurst, Editor
Cover Photo © 2015 Michele Kempees. All rights reserved - used with permission.

Outskirts Press, Inc.
http://www.outskirtspress.com

ISBN: 978-1-4787-4803-8

Outskirts Press and the "OP" logo are trademarks belonging to Outskirts Press, Inc.

PRINTED IN THE UNITED STATES OF AMERICA

In memory of my mother, Genevra Kellogg Weidenbach, who lovingly cared for our family through the Great Depression.

Acknowledgements

Thank you to Toni Grove for suggesting I develop my simple short story into a novel. You encouraged me to create characters and situations. I kept you looking over my shoulder all the way.

Thank you to my teacher and fellow classmates in the Senior Center Writing Class, for despite all your teasing, I learned. It was jolly-good fun.

Thank you to Whidbey Writers Group for taking in a novice. I appreciated your patience, encouragement and friendship. Let's keep writing!

Thank you to my family and friends for your interest and support, and especially to my husband, George, who so often thought of just the right words. He kept me going by saying, "I can't wait to see what happens next."

Chapter One... A Big Decision

Pauline heard Fred stomping his boots on the porch. He came into the kitchen, shrugged off his mackintosh, tossed it over the back of a chair and announced, "I'm out of work."

"You were fired?"

"No, John didn't fire me, but no one can afford new cabinets these days and he can finish up the Barron's job by himself. He needs the work more than I do since he and Martha have the three kids." He took his hat off, went to the stove, poured a cup of coffee and sat at the table. "Tomorrow I'll start looking for work."

Pauline brushed her wet hands down the front of her apron and went over to him. "We'll be okay, dear." She hugged his head against her chest and kissed his thinning hair. "I've been afraid this day would come ever since Glenn lost his job. I've been putting a bit aside from my pay checks just in case."

"In case I lost my job?"

"Yes." She nodded at his puzzled tone.

"Pauline?" He pushed her away and held her at arm's length with an intense look. "It's not like you to keep something from me. Where do you keep it?"

She reached to a top shelf for a red tin can. "When I first started working at Elgin's, Dad told me a penny saved..."

"Is a penny earned," Fred finished. "Ben Franklin coined that phrase."

"Yes, well, Dad gave me his old Prince Albert tobacco can. I saved my pennies and anything I hadn't spent by the end of the month. It got to be a habit. Since Marie and Glenn lost their money, I don't trust the bank. I've been putting aside a dollar or two each pay day. I'm sure we have plenty to keep us until things get better."

"How much?"

"I don't know. Dad made a cut in the top to slip the money through. Here, you open it."

Fred pulled on the lid. "It's really tight. Hand me the screwdriver." After he pried the lid off, bills fell to the table, coins rolled and dropped to the floor. "Wow! This is quite a pile of money."

Pauline picked up the scattered coins.

"At a dollar or two every two weeks since '29... Let's see... It could be over two hundred dollars, a lot of cash to have in the house."

"Yes, enough to pay the rent for a year and more."

"Dear, I can't believe you did this. It's amazing." He drew her close on his lap as they sorted the coins and counted the bills. "This is such a great help."

Pauline glowed at the relief in his voice.

"Look! Two hundred eighty-nine dollars! And to think you've only been making twenty cents an hour. You're always good at keeping our budget."

"And now you find out I'm good at keeping a secret, too."

Fred smiled and ran his hand up her back to her blonde curls. "Well, this is one secret that worked and I guess I better tell you, I have a secret, too. It's something I've been thinking about. You know the letters we got from your brother out in Washington?" Pauline's eyes grew wide. "I think we ought to do it." She got up from Fred's lap, walked away and stood with her back to him. He continued, "And now with this money, we could buy the land."

"Really Fred, we don't know anything about the place," she countered, crossing her arms against her chest.

Fred jumped up. "Okay, let's find out more about that Whidbey Island. We need our map." He searched the desk and found their prized map of the entire United States with its colored states and lakes. He carefully unfolded and spread it out on the kitchen table. They pored over the map and located Washington State and Puget Sound.

"Which one of those squiggles is Whidbey Island?" Pauline frowned. "I wonder how salt water feels on your skin. I don't know about this…"

She found the two letters from her brother, Will, who had moved to Whidbey Island many years earlier with his wife, Marian, and their daughter, Jenny, and began to read the first one.

Dear Pauline and Fred, I know you're having a hard time making a go of it and I think you should come to Washington. Just up the road from my place are a few acres vacant for a number of years and they can be bought by paying the back taxes. There's a house and shed, a bit run down, but it would be a place to raise animals, and like they say, farmers always have meat on the table. Her voice trailed off as she read to herself. "No, Fred, I don't think..."

Fred had answered Will's first letter explaining that although jobs were scarce, he picked up work now and then, and that Pauline still worked at the shirt factory and wasn't keen on the idea of moving. He had asked if there was work out there for a carpenter. He had asked about the weather and how much he'd have to pay for the land.

Will replied with encouraging words. *Fred, The weather out here is mild, reminds me of Michigan. In fact, there are many folks farming here who came from Michigan. I know you don't know much about farming, but Cornet is a small community of farmers who love giving advice. The Martin brothers who came from Bay City live at West Beach only four miles from me. Maybe you know their cousins. You can stay with us while you get your place fixed up. Just come.*

There was also a note from Marian. *Pauline, do you realize you haven't seen our Jenny since she was five years old? She's working for her room and board with a family in Bellingham while taking classes at the college. We have plenty of room and would enjoy having you with us. Love, Marian.*

"Let's think about it, dear. You know I'm not a rash type. Let's sleep on it and then we can decide."

Pauline retorted, "You can sleep on it. That's wilderness out there."

"Well, I might be able to get work making cabinets or even work in the woods."

Pauline chuckled. "Oh, Fred, you've never worked in

the woods."

"No, but I bet I could swing an axe as well as the next fellow."

"Dear, I don't want you working in the woods, it's too dangerous."

Fred, quiet and patient, mulled it over for several days, and as Pauline left for work one morning, he told her, "I'd like to take Will's advice."

"You're really serious?"

"Yes. I'm tired of jumping from job to job. Delivering milk, security job at the prison… never anything permanent. I want to work with my hands, build cabinets. This job with John has been the best in a while. My skills are sharpened now and I'm ready to do more."

"But we don't know if you'll get that kind of work out there."

"If there are new homes, they will need cabinets. Think about it, Pauline."

"I don't see any new homes going up around here."

"The economy might be different there. I'd like to take the chance."

That evening, home from a long day of work, Pauline found Fred waiting at the door and forgoing the usual kiss, he asked, "Have you thought about Will's letters?"

"Oh, Fred, it's been on my mind all day. I'd miss my friends, my work. I've never lived anywhere but here in the city, and moving to a strange place…"

"But think how nice it would be to live near Will and Marian, and to see little Jenny. She's all grown-up.

You haven't seen your family since our wedding thirteen years ago."

Pauline shrugged, walked away and hung her coat in the closet. "I'm going to start supper."

Fred followed her to the kitchen. "You don't have to make up your mind tonight."

Pauline toyed with the food on her plate. Later, she pulled the family picture album from a shelf. She rocked in her favorite chair and thumbed through the pages smiling at the fun times with Will, and there was Jenny in a red wagon cuddling a small furry puppy named Rags. *Jenny's not little any more.* Pauline moved to the couch and snuggled up to Fred. "We've been happy here, I hate to leave."

"Yes, we've had a wonderful life here, but maybe it's time for us to move on." He took his arm from around her shoulder, caressed her cheek, kissed her and murmured, "It will be all right." He got up and unbuttoned his shirt. "Guess I'll turn in."

The next day at the shirt factory, Pauline had a hard time concentrating. She looked up from her sewing machine at the women bent over their work. She enjoyed her position as floor boss and was saddened when a month ago Mr. Elgin had warned the shop would close at the end of March. He had no more orders to fill. The whirring buzz of machines filled the open spaces already vacated by many women he had let go.

The old wall clock struck six. Her co-worker, Marie, called, "Come on, Pauline, that shirt will be there tomorrow. I'll walk you home on my way to get the kids."

Pauline left her machine and went to the coat room where women were scrambling to put on their coats and overshoes. She sat on a bench, struggled with her galoshes, buttoned her coat, and walked out with her friend.

They stepped out into the darkening evening and walked with their hands in their coat pockets. "Brrrr, it's colder tonight," said Marie. They reached the corner where they would part. "Pauline, you seem distracted. What's on your mind?"

"We have letters from my brother. He wants us to come to the island where he lives. He says we could buy a little farm. Fred thinks we should go, but way out to Washington?"

Marie put a hand on Pauline's arm and looked into her eyes. "Go! I'd do it in a minute."

"Really? Leave your home and all your friends?"

"You bet! Glenn and I'd pack up the kids and be on our way. Tell Fred yes before he changes his mind."

"Oh, he won't change his mind. I'd miss you."

"We can write. Maybe someday Glenn and I'll pop in and rest on your front steps."

Pauline embraced her. "You're the dearest friend. You'd be welcome anytime."

She saw Fred sitting on the top step of the porch, and as she went up the walk called, "Okay, dear, Marie helped me make up my mind. I'll go if you're sure the move is right for us."

Fred jumped up, came down the steps, grabbed Pauline, twirled her around and exclaimed, "I'll write tomorrow and tell Will to go ahead and buy the land for us!"

"Okay, okay," Pauline laughed. "Put me down. I have lots to do."

He set her down. "You know, darling, you're as light as a feather."

"Flattery will get you supper, Mr. Gunther." They walked hand in hand up the porch steps.

Fred stepped back and put out his hand. "After you, my lady."

Pauline laughed. "Always the gentleman."

After supper Pauline rummaged through their bedroom closet, opening boxes that had sat on a high shelf and not been touched since her father died several years earlier. She took one out to Fred. "Look what I found in the back of the closet. This is a treasure I have to take. It's Dad's special box." She handed him the ornately carved box. "He kept it on his dresser. He had a key, but I've never found it."

Fred closely examined the wooden box, turning it over and over. "Ah, a hidden drawer that slides out of the bottom."

"Oh, that's the trick!" Pauline grew excited. She watched him push the little drawer out, remove a silver key, turn it in the lock and lift the lid. She picked up a small black velvet box. "It's my mother's wedding ring and Dad's tie stickpins."

"Looks like your dad had some stocks. They're probably worthless." He shuffled through papers. "Here's his birth certificate, and your mother's, and yours, too."

Pauline held up a leather pouch. "I remember this. He kept old silver dollars in it." She shook it over the table and coins and a roll of bills held with a rubber band fell out. "Oh, my goodness!" She drew in her breath and handed the roll to

Fred. "You count them."

The old band snapped and he sorted the bills into piles on the table. "Five hundred sixty-three dollars."

"My gosh! Fred, we're rich!" She gave him a big squeeze.

Chapter Two... Bay City to Seattle

With a clang of a bell and the hissing of steam, the Great Northern train pulled away from the station starting its four-day journey to Seattle. Each chug of the engine took Pauline from the only home she knew. She wiped a smudge from the window with her coat sleeve. Pressing her forehead to the grimy glass pane, she mouthed *I love you* to her friend Marie, who stood on the platform holding the mittened hands of her children, Little Pauline and Charlie.

Pauline dabbed at her eyes with a handkerchief and turned to her husband. "I'm going to miss them, Fred."

"I know, but you can write. Maybe they'll visit someday."

They watched other passengers stow their bags and boxes, getting settled in the coach seats for the long ride.

"Just think, I'm 33 years old and this is the first time I've been away from Bay City, except, of course, on our honeymoon."

He took her hand. "I had fun showing you a good time."

"Yes, it was wonderful."

Fred leaned back in his seat. "I'm going to take a little nap."

Too excited to nap, Pauline looked out the window at the gray industrial buildings. As the train picked up speed leaving the city, she clasped Fred's warm hand. "You've always known what's best for us." She smiled and closed her eyes. Her thoughts turned to when they had first met at Bay City High.

Good thing Marie already had a date with Glenn or she might be Mrs. Fred Gunther. I wonder if Fred remembers our first date. Dad gave me money to buy material to make a new dress and I struggled to make it perfect. Actually, it turned out pretty well... light blue taffeta with big puffy sleeves and net over the full skirt. I wore Mom's pearl necklace and Fred's mother bought a wristlet of tiny pink rose buds for me.

Pauline felt Fred stir and saw his eyes were open. "Fred, do you remember our first date?"

"Sure do. You wore a blue dress."

"Yes, and you sang a song to me."

Fred started singing. "If you were the only girl in the world, and..."

Pauline put her hand over his mouth. "Shh! People will hear you."

He laughed. "I fell in love with you that very night."

"I'm still in love with you. I used to dream of being Mrs. Fred Gunther."

"I had my share of dreaming of a brown-eyed girl with freckles on her nose." He put his hand under her chin and turned her face to him. "Whatever happened to all those freckles?"

"Oh dear, I don't know. They just disappeared with

age, I guess."

Fred sniffed. "Something smells mighty good. Are you hungry?" He looked around the coach and saw other passengers opening lunch boxes. "Let's eat." He pulled their basket from beneath the seat.

Pauline munched on her ham sandwich. "I used to stop by your store on my way home from school just to see you. I really liked your dad even though he teased me."

"Yeah, I could have gone to college, but Dad really needed my help. Then we got into the war and my friends were joining up. When I told Dad I wanted to join the army, he couldn't say no."

"Marie and I cried when we said goodbye to you and Glenn at the train station on your way to Camp Sherman. Ohio seemed so far away. I wondered if I'd ever see you again. Sewing shirts at the factory helped keep me thinking I was helping you. All of us girls thought we were being patriotic. It was the first money I ever earned…fifteen cents an hour."

Fred teased, "Maybe I wore a shirt you made."

"You're silly, but I did make hundreds of shirts. I wrote to you every night while sitting with my dad by his radio. We were anxious for news of the war. Did you know he tacked a world map on the wall so we could keep track of the fighting?"

"My dad did too. I imagine a lot of homes had a map on the wall."

"The day we heard church bells ring and factory whistles blow we stopped working and ran out into the street. People waved flags and yelled an armistice had been signed. We sang and danced far into the night and again the next day. I'll never forget November 11, 1918. It's kind of etched in my mind."

Fred squeezed her hand. "If I'd been home, I would have danced your legs off." He played with her ring. "When I came home from France, I sure wanted to get married."

"But it's good we took Dad's advice and waited until you had work."

"If we hadn't, I'd probably have taken any old mediocre job. You know, at Johnson's I discovered I really like working with wood and I like the smell of it. I get a lot of satisfaction when I've completed a project."

"And for me, working at Elgin's making white shirts again was a welcome change from the army brown. I saved all my money for our wedding. We had such exciting times. Saturday nights seemed like celebrations."

"Yeah, those were fun times. Remember the Avalon Dance Pavilion? We learned all the new dances like the Charleston, and my favorite, a fast Turkey Trot."

Pauline looked at Fred. "Did I ever tell you I was a bit jealous when Marie got married? You stood beside Glenn and I wanted to be a bride instead of the bridesmaid."

"You were a beautiful bridesmaid." Fred put his arm around her, kissed her ear and whispered, "And two months later you were my own gorgeous bride."

Pauline smiled and snuggled against his shoulder. Fred started dozing and she closed her eyes and thought back to their wedding day, June 20, 1920.

I had just had my birthday. I was twenty and Fred, twenty-three. I wore my mother's white-lace wedding dress. No one back then had big weddings. Will got all gussied up in his old suit to be Fred's best man and Marie wore her prom dress. Dad treated all of us to lunch at the Palace Hotel and then we left in Fred's Model A Ford for the five-hour drive to Port Huron, Michigan.

We sang our favorite songs, laughing at our mistakes and trying again. It seemed Fred drove too fast, but he said thirty-five wasn't so fast.

When he said we would stay the night at the Thomas Edison Hotel, I thought it was too expensive. He told me to hush. He didn't want to hear another word about money. He had saved especially so we could have a wonderful time on our honeymoon. And we did.

We got up early the next morning, just as the sun rose, to board the Lady of the Lake. We walked the decks hand-in-hand and when Fred asked me, "Are you enjoying the day, Mrs. Gunther?" I giggled, "Oh, yes, Mr. Gunther, I'm so happy." When I danced away from him, he chased me. People just smiled and stepped back.

He said Mrs. Gunther was having too much fun. I loved it when he called me Mrs. Gunther. Oh my, we hugged and kissed and didn't care what the other passengers thought.

After lunch, when he said he would like to take a little nap, I told him, "You can take a nap, but Mrs. Gunther isn't tired." He laughed and then rested in the lounge chair while I wandered to the back of the boat and leaned over the deck rail. The flying seagulls seemed to float above the foamy wake. I waved to passengers on passing boats and they waved back.

When I heard the Lady of the Lake's horn announcing the

arrival at Goderich, I ran to Fred. I hated to wake him, but it was time get off the boat.

The little town was pretty with all the trees along the streets. We looked in the windows of the shops and went down to the beach while waiting for the ferry. We took off our shoes and played wave-tag. Oh my, we had fun. I thought we would go right back home after returning to Port Huron, but Fred said he had one more surprise...we would go to the theatre to see Charlie Chaplin. Goodness, we laughed until our tummies hurt.

Chapter Three... Seattle to Whidbey

"We're here, Pauline." Fred nudged her. "Wake up, we're in Seattle." The Great Northern pulled into Union Station, steam drifting away from its cylinders. The coach car became noisy as tired passengers retrieved their belongings.

Pauline peered out the window hoping to see her brother standing on the platform. "Look! There's Will!" She tapped on the window and then made her way up the aisle. "Come on, Fred."

After kisses and hugs, Will guided them through the parking area to his black Model T. "I know you're tired. We're going to spend the night at a hotel and drive to Whidbey in the morning. It'll take about three hours to get there. Paulie, how would you like a nice soak in a big bath tub?"

"I can't think of anything more heavenly. We haven't slept in a hotel since staying at the Thomas Edison on our honeymoon."

"Marian said to take you to the Bergonian. It's one of the newer hotels, built in 1927."

"Look at the tall building to the left, Pauline," said Fred. "It certainly stands out above the others."

"The Smith Tower," said Will. "Tallest building west of the Mississippi, almost five hundred feet tall, built in 1914."

"Is it a hotel?"

"No, it's filled with business offices. Someday Marian and I will bring you back here and we'll explore the city."

Will pulled up to the entrance of the luxurious Bergonian Hotel. Pauline exclaimed, "Fred, isn't it beautiful?" She nudged him when the bellhop met them at the car and took their suitcases.

A doorman held the glass door open and they stepped onto a shiny white marble floor. *Oh my, this is so exciting!* Will checked in with a man behind the long mahogany reception desk.

The bellhop carried their suitcases and showed them to their room. Pauline went to the window, drew a curtain aside and looked out at Seattle. "Fred, come here. We can see the water and the far away mountains."

"Hmm…across the water, those must be the Olympics we saw on the map."

Will said, "That's right, and tomorrow I'll point out Mount Rainier to the south."

Pauline said, "I just love this room with its thick maroon carpet, and Will, you promised me a bath."

"Okay, Paulie, and then we better get some supper in the dining room."

She opened the door to the bathroom. "My word, isn't this just too grand?" The walls were a soft green that coordinated with the small green and white square floor tiles.

Fred looked at the porcelain tub standing on its claw feet. "Fit for a queen, Pauline."

She soon immersed herself in the large tub filled with scented warm water. After peacefully relaxing and almost falling asleep, she heard Fred tap on the door and say, "Hey, we're hungry."

Stepping out of the tub, Pauline wrapped herself in a fluffy white towel and called, "I'll be ready in ten minutes."

On the way to supper, she told her brother, "That was the best bath I've ever had."

They entered the dining room and were seated at a round table covered with white linen. Crystal goblets sparkled in the light of chandeliers hung from polished brass chains. Pauline's eyes glowed with excitement. "This is so elegant, Will. Are you sure we should…"

"Now Paulie, don't even think the word expensive. This is my treat."

Fred and Will ordered the special of the day, corned beef and cabbage. Pauline said, "I'll have the chicken pot pie."

While enjoying their meal, she pointed out details of the room—the textured wallpaper, the heavy maroon drapes held back with golden cords, the landscape paintings in ornate gilt frames.

Always nearby, their attentive waiter removed their finished dishes and suggested a selection of desserts. "No, no dessert for me," said Pauline. "I'm tired. That four-poster bed with the down pillows looked very inviting."

After a quick breakfast the next morning and a last glance around the lobby, Pauline followed Will and Fred out of the hotel. She remembered to ask Will to point to Mount Rainier. The sun shone on the snowy mountain top. Pauline said it was gorgeous and looked just like a picture postcard. They stopped at the train station, arranged for their trunks to be shipped to Whidbey, and then started the eighty-mile drive north on Highway 99.

Will answered their many questions as they travelled over the paved highway. "Everett is a sawmill town. Logs used to be floated down the rivers, but now, most are trucked down from the surrounding forests."

As they neared Silvana, Will veered off the highway and parked his Model T by a monstrous tree stump. "Time to stretch the legs."

They got out of the car. "Wow! Look, Fred," said Pauline.

Will explained, "Loggers cut down a gigantic cedar leaving this sixteen-foot stump, then it was brought here and they cut an arch big enough to drive through."

"Wonder how old it was," mused Fred as he and Pauline stood inside the cavernous burned-out stump.

"Oh, they say it's over a thousand years, maybe twelve hundred," said Will.

Pauline felt the thick rough bark. "Can we drive through it?"

"As soon as you get back in the car, Paulie."

On the two-lane highway again, Will answered Fred's questions. "The farmers in Skagit County grow vegetables for seed, and the valley is beautiful in the spring with fields of tulips and daffodils grown for the bulbs."

When they reached the Swinomish Channel, Will stopped behind several cars. "We have to wait for the drawbridge to open."

Pauline asked, "Can we get out and watch?"

They walked close for a clear view of the tall structure. Fred studied the construction of the towers as Will explained about the concrete block counter-weights. "Cables are attached to wheels at the top of each tower. When the operator in the gatehouse pushes a button, the cables pull up the middle section. Masts on some of the boats are too tall to go under the unopened bridge. Boats always have the right-of-way. Sometimes it stops road traffic twenty or more minutes. Look to your right and you'll see a purse seiner fishing boat coming through, probably taking a morning catch of salmon to the cannery in La Conner."

Pauline called, "Hello!" and waved to the men on the boat deck as it chugged through.

When the gatehouse came down, they got in the car and were on their way again.

"That was fun. Did you see the men wave back to me?"

"There's more excitement coming, Paulie," said Will as he drove over the bridge. Now we're on Fidalgo Island. Soon we'll be at Dewey Beach to take the *Cup and Saucer* over to Whidbey."

"*Cup and Saucer?*"

"Yep. It's what the local folks call the little ferry. It depends on the tide what kind of ride we'll have. I think we're going to hit it at slack tide."

"What do you mean?" asked Pauline.

"Well, do you remember the high tides and low tides when we were at the beach at Lake Superior?"

"Yes, I remember them, but what's slack tide?"

"When the water is flowing in, we call it high tide. When the water is going out, it's called an ebb tide or low tide.

At slack tide the water kind of stops flowing in or out. You might say when the water is calm, it's resting. When it's not slack, the water rushing through the narrow passages creates large whirlpools with sunken centers. It can be dangerous, especially in a small boat, and depending on the tide, if there's a storm the ferry won't run."

"What you're saying is slack tide is between the incoming and outgoing tides."

"Right, Paulie. When we go to West Beach there will be sandbars if the tide is real low. If it's a minus tide, we dig for clams. At real high tide you won't be able to walk on the beach because the water will be up to the driftwood."

"What if it's not slack tide when we go on the ferry?"

Will grinned at Fred. "Then you'll see whirlpools that will suck you under if you fall in the water."

Pauline looked at her brother. "You haven't changed a bit, Will, still a big tease. Has anybody actually been sucked under?"

"You should talk to old man Jorgen. He can tell you everything about the water. He was born here and has fished all his life. He's a great story teller. It's fun to visit with him."

Pauline sat back and listened while Will told about the town of Anacortes and the little settlement called Dewey Beach. Driving down to Blout's Point they saw the large sign "Blout's Bazaar, Gas, Oil and Other Stuff."

"Here we are, and it looks like the tide is coming in. We timed it just right," said Will.

Pauline and Fred looked at the flat-bottomed boat that could take several cars on each side of a small elevated booth where the captain navigated. Pauline noticed a rowboat hung from two wooden posts on one side of the deck. "If that's the lifeboat, it sure won't hold many people."

Will said, "I've never heard it needed to be used." After paying the fee, he drove onto the ferry.

"I'd like to get out of the car."

"Go ahead, Paulie, but the deck will be slippery. Better get out and hold on to her, Fred."

Will got out too, and they stood beside the car. Fred put an arm around Pauline's waist and draped his other arm over the open window in the door. The diesel engine came to life and the ferry started its slow journey across the green water.

The boat rocked up and down in the small swells. Wind blew Pauline's hair in her face and she tasted salt in the water spray. She rested her head against Fred's shoulder taking in the view and listening to the men talk.

Will explained, "In another year or so we'll have a bridge. Actually, there will be two bridges. See the little island there between Fidalgo and Whidbey? It's called Pass Island. There's a channel of water on each side of it. One span will connect Fidalgo to the small island and from there a second span will connect to Whidbey."

Fred asked, "How long has the bridge been in the works?"

"Talk of it started a long time ago. Captain George Morse, who settled in Coupeville, thought there should be a bridge to connect Whidbey and Fidalgo Islands. Way back in 1907, as a state representative, he introduced a bill for $90,000 toward building a bridge. Studies were made and plans were drawn. In fact, someone built a large model bridge which was displayed at the 1909 Alaska-Yukon Expedition in Seattle."

"I suppose some people were against a bridge."

"You're right. Berte Olson, the ferry boat captain really fought it, but she lost the battle."

Pauline asked, "A woman is the captain?" She looked through the window into the small cabin at a husky, buxom woman. "I thought she was a man. She sure dresses like one."

"You would too if you worked out in the cold." said Will. "Yep, she's one smart woman, designed two car ferries, this one and another that runs farther down the island over to Camano Island. After WWI the American Legion formed the Deception Pass Bridge Association and in 1923 the state designated the area as a park. The Legion has been holding potluck picnics every year and making speeches trying to get people interested in a bridge. About five years ago the state legislature finally passed the Bridge Bill and last year they gave the Parks Department permission to build a toll bridge, but no one wanted to pay money to use a bridge."

Fred asked, "So how did they get the money for a bridge?"

"Oh, finally the legislature came up with about $250,000, the county chipped in $150,000 and they got about $80,000 from the Federal government."

Fred said, "Quite a bit of money."

"Yeah, but the bridge is going to be worth every penny."

Pauline said, "Here comes another fishing boat."

The *Cup and Saucer* slowed, letting the motor idle while the seiner passed. Waves splashed onto the deck as the ferry rocked back and forth. Pauline waved to the crew. She lost her balance and Fred tightened his arm around her. She felt safe. She stretched her neck looking up at the evergreen trees clinging to the jagged rock walls. "Isn't it beautiful?"

"Yes, it is."

Will said, "See those white heads in the trees?"

"Eagles," said Fred.

"Yep, they're everywhere around here," said Will. "Earlier this spring men started blasting rock to make room for the approaches to the bridge. You'll probably hear the blasts and the sound of jackhammers. My friend, Hank Martin, is the county road supervisor overseeing the work on the Whidbey side. Many of the local farmers are picking up extra money working on the roads and the CCC's are…"

Pauline interrupted, "What are the CCC's?"

"The C's stand for the Civilian Conservation Corps. President Roosevelt started the program to put guys to work during these hard times. There are about two hundred men living down at Cornet Bay. Years ago the local folks built a bath house, a kitchen and trails as well as a couple roads, but now the CCC's are at work making improvements throughout the whole park. We'll have to hike down to Cranberry Lake to see what all they're doing."

Will pointed out Ben Ure Island and then said, "Look up at the cliff behind us on Fidalgo Island. There used to be a prison up there for convicts sentenced to hard labor. They were here to quarry rock. They operated rock crushers on the face of the cliff up there. The rock dropped into a huge wooden bunker and went down a chute onto scows below. Then it was taken to the Seattle waterfront to be used as landfill."

"Dangerous place to work," said Fred. "Anyone ever get killed?"

"Didn't hear of anyone, but one time they put too much

on one side of a barge and it flipped over and dumped its load. About fifteen years ago, Joe Andrews, who lives near me, and his brothers tore down all the structures. Most of the lumber was barged to Seattle. But later, Joe rowed his boat out, and with Hank Martin's help, tied a bunch of the boards together and towed them into Cornet Bay. Joe built a chicken coop with them."

The *Cup and Saucer* slowed and they got in the car.

As Will drove off the ferry, he pointed and said, "See the round saw blade hanging over there from the pine tree? If the ferry is on the other side, you pound on it with a big mallet to call attention that you want to cross. We usually have to wait twenty or so minutes if the ferry is on the other side. Just depends on the tide."

As they continued on Cornet Road along the shore, Pauline asked, "Do you have a boat?"

"No, but I've gone fishing with Bill Jorgen a few times. I love catching the big salmon!"

Turning up Ducken Road, he said, "We'll be home in about five minutes and Marian will have lunch for us."

He honked the horn as he drove into the yard. Pauline saw Marian, wearing an apron over her everyday house-dress, come flying out of the house letting the screen door bang shut and hurry down the porch steps to the car. "Oh, Pauline and Fred, you're finally here!"

During lunch Marian asked many questions about their trip.

"I liked watching the drawbridge with the Indian name go up and down," said Pauline. "But the ferry ride was the best. The rock cliffs are beautiful and we saw eagles perched in the trees."

Will interrupted the women's chatter. "I know you're anxious to see your new place, Fred. Jorgen helped Marian milk the cows last night and this morning, but I need to clean out the floor gutters before milking tonight. You and Pauline take the car up and explore. I'll see you for supper." He gave Fred directions to their property and left for the barn.

Chapter Four... Their Property

Fred drove from Will's house out to Ducken Road and the half-mile up the graveled road to a barbed-wire gate. He turned off the motor and they sat for a moment looking at a rusty three-strand fence held up by rotted posts. "Looks like this is it," said Fred. They got out and as he opened the gate, a broken wire caught on his trousers. He bent to untangle it.

Thistles and dandelions covered the ground. Clumps of snowberry bushes and Oregon grape growing around rock piles dotted the hillside. Fred took Pauline's hand as they walked up the slope. Wild blackberry vines caught on their shoes. Pauline ran her hand down her leg. "Nerts! My stockings will be ruined."

Fred stood with his hands in his pockets. Pauline held his arm. They saw the roof of a building above overgrown bushes and weeds.

"Is that the house with all those bushes around it?" she asked.

"I think so."

Pauline slowly shook her head and said softly, "Goodness,

Fred, what have we bought?"

"A lot of work." As they walked closer to the building, he pushed bushes out of their way. "This lean-to must have been added." A jumble of rope, a pitchfork and an old bucket were strewn about in a pile of matted straw. "Looks like it was used as a barn."

"Are we going to have animals?"

"Depends. Would you take care of them?"

"I've never taken care of any animals. Maybe I could have chickens. They probably don't take too much work and it's good to have fresh eggs."

"I know I don't want to milk any cows," said Fred. "Will told me we would find a spring about half-way up to the southeast corner. I'd like to find it. Want to come?"

"No, I'm not dressed to go tramping through brush. I'll wait for you. Maybe I can look in the house."

"I won't be gone long." He pushed his way through the overgrown scrub.

Pauline picked her way through the tall weeds. She felt a sharp scratch on her leg. "Ouch!"

Chunks of old split wood lay scattered near a large round block used for chopping. She broke off brittle branches of a lilac bush and found the porch. Weeds grew between the cracks of the thick moss-covered boards. She put a foot on a plank step, decided it was strong enough, and climbed two more steps onto the wide porch. Closed-in on both ends, it fronted the width of the house. Leaves lay in piles in all four corners.

The door came open with a tug on the rusty door handle. Stale, musty air whooshed out at her. Cobwebs formed netting over the opening. She picked up a broom and batted them down, then stepped inside the one-room house onto dirty, faded, brown and green linoleum. Ropes of cobwebs hung from the open-beam rafters. Sunlight streamed through a cracked window pane highlighting suspended dust mites in the air. Old wool socks and towels hung from a wire strung from one side of the room to the other.

Pauline saw three straight-backed kitchen chairs pulled up to a small table coated with dust. A fourth chair was tipped over on the floor. A large wardrobe stood in one corner of the small room, a bed in another. Dirty light bulbs hung on black cords from rafters. She pulled on a chain, but no light shone. Hearing Fred, she went out on the porch. "Any luck? Did you find the spring?"

"Yep. There used to be a trail, but now it's pretty much covered with salal and snowberries. Had to step over rotting logs and go through thick undergrowth, but I found it." He came up on the porch and showed her his scratched hands. Pauline brushed leaves and twigs from his shirt. "Water bubbles up and pools around mossy rocks. Looks like plenty of water flows from it."

"Is it good to drink?"

"I scooped up a bit in my hand. It doesn't smell and it tasted fine. Lots of horsetail and those little yellow buttercups grow where water seeps down the slope. It's a long way to carry water."

"The house is a mess. Come see inside."

Pauline's heel caught in a crack in a board and she walked out of her shoe. She held Fred's arm while he slipped it back onto her foot. He followed her through the door.

She said, "I used an old towel and wiped the windows. There are trees in bloom."

"Apple trees, maybe pear."

"If you look out the broken window, you can see water over the tops of the trees."

Fred said, "That's west and those dark hills must be more islands. We might have good sunsets."

Pauline brushed at her hair. "Yuck! It feels like spiders."

Fred grabbed a long cluster of cobwebs and pulled it down from a rafter. He looked at the table and chairs. "We might be able to use some of this stuff."

"It's shabby and dirty."

"Hold on a minute." Fred turned the chairs this way and that. "There's no reason we can't use these." Putting his hands on the table, he tried to jiggle it. "The table seems strong. We can throw a coat of paint on it and the chairs. They'll do fine until I can make something better." He brushed his hands together.

Pauline lifted the corner of a rumpled blanket on the bed. "Yikes!" Mice scampered to dark corners. "I won't sleep on this filthy mattress."

"No, it will have to go. The wrought iron bedstead will probably be okay, just needs a new mattress." Fred pushed his hat back and scratched his head as he scanned the room. "We have a lot of work ahead of us. I'll ask Will to help take out the big stuff. Whoever lived here tacked up cardboard and newspaper between the studs to keep out the wind. It must have been mighty cold."

"Maybe that's why they left."

"I'll get plywood to cover the walls. We can stuff newspaper in between. We'll paint everything."

Pauline said, "It's going to take a lot of scrubbing with hot water and soap."

"Yep, it will, but your brother said he'll help us. Tomorrow I'll take a look at this old stove. It's getting late, let's go down to Will's place. Marian said she likes to have supper around six."

While eating, the conversation centered on the house and what needed to be done. Fred said he'd like to climb up on the roof and check it out. "There are about two inches of moss on the north side and shingles missing on the west."

Will asked, "Have you checked the foundation?"

"No, but I will. The whole house is surrounded by vegetation. There's a small building, looks like a shed, but the door's nailed shut. There's also an outhouse almost completely covered with vines and fireweed. It will have to be one of my first jobs. But then, maybe I should just burn the whole thing down and build a new one."

Pauline sat quietly, playing with her fork on the table cloth.

Marian asked, "What are you thinking, dear?"

"Oh, I'm just planning what I'm going to do first."

"And what will that be?"

"While Fred's busy with the roof and outhouse, I'll clean the house."

Fred said, "I'll cut the brush from around the porch, then you can get in and out easier."

Pauline said, "There's so much work to do, Marian, and

I didn't bring any old clothes."

"You can wear a pair of my pants and an old shirt. You know there are many men who need work. Why don't you hire someone to help?"

Pauline glanced at Fred. "No, we can do it."

He looked at her and grinned. "Yeah, we can do it."

Chapter Five... Checking the House and Shed

At breakfast the next day, Will swallowed the last of his coffee and then said, "I'm anxious to see what you've got up there, Fred. I walked around the place a bit before I wrote to you about it being for sale, but didn't look in the buildings. I knew it would take a lot of work to fix up, but I think it's worth it." He pushed back from the table. "Shall we go?"

"You bet!" said Fred. "Do you have a ladder long enough to reach the house roof?" As the men went out, they talked about what they needed to take with them.

"Why didn't they wait for me?" Pauline complained to Marian when she came out of the bedroom dressed in Marian's trousers and a flannel shirt.

"They're excited." She looked at Pauline. "My sakes, but those are too short for you. You're at least three inches taller than me."

"Beanpole. That's what the girls called me in gym class. *Give the ball to Beanpole.* I was pretty good putting the ball through the hoop, but I liked playing field hockey better. Did you like sports?"

"Not much. I think I spent most of my time in the library.

I'll drive you up."

"Thanks, but I can walk. I need the exercise after sitting on the train for three days. See you later."

It was a sunshine and blue sky day. Black-capped chickadees perched on the fences along the road kept Pauline company. She hummed a tune and enjoyed the walk to her house on the hill.

She heard her brother's loud voice as she neared the shed. "Look at all this stuff! You've sure got a bunch of tools here, Fred."

"Good the door had been nailed shut or someone would have helped themselves."

"Well, this far off the road, no one probably ever came up here. Old man Jorgen is about the only person I see walking on Ducken Road. He lives over on Monkey Hill Road."

Amused by their enthusiasm, Pauline watched through the open door. Fred said most of the tools were pretty rusty and needed sanding and oiling. He looked through a bunch of gunnysacks, letting them slide to the floor. "Look here."

"Shakes. You might need those to patch the roof. Did you see this splitting axe? You'll need it to keep Pauline supplied with firewood," said Will.

"Yeah, that's for sure." The men laughed and pointed out treasures as they checked all the boxes on the shelves and workbench. There were screwdrivers, a hammer, an old coffee can half-full of nails, another with nuts and bolts, and other stuff men seem to collect.

Will said, "Hey, look up."

Pauline stepped through the door. "What's up there?"

An eight-foot long saw with wooden handles lay on the

rafters. Will said, "It might be the saw used to cut down the huge firs in your woods. It took two men to work it."

Pauline said, "Sounds like hard work."

"That's why they call it a misery whip."

"Did you know the people who lived here?"

"Nah, they left before Marian and I bought our land. Maybe the fella got tired of trying to make a living here. Logging is hard work and there are a lot of accidents."

Fred said, "Maybe I'll use it to saw a log someday. Pauline can be on one end." He looked at her and chuckled, "Right, dear?"

"Don't think I couldn't do it," she retorted. "I'm pretty strong."

Fred grinned at her spunk. "Will, come see the house. I know the roof needs work, but let's take a look at the foundation."

Pauline watched her husband and brother pull brush and tall weeds away from the house. Thick-cut cedar shakes of different widths had been nailed to the bottom of the fir planks of the outer walls. Fred crouched down, pulled a few off and tossed them aside. He and Will peered under the house. The ends of peeled logs had been placed on large rocks in each corner. The logs supported three-inch thick by fifteen-inch wide fir boards, their ends placed on top of the logs from one side of the house to the other making the floor.

Will stood up. "The fellow who built this knew what he was doing. It was a smart way to build the floor up off the ground."

"Yeah," Fred agreed, "and the shakes help keep the wind

from blowing under. Let's check out the roof."

Will carried the ladder from his truck and Fred helped set it against the house. They climbed up and crawled over the mossy shakes pointing and nodding their heads as they talked.

Pauline called, "Is it okay?"

Fred said, "It needs a new roof."

"It's in pretty poor shape," agreed Will. "You've got a great view from up here."

Pauline called, "I'm coming up."

Will looked down at her. "Paulie, are you sure?"

"I can climb ladders as well as you." She was on the third rung of the ladder when one foot slipped. "Rats!" The ladder slid sideways. She jumped off and back as it landed on the ground.

Standing with her hands on her hips, she looked up at them.

"Pauline, set it back up against the wall," said Will.

She struggled to lift the wooden ladder while Fred and Will yelled advice. "Nope, I can't do it. Guess you'll be up there for a while. I'll walk down and get Marian to help me. I'll hurry."

Marian, working in her garden, laughed as Pauline told her about leaving them on the roof.

When they drove into the yard, the men were standing on the ground.

Pauline said, "How did you get the ladder up?"

"Did you really think we'd stay up there and wait for you?" asked Will.

Fred said, "Your brother is quite an acrobat."

Will said, "It's only a ten-foot drop. Just bend your knees as your feet hit the ground." He gave Marian a superior look. "Come on, dear, let's go home and let these two get to work, I've got chores to do."

Pauline watched them drive away, Will in his truck and Marian in her car. She turned to see Fred climbing the ladder. "Now what?"

"Now you come up and look at this view. I'll hold the ladder. You can see the San Juan Islands. Come on up, you boasted to Will you can climb ladders."

"I *can* climb the ladder, but the roof might be slippery."

"No, the moss is dry. I'll help you."

She climbed the ladder to the top and Fred helped her onto the roof. She crawled on her hands and knees to the ridgeline and looked down at the trees.

They sat together. "See all the islands?" Fred asked. "We saw them on the map at the library. Will said Lopez is to the north of us and the dark blue shape farther out is Vancouver Island in Canada." He pointed southwest and said, "The small spot that looks like a ship is Smith Island."

Pauline said she remembered the map and turned to look northeast. "That must be Mount Baker. The snow is beautiful against the blue sky. Marian told me they've picked wild blueberries in the meadows in the fall." She wiped her forehead. "I'm too warm. I shouldn't have worn this flannel shirt. Look, someone's down by the trees watching us."

Fred scanned the trees below. "I don't see anyone."

"Well, he's gone now, but I saw a man by the bushes."

"Probably a deer. Will said we'll see a lot of them."

"Hold the ladder, Fred. I don't want it to slide." She

scooted on her bottom down to the ladder and he held it for her. Safely on the ground, Pauline held the ladder for him.

He said, "Let's start taking what you call 'dirty old junk' out of the house." Feeling inspired and ready to have at it, they went into the house. "Will said he'll haul away anything we don't want. We'll just set it outside."

They put the table, chairs and a small dresser out on the porch. Pauline said she could help move the bed. They dragged all the bedding and the stained cotton mattress outside and made a pile.

"This couldn't have been a comfortable bed," said Fred, as he carried out the springs. They dismantled the iron bedstead.

Pauline opened the door of the old wardrobe. Inside they found a woman's black wool coat, housedresses, and a child's winter coat on wire hangers. Pauline took dusty lids off boxes filled with undergarments, hats and mittens. Mice had eaten holes and nested in towels and blankets on one shelf. Shoes and rubber boots lay on the floor.

Fred stooped and took an armload outside. "Whoever lived here sure didn't bother to take all their clothes. They must have left in a hurry."

"I wonder who they were," said Pauline.

"I might as well take everything out, or do you want to wear something?"

"You are being silly, Fred. You know I wouldn't wear any of it. Whoever wore these clothes wasn't very tall." She held up a dress. "It doesn't even come to my knees, but the material is still good. I can use it for my braided rugs."

Fred looked at the black wool coat. "The moths loved

this. I'll throw it out."

"Wait, let me check the pockets." She pulled out an ornate silver locket on a long chain. "This is beautiful. Why would a woman leave this behind?" She found the clasp and popped it open to see a picture of a young couple. "I think this picture was taken a long time ago. Women don't wear big hats with feathers anymore. I wonder who they are. Someone must be able to tell us. Maybe Marian will know." Pauline hung the locket on a nail in the wall of the wardrobe.

Fred said, "Let me get the stuff off that high shelf." He stepped in front of her and reached up. "Here's a basket of some sort."

"It's a sewing basket." She opened it and found pillowcases. The embroidered roses and leaves hadn't been finished and the tatted lace edging hadn't been sewn on. "It's beautiful work, the stitches are so tiny. We shouldn't throw it out, but I wouldn't feel right finishing someone else's work. I'll look through it later."

"The wardrobe smells so musty, Fred. Can we get rid of it?"

"Yeah, we'll take it out and someday I'll build a nice closet."

It was a struggle, but by pushing and rocking the wardrobe from side to side they moved it onto the porch. Fred said, "I'll have Will help me take it to the shed. I can keep my tools in it." He looked at his watch. "It's time we see if Marian has some lunch for us."

They took one last glance around the room, closed the door, and walked down the hill.

After a quick lunch, Fred headed back to clear away

more brush. Pauline washed the dishes. "I'd rather wash your dishes, Marian, than those in the sink up at the house. Besides, I don't have any water," she laughed, "but I did find a small plate inside a box of NuBora soap."

"Well, that's a good find," said Marian." By the way, Will's going to fill milk cans with water and take them up to your porch."

"Wonderful! I can use it. I better go so I can get started cleaning the messy kitchen."

"Nerts!" Pauline looked at the dirty pans and utensils in the sink. "I'm not going to keep any of this rubbish." Dusty plates, bowls and cups were stored on open shelves on each side of the window. She took down opened food boxes. Mouse droppings littered the shelves, windowsill and counter. "Yuck! What a mess!"

She found wooden orange crates under the counter, reminding her of those her father had used as shelves in his workshop. The crates held odds and ends of kitchenware and jars of canned fruit turned black from age.

A large galvanized washtub hung on the wall. She got it down, put the jumble of stuff into it, and then pulled it out to the porch. On second thought, she decided if there weren't any holes in the tub, it would be useful. She emptied it, adding everything to the pile Will would haul away.

"Fred," she called, "You-hoo! Fred!"

"I'm out here."

Walking through the weedy yard, she stepped on a hard object. Pawing the dirt she found a toy car. Fred was using a pick and a shovel to dig up the brush growing around the outhouse. She held out her hand. "Look what I found."

"Must have belonged to the little boy who left his boots in the wardrobe."

"I wonder what happened to him."

"We'll probably never know. Want to help? You can carry this stuff over to that pile."

Pauline dragged the vines and brush to the pile a short distance away. They worked until she said her arms were tired. "I'm not used to using these muscles and I've got scratches all over my hands. I told Marian I would help with supper tonight. We can get an early start tomorrow."

"Okay, but first I'd like you to see the spring. Come with me."

Pauline ducked her head as Fred held back blackberry vines and rosebushes. As they came to a small clearing, she heard the faint sound of rippling water. "Look, someone planted daffodils. This is a lovely spot."

She knelt in the grass, reached down over the rocks, washed her hands, and then cupped water in them and took a sip. "It does taste good."

They sat on the rocks for a few minutes and then walked past their house on the way to Marian's.

Chapter Six... The Stove

Back at their house the next morning, Fred said, "I'd like to take out that old linoleum." They started rolling up the worn floor covering. Fred lifted the corners of the stove one at a time so Pauline could pull the linoleum off piece by piece. They took the scraps out to the yard.

"I can replace these boards," said Fred, looking at the wide floor planks. "What do you think?"

"I kind of like them. After they've been cleaned and varnished, I can dress them up with my braided rugs."

"Okay, that sounds like a good plan." He lifted the lid on the stove and poked at the grates. "The rust stains on the chrome can be polished. It's like the one my grandmother had, except hers had a reservoir for hot water."

A blackened teakettle and a white enamel basin with red trim sat on the old Monarch stove. Worn potholders lay on top of the warming oven above the stove top. "Here's lunch!" joked Fred, playfully holding up a dried mouse by the tail to show Pauline.

"Yuck!" She slapped it out of his hand to the floor, and then picked up a black and silver object. "What's this?"

"It's used to lift the stove lid." Fred inserted the blunt end of the curled chrome handle into the hole in the round lid. "See how this door opens?" Ash dust fell to the floor. "The box needs to be emptied. I'll put the ashes into one of those old pots and save them for our garden. Ashes are ideal for growing potatoes."

"How do you know?"

"It was my job to empty the ashes and carry in wood for Aunt Minnie when I lived at Uncle Jack's farm." Fred drew his pocketknife from his overalls pocket and began cutting on a cedar stick. "At night my dad sat beside the stove and cut the kindling for the morning fire." Pauline watched as Fred feathered out the ends of several sticks. "The chimney might need cleaning, but I'll take care of it later. Bring me some of that old newspaper and I'll start a fire." He wadded the paper, stuffed it in the firebox and placed the cedar sticks on top. He lit a match to the paper. Flames came up through the kindling, crackling and spitting up sparks. Fred was about to put chunks of dry fir wood on top of the burning kindling when smoke billowed out of the seams of the chimney pipe. "Oh, shucks! I should have checked the chimney first." He shut the damper down tight to put out the fire.

Pauline ran out of the house and called back, "There isn't any smoke coming out of the chimney."

"Okay, it's back up on the roof."

Pauline held the ladder and Fred climbed up and looked down the chimney. "Yeah," he called, "we have a problem. Looks like birds have been building nests for some time." Reaching in the length of his arm, he pulled sticks and dried grass from the chimney. "I'm going to have to use the ol' gunnysack trick. I'm coming down."

"You seem to have lots of tricks up your sleeve." She followed him into the house.

"Look here." He got on his hands and knees by the bottom of the chimney. "There should be a hole in the chimney so the soot can be cleaned out. It looks like it's built-up inside." He slipped the point of his pocketknife along the mortar of a couple bricks. It was loose enough so he could pry out four, leaving a hole. Soot flowed onto the floor. "It makes a mess, but it has to be done. Now I need to go back up on the roof."

He took a gunnysack from the shed, put a few rocks in it, tied the top with a piece of rope, and then started up the ladder. While Pauline held it steady, she glanced down the hill and saw a man with his hands in his pockets, standing by the trees looking up at them. "Fred! There *is* someone watching us!"

He set the sack on the roof and turned to look. "I don't see anyone. Like I said earlier, it could be a deer or just someone passing through. Let's get this chimney cleaned out." He put the sack into the chimney, pulled it up and down, up and down. As it rubbed against the walls, black sooty dust enveloped him. He stepped back, coughing and clearing his throat. Coming down the ladder, he said, "I'll have to take the stove pipe out to the yard."

Pauline laughed. "You look like you've just come up from a coal mine."

Fred used old rags to clean the stove pipe. He put it back together and pushed one end into the back of the stove and the other into the hole in the chimney above. He put the bricks back in place. "Now we're all set."

He showed Pauline how to use one end of the lid opener to shake the grates in the firebox. She watched the ashes fall into the box below. "Now you start the fire. Do it like I showed you."

Pauline lit a match to the feathered cedar kindling. Bright orange flames jumped up through the sticks. She heard her brother come into the house, but watched the fire.

"Hey, what are you two up to? Fred, you look like you've been working in a coal mine."

"Exactly what I told him, Will."

"Marian sent me to bring you down for lunch, and then we can bring up water."

"Okay, but I have to close the damper first. Right, Fred?"

"Yep. You learn fast."

"That's my sister, fast learner," said Will.

After lunch, Will brought milk cans from his barn. He and Fred filled them with water and loaded them onto the truck.

"I'll ride on the back," Pauline said, and she crawled up on the truck bed and leaned her arms on the cab while Will drove to the house.

"Paulie, you shouldn't try to carry those cans. I have time to help Fred. You get your fire going and we'll get the tub filled."

Pauline built up the fire, put the tub on the stove, and the men filled it with water. She helped carry rubbish to Will's truck, and after he drove away, she and Fred set to work.

Fred swept the cobwebs from the ceiling and Pauline took down the faded curtains from the windows. Dust filled the air. They washed the windows, shelves, counter and sink with the NuBora soap and warm water. "It's coming along," said Fred.

"Yes, but look at my hands." Pauline held out her red puffy hands.

"I have just the ticket to soothe them," said Fred. He went out, but quickly came back with a small green can labeled Bag Balm. "I found this on a ledge in the lean-to." He pried off the lid, stuck a finger in the salve and rubbed it on his hands. "It feels smooth. Try some. Uncle Jack used it to keep the cows' teats soft."

"Does it smell?" He held it to her nose. She took a small sniff. "Hmm, kind of a sweet smell. I'll try it." She rubbed some on her hands. "It is smooth. I like it."

While cleaning up the supper dishes, Marian asked, "Is something bothering you, Pauline? You've been so quiet."

"Yes, the other day while we were on the roof, I thought I saw a man down by the trees watching us. When I looked again he had gone. Fred said it was probably a deer, but I know a deer doesn't wear a plaid shirt and dark pants."

Marian laughed. "Now that would be an interesting sight. Did you see his face?"

"No, but I think he's young. Do you see men walking around here?"

"Oh, once in a while, but we're kind of out of the way. Mr. Jorgen goes by. He keeps his fishing boat at Cornet Bay."

"Well, maybe that's who I saw." She hung the damp dishtowel on a rack. "You know, I feel sad leaving behind the furniture Fred had from his family, but it cost too much to bring it. His cousin, Irene, planned to marry soon, so we gave it all to her. Is there a place in Oak Harbor that sells second-hand furniture?"

"Yes, and you can probably find some good bargains. A lot of folks are having a tough time and are selling things they don't need."

"All we really need is a new mattress and springs for that iron bedstead."

"We have two easy chairs in the basement. Will can take them up when you have the house ready."

"Thanks, Marian. I'm glad Fred shipped my sewing machine out. When it gets here, I'll make curtains."

Chapter Seven... First Trip to Oak Harbor

Pauline sat between Will and Fred in her brother's old truck. She held her legs away from the gear stick so Will could shift. "How far is it to town?"

"About six miles," said Will. "We'll go to the lumber yard first and get the plywood."

He parked by the entrance to the Columbia Valley Lumber Yard. Fred helped Pauline from the truck and they went into the immense yellow building. "Hey, Bill!" Will shouted.

"Yeah, be right with you." A tall muscular man came from around a stack of lumber. "Haven't seen you for a while, Will."

"Bill, my sister, Pauline, and her husband, Fred Gunther. They bought that old place in the woods up the hill from me."

The men shook hands. Pauline listened to them talk. After they decided how many sheets of plywood Fred would need and it had been loaded onto the truck, they shook hands again. Fred told Bill he would be seeing him soon to get lumber for cabinets.

Will said, "Okay, it's off to the Co-op. They carry about everything you need from groceries, hardware, clothes... you name it, they've probably got it."

Fred and Pauline followed Will into the store. The walls and counters in the large building were illuminated with big white globes hanging from the high ceiling. Will pointed to where they could find the paint.

The worn oiled floor boards creaked with every step as they walked from aisle to aisle of hardware, farm tools and groceries. Pauline spied dry goods and headed in that direction, but Fred caught her arm. "Come along, you need to choose the paint."

It didn't take her long to decide on a color. "I always liked my bright yellow kitchen back home."

Fred selected a brush, turpentine and two gallons of paint. "I hope this will be enough. It should keep you busy for a while."

"Me? No, no, Fred. Buy another brush."

"Just teasing, dear. We'll do it together."

They found Will waiting for them. "Are we going straight home?"

Fred urged, "I think we should go home, Pauline. I want to start nailing up the plywood."

"I'd like to see the town."

"You'll have to wait, Paulie," said Will. "There will be plenty of other times to look in the stores, and I have time now to help Fred for a couple days."

"All right," she said, but when Fred held the truck door for her, she made a face at him.

He laughed and got in the truck. When they arrived at the

house, the men pulled the plywood from Will's truck, carried it inside and began working.

Pauline helped and when her arms got tired holding the four by eight boards in place, she pushed against them with her back. Sometimes Fred handed a hammer to her. Later, she showed Marian a black thumbnail, but said she usually hit the nail on the head.

By mid-afternoon of the next day, they finished and stood back and admired their work. Fred thanked Will for helping, and said that he and Pauline would start painting right away.

"Okay," said Will as he went out to his truck.

"Tell Marian I'll do the dishes," Pauline called after him.

Fred shook his head a little and said, "You really like to do dishes, don't you?"

"I've never minded doing dishes, and Marian needs to rest after cooking for us."

Fred opened a can and stirred the paint with a long stick. "Here's your brush. Watch." He dipped the brush into the paint. "Don't wipe it against the side. Just turn it a little so it won't drip."

"Fred, I know how. I painted our kitchen back home, remember?"

"Yes, of course, and you did a great job."

Pauline enjoyed working with Fred. He whistled, and once in a while, sang the melody to songs they had sung many years earlier. After an hour she said, "It's been too long since I've done this. I need a little break to rest my arm."

She went out on the porch, looked around, turned and went back in. "The man is down by the trees again. I hear him whistling."

"I think he's harmless, probably on his way home from somewhere. Not everyone has a car or truck. Many people have to walk. He might be taking a short-cut."

"I think he's spying on us."

"Let's call it a day and go for a walk." Fred put the brushes in turpentine."

They went up to the spring. "It's sure peaceful. I like the musical sound of the water as it makes little ripples around the rocks," Pauline said. Sitting on a boulder with her arms around her drawn-up knees, she mused, "I can imagine a child playing in the water, watching little sticks float over the pebbles to the pond."

Fred moved from where he was standing and sat next to her. He put an arm around her shoulders. She turned to him. Her misting eyes and tone of voice told him she was thinking of the child they both wanted. "I'm so sorry," she whispered.

"Me too, darling," he said, pulling her close and brushing her forehead with his lips. "I love you, Pauline."

After a quiet time, they walked hand in hand down the hill to Marian's. As they passed their house, she said, "I'll make our little house into a wonderful home for us."

Fred squeezed her hand.

Pauline woke with the sun the next morning, dressed quickly and found Marian in her kitchen mixing batter for hotcakes.

Marian greeted her. "Well, look at you! Up so early?"

"I feel good and it's going to be a great day. We're almost finished the kitchen walls and I'll paint the furniture while Fred is cleaning the outhouse. Soon we'll be ready to live in our house. You and Will have put up with us long enough."

"Pauline, I've liked having you here. Pour a cup of coffee and read Jenny's letter. She's anxious to see you and will be at the Grange Picnic in a couple weeks."

"Does she have her own car?"

"Oh no, she knows how to drive, but we certainly can't afford another car. She gets rides with her friends to Dewey and then takes the ferry. Will or I go pick her up."

"Well, it will be wonderful to see her. I've been looking at the pictures on your fireplace mantel. She's a beautiful young lady."

"I think so, too," said Marian. "I think she resembles her Aunt Pauline."

"Oh, that's sweet. Now I really am eager to see her."

Chapter Eight... The Outhouse

Working together, Fred and Pauline finished painting the walls that morning. "Are you happy with it?" he asked.

"Yes! It's like the house is filled with sunshine."

Fred told her they should flip a coin to decide who would clean the outhouse.

"I'm not doing it. That's man's work and I know just the man who is going to do it, and while he does it, I'll paint the table and chairs."

"Yellow?" asked Fred. "We can buy a different color."

"We have enough left and I like yellow."

Fred hemmed and hawed while looking at the chairs and table.

"Okay, if it's what you want."

"It's what I want."

"Well, guess I can't put if off any longer." He strode out the door and went to the outhouse.

"Have fun, dear," she teased.

Pauline hummed as she painted the table. "Finished already?" she asked when Fred returned.

"Over the years the fir boards have dried and there are

cracks that let the sun and rain come in. The door is hanging by just one hinge. You know some outhouses have two holes, one for big people and one for kids."

"No, dear, I didn't know that. I've never had to use an outhouse."

"Well, this one has just one hole and it has a hinged lid, so it's a bit more modern than the one at Uncle Jack's farm. There are bird nests in the corners near the roof and piles of their droppings on the bench. It's a mess with old catalogue pages and dried leaves covering the floor."

"Does it have a moon cut in the door?"

"Yep, wouldn't be an outhouse without one. I came back to get the broom. I've been thinking about what I need to do. I remember the outhouse at Uncle Jack's smelled awful. Flies and sometimes bees buzzed around. I always put off using it as long as possible." He used his foot to push the paint can closer to her. "I'll get small strips of wood to cover the cracks, cut holes for ventilation and cover them with screens. The ceiling and walls can be cleaned up with whitewash to make it lighter, and you know what that means."

"What, I'm going to help?"

He laughed. "Well, you're good with a brush."

"Unh-uh. I have enough to do in the house."

"I think you can dress it up a bit by hanging a few magazine pictures on the walls."

Pauline smiled as she dipped her brush in the paint. "You've thought of everything, even a little art gallery."

Fred stood around watching her, hands in his pockets. "I'm going to get goats. They eat about anything and can help clear the brush. I can tether them out during the day, but keep them in the lean-to at night."

"Goats will be fun, and I'd like to have chickens."

"They'll need to be penned-up at night, too. Will told me there are foxes lurking around during the night."

Chapter Nine... Looking Through the Trunks

Fred and Will brought Pauline's trunks into the house. "Marian sent these two chairs and a bed for you until you get around to buying your own," said Will. He looked at the tables and chairs. "That's a lot of yellow, Paulie."

"A bit maybe, but when Fred puts up the bedroom walls, I'll wallpaper them with pretty flowered paper."

"That will be a while," said Fred.

"Marian is anxious to see all you've done and might be up later," said Will. "Well, Fred, let's go clean out that lean-to."

Pauline kneeled by the three trunks and decided to start with the largest. She unbuckled the leather straps and with some effort pulled up the top. Lifting out a blanket, she sniffed it and immediately knew she needed a clothesline. She went to the porch and called, "Yoo-hoo!"

Fred stuck his head around the corner. "What do you want?"

"I need to air out the bedding. Can you make a clothesline for me?"

"Just give me a minute. I saw a roll of wire in the shed."

Will helped Fred fasten a long wire from a porch corner post to an apple tree trunk.

Pauline washed it with a wet rag and hung blankets and sheets. The slight breeze and warm sun would make them smell fresh.

Back in the house, she knelt by another trunk and picked up the hand-stitched Double-ring wedding quilt and thought of her mother. She caressed the crocheted afghan her grandmother had made. Then she turned her attention to the last trunk, but decided to leave the things in it until Fred had built the closet and drawers. They would live out of the trunks for a while.

Among the clothes, she had packed the family picture album and her red velvet-lined jewelry box, a gift from her father on her sixteenth birthday. She took out her grandfather's mantel clock, traced the ornate woodcarvings with her finger and then placed it on top of the wedding quilt.

Hearing footsteps on the porch, Pauline turned and saw her sister-in-law. "Oh, Marian, come on in. I'm looking in the trunks. It's been a while since we packed them and it's fun to see what I brought."

Marian got on her knees beside Pauline. "This is cute," she said, as she picked up a small porcelain clock painted with a Swiss boy and girl.

"It's a souvenir from our honeymoon," said Pauline.

Marian looked around the room. "You've spruced it up in just a few days. No wonder you're tired at night. Painting the table and chairs to match the walls was a good idea."

"Thanks. Will thought it a crazy idea, but I'm glad I did it. As soon as I get my Singer, I'm going to sew Priscilla curtains like we had back home. Maybe you can take me to town to buy material."

"Sure, we can have lunch and maybe stop in and see my friend, Thea."

"That'd be fun. I'd like to meet your friends." Pauline closed the trunk and motioned with her hand. "What do you think of the floor?"

Marian said, "Someone gave it a good scrubbing."

"Yes, Fred spent hours on his hands and knees. Now I need to put a couple of coats of varnish on it." Pauline took three braided rugs from the bottom of the large trunk.

"Did you make these?"

"Yes, I like working with my hands. It gives me something to do in the evenings."

After admiring the rugs, Marian said, "You do nice work." She walked over to the stove. "I had my doubts about this old stove, but you've done a great job cleaning it."

"Hey, ladies, what's going on in here?"

Marian looked up at Fred standing in the door. "You and Pauline have done wonders for this old house."

"Yeah, it's coming along. Will said I can use his truck to pick up a couple of goats. Want to come, Pauline?"

"Of course I do. Are you going now?"

"Yep, right now. We'll take Marian and Will to their house first."

Since there wasn't room for all of them in the truck, Marian and Will got up on the truck bed for the short ride. After dropping them off in front of their house, Fred rolled down the window and listened as Will gave directions to Gerald Lamb's place. "Go on Monkey Hill and turn left onto

Tea and Coffee."

"You mean Troxell Road," said Fred.

"Yep, the old Tea and Coffee Road. It goes on out to Ala Spit where the Troxells used to fish trap," said Will.

Pauline looked back as they drove away and heard Marian call, "Have fun you two."

Chapter Ten... Nanny and Billy

"Tea and Coffee, Monkey Hill." Pauline laughed. "They certainly have strange names for roads around here."

Fred, concentrating on driving, told her, "We're looking for Gerald Lamb's mailbox."

Amused, Pauline said, "I think Mr. Lamb should be raising lambs rather than goats."

Fred drove onto a rutted driveway and parked a short distance from a ramshackle house.

Dogs, awakened from their naps, started barking. Sticking his head out the door, a man yelled at the dogs to be quiet. The noisy dogs jumped about him as he came down the porch steps. He adjusted a scruffy hat over his disheveled gray hair. Pauline noticed his scraggly beard and dirty overalls.

Fred stepped out of the truck and was immediately surrounded by the barking, jumping dogs. "Down boy, down!" he told them.

Pauline said, "I'll stay in the truck." She rolled down a window to hear the men talk.

Fred tried to walk away from the dogs, but they kept

jumping and sniffing at him. The man whistled the dogs off.

Fred called out, "I'm looking for Mr. Lamb. I heard he has goats for sale."

"Always do. I'm Gerald Lamb."

"Fred Gunther." They shook hands. Gerald pushed the dogs away with his feet.

"I need a couple of goats to help clear brush."

Gerald nodded toward a building made of scrap boards and led the way.

Pauline watched goats nibble at tufts of grass in the yard and laughed when two started jumping and butting heads. She saw Fred take his wallet from his pocket and hand a few bills to Gerald who stuffed them into his overalls pocket.

Gerald put one leg over a pole fence and then the other. He scooped up a small white goat, cradled it in his arms and carried it into the little shed. He did the same with a second goat. He came out with a gunnysack tied shut.

Fred came to Pauline's side of the truck and opened the door. "You're going to have company on the way home."

Pauline moved over a bit as he put the gunnysack beside her feet. The goats thrashed around.

Fred got in, started the motor, and called out his window, "Thanks, Gerald."

"Anytime," said Gerald, as he tipped his hat.

The goats lay still. Pauline said, "They're so little. Are they babies? Are they girls or boys?"

"They've been weaned a few days. Gerald said they'll grow pretty fast. We have a billy and a nanny. He said they'll eat right out of our hands. The billy has been castrated."

"I guess that means he's been spayed like my cat."

"That's right."

"We have to give them names."

"They already have names. Nanny and Billy. Okay?" He smiled and looked to her for approval.

"Okay," she agreed.

Back home, Fred set the sack in the lean-to, untied the string and let the goats tumble out. They lay still, blinking their eyes. Pauline rubbed their backs and soon she was on her hands and knees playing with their floppy ears and petting their necks. They licked her fingers. "Fred, our little goats are tame and their hair is as soft as down on a duck. They're just like little puppies." She snuggled them in her lap.

"They sure are. The smaller one is the nanny."

"Look how their short tails stick straight up. They're pure white, but Billy has a black spot on the underside of his fat little belly." She held Nanny's head in her hands. "Such beautiful blue eyes."

Fred tied ropes around their necks. "I'll stake them out during the day when the sun's out. They like to forage on grass and brush." He got a bucket and headed for the spring to get water for them.

"Hi Paulie."

"Hi Will. See what we've got." She put her arms around the goats.

"Paulie, you surprise me. I thought you didn't like animals. You never played with my dog. Only paid attention to your cat."

"Snowflake was special. I liked your black puppy, until he chewed on my Raggedy Ann."

"You shouldn't have left it outside."

"My goats are just babies and have sharp toes. Feel these little bumps on their heads."

"Kids, Paulie. Baby goats are called kids."

"I know that, Will."

He squatted beside her and rubbed his hand over the billy's head. "The bumps are called nubbins. He might grow horns."

"Well, I hope these sweethearts don't grow up too fast. Fred is going to buy collars for them. These old ropes might hurt their necks."

"I'll find bells to put on the collars and then you'll always know where they are."

"Good idea. I wouldn't want to lose these darlings." She kissed Nanny's head and stroked Billy's back.

Will stood up, smiled down at his sister, and asked, "Where's Fred?"

"He went to the spring for a bucket of water." She looked up at Will. "Do you know he wants to dig a well?"

"Yeah, but this ground is mostly hardpan clay and rocks. It would be a hard job."

"If I know my husband, he'll try anyway, and here he comes."

"Ah, Will," said Fred. "You didn't have to walk up to get your truck. I was going to bring it down at supper time."

"Oh, I saw you drive by and thought I'd come up and see the goats. These Nubians won't get real big, so they might not eat your brush down very fast," said Will

Fred replied, "No, but Pauline will have fun with them." He filled a small pan with water. "You take the truck and we'll walk down after a while."

"Yeah, see you later." Will looked back over his shoulder as he went to his truck. "Maybe we can play cards after supper."

"That sounds like fun," called Pauline.

Fred fluffed hay in one corner of the lean-to and tied Billy and Nanny to a corner post. Pauline gave them a final pat and closed the gate. "The sheets and blankets are still on the line. Come help me bring them in and we'll make the bed."

Fred tossed the blankets on the bed. Pauline teased, "Not yet, silly, the sheets go on first. Mmm, I love the smell of fresh sheets."

They laughed as they made up their bed, tucking in the corners just right.

With a twinkle in his eyes, Fred said, "I think we should try it out."

"We have to go to supper."

"They can eat without us."

Pauline giggled and kicked off her shoes. "Last one in is a…"

At Marian's house the next morning, Pauline bent over to tie her shoes, and looked up when Fred came in.

"Hey, sleepyhead, you must have worn yourself out yesterday playing with the goats."

"I'm not sure that's all that wore me out."

Fred laughed, his eyes sparkled. "We know when to have fun."

Pauline said, "Yes, but we were late getting back here to

supper. It was nice that Marian kept it warm for us."

"Yeah, and this morning she said to let you sleep. They've eaten and gone out to do chores." He walked aimlessly around the room, picking up a hairbrush, putting it down, then picking it up again, looking in the mirror and brushing his hair. "I'm losing it."

"You have lots to lose, I wouldn't worry about it."

He set the brush on the dresser.

Pauline studied him. "What is it, dear?"

"I think it's time we buy a truck."

"Uh, Fred, we agreed to save money for a car."

"Yes, I remember. But, Pauline, I really need a truck so I can haul stuff. I can't borrow Will's all the time. If I get a job building cabinets, I'll need to carry my tools and haul lumber. We'll be buying feed for the goats and if you get chickens…"

"Yes, I do want chickens. I suppose a truck would be more practical and we do have Dad's money."

"Great! I knew you'd see it my way," Fred said, rubbing his hands together. "This is swell. Will recommends I go to Olson's who takes in cars and trucks. He can take me to town this morning."

"I want to go with you. Maybe this time I can see something of the town."

Chapter Eleven... The Double A

Coming from the bedroom, Pauline said, "Thank you for loaning us a bed for our new house, Marian." And then she giggled.

"What's so funny?"

"Oh, nothing. Fred and I made it up yesterday. It's all ready for tonight."

Marian gave her a knowing look and smiled, "So that's why you were late getting here for supper."

Pauline blushed and said, "Yep." She cinched the belt on her cotton dress. "I've lost an inch or two."

"It's all that work you've been doing, climbing ladders and scrubbing your house. You eat like a bird."

"Oh, I eat enough. I feel healthy." She slipped into a light jacket. "Marian, is there anything I can get for you in town?"

"Actually, I do need groceries and it'll save me a trip."

"I'd love to shop. It'll be the first time I've bought groceries since Bay City. Just give me a list."

Marian looked through her cupboard and jotted down a few items. "Let me get my purse."

"Oh, no, you don't! It's my turn to buy groceries. I insist."

"Well, all right. I usually buy at the Co-op, but you'll need to go to Morton's Meat Market for the chops. My shopping basket is on the porch."

Pauline gave her sister-in-law a gentle hug and picked up the basket on her way out to Will's truck. She sat between her brother and husband.

"Move your legs, Paulie. I need to shift gears."

She moved her legs closer to Fred's. He put an arm around her shoulders.

As usual, Will parked in back of the Co-op. "We'll meet you here in about an hour, Paulie." Then he and Fred hurried off to look at trucks.

Pauline took her time looking in shop windows. She smiled and said hello to shoppers walking toward her. A display in the Fabric Shoppe window caught her eye. A bell tinkled as she pushed open the door. An elderly woman, her hair drawn back in a tight bun and wearing a black dress down to her ankles, came slowly from the back of the room.

Pauline smiled and said, "Hello, I noticed the beautiful prints in the window. I'm looking for curtain material. I can't buy any just now, but someday I will."

The woman turned and walked over the creaking wood floor to a dark counter, and then hoisted herself onto a stool. Pauline felt uncomfortable as the woman watched her wander from table to table admiring the pretty fabrics. She stroked a bright floral cotton she thought would be perfect for her little house. As she went out, she looked back and called thank you, but the woman had disappeared behind a dark curtain. The bell tinkled as she closed the door.

Pauline crossed the street. When she heard a sharp whistle

and Fred call yoo-hoo, she realized she had lingered a bit too long looking in windows. She hurried over to the Co-op and checked her watch. "You're early. I haven't bought groceries and I need to go to the meat market. Marian wants pork chops for supper."

Will said, "Tell you what, give me Marian's list and you and Fred go to Morton's Meat Market in the next block. I'll meet you at Fred's truck."

Pauline looked from Will to Fred. "Oh, you found one! Where is it?"

Smiling broadly, Fred said, "Up the street a couple of blocks. It was a terrific buy. A widow woman brought it into Olson's Garage a few days ago. She's moving to California to live with her son."

"You're going to like your truck, Paulie," said Will. "Here, give me the list and the basket. It won't take me long."

Fred said, "Okay, see you in a bit at *my* new truck!" He started walking toward the meat market and Pauline tried to keep up. "You go on in," he told her. "I'll wait for you at the truck. It's just in the next block."

When she entered the shop, the smell reminded her of the meat market back home.

Happy with her purchases, she left and saw Will ahead of her. "Will," she called. He turned and waited. She took his arm. They walked past several old cars and stopped by a shiny black truck. "This is it, a 1929 Model Double A," said Will, slapping his hand on the hood. He stood back jiggling coins in his pockets admiring the truck.

"It's so new!"

"Yep, you're really going to ride in style."

Fred walked around the flatbed truck. "Isn't it a beauty? I'll be able to haul lumber and anything else we need."

"But Fred," she said, caressing the black, shiny fender, "it must have cost a lot."

"I bought it for half of what her husband paid. He died shortly after he got it and it's been sitting in a shed for four years. Here, get in." He opened the door and held her arm while she stepped up onto the running board. She squirmed around on the seat to get comfortable.

"A new truck! Gosh, what will people say? Will they think we have lots of money?"

"I wouldn't worry about that," said Will.

Fred shook his hand. "Thanks for all your help. It's a great truck. Now we're going to the lumber yard. I want to build our cabinets."

Will started to walk away, but stopped. "Oh, Pauline told me she wants chickens. On your way home, stop at Jens Meyer's place on Troxell Road. He posted a note on the Co-op bulletin board that he has chickens to give away." He waved and walked toward his truck.

Fred cocked his head and listened to the motor start. Pauline watched him change gears as he backed out of the parking space and drove down the street. She ran her hand over the dashboard and rolled the window up and down. "It's so nice," she marveled, and then asked, "Did Will say something about chickens?"

"Yep. It seems a poultry farmer is giving them away."

"Let's get some."

"Okay, after we get the lumber we'll stop and see Mr. Meyer."

Fred parked by the yellow Columbia Valley Lumber Yard building. They heard the loud screaming of a buzz saw cutting wood. The sweet smell of fresh sawn lumber wafted out as they walked into the cavernous building.

They waited to be seen. When the saw had been turned off, Fred said, "Hello, Bill. I was in a few days ago and bought plywood."

The big man answered, "I remember you," and taking off a work glove, wrapped a large hand around Fred's.

Bill tipped his hat to Pauline. She smiled and said, "Hello."

"What can I do for you today, Fred?"

"I need lumber for kitchen cupboards and bedroom closets."

"Follow me. I have two grades of plywood brought in from the Anacortes mill. Many folks use it. Just put on a couple coats of varnish or paint for a nice finish." He pointed and walked to different stacks explaining each type and thickness.

Fred took his time looking over the fir two by four boards and sheets of plywood. He studied the drawings he had made on an old envelope.

Pauline walked over to the pine boards. "Dear, I like this knotty pine."

Bill told him the price and then Fred did more figuring. "I can use it for the doors on the shelves above the sink and the fronts of the drawers, but get plywood for the closets."

Pauline touched his arm. "I'd like the closet lined with cedar. I like the scent and it keeps moths from eating holes in our woolens."

Fred did a bit more figuring and added cedar to his order. He paid with cash. The men loaded the lumber onto the truck bed. Bill walked around the Ford. "This truck looks familiar."

"It's been mine for about an hour. Bought it over at Olson's Garage."

"So Harry's widow finally decided to sell," mused Bill. "I know several fellows who wanted it, but Thelma said Harry's dream truck wasn't for sale. It's the only Double A on the island."

"Fortunately for me, she changed her mind. She's going to live with her son in California."

The men shook hands. Fred helped Pauline into the truck.

Fred rolled down his window. "Say, Bill, do you know anyone who needs a carpenter? I'm anxious to work."

Bill rested one foot on the running board and leaned on the window ledge. "Otto Van Zef might need someone."

"Where can I find him?"

"I know he's working on a house out at West Beach. Tell him I sent you."

"Great. Thanks. I'll be seeing you again." Fred drove to Oak Harbor Feed Store and parked. "I'll only be a minute," he assured Pauline.

He returned with a sack of grain for the chickens, hoisted it into the back of the truck, and they were soon on their way.

As Fred turned the steering wheel to go up Telephone Hill, Pauline noticed the telephone office. "We need a telephone."

"Someday I'll ask for a line up to the house from Ducken Road."

Pauline asked how much he had paid.

"For the grain?"

"No, for the truck."

"Two hundred sixty-five. Much less than I thought I'd have to pay. Thank your dad again for being a saver."

"Yes, it's like Dad was looking out for us." She sat back thinking of how hard her father had worked in the shipyards and wondered what he would think of her now.

Chapter 12... Chickens

Fred drove up Monkey Hill, came to a cross-road and turned onto Troxell Road.

Pauline pointed and exclaimed, "There! I bet that's it with the chicken painted on the mailbox!"

Fred slowed and turned through the gate. The truck bounced over the winding gravel road between tall Douglas fir and cedar trees. He stopped in a clearing with several small chicken coops. Birds walked in the yard and driveway and scratched in the grass and dirt. He got out and opened Pauline's door. "Coming?"

"Try and stop me!" She jumped down. "Did you ever see this many chickens?"

A man stood in the yard with his hands in the bib of his overalls. Lying in the dust, two black dogs perked up their ears and bounded over to Fred.

"Mr. Meyer," called Fred to the man. "I'm Fred Gunther and this is my wife, Pauline. She's anxious to get some chickens."

The two men shook hands as Jens replied, "Good! I have too many."

Pauline smiled hello and then bent to pat the dogs' heads. The Spaniels brushed their wagging tails against her legs. "Nice dog, good dog," she praised them. Jens shooed them away.

"You certainly do have a lot of chickens, Mr. Meyer, and so many different colors. I like the bright red ones with the shiny green and black feathers in their tails," said Pauline.

Jens said, "Those roosters are Rhode Island Reds. The Rhody hens lay brown eggs. This orangey lady, here by the truck, is a Plymouth Rock. Her eggs are blue or sometimes green."

"I like that red one, but I only want hens, no roosters." She smiled. "They might wake me up."

Jens went to a small shed and brought out a gunnysack and a long pole with a wire hook on one end. He handed the sack to Fred, took a handful of grain from his pocket and threw it on the ground. The chickens scrambled to peck the grain by Pauline's feet. She laughed when they snatched at her shoelaces.

Jens reached out with his pole and hooked the wire around the leg of a Rhody. It beat its wings in the air, squawking loudly. He pulled it to him, bent down, grabbed its legs, and then cradled the bird in his arms against his chest. "Calm them down and they're easy to hold." He stroked the Red's neck and back. It nestled in his arms. He held it out to Pauline. "Here, now, hold her close."

Pauline held the hen against her chest and stroked its soft feathers. "She seems to like me."

"Okay, let's put her in the sack," said Jens. Fred held it open. The hen flapped its wings in Pauline's face. She let go, but Fred caught it and put it in the sack.

Jens hooked another and put it in the sack. It flopped around and then lay still. He said, "Chickens settle down and are quiet in the dark." He held the pole out to Pauline. "Your turn."

"Me? Well, I'll try." She took the pole and jabbed it at a Red. It lifted its wings and jumped over the pole. She laughed and tried again, but the hen squawked and scurried away. "I'll catch you," she called, taking big strides with her long legs. Chickens skedaddled, clucked noisily.

Pauline heard Fred chuckling. She scrambled after one chicken and then another, and fell down on her knees. "Ouch!" Chickens clucked as they ran every which way. Jens reached out to her. "Oh, I'm okay," she said, getting up and brushing hair back from her face with a dirty hand.

Jens threw out another handful of grain and suggested she walk slowly, keeping the pole close to the ground. After several attempts, she hooked the wire around a hen's leg and pulled it to her as the bird squawked. Pauline turned her face away as the hen's wings lashed at her. She let go. It landed on its feet and scudded away, cackling and causing a racket as chickens scattered. "Nerts! I'm not a good chicken catcher."

Pauline handed the pole to Jens. "I like that one with the purple and black feathers."

Jens took the pole and caught the Barnevelder. "Are you sure you want a rooster?"

"Oh, this is a rooster? No, I'll just take hens."

Jens let the rooster go, hooked a Barnevelder hen and held it up to Pauline.

"Ah, you're pretty." She stroked the hen's feathers. "I

think we have enough… after all, how many eggs can we eat?" She took one more look at all the hens running around. "Oh, but, I'd like a Bantam."

"Of course you need Bantams." Jens caught two and put them in the sack. "They're pullets and won't start laying for another couple weeks."

"Pullets?"

Jens explained, "Young hens, like teenagers."

"I have a lot to learn about chickens."

Pauline told him about the orange crates she had found in her house. He said they would work fine for nests and she should line them with straw.

Fred bunched the end of the sack together, tied it with a string, and opened the truck door for Pauline to get in. He put the chickens by her feet, turned and thanked Jens. The men shook hands.

Pauline rolled down her window. "Thank you, Mr. Meyer. You're welcome to come visit your hens anytime."

Jens said he would visit if she had coffee.

Pauline replied, "And cookies, too."

Fred started the truck, but Pauline said, "Wait, Fred," and then called, "Mr. Myer, how did Monkey Hill get named?"

"Monkey Hill? Well, the way I heard it, the farmers had a hard time getting their horses to pull loaded wagons up the hill. They had to kind of zigzag on the way up or sometimes leave part of their load at the bottom and go back down to get it. One fellow said it was a lot of monkeying around and so they all started calling it Monkey Hill. Some guys put their cars in reverse and backed up."

"Well, I think that's a good name for it then. We'll see

you again." As Fred drove away she asked, "Why did they back the cars up the hill?"

Fred explained, "A Model T has a lower gear in reverse than when it goes forward. Now, maybe the guys with Model A's don't have that problem. The newer Model A's have more power."

"Oh," she murmured, trying to understand.

The hens stayed quiet in the sack by Pauline's feet.

At home she and Fred carefully set the sack on the ground in the shed and untied it. The chickens emerged hesitantly and explored their new surroundings. Pauline gave them a dish of water while Fred unraveled the string on the grain sack. She tossed out handfuls of grain. He used a sturdy stick to rig up a temporary roost in a corner.

"They'll be ok here in the shed until I get the coop repaired in the lean-to," he said. "I'm hungry. Let's get to supper."

At Marian's house the next morning, sun poured through the bedroom window. Pauline blinked her eyes open. "My chickens," she murmured to herself. Careful not to wake Fred, she crept out of bed, dressed and dashed off a note. *I'm checking on the hens—be back soon.*

She walked briskly up the hill and opened the shed door. The hens cackled and ran to one corner. "Here chick, chick," she cooed as she sprinkled grain on the floor. One by one the hens ventured closer and started pecking the wheat. "Nice chick, chick," she said as they stepped around her feet.

After a few minutes, she walked back to Marian's. As she entered the kitchen, she said, "The hens are happy."

"Oh good. Maybe you can settle down and eat now,"

teased Marian. "How about some hotcakes?"

"You got an early start this morning," said Will.

Fred took a last swallow of coffee. "Pauline, as soon as you eat, I'll get to work on fixing their coop."

Pauline started to open the shed door, but was interrupted by Fred calling, "Hey, come on. The work's over here."

"Okay, what can I do?"

"You can help by holding the boards steady." She held them while he sawed and then held them in place while he nailed. He brought a roll of chicken wire from the shed.

"What are you going to do with that?"

"We'll use it for the top half of the wall to let in more light. I'll make a door for you to take in the water and grain."

"And gather the eggs."

"No, I've decided to cut a hole in the wall and mount a long nest box outside so you can gather the eggs without going into the coop."

"But the nests will get wet when it rains."

"No, I'll make a roof to keep them dry, and keep predators out."

"What kind of predators?"

"Raccoons, rats, maybe crows."

Fred hummed a little tune as he worked. Sometimes Pauline joined in, singing the words. They measured for the hole and after it was cut, built a rectangular box to hold the straw nests, and then nailed it to the outside wall. Fred found an old piece of plywood and made a hinged sloping roof.

"Look here. You open the roof like this to collect the eggs. Now I have a job you can do by yourself. The hens need a ramp to walk up to get into their nests."

Fred gave her short, narrow strips of boards to nail cross-wise onto a long, narrow plank. "Do it like this. You're making stairs for them."

Pauline pounded nail after nail, sometimes missing and hitting her thumb. She put straw in the nest boxes.

Fred said, "I'll make a little door near the floor in the outside wall so the chickens can walk out onto the grass during the day. They like to scratch in the dirt and eat seeds, worms and bugs. They eat grit, little pieces of rock and sand, to help them digest their food."

Pauline giggled. "I'm glad I'm not a chicken."

"I'm glad too," he joked. "Actually, their food goes into a little sack called a crop and the bits of grit help grind up whatever they find to eat."

"I think you're teasing me."

"No, it's the truth. Remember, I learned a lot from Uncle Jack."

Then the fun began. Fred and Pauline went to the shed to catch the chickens. They cornered and caught them and took the squawking hens to their coop. One hen flew out of Pauline's hands into the tall grass. "Fred, a Bantam got away!"

"It'll want to come back for the grain," he assured her.

When they finished getting the hens settled in their coop, Pauline looked at her hands and bare arms. "Look, Fred." She showed him small streaks of blood where the hens' claws had made scratches. "My dress is a mess. I need trousers."

"Yes, you do. Next time we go into town you can buy a

pair at the Co-op. You better wash, and then use Bag Balm on those scratches."

With the hens settled in their lean-to coop, Fred worked in the shed building cabinets for the house. Pauline liked helping by holding boards and getting tools he needed. He said, "We make a good team."

She kept him amused chatting about the chickens, calling them "my girls" and thinking up names to match the color of their feathers or their personalities.

"I didn't know chickens had personalities," kidded Fred.

"Sure they do. Buffy picks on Candy and Taffy, the Bantams. She flies at them to shoo them away so she can have the best grain. I have to think of a different name for her."

"How about Greedy or Bossy?" he teased.

Pauline heard a "cluck-cluck-cu-docket," and ran to the coop to see if a hen had laid an egg. "Fred, we have our first egg!" She picked it up and ran back to show him the brown egg. "It's from one of the Rhode Island Reds."

Fred admired the large egg and said, "I'd like a scrambled egg for breakfast."

Chapter Thirteen... Another Trip to Town

On her way to the spring, Pauline petted Billy and Nanny who were staked out in the brush. As she continued up the rough path, she heard a noise. She stopped and peeked through the bushes. A man sat on a big rock throwing pebbles into the pool. She backed away, turned and started running, trying to avoid the blackberry vines. "Ouch," she whimpered when she tripped and fell on brush stubble, but she got up quickly and ran to the shed. "That man, Fred! The man I saw by the trees is at the spring. I know it's the same one. He's wearing the same shirt. Go see him!"

Fred said, "Okay," put down his hammer and hurried up the slope. Pauline went to the house to wash her arms and legs. Fred returned shortly. "I didn't see anyone. Perhaps he heard you and left. Here, let me help." He rubbed salve from the green can on her cuts.

"I wish he would just come to the house and talk to us."

Fred shrugged a little and looked concerned. "I'll ask Will. Maybe he knows about someone who might be coming around. I don't like you to be frightened. Maybe you should stay with Marian when I'm not here." He gave her a hug. "Now I need to go to the Co-op for more nails and buy more sheets of plywood so I can get started on a wall to set off our bedroom."

Pauline said, "Well, I'm going with you."

"Yes, of course. Wouldn't think of going without you."

"Why so quiet?" asked Fred as he steered the truck down Telephone Hill.

"I'm just thinking we could buy groceries and start living in our own house. Wouldn't it be fun?"

"Are you going to unpack your dishes and cooking pots?"

"Yes, a few, they're easy to take out of the trunk. We do need to buy a coffee pot."

"We can get everything you need at the Co-op. I'd like to check out Maynard's Hardware. You'll have plenty of time to look for curtain material if you want."

Fred parked the truck. Pauline got out and started directly to the Fabric Shoppe. The little bell tinkled as she opened the shop door and seeing the same elderly woman, Pauline smiled and said, "Hi! I'm back again. I hope the material I like is still here."

The woman mumbled hello and came forward from behind the counter. Pauline held out her hand. "My name is Pauline Gunther."

The woman put her soft hand into Pauline's. "Mrs. O'Dell."

Pauline went to the counter where she had seen the dotted Swiss cloth. She started to pick up the roll.

"I'll get it," the woman said, and stepping beside Pauline, lifted the roll and carried it to the tall brown counter.

"I need enough for six windows. They're not big, about…

oh, let's see." Pauline held her arms out to show the width of each window. "I think they're about two feet wide, and since they're square, two feet high. I like frills. I'm going to make Priscilla curtains with tie-backs."

Mrs. O'Dell reached for a paper pad and pencil. "With the ruffles you need several yards." She measured with a tape.

"Do you have oilcloth? I need to cover my table."

Mrs. O'Dell pointed to a counter. Pauline chose a pattern with yellow, red and blue flowers, carried the bolt to the counter, and watched Mrs. O'Dell's scissors snip through the cloth.

Pauline paid for her purchase. "Thank you. It was nice meeting you, Mrs. O'Dell. I love to sew. I'm sure I'll see you again."

Mrs. O'Dell nodded with a tiny smile. As Pauline closed the door, the little bell tinkled.

She found Fred waiting at the Co-op. "I'm going to buy overalls for when I'm working with you, and I have a list of groceries we'll need. While I get them, could you find a coffee pot?"

"Do you trust me to get the size you like?"

"Yes, a six or eight cupper."

Pauline looked through the stack of overalls, but couldn't find her size. *Oh well, I'll get a new pair for Fred and I can wear them with the legs rolled up.* She walked around the aisles of clothing over to the grocery section. A large rack mounted on a post against the back wall held metal leaves opening like a book. Shelves against the wall held canned meats, vegetables and fruit. She jumped when a man's deep voice ask, "Can I help you?"

Pauline looked up to the smiling face of a man old enough to be her father. "Oh, yes. I have a long list. I'm Pauline Gunther. My husband and I are moving into our house. I'm anxious to start cooking."

"I'm Bernard Gilbert, but everyone calls me Bernie."

Pauline handed her list to him and watched as he used a clamp mounted on a long pole to reach cans on high shelves. He brought sacks of flour and sugar from the cupboards below the counter. He checked all the items off the list and then asked, "Will you need salt and soda and maybe baking powder?"

"I forgot those," Pauline said. "I'm glad you thought of them."

"If you're going to bake bread you'll need yeast, or maybe you would like to shop at the bakery down the street."

"Oh, I like to bake our bread… cakes and cookies, too. Of course, I have to learn how to use the oven. I've never used a wood cook stove."

"It takes practice," said Bernie. "Now then, can you think of anything else you might need? Dried beans?"

"Fred likes baked beans. I think I should get some of those pink and white peppermints, too. They're Fred's favorite candy." Hearing footsteps on the hardwood floor, she turned. "Oh, here he is. Fred, this is Bernie."

Fred said how do you do and the men shook hands.

"He's helped me with what I need to start cooking. I would have gone home without baking powder for your biscuits or yeast for bread."

"After helping housewives with their groceries for

thirty-seven years, I know what they need," said Bernie, as he wrote the items and prices on a paper pad.

Fred held up a percolator coffee pot. "Is this what you had in mind?"

"Yes, that's just what I wanted!"

Bernie put the groceries into boxes. "Do you want to charge this until the end of the month?" He pointed to the big metal book on the wall with the yellow slips of paper attached.

Pauline looked at Fred.

He said, "Yes, that's a good idea."

Bernie wrote Fred's name on the paper and asked for his address.

Fred said, "We don't have our own mailbox. Our mail is delivered to Pauline's brother's box, Will Ansbach." He looked at Pauline. "We should really get our own mailbox while we're in town."

"We all know Will. He's a dependable customer," said Bernie as he tore the papers from the little charge book and handed the top one to Fred. He flipped the metal book pages on the wall and put the yellow carbon copy under a clip, "Okay, you're all set."

Pauline and Fred walked out of the Co-op with their arms full. She said, "Bernie was helpful. Now, let's go to the meat market."

After putting the boxes of groceries in the truck, they walked to Morton's. Pauline followed Fred through the door. She said, "Does it remind you of the meat market back home?"

"Yep, the smell of sawdust on the floor, sausages and

hams hanging on hooks from the ceiling, just like Oscar's Market. I would sure like bacon for breakfast tomorrow."

Pauline stepped up to the counter and looked at the different meats under the glass. When Mr. Morton came from a back room, she introduced herself and Fred. After buying bacon, hamburger for meatloaf and an oxtail for soup, she watched the butcher wrap the meats in white paper, pull string from a cone hanging from the ceiling and tie the packages.

They stopped on the way home and told Marian they had bought groceries and would start living at their house.

"Are you sure, Pauline?"

"Yes, we've loved staying with you and Will, but we're ready to be on our own. We need to take care of our goats and chickens, too."

"Well, I want you to come have supper with us Friday. It will be a little celebration."

"And just what will we be celebrating?"

"Jenny is coming home for a few days. She's excited to see you."

"Oh good." Pauline hugged her sister-in-law. "It's been so long. Will I recognize her?"

"Of course, she hasn't changed from her high school graduation picture."

While driving up to their house, Pauline chatted about what she would fix for supper.

Fred said, "You seem excited about living in our own house."

"Oh, I am, Fred. I like just the two of us together."

"Me, too. You know, Marian's a good cook, but I've missed your cooking."

"It might take me a while to learn to use the stove, so tonight just I'll open a can of soup. Tomorrow I'm going to make oxtail soup and biscuits."

"Do you remember how to start a fire?"

"I think so. Wad some paper, put in a few sticks of kindling and then light the paper. When it starts burning I'll add the big pieces of wood. Maybe you can help me the first time with the damper."

"Sure. Have the damper open when you start the fire and as it gets going good, pull the little handle back to close off the air. If you close it too tight, the fire might go out. It takes practice, but you'll figure it out."

As they drove into the yard, Fred said, "Something's wrong. I don't see the goats. I staked them out to eat the nettles by the little fir tree."

"Maybe the man I've seen took them."

Fred parked the truck, got out and started walking up the hill. He called, "I see them lying in the grassy area by the spring. I wonder who staked them up there."

Pauline followed him to the spring. She got down on her knees by Nanny, "Little girl, are you okay?"

Fred pulled up the stakes. "Let's take them back to the lean-to."

They got the goats settled and carried the groceries into the house. Fred said he'd get fresh water while she made supper.

Fred whistled or hummed as he worked steadily the next three days building a closet.

"I'm glad you like your work, Fred, and I know you're happy, but something else is going on. What haven't you told me? Are you keeping a secret from me?"

He smiled, his blue eyes twinkling. "I met Otto Van Zef at Maynard's. We got to talking about work. He'd like me to come see a house he's building out by West Beach. I told him I'd come after I've finished your cabinets."

"That's wonderful, dear. What kind of man is this Mr. Van Zef?"

"He's about sixty years old and has the biggest gray mustache I've ever seen. He must have a lot of hair on his head, too, lots sticking out under his hat. We talked quite a while and I think I'll like working with him. Hey, I have enough lumber for a vanity dresser, would you like one?"

"Well, as you know, I'm not one to dawdle much over how I look." She ran one hand through her blonde curls. "I'd rather have drawers for towels and linens."

Will stuck his head into the shed. "Guess what? I've got

a surprise for you."

"A surprise? What is it?" asked Pauline.

"I was picking up feed at the dock and Clarence told me there was a box for you. I put it in the house."

"Oh, my goodness! It must be my sewing machine!" Pauline clapped her hands together. "Now I can sew the curtains."

Fred said, "You're here at the right time, Will. I can use your help. Pauline varnished the cabinets, gave them two coats and they're dry now. I think she did a pretty good job."

Will felt the smooth varnished wood. "They look great. Do you want to take them in now?"

"Yep, we took the old counter out. Want to grab the end of this one?" They carried the cabinets to the house and nailed them to the wall, one on each side of the window above the sink.

"I have something for the top of the sink counter," said Will. "I'll get it from the truck."

He returned with a large piece of linoleum. "I figured you'd need something on top of the counter and brought this up. What do you think, Paulie?"

She frowned at the pattern. "It looks like the kitchen floor in your house."

"It's leftover, but will make a good countertop."

Pauline looked perplexed. "I don't know. Linoleum on the counter?" She ran her hand over the small black and white squares. "What do you think, Fred?"

"It's a good idea, better than bare wood."

Pauline said, "Okay. I guess you're right."

When it had been cut and nailed down, they stood and

admired Fred's cabinets.

Pauline said, "Now they just need handles."

Fred replied, "Next time we're in town you can get them at the hardware store."

"I better get going," said Will. "I told Marian I'd help her in the garden."

"Will, Fred and I are happy here. I love being close to you and Marian."

"I'm glad. We've lived apart for too many years." He started to walk away, hesitated, and then gave his sister a bear hug. "Well, I'll see you later."

"Thanks again for helping," said Fred.

"Sure, anytime. Just give a holler."

Pauline woke to the smell of coffee. She stifled a big yawn. "Gracious sakes, Fred, you're up early."

"I'm excited. It's my first day working for a salary since we left Bay City. Can you make me some oatmeal while I stake out Billy and Nanny?"

Fred ate a hurried breakfast and put on his jacket. "Are you going to be okay?"

Pauline laughed, kissed him and said, "Yes, I'll be fine as long as you keep me supplied with wood and water."

"The drive is only about three miles," he said as he went out the door. "I'll be home for lunch." Pauline followed him and waved from the porch as he drove out of the yard.

Each morning after Fred left for work, Pauline took care of the chickens. She reached under the hens' warm bodies to find their eggs and delighted in finding the different colors. Resting her arms on the bottom part of the

Dutch door Fred had made, she watched and listened to the hens' soft, contented sounds as they walked around, lifting one foot, gently putting it down, and then doing the same with the other foot.

One morning after fastening the latch on the nest roof, she heard footsteps and quickly turned. She gasped, put her hand to her mouth, dropped the egg basket and exclaimed "It's you!" She looked up to a freckled-faced young man sporting orange-red hair. "I've seen you walking down by our trees and up by the spring."

"Yes, ma'am."

"Who are you? What do you want?" she asked, shielding her eyes with one hand from the bright morning sun.

"My name's Rupert. I'm sorry I scared you. I used to live here with my ma and pa." He took off his cap and looked down at her.

"Rupert?" she repeated.

"Rupert Long."

Pauline looked at his clothes. *Why he's hardly a man, just a tall boy dressed in jeans and a plaid shirt with frayed cuffs, and wearing scuffed leather shoes. Should I be afraid of him?*

Rupert reached for the basket and saw the broken eggs. "I'm sorry. I should have called hello."

"Well, never mind," said Pauline, taking the basket, more interested to learn about him than worry about the eggs. "When did you live here?"

"I was born there," Rupert said, pointing to Pauline's house. "My pa and ma lived here until she died. Then Pa and

I went to Pennsylvania to live with my gramma and grampa."

"How old were you when you left?"

"I was five years old, but I'll be twenty-one on the Fourth of July. Pa told me I was a patriotic baby. We left here in 1917."

Then remembering she had started bread to rise, she told him she had work to do.

"Well, if it's okay with you, maybe I can wait until your husband comes back. I'd like to talk with him."

"No, you can't hang around. Come back in the evening around seven. I'll tell him you came today and want to talk with him, but you go now."

"Okay, I'll be back," Rupert said, and told her again he was sorry he had scared her. He sauntered toward the road with his hands in his pockets, whistling a little tune. Pauline watched him walk away, then picked up the broken eggs and threw them onto the dirt floor in the chicken coop. The hens clucked noisily as they scurried to start pecking.

She felt anxious for Fred to come home and hurried back to the house. Her mind kept going back to Rupert as she kneaded the soft dough and formed the loaves. *He was polite and seemed harmless, yet....*

When Fred drove into the yard for lunch, she rushed to meet him.

"Well, my pretty wife, you seem eager to see me." He put an arm around her slim waist.

"Fred, the man I told you about came today. He nearly scared me to death and I dropped my basket of eggs."

"Just a minute, here, slow down and tell me what happened."

After taking a deep breath, Pauline told him about the encounter with Rupert.

"And you say he moved away seventeen years ago?"

"Yes, and he said he'll come back around seven tonight when you're home. I don't want him here when I'm alone."

Taking her hand, they walked to the house. "Do I smell fresh bread? I'm sure hungry."

Fred smeared butter on a thick slice of warm bread and enjoyed it with a bowl of Pauline's hearty vegetable beef soup. "You sure are a good cook."

"I like cooking for you." And after a pause she asked, "Do you have to go back to work?"

"We're trying to finish a job today. Would you like me to drop you off at Marian's and pick you up on the way home?"

"Yes, I'd like that."

That evening, she told Fred that Marian and Will had invited them to go to the Grange Potluck on Saturday. "It would give us a chance to meet some of our neighbors. Can we go, or do you have to work?"

"Otto doesn't work on weekends and I'd like to meet our neighbors, too."

"Marian said I don't need to take anything, but Will reminded me of the rhubarb cobbler our mom used to make. He said he saw some growing over by that rusty wire fence."

After supper Pauline sat at the table engrossed in writing while Fred was comfortable in his chair reading Will's latest *Successful Farming* magazine. He glanced over at her. "What have you got there?"

"This is my little book I use as a journal. Remember I

had it on the train?"

"If I remember correctly, you did a lot of day dreaming on the train reliving our whole life together."

"Well, I don't write every detail, but I do want to write about Will meeting us in Seattle, the ferry boat ride to Whidbey, living with Will and Marian, the house, the chickens and..."

"You have a lot of catching up to do."

"I might need your help remembering everything."

"All you have to do is ask. I have a good memory."

Pauline wrinkled her nose and laughed. "Yes, I know you do."

He went back to his magazine and she to her writing.

Rupert had not come by eight o'clock. Fred stood and stretched. "I don't think that fellow is going to show his face tonight. I need to turn in, dear."

The next day before Fred went to work, he held Pauline a bit longer than usual. "If he shows up, tell him to come back when I'm home for lunch."

Chapter Fifteen... The Grange Picnic

Pauline glanced at the mantel clock when it struck on the half-hour. *Nine-thirty already. I better hurry if this is going to be ready by eleven-thirty. I'm glad Fred started the fire for me and is taking care of the hens.*

She cut chunks of rhubarb into a casserole dish, added sugar, a handful of flour, a bit of nutmeg, a bit more to please Fred, and added dots of butter. She mixed the batter and dropped it onto the rhubarb. After testing the temperature with her hand, she put the cobbler in the oven.

The dishes were washed and the counters were clean when Fred came in and asked, "How's the cobbler? I hope you used nutmeg."

"I put in an extra amount just for you." She opened the oven door, leaned back from the hot air and looked at her creation. "The juice is bubbly and the crust is browning, just needs a few more minutes. I'm going to put on a clean dress. Are you going to change?"

Fred looked down at his overalls. "These are clean. We're just going to a picnic. No need to dress-up." He sat down at the table and picked up a *Farm Journal,* another of

Will's magazines.

Pauline took off her soiled apron. Pushing hangers back and forth, she decided to wear a blue and white checkered print with long sleeves.

"The cobbler sure smells good. Shall I take it from the oven?"

"Yes, take it out," she mumbled, slipping the dress over her head.

Looking at the cobber, Pauline said, "Oh dear, how am I going to carry this? I wish I had a picnic basket."

Fred got up from the table. "Here let me help you. Bring me a dishtowel."

Pauline gave him a towel made of a flour sack that she had decorated with embroidered blue flowers. He spread it on the table, put the cobbler in the middle, brought up two opposite corners of the towel, tied them and did the same with the other two corners.

"There," he said, "just like my mom did. The knots make a nice handle."

"Very clever, Fred. I'm ready. I'm so excited to see Jenny!"

They heard Will's car. "There they are!" Fred followed her with the cobbler.

Jenny jumped out of the car and ran to Pauline. They embraced and looked each other over. "You've grown up and you're so beautiful!" She gave her niece another big hug and kissed her cheek. "Oh, it's good to see you, Jenny. It's been so long."

"Yes, since your wedding."

"My just look at you." Pauline stood arms-length away

from her. "You're as tall as me and your hair is just as blonde as mine. Fred, see how tall she is?"

"Come here, Jenny. Give your old uncle a hug!" Fred slipped his arms around her slim back. "You look like you could blow away in the wind. Don't they feed you up there?"

Jenny laughed and said, "Oh, Uncle Fred, I eat plenty."

"Come on guys, you can talk in the car," Will called.

"I want to hear all about your life in Bellingham," said Pauline. "Where do you live?"

"I'm living with a doctor's family and help with chores for my room and board."

"What kind of work do you do?"

"I iron sheets and Doctor's shirts and do the dishes after supper, only they call it dinner. I set the table with china and candles every night. Doctor Shubert and Mary, that's his wife, eat in the dining room, but I eat at the kitchen table by myself."

"Really? By yourself? Do you like that?"

"It makes me feel like a maid, but I love taking care of Lil' Lise. She's just fifteen months. She welcomes me home every day. She holds her arms up to me and calls me Enny. She's so cute when she waddles on her fat little legs."

"She sounds sweet."

"Yes, she cries when I leave for school in the morning. I walk about a mile on Garden Street up to school, but sometimes if it's raining hard, Mary gives me a bus token so I can ride the city bus. Last January we had lots of snow. Doctor said he couldn't remember when they had so much. I'm glad Dad gave me boots at Christmas."

"I remember our cold winters in Bay City. Your dad kept

busy shoveling snow from our sidewalks and earned a few pennies from the neighbors by clearing theirs."

Marian asked, "Jenny, do you remember the deep snow we had in Bay City?"

"I remember that time Dad pulled me on the sled. It turned over and I rolled down the big hill. You said I looked like a snowman," she said.

Arriving at Hank's West Beach picnic grounds, Will parked his Model A on a grassy strip by a few other cars. Fred helped Pauline and Marian out of the backseat. Will came around the car and took Marian's picnic basket. They walked a short distance and through an opening in a hedge of native rose and snowberry bushes.

"You can't catch me!" yelled a boy as he ran zigzag around other boys. Fred caught Pauline's arm and pulled her away before the boy fell at her feet. He got up and ran away.

"Kelly, come over here," called his dad. "You know better, son, watch where you're going."

The young boy hung his head, and then looked up at Pauline. "I'm sorry."

Pauline smiled and laughed. "I'm okay, but you better hurry or you'll get caught."

Kelly asked his father, "Can I go now?"

"Yes, go play with the boys in the sand dunes."

Will said, "Hank, this is my sister, Pauline, and her husband, Fred Gunther." As they shook hands, Will added, "I think I told you, Fred, Hank is the county road supervisor. He has a lot of men working on the approaches to the bridge."

Just then a girl bumped between Pauline and Jenny. Jenny whirled to see her friend. "Suzie! I was hoping you'd be here!" The girls hugged and Jenny introduced her. "Aunt Paulie, this is my friend from high school."

Pauline took Suzie's hand and said, "It's nice to meet you."

Marian asked, "Is your mother here, Suzie?"

"Yeah, she's over by the food tables. Jenny, come see Ellen and Harriet."

Marian took Pauline's arm. "Come, I'll introduce you to the ladies." Fred handed the cobbler to Pauline and Marian took her basket from Will. Stepping over yellow-blooming sand verbena, they walked into a grassy clearing where women arranged picnic food on a table made of long planks set on saw horses.

"Hello, ladies," said Marian. When they looked to her, she said, "I'd like you to meet my sister-in-law, Pauline Gunther. She and her husband, Fred, moved from Michigan to make their home up the road from me." The women gathered in a semi-circle, and as Marian said their names, they responded with welcoming smiles and handshakes. Pauline repeated their names as she tried to connect each name with a new face.

As more picnickers arrived, they set their casseroles and bowls of salads on the table in the open, sunny space. Soon someone announced, "Time to eat!"

Children of all ages and sizes came running, jostling one another for a place in line. Mothers scolded them to behave while helping little ones with their plates of food, and then directed them to sit at the tables nestled under the canopy of wind-blown wild crabapple trees.

Adults lined up to fill their plates with fried chicken,

baked beans and a variety of salads.

"Where's the sauerkraut?" a man asked.

"We used up our kraut months ago," someone replied.

"Our cabbage is making heads," said a woman. "Won't be long and we'll be filling the crocks again."

Fred stood with Pauline. "I smell fried chicken. Maybe one of your hens would be good eating," he teased.

"Oh, no, not my girls."

Marian whispered to her, "Try Gev's potato salad in the big yellow bowl. She makes a boiled dressing."

The men congregated on benches in the open area, eating and laughing at each other's jokes. Pauline enjoyed listening to the women chat and answered questions about where she had lived in Michigan and if she liked Whidbey Island. She told them about her work in the shirt factory and that she had lived all her life in Bay City.

"Come on guys. Let's go play ball." Pauline heard Kelly's voice and watched the boys scramble out of the picnic area.

The men stood, stretching and patting their full bellies, bantering back and forth, and headed toward the beach, a few holding the hands of their younger children. One young man hoisted his little boy to his shoulders.

"As usual we're left to clean-up," said a women as they all began collecting their own dishes and utensils. "I think the men have much to talk about."

"The bridge is the main topic these days," said the woman standing beside Pauline.

Soon everything was in order and one of the women said, "Looks like that about does it. Shall we go to the beach?" They started walking, some carried babies in their arms and others pushed strollers.

They reached the end of the road where the men were sitting on large logs that had been thrown up by high tides. Some women gave their children to their husbands to look after, others took their young ones down a path to the sand.

Pauline stood beside Marian, breathing the fresh salty air. She turned her head from side to side, taking in the whole view. Mounds of sand left by the low tide lay exposed to the warm sun. White foam sparkled as low waves broke on long sandbars. "It's so beautiful, Marian."

"Yes, it is. We have an extremely low tide today. The water will warm up as it washes over the sandbars. The kids like to dig big holes and sit in them like they're in a bathtub. Do you see Jenny and her friends way out on the far sandbars? They have so much fun playing games and swimming between the bars. Well, shall we find a log and sit with the ladies?"

"You go ahead. I'll mosey on down and wade in the water with the kids." She picked her way around the driftwood onto the sand, took off her shoes, stuffed her stockings into them and set them on a log. She walked to the water's edge and dug her feet into the coarse sand. Gentle waves washed the gravel back and forth.

Women held the hands of little tots jumping about in the small waves. Children plopped themselves down onto the sand and dug holes with their hands and clam shells. They laughed and splashed water onto each other. A woman joined her. "Hello, Pauline. I'm Gev Martin. I'm sorry my rambunctious boy almost knocked you down."

Pauline laughed. "Oh, he was fine."

Gev bent and picked up a stone and passed it to Pauline. "This is the best beach for finding agates. Hold it up to the sun and you'll see your finger through it."

Pauline held the stone up and peered at it. "Oh, I see." She looked down at the gravel and picked up a small whitish stone.

"That's a sugar agate. It's a different kind of rock. We tease the kids that maybe it will be an agate in another million years," said Gev, smiling.

Pauline commented, "It's quite different than the agates at Lake Superior. Those are dense. You wouldn't see a shadow through the browns and yellows. Some have stripes and patterns. People use them to make jewelry." She drew a chain from around her neck. "I have one. See my pendant."

Gev admired the red and yellow stone in the gold setting. "Yes, it's lovely."

Picking their way around mounds of gravel, they watched children lying on logs floating in the water, kicking as the logs rose and fell with the gentle swell of the waves. Older boys played on a log raft they had fastened together with old rope.

Gev asked, "Do you like to swim?"

Pauline answered, "I do. When I was young, my folks took my brother and me to the lake. I didn't know any fancy strokes, but enough to get away from Will when he came after me."

Brown kelp floated in small pools around seaweed-covered rocks. Pauline squatted for a closer look at the limpets and barnacles clinging to the rocks. Green sea anemones lay open in the sun-warmed water, and little shore crabs scurried sideways to find safety in the algae. A flash of light caught her attention. She pointed to a glass ball bobbing in the water a short distance away. "Look!" She pulled her skirt up and waded into deeper water. "I got it!"

Gev explained, "It's a Japanese fishing float. The fishermen tie them to the edges of their fishnets. My son, Chris, has many of them. He hunts for them after winter storms."

"Here, he can add this to his collection," said Pauline.

"No, it's finders keepers. You keep it."

At the sound of a sharp whistle, they turned and saw Hank, his hands cupped around his mouth. "Time for ice cream!"

"Is it homemade?" asked Pauline.

"No, Hank has the Darigold truck deliver it when the milk cans are picked up in the morning. It's packed in dry ice in heavy canvas containers."

Pauline said, "Look at the kids come running! It didn't take long to get them out of the water."

"They know Ted always brings a case or two of soda pop and they hurry to get their favorite. Orange and grape seem to be the most popular. I like the Cream Soda. The kids like to take the corks from inside the bottle caps and fasten them to their hats."

Pauline said, "I like Root Beer."

They retraced their steps to the picnic grounds. Women opened their baskets and brought out their favored desserts: Mildred's chocolate devil's food cake, Thea's white cake covered with whipped cream, Alice's molasses cake, and Marian's lemon pie.

"What surprise did you bring, Pauline?" asked Alice.

"Just a rhubarb cobbler," she said as she undid the knotted towel.

"I know one man who will be happy for a new addition to our dessert table," said Alice, and she teased, "Gev, are you keeping something from us? It wouldn't be a Grange picnic without your mile-high strawberry pie."

Gev smiled as she put her pie on the table. "Hank and the boys picked the berries yesterday."

On their way home, Jenny said, "I'm so glad I got to see all my girlfriends."

Marian asked Pauline if she had a good time.

Pauline's face lit up with a big smile. "Yes, I did. All the women are so friendly. Gev Martin walked with me on the beach. She told me Otto built their house and they've been living in it for a few years, but the upstairs isn't finished yet."

"She hangs blankets on the unfinished walls between the hall and the three bedrooms."

"And Alice asked me to come for coffee, but I don't know which house."

"She lives in the white house across the road from us."

"Oh, I love that big house," said Pauline.

"How about you, Fred?" asked Marian.

"Hey, I think I met a lot of good cooks, and there's no problem talking with the men. They're all easy going. Seems they like to tease each other and that's fun. Of course, they talked about the bridge. Hank said they have tons of rock to move so we'll hear a lot of blasting."

Pauline said, "Well, I like the little ferry."

"Yeah, Paulie, it's fun," said Will, "but we need the

bridge. Now the farmers have to take their produce to Maylor's Dock to be shipped out. The ferry can't handle big trucks and equipment."

They all sat quiet for a few minutes and then Fred said, "One of the men said the Three C's are doing good work in the park."

"Three C's?" asked Pauline.

"The Civilian Conservation Corps that President Roosevelt started," said Fred.

"Oh, the men working down by the park. I wonder..."

Fred looked back at Pauline. "What are you thinking, dear?"

"Do you suppose Rupert is with the Three C's?"

"Yes, he certainly could be."

Jenny asked, "Who's Rupert?"

"Oh, he's a young man who lived in our house when he was little."

Chapter Sixteen... A Visit with Alice

Pauline and Fred got on with their daily routines. Fred staked Billy and Nanny to new patches of brush, brought water from the spring, and after breakfast, left for work. Pauline took care of her hens and busied herself with housework and sewing projects. She and Fred enjoyed Saturday trips to shop at the Producer's Co-op and Morton's Meat Market.

The hens were laying four or five eggs a day, more than Pauline could use. She gave some to Marian and had Fred take a few to Otto. She loved her hens and often talked to them. One day she told them, "I'm going to take some of your colorful eggs to Alice."

Pauline put on a fresh cotton housedress, nestled five colorful eggs into a linen napkin inside a Pyrex bowl and set out down Ducken Road. Yellow dandelions bloomed in the green grass along the sides of the road. Water from the June rains sparkled as it trickled over rocks in the ditches. Pauline hummed a little tune as she walked on the narrow gravel road.

When she came to Alice's white picket fence, she lifted the latch on the gate and walked on the concrete sidewalk around to the back of the old farmhouse. White lattice walls enclosed a large porch and bright red geraniums hung in pots from rafters. She tapped on the door, and when Alice opened it, Pauline got a whiff of something good baking in the wood stove oven.

Smiling, Alice said, "Well, hello, Pauline. You're a nice surprise."

Pauline handed her the bowl of eggs and went into the warm cheery kitchen. While sitting at the oilcloth-covered table and enjoying coffee and cookies, they chatted about this and that like women do. Pauline asked, "Alice, did you know the people who lived in our house?"

"I know a family lived up there in the woods, but they stayed to themselves and we didn't get to know them."

"Well, the other day while I fed my chickens a young man came up behind me and about scared me to death. His name is Rupert Long and he said he was born in our house."

"I don't remember that name. Mama didn't do much neighboring because we had so much work at home. My dad's legs were broken in a logging accident when he and Hank were skidding logs from the woods."

Pauline put a hand to her face. "Oh my, how terrible."

"Yes, he was standing on the wrong side when the logs whipped around a tree and hit him. Hank had to go for help. They put Dad in a wagon and brought him to the house and the doctor kept him in bed for a year. Hank stayed home from school so he could help Mama take care of the farm. She called him the bread winner in the family."

Pauline put a hand on Alice's arm. "It must have been a hard time for your family, Alice."

"Yes, it was." She went to the stove, added a stick of wood to the fire and took the coffee pot to the table. She filled their cups and sat down again. "Ted, Thea and I all had chores to do. Mama and Hank milked the cows in the morning and I helped at night."

"Did you like milking cows?"

"Oh, sometimes I didn't want to, but it had to be done. I guess I didn't mind too much." Alice laughed. "The cows were gentle and warm when I leaned my face against their sides. Sometimes a tail would swish into my face. When I think about it, I can almost smell the warm milk."

Pauline commented, "Marian helps Will milk their cows but I've never tried it."

Alice stirred sugar into her coffee.

Pauline said, "I've been thinking about the big stumps in our woods. Some of them have big chunks cut out on their sides."

"Yes, when the trees were cut down, each man had his own springboard. He used an axe to cut a v-shaped notch in a tree trunk and put one end of the board into the notch. Then he stood on the board. Notches were cut on both sides of the tree. Like this." Alice drew a picture on a piece of scrap paper.

"Oh, I see," said Pauline. "Those notches are so high. Why didn't the men just stand on the ground?"

"Sometimes the ground wasn't level, or maybe they didn't want the lower part of the tree because it had a funny shape. They wanted straight logs for lumber and telephone poles. They used a long saw with a handle on each end to cut through the tree."

"Fred found a long saw in our shed. Will called it a misery whip because using it is such strenuous work."

"Yes, those saws are hard to pull back and forth." Alice pushed a stack of magazines to Pauline and asked if she subscribed to any.

"No, not right now, maybe someday."

"I was cleaning out the attic. These are old, but they have interesting stories. They're mostly *Pictorial Review Magazine* and *Ladies Home Companion.*"

Pauline's eyes lit up. "The *Pictorial?* I haven't seen one of these for ages. I loved cutting out the Dolly Dingle paper dolls, and Mom drew dresses for them." She opened a copy and searched the middle section for a paper doll page. "Oh, look. It's *Dolly Dingle and Her War Garden.* Isn't it darling? I love the wheelbarrow filled with vegetables."

Alice asked, "Would you like to cut it out?"

"Oh, yes," said Pauline, smiling.

Alice took her scissors from a kitchen drawer.

Pauline carefully cut out Dolly and her outfits. She reminisced about her paper dolls from childhood. "Those were special times with Mom. She died when I was almost thirteen." Pauline's eyes grew misty. "I really missed her and she didn't get to meet Fred."

A comforting smile played on Alice's face. "I think she would like him."

Pauline said, "I know she would. Dad and I had quite a time cooking and keeping up the house. Will and Marian still lived in Bay City and they helped us a lot. It's good to be with them again." Pauline looked up at the walnut kitchen clock. "Oh my, I better go home and start supper."

They got up from the table and Pauline buttoned her sweater. Alice put a few cookies in Pauline's blue bowl. "You can put these in Fred's lunch box."

Pauline gave Alice a hug and promised to visit again.

Chapter Seventeen... Smelting

Fred closed the door and hung his hat on a peg. "A beautiful sunset tonight, Pauline. Did you see it?"

"I missed it, dear. I've been reading. Alice gave me all those magazines." She pointed to the stack on the counter. "She sent cookies for you."

"I'll thank her next time I see her."

After supper they sat in their easy chairs. Pauline looked through the magazines and Fred chuckled while listening to *Jack Benny* on his Philco.

Pauline looked up and cocked her head. "Fred, someone just drove into the yard."

He went to the door and opened it to see Gev, dressed in a pair of Hank's overalls, a big wool jacket, stocking cap and rubber boots, walking up to the porch.

"Gev! What brings you out on a cool night like this? Come in."

"Hank is waiting in the truck," she said, stepping into the warm kitchen. "We would like you to go smelting with us. Will and Marian are coming in their truck."

Pauline asked, "Smelting?"

"Catching little fish," said Fred. "That sounds like fun."

Pauline and Fred put on their jackets and boots and followed Gev to Hank's Whippet truck.

Hank slid out of the cab. "Jump up in the back. We're just going down to Cornet Bay. Here, Pauline," said Hank. He cupped his hands together for her to step into and gave her a lift up onto the bed of the truck. "You both better sit down. Be careful not to trip over the rakes." And not waiting for them to get settled, he drove out of the yard onto Ducken Road.

"Whoops!" Fred exclaimed as both he and Pauline nearly lost their balance. He helped Pauline sit down and they leaned against the back of the cab. Fred put an arm around her. "This is going to be a bumpy ride. Hank doesn't seem to slow down for chuckholes."

"Do you know what we're going to do, Fred?"

"I overheard a guy tell Otto the smelt are running. We're going fishing. I haven't been fishing for smelt since I was about twelve years old when my family fished along the shores of Lake Superior."

"We never went fishing at night," said Pauline.

"It's fun. Smelt are small and come to shore to lay their eggs in the sand at high tide."

"Do you like to eat them?"

"Sure do. Dad took us out to the lake whenever Uncle Jack came for a visit."

The truck bounced along over the pot holes on the dirt road and made a sharp right turn. "We must be turning onto Cornet Bay Road," said Fred.

"I think I'm going to have a sore bottom," said Pauline

as the truck jolted to a stop behind the logs along the bay. Hank and Gev got out. Fred and Pauline scooted to the edge of the truck bed and Hank helped Pauline to the ground.

He lit a kerosene lantern. "Here," he said, handing the lantern to Pauline. "Fred, you can bring the buckets." Hank carried a long pole with a rake he had fashioned from an old window screen.

Gev carried a basket on her arm. "Careful going over the logs, we don't want any broken legs," she said.

"It's about time you got here, Hank," someone called. The glow of lanterns cast shadows of men standing along the shore.

"Come this way, Pauline," said Gev, and they joined several women who were sitting around a bonfire and poking long sticks at the burning logs. Sparks glowed in the dark sky each time another log was thrown onto the fire. It reminded Pauline of the lightning bugs back home. The women talked in soft voices about their day. Several had been weeding and watering their gardens.

Pauline heard Fred and Will laughing with the men along the shoreline. Then one man shouted, "Look! They're coming!" The women buttoned their coats, pulled on their hats and scarves and hurried toward the water to join the men.

There was a hushed "Shh...they're here!" as smelt came skimming under the surface of the water. The little fish flashed in the moonlight as they came closer to shore.

The men stepped into the water carrying long-handled basket rakes. They reached out with the rakes, then pulled them back to shore and emptied the baskets. Silver fish slipped onto the beach and thrashed around on the sandy gravel. The women scrambled to pick them up.

Fred squatted beside Pauline. "Are you having fun? Did you know catching fish could be so exciting?"

Pauline laughed. "They're slippery little devils. They jump right out of my hands! Look at their black, beady eyes."

Men all along the shore called back and forth, "They're coming fast!"

"I can't rake fast enough."

"Hey! I got more than I can handle."

"The fish are small this year."

As they pulled the rakes in, many of them empty, some-one said, "They're moving out with the tide, guess that's all for tonight."

Everyone gathered their rakes and buckets of smelt and walked up to the fire. Sparks rose into the black night as sticks and logs were thrown onto the burning embers. Husbands and wives sat together on logs. They opened baskets, poured hot coffee from thermos jugs into aluminum cups, and passed tins of cookies and cinnamon rolls.

Light, reflecting from the crescent moon, quivered on waves lapping on the shore. Occasional splashes could be heard as fish jumped and fell back into the water. Pauline enjoyed the quietness of the evening with her new friends. She asked Gev, "How do you cook smelt?"

Gev explained that she would keep them cool outside for the night and then cook some for breakfast. "Hank likes them rolled in flour with a little salt and pepper and fried in butter. It doesn't take long to get them crisp and brown in my iron skillet. These smelt are small so we don't take out the bones. Hank eats all but the tail."

"Even the head?" asked Pauline. Much laughter followed.

"No, I cut off the heads with scissors before I roll them in flour."

Hank and his brother, Ted, took harmonicas from their pockets and started playing "Turkey in the Straw." Men and women suggested their favorite songs and crooned in unison "When Irish Eyes are Smiling" and "By the Light of the Silvery Moon."

"Ten o'clock!" someone announced and they all sang "Goodnight ladies, goodnight gentlemen, goodnight ladies, it's time we head to bed."

The men knocked what remained of the log fire apart making a game of throwing glowing logs into the water. They carried buckets, rakes and lanterns to their trucks and cars and called out goodnight.

Fred teased, "Are we going to have another bumpy ride, Hank?"

In good humor, Hank said, "I'll try not to shake you up too much." When they reached the little house on the hill, Fred helped Pauline off the truck. Hank asked, "What do you think of smelt raking, Pauline?"

"I liked the whole evening. I loved singing around the fire." As she walked toward the house she called, "I'll try Gev's recipe." But, she thought to herself, *I'm not sure I'll like the little fish.*

Chapter Eighteen... Pauline's Accident

A week had passed since Pauline had visited Alice, so she decided to take eggs to her friend. She bustled around doing her morning chores and then left the house with a few eggs in her basket. As she stepped down from the porch, she felt a sprinkle of rain so went back into the house to get her red scarf. She stuffed it into a coat pocket and started on her way.

After leaving the shelter of the woods, the wind picked up and blew rain on her face. She tied the wool scarf under her chin and turned up her coat collar. *Should I turn back? No, it's just a late June shower. I'm closer to Alice's house than mine, and her kitchen will be cozy warm.*

Large drops of rain pelted her. She bent into the wind, held her new basket in the crook of one arm and put her hands in her pockets. The wind whooshed through the bushes on the sides of the rutted road. Thunder rumbled in the distance. The wind snatched her scarf and her hair fell across her face. She held up one hand to shield her eyes. She stumbled, lost her balance, dropped the eggs, and landed on her hands and knees. "Nerts!"

Someone bent down beside her and put a hand on her back. "Here, let me help you!" She looked up and saw Rupert, his red hair falling over his face. "Come," he yelled, and with his help, she stood up. He held her steady with one arm around her waist. Twigs and leaves, chased by the howling wind, hit their legs.

Pauline brushed her wet, matted hair from her eyes and yelled, "Thank you. I stumbled."

"Yes, I saw you."

She rubbed at tiny bits of rock embedded in her skinned hands and then pointed to Alice's house. "Let's go...white house!"

They made their way toward the big house, their heads down against the stinging rain. Rupert fumbled with the latch on the gate, opened it, and they climbed four wooden steps to the porch. He knocked on the leaded glass in Alice's front door. Pauline looked down at her wet dress and saddle shoes. She put a hand to her head, "I lost my scarf."

"And I lost my cap," said Rupert.

"I wonder if Alice is home. Knock again."

He knocked. Pauline saw Alice peek through the lace curtains on the window, and then the door opened. "My goodness, Pauline. Come in. I thought I heard a knock, but figured the wind was blowing the hanging basket against the house."

Pauline and Rupert stepped in, water dripping from their shoes onto Alice's floral carpet. Pauline blurted out, "I fell and Rupert helped me up. Rupert, this is Mrs. Andrews."

Alice looked at Rupert and then back at Pauline. "Let's get you out of those wet clothes, Pauline. Whatever were you thinking going out in a storm like this? Both of you take off your wet coats and then sit down and take off your shoes."

"Alice, I shouldn't sit on your nice couch."

"Come in my bedroom, Pauline."

Rupert took off his jacket, looked at the plush, upholstered furniture, and then sat on a plain straight chair. He bent over and took off his leather work shoes. He smiled when Pauline came out wearing a pair of Alice's flannel pajamas and plopped down on the couch.

Alice said, "Wrap up in the afghan, Pauline. We don't want you to catch a cold."

"I'm okay, a bit chilled is all," she said, but snuggled under the soft knitted coverlet.

"I have coffee on the stove," said Alice, and looking at Rupert told him, "some for you, too." She bustled out to her kitchen.

Pauline looked at Rupert. She brushed her hair back. He brushed his back, and then they laughed. Alice brought two cups of steaming coffee and set them on a small table. Rupert thanked her and held the hot cup with both hands. Pauline sipped the coffee.

"Are you feeling better?" asked Alice.

"I'm fine. I didn't expect so much wind."

"It's unusual to have such a bad storm come up this time of year."

They heard a knock on the door. Alice opened it to find Fred. "Hi, Alice, is Pauline here?"

Pauline called, "Yes, Fred. I'm here."

Rupert stood up. Fred took off his hat and then stepped in.

Pauline asked, "Why aren't you working?"

"We quit work when the lights went out. Otto said he couldn't remember such a storm in June." He looked at his frumpled wife on the couch, "What happened to you?"

"That wicked wind blew so hard and I couldn't see through the rain. I tripped on something and the next thing I knew I was on my hands and knees on the road. Rupert helped me walk here."

"Are you hurt?"

Pauline laughed. "Goodness no. I'm not hurt, just feel like a silly goose. I got soaking wet and now I'm wearing Alice's pajamas."

"If it hadn't been for your red scarf tangled in an alder branch by the road, I would have just gone home." He glanced up. "You're Rupert?"

Rupert nodded and said, "Yes, sir." He sat down and put on his wet shoes. "I should get going. I want to find my cap."

"Wait, where are you going?" asked Fred.

"Back to camp."

"Are you with the C's?"

"Yes, sir." He stood and reached for his wet jacket.

Fred said, "I'll drive you down in my truck." He gazed at his wife, "I'll pick you up on my way back."

Pauline called, "Thank you, Rupert," as the men went out the door.

Alice brought her coffee pot and filled Pauline's cup and a cup for herself.

Soon Fred was back. "Well, now," and with an amused smile, looked at Alice, "What am I going to do with a wife who goes out on such a stormy day?"

Pauline gave him a quirky smile and laughed. "Fred, I needed to get out. When I left the house there was only a little sprinkle and just a little breeze. It felt refreshing. I wanted to walk."

"You should have turned back and gone home. The roads are covered with branches. Come. Let's go home and see what damage we have."

"Just a minute," said Alice. She put Pauline's wet clothes in a bag and took a coat from the closet. "Here, wear this."

Pauline gave Alice a hug. "I'm sorry to be such trouble."

"You're no trouble, Pauline. I'm glad you didn't get hurt."

"Fred, my shoes."

Before she could say more, he grabbed her shoes, picked her up, carried her out into the rain and put her in the truck. Starting the motor he said, "You're lucky Rupert came along."

She watched the windshield wiper squeak back and forth across the glass while he concentrated on driving.

Fred parked the truck close to the house. "I'll carry you in."

She laughed. "This is like coming home from our honeymoon."

"The house is cold. You're shivering, better get in bed until it warms up." She slid between the cold sheets and pulled the quilt up to her chin. Fred poked at the fire. "Pauline, did you remember to bank the fire before you left?"

"Nerts! No, I didn't think of that." She buried her head in the down pillow.

"Well, never mind. It won't take long." After getting a

hot fire going, he asked, "Did you have anything planned for lunch?"

"There's a bowl of leftover chicken soup in the cooler. Bread and butter would be nice."

"I'm going to check on the animals, and when I get back, I'll heat up the soup."

She heard Fred return and after a few minutes, he came over and stroked her hair and kissed her forehead. She sat up and put her arms around his neck. He held her and whispered, "Come on, the soup is hot. Let's eat."

"I'm so glad Rupert helped me."

"Tell me about him. Was he coming down the hill from our place?"

"I don't know. He surprised me. When I couldn't get up by myself, he bent down and pulled me to my feet. I got gravel in my knees and hands. My feet squished in my shoes."

Chapter Nineteen... A Sunday Trip

Pauline woke early Sunday morning to the sound of rain on the windowpane. She crept out of bed, careful not to wake Fred, and peeked out the door. "Nerts! Now we can't go down to the camp." She crawled back into bed and Fred's warm arms pulled her close. "It's raining," she whispered. "I guess we'll be staying home."

Later, after a breakfast of pancakes with blackberry syrup, Fred put on his boots and told Pauline, still in her pink robe, "I'll feed the chickens and take care of the goats."

As Pauline cleared away the breakfast dishes, she thought about Rupert. *Only five when his mother died. How sad for a little boy. Does he remember anything about her? Why didn't his father bring him back here to their land?*

Fred came in with a few eggs. "The rain is letting up and it's clearing in the west. I think we can go down and look for Rupert, give us a chance to see the work the men have been doing. Would you like to take our lunch and eat by Cranberry Lake?"

"Sounds good to me, I'll get dressed and make sandwiches."

"Okay, I'll fill the thermos with coffee."

As Fred drove down Ducken Road, Pauline kept up a constant stream of chatter. "I wonder if Rupert's father lives in Pennsylvania? Don't you think it strange to walk away from your land and never come back?"

Fred answered each of her questions with, "I don't know, Pauline." He turned onto the road leading to Cornet Bay. "You've got a lot of questions for Rupert. Help me find the road to the camp."

"Turn there, by the big stump covered with salal."

He drove onto the road, twisting around the old firs and cedars populating the virgin forest. They came to a graveled parking area marked off by peeled logs. Fred pulled up beside a truck at the back of a long wooden building roofed with shakes. Pauline stepped down from the truck and over a puddle. Rain dripped from the great cedars.

"It's so quiet. Is anyone here?"

"Well, it's Sunday. Maybe the fellas are away or resting in their cabins. Let's look around a bit."

Following a worn path, they walked past the end of the building and down a slope to a large open space with a well-used baseball diamond laid out in a grassy area. Small bunkhouses erected by the C's stood on each side of the field. They saw several canvas tents set among the trees. The Stars and Stripes hung loosely on its pole. Fred took Pauline's hand as they walked across the wet grass toward the bay. They reached knee-high, gray-green beach grass growing along the edge of the field and sun-bleached driftwood logs in jumbled piles. Seaweed, small sticks and shells marked the last high tide on the rocky beach. Steep cliffs of jagged rock formed the sides of the bay. Stunted firs growing precariously among the stark rocks, cast shadows on the calm dark water. "It's so beautiful," said Pauline.

Fred agreed and as they walked back up the slope to the long building, they saw a man lying in a hammock on the porch reading a book. He looked up as they approached.

Fred called out, "Good morning!"

The young man returned the greeting, rolled out of the hammock, and came down from the porch. "What can I do for you?"

"I'm Fred Gunther and this is my wife, Pauline. We're looking for Rupert Long."

"Dave Felding." They shook hands. "I think Rupert is with a group at Cranberry Lake."

Fred said, "I hear the men are building picnic shelters over at the lake picnic area."

Dave smiled. "Yeah, I'm learning to cut stone for the shelter foundations. Working with the rock is challenging, but I like it. I think Rupert's been working with the blasting crew. Some of the guys are cutting trees and peeling logs." He motioned with his hand. "This building was our first project. Want to have a look?"

Pauline and Fred followed Dave up the steps and into a large open-beamed room. He said the men lived in tents while putting up the building. "And some of us are still living in tents until more cabins are ready." He said the planed boards for the walls were brought in from a local mill. "Everything you see here, we built: tables, benches, kitchen cupboards and counters. We all have assigned times for kitchen duty and eat our meals here. Classes are held here, too, for guys who want to finish high school."

Pauline scanned the bulletin board covered with notices informing the men of classes and activities. "Look at this, Fred. Here's a picture of a baseball team in their uniforms. I wonder if Rupert plays ball." She moved a finger over the pictures looking for him and then put her hand on Fred's arm. "Here he is. The tall one in the back."

Fred took a close look. "Yep, that's Rupert all right."

"We're proud of our baseball team," boasted Dave. "They've had games at three other camps and always come back winners. We've got some good wrestlers and boxers, too."

Pauline gave Fred's arm a squeeze. He took the hint, thanked Dave and told him they would go over to the lake and look for Rupert.

Fred parked the truck in an area set off with logs. When they got out, they heard yelling, and looking toward the lake, saw men in row boats. "Let's eat and wait for them to come to shore," said Fred.

They sat at one of the newly-made wood tables which had a top made of a log sawn in half lengthwise. Fred took a big bite of his ham sandwich. "Mmm, this is tasty."

"You're just hungry," teased Pauline, as she poured coffee into tin cups. "Remember on our honeymoon when we splashed each other trying to row the boat?"

"Yeah, lucky we didn't tip over."

Pauline laughed. "I wasn't a strong swimmer. I would have drowned."

Fred's eyes twinkled. "No, the hero in me would have

saved you."

Pauline smiled. "My hero? Yes, you are," giving him a little nudge. "Oh, look! The boats are almost to the shore."

One row boat scrunched on the sandy shore. Two men climbed up onto the dock waving their arms and shouting in triumph. The other two boats beached beside the first. The men slapped each other on the back, laughing and joking.

"I see Rupert," said Pauline. "Let's go meet him. We could invite him to have dinner with us next Sunday."

"Sure. I bet he would like a home-cooked meal."

Pauline waved and called hello. Rupert looked up and waved back. Taking long strides, he met them with a cheery grin. "Hi." He and Fred shook hands.

"You fellows seemed to be having an exciting race," said Fred.

"Yeah, the guys in my cabin challenged guys in a couple of other cabins."

"We came to thank you for helping Pauline."

Rupert grinned at her and she laughed. "I felt so ridiculous."

"Pauline told me you lived in our house when you were a boy."

"Yes, I remember living there. I've wondered if I might find anything. When my pa decided we would leave, we didn't take everything."

"We did find a sewing basket," said Pauline. "Would you like to come up and join us for dinner next Sunday?"

"That would be great." He looked down toward the lake. "The guys are leaving. I better go while there's still something left to eat." And he jogged off to catch up with his friends.

"We have dinner at noon," Pauline called, and saw him wave back to her. She turned to Fred, "It will be interesting to find out about Rupert's family."

"Don't get too excited, after all, he was just a young boy when his father took him to his grandparents' home."

"What shall I fix, maybe something different than he gets at camp?"

Fred teased, "He'd probably like your famous rhubarb cobbler."

Chapter Twenty... Cows and Driving

Pauline, excited to tell Marian about Rupert, walked into Marian's yard to find her on her hands and knees weeding her flower garden. "Well, hey! What brings you here so early?" asked Marian.

"We went down to the CCC Camp yesterday to find Rupert."

Marian continued scratching in the soil with a garden fork. "Did you find him?"

"We did, and he's coming to dinner next Sunday."

Marian got up, put her hand tools in a bucket and pushed the wheelbarrow across the yard toward a pasture. "I'll dump this and then we'll have a cup of coffee and cookies."

"That sounds good," said Pauline.

Marian threw the clumps of grass and weeds over the fence. Cows came running, their udders swinging back and forth. They crowded along the barbed-wire, swishing their tails to drive away the flies and using their heads to boot each other out of the way.

Pauline stepped back from the fence. "They're mean to each other."

"Bessie's a brat and always first through the gate."

"Which one is Bessie?"

"There's Bessie with the white spot on her head, and that cow next to her, I call Moonshine, because she has a white crescent moon on the side of her belly. Before they can be registered I have to draw the pattern of their markings on an outline of a cow. Will tags each cow, records how much milk she gives and sends everything to the Guernsey Association."

"I don't know much about cows, but they have such pretty brown eyes."

Marian said, "Yes, they remind me of a song." She began to sing...

They strolled down the lane together.
The moon shone bright above.
He looked into her brown eyes, and they were
*   full of love.*
They reached the gate together.
There was nothing between them now,
For he was just a country lad and she a Jersey cow.

"Sing it again, I want to sing it for Fred." Pauline joined in as Marian sang it again, and then again.

When Marian pushed the wheelbarrow to the shed, Pauline noticed Will's truck. "I've never learned to drive. I'm going to ask Fred to teach me."

"Oh, no!" Marian exclaimed. "Husbands are the worst teachers. Let me teach you."

"You'll teach me to drive?"

"Sure, it's not difficult. Do you know anything about driving?"

"Not really. My dad turned a crank on the front to make his car start. Fred just pushes a button."

Marian motioned to the truck. "Let's give it a try."

"Shall I get in?" asked Pauline.

"Yes, on the passenger side. First you watch me, then it's your turn. This used to be a Willy's Whippet car, but Will converted it into a truck. Look. Here's how we start the motor."

Pauline watched as Marian pointed out the different buttons and explained what they did. Then Marian started the motor, looked over her shoulder, backed the truck out of the shed and drove into an open field. "You can practice here where you won't run into anything." She turned off the motor. "Okay, let's trade places."

They got out and walked around the back of the truck. Pauline grabbed the steering wheel to pull herself up onto the seat. Once again, Marian explained how to start the engine. With the motor going, she pointed out the pedals on the floor. "To go forward you have to let the clutch out slowly and press on the gas at the same time."

Pauline tried. The truck lurched forward and died. Marian told her to try again. The engine coughed, sputtered and quit abruptly.

"Nerts, I'm sorry. I'm such a dummkopf."

"No, you're not. It takes practice. Try again."

After several tries the truck moved forward coughing and sputtering. Pauline gripped the steering wheel for dear life.

"Now give it a bit more gas, and try to hold the steering wheel steady. Don't move it back and forth. We'll go straight toward the woods, turn and come back."

The truck zigzagged across the field. When they were twenty or so feet from a fence, Marian told her, "Start turning away from the fence." She put her hand on the steering wheel to help Pauline turn the wheels. They crawled back across the pasture. Nearing the gate, Pauline took her foot off the gas, the truck jerked to a stop. She sat back. "Whew! I did it!"

"Yes, you did a great job. That's enough for the first time. Are you keeping this a secret from Fred?"

"Yes, oh, yes! Let's keep it a surprise from Fred and Will."

"Then I better drive the truck back to the shed before Will comes in from the barn."

After the truck was safely put away, Pauline, delighted with her first lesson, clapped her hands and gave Marian a big hug, "Thank you! Thank you! Can I come for another lesson tomorrow?"

"I'll come up in the afternoon and we'll drive out to Ala Spit on Troxell. There won't be many cars on the road."

"I'll be ready any time. I better go home now before Fred comes for lunch."

"Wait a minute, Pauline. It's Sewing Circle day on Thursday. When Thea called to remind me, she said to bring you. I'll take Alice, and Gev and Mildred will be there. Would you like to go?"

"I'd love to. It's so nice to be included."

Pauline hurried home. She had lots to write in her journal.

During lunch Pauline told Fred she had been invited to join the Sewing Circle. He smiled and said, "I know you'll enjoy that, but you have a lot going on this week. And Rupert will be here Sunday."

"Oh, I like to keep busy. Hmm, I just have to decide what to fix."

"I bet he'd like fried chicken."

"I know you, Fred Gunther. That's what you want."

"Yeah, you know me all right. I'll stop by Jens Meyer's place on my way home from work on Friday and get a nice young fryer. Okay?"

"Okay, fried chicken it will be."

"Well, it's off to work for me." He gave her a quick kiss and grabbed his hat as he went out the door.

Pauline had her Tuesday afternoon driving lesson in Marian's car on Troxell Road out to Ala Spit. After a few jumpy starts she learned to shift gears without killing the motor and Marian let her speed up to twenty miles an hour. They turned around at the Monkey Hill and Tea and Coffee intersection, and drove down to Ala Spit again before going home. Pauline practiced backing up in the pasture until Marian said, "That's enough for today. You're doing well."

"Thanks, Marian, you're a wonderful teacher."

"Remember, I'll pick you and Alice up about noon for Sewing Circle on Thursday.

Wednesday night Pauline checked her sewing basket. She had purchased embroidery thread the previous Saturday at the Fabric Shoppe. She thought about Mrs. O'Dell. *What a strange lady. She's so somber. In town, everyone smiles and says hello. Maybe I need to ask her some questions to start a conversation.*

When Fred left for work Thursday, he told her to have a good time. "I'll have lunch with Otto in town today, but I'll miss coming home to have lunch with you."

"Me, too, dear."

She gave him a hug and tucked a surprise Baker's Chocolate bar into his shirt pocket.

Fred went out to his truck. "See you for supper!

Chapter Twenty-One... The Sewing Circle

Pauline knotted the blue thread on the needle, looked up from her embroidery work and over at Thea. "Thank you for inviting me, I love coming into town."

Marian chuckled. "It gives her a chance to practice her driving."

Thea and Alice smiled at Pauline's sparkling eyes. "Marian is teaching me. I had a lesson on Monday driving Will's old Whippet in the pasture, but Tuesday I drove Marian and the Model A on the road to Ala Spit. It was scary when a truck came toward me. I steered into deep gravel on the side of the road. Marian and I had to get out and push the car backwards onto the road. Lucky I didn't go into the ditch." She grinned at her sister-in-law. "Marian is quite patient with me. Today she let me drive into town."

"You did a fine job," said Alice. "Didn't she Marian?"

"Yes, she didn't make any mistakes. Just a good thing we left early."

Pauline's face glowed with happiness. "Won't it be fun the first time Fred sees me driving? I can hardly wait to see the expression on his face."

The women laughed and agreed it would be quite a surprise for Fred. Enjoying their companionship, the women worked on their projects: Gev embroidering a square for a baby quilt, Mildred knitting a new sweater for her daughter, Alice darning her husband's socks and Thea tatting lace for a handkerchief.

Pauline cut her thread with her teeth, and said, "The lady at the Fabric Shoppe is not very friendly."

"You mean Mrs. O'Dell?" asked Thea.

"Yes, I visited the shop last Saturday. I needed thread to match the color I'm using on these pillowslips. She didn't say anything to me when I said good morning. She never asks if I need help, just sits behind the big counter and watches me like a hawk…but she does have a better selection of thread than the Co-op."

Alice glanced at her sister, Thea. "Olga O'Dell has never been a very happy person."

"No," Thea agreed. "She keeps to herself."

"Has she always lived in Oak Harbor?" asked Pauline.

Thea answered, "Olga came about fourteen or fifteen years ago."

The shrill whistling of the teakettle on the wood cook stove ended the talk about the shopkeeper. Thea put aside her tatting and bustled out to the kitchen to make coffee.

Gathered around the dining room table set with Thea's Haviland china cups, the women continued their chatty conversation. All too soon, Marian suggested it was time to start home.

On their way to the car with Alice, Marian asked Pauline if she wanted to drive. "Oh, yes."

"All right," said Marian. "Take us home."

Gev, Mildred and Thea stood on the porch watching as Pauline started the motor, put it in reverse and backed down the driveway.

"Turn a little. Don't give it too much gas," cautioned Marian. But it was too late. The car hit the corner of a rock wall.

"Nerts! Oh, Marian, I'm so sorry."

"Well, turn off the motor and we'll see if anything is damaged."

"Are you hurt?" called Thea from her front porch.

"No, we're okay," Alice called back to her sister.

"No real damage," Marian observed. "Only a broken reflector. We can stop at Al's garage to get a new one. Will won't notice the difference."

Pauline kept saying what a dummkopf she was and she better not drive any more.

"Nonsense," said Marian. "When you fall off a horse you get right back on. Now figure out how you'll get onto the road."

Pauline got into the car, thought for a minute, started the motor, put it in gear and slowly went forward. She turned the wheel a bit to straighten out, changed gears and looked in the mirror as she backed onto the road.

Pauline asked, "Did I do that right, Marian?"

"Yes, you did fine. Let's turn right at the corner and go down the hill through town. Al's garage is at the other end of town past the Lighthouse Tavern."

It took Al just a couple minutes to put in a red reflector. Pauline gave him a dime from her change purse and thanked him. "I'm always available to help the ladies," he grinned.

Pauline turned and said, "You drive, Marian." She went to the passenger side and explained to Alice, "I can't take a chance Fred might see me driving."

Alice's brown eyes twinkled. "My lips are sealed."

When Fred came home Friday, he told her he knew about her little secret.

"What secret?"

"Oh, word gets around, and Al doesn't sell many reflectors."

Pauline gasped, "Who told?"

"I believe it was Al who told Otto and he, of course, told me."

"Are you mad, Fred?"

"I'm disappointed you didn't ask me to teach you."

"Well, Marian said…"

"It doesn't matter what Marian said. You could have had a terrible accident with Will's truck. It's my responsibility to teach you."

Pauline's face turned red. "Fred Gunther, I'm a grown woman. I don't need you to look after me. Besides, it's Marian's truck, too."

"Stop, Pauline." Fred stepped up to her and put his hands on her arms. "Look at me. I love you and don't want anything to happen to you."

Pauline scowled. "I know…and I love you, but I wanted to surprise you."

He put his arms around her. "Maybe you can think of another way to surprise me."

"Will you show me how to drive our truck?"

"Yes, I'll teach you, but not tonight."

Hugging him, Pauline whispered, "Okay, supper will be ready in a jiffy."

Chapter Twenty-Two... Sunday Dinner

After a restless night with thoughts of Rupert coming for dinner, Pauline awoke Sunday morning to the smell of coffee. "Why did you let me sleep so long? I have so much to do."

"Darling girl, you tossed and turned most of the night. You finally settled down about daybreak. I've taken care of the goats and your hens. Come have your coffee while I flip the hotcakes."

"Yes, I did need the rest. You're always so thoughtful. You're even making breakfast! Thank you, dear."

When she started to make the cobbler, she decided to make Fred's favorite coconut cake, too.

Rupert knocked on the door a few minutes before noon. Amused at how eager Pauline was to greet him, Fred sat back in his chair and watched. He smiled as she took off her apron, hung it on a peg, smoothed down her dress and brushed her curls back from her face. She opened the door. "Hi Rupert, come in."

He wiped his feet on the mat and stepped into the warm kitchen.

Pauline noticed his large hands as he removed his ball cap. She pointed to a hook on the wall for him to hang it.

"Sure smells good in here, reminds me of my gramma's kitchen," he said.

"I hope you like Southern Fried Chicken."

"I do. The guys down at camp would be jealous. Guess I won't tell them."

Pauline smiled and said, "Dinner will be ready soon."

Fred stood up and the men shook hands. He pointed to Pauline's red easy chair and sat down in his. He asked, "How's the work going at the quarry?"

"We're moving a lot of rock. It's hard work. The past couple days I've been the powder monkey."

Pauline said, "That sounds silly. What's a powder monkey?"

"I carry the dynamite from the storage shed to the quarry and put it in the holes drilled in the rock."

"Isn't that dangerous?"

"It's very dangerous work," said Fred.

"Yeah, I'm doing it, but I'm not crazy about the job, and you can bet I don't hang around after I've put in the blasting cap and lit the fuse."

"It's a job for an unmarried man who has no long range plans," quipped Fred.

"That's sure not a nice thought, Fred," said Pauline, as she set the platter of chicken on the table.

Rupert answered many questions about his work, and when Pauline urged him to have more mashed potatoes and gravy, he helped himself to the last drumstick. "This chicken is the best, Mrs. Gunther."

Fred winked at Pauline. "Yep, she's a great cook. That's why I married her."

Pauline laughed. "That's not entirely true."

Rupert asked, "How did you get this house?"

"I didn't have work in Bay City. Pauline's brother told us no one had lived on this property for many years and that it was for sale. We only had to pay the back taxes. Pauline wasn't too keen on the idea of leaving her home and friends, but thought it would be nice to live by her brother, so we came to Whidbey."

Pauline asked, "Why did your family leave, Rupert?"

"After my ma died—I think she had pneumonia—Pa wanted to go back home to Pennsylvania. We lived with my gramma and grampa." Rupert put down his fork and finished his glass of milk. "I remember there was a lot of snow, and Pa's friend took us to the railroad station. Pa told him he could have our truck, and our cow, too."

Pauline said, "I'm sorry you lost your mother. Do you remember her?"

"Yeah, she was always saying 'I love you to pieces' and giving me hugs." He paused and smiled, and then continued, "We used to take our cow up to the spring for water. I remember playing with a little boat my pa carved for me. When Pa cut wood for the stove, he put me on top of the wood in the wheelbarrow and gave me a ride to the house."

Fred said, "Why didn't he come back or sell the property?"

"Pa died in the war—in France, I think. After Grampa died a few years ago, my gramma and I raised chickens, but we didn't do very good. It was hard to get by, so when I heard about the CCC, I sent in an application right away.

Now, Gramma gets twenty-five dollars a month."

Fred leaned back in his chair. "I served in Europe, too. Do you know which division your father was in?"

"Grampa said Pa served as an infantryman in the trenches. I've learned a lot from reading about the war, and I don't like to think about my pa being in it." Rupert looked down at his hands and twiddled his thumbs. "My pa had a little fiddle and I was hoping it might still be here. When he played it, my ma would take my hands and we danced around."

"We've never found a fiddle, Rupert, but goodness gracious," Pauline put both hands to her head, "I just remembered, when we first came I found a locket in a coat pocket. Fred, I think I hung it on a nail in that old wardrobe."

Fred pushed back his chair. "I'll see if I can find it."

"Thank you, dear. Also, Fred, bring that sewing basket. I put it in a cardboard box. There are a couple toy trucks in the box, too."

She turned to Rupert. "The locket has a nice picture of a man and a woman, maybe your mother and father."

"I don't have any pictures of my ma, just my pa in his uniform." He looked down at his folded arms.

Pauline reached out and rested her hand on Rupert's arm. "What were your mother's and father's names?"

"Pa called my ma Honey or sometimes Ruby. Pa's name was Ralph."

Fred brought the box, and dangling from a finger, the locket.

Rupert opened his mouth in surprise and took the locket. "I remember this. Ma wore it." He turned it over and over, opened the clasp and looked at the picture. "I don't know these people."

"Perhaps they're your ma's mother and father," said Pauline. "Do you know where they live?"

"No. I don't remember them. They didn't come visit us. I don't have any idea where they live or where Ma grew up. I don't know anything about them. My gramma said maybe they live here and I should look for them, but I wouldn't know where to start looking.

"Well, that's too bad. It would be nice if you could find them." Pauline opened the box.

Rupert picked up the rusty iron trucks, examined them and smiled. "I played with these in the dirt out in the garden." He opened the basket. "My ma did like to sew."

Fred said, "Say, Pauline, how about that cobbler?"

She got up and brought the cake to the table. "I've got a surprise for you."

Fred looked at the mound of coconut on the top and licked his lips. "Wow, look at that, Rupert. Do you like coconut?"

"I sure do. My gramma makes good cakes, and pies, too."

Pauline cut big pieces for them.

Fred laughed when Rupert licked his fork and suggested he have another piece.

Rupert grinned. "Sure."

Pauline cut another slice. She sipped her coffee and watched him eat. He picked up the locket, opened it and studied the picture. "Thank you for keeping this and thank you for the good dinner, Mrs. Gunther. I think I should go back to camp." He put the locket in his pocket and got up from his chair. "I better not take the sewing basket. It wouldn't fit in my locker and the other guys might laugh."

"We can put it back in the closet."

"Yeah, that would be nice. The trucks, too."

Pauline watched from the door as Rupert walked toward Ducken Road. Then she began clearing the table and told Fred, "Wouldn't it be nice if I could find his mother's folks?"

"It would. How do you propose to do it?"

"I could ask people."

"What would you ask? You don't know their names or anything about them."

"Yes, I see what you mean." Pauline thought for a minute. "I know! The locket! I can show people the picture. I'll ask Rupert if I can borrow it."

"Okay, you have a mystery to solve. By the way, Hank Martin stopped by to see Otto on Friday. We got to talking and he asked if we would like to come out to his place sometime and ride horses with them on their beach."

"I don't know about riding a horse, but it would be fun to try."

"That's my girl. I told him we would come."

Chapter Twenty-Three... A Saturday Ride

"Can I ride a horse?" Pauline asked in reply to Hank's question. "Well, I rode a pony on the merry-go-round. Does that count?"

He laughed. "I guess that counts." The palomino mare jerked her head and worked the bit with her tongue. Hank adjusted her bridle. "Easy girl." She settled down and he handed the reins to Pauline. He tightened the saddle girth around Dixie's belly. "How about you, Fred, have you ridden much?"

Already in the saddle on Peanuts, a little brown mare with a black mane and tail, Fred said, "When I spent summers on my uncle's farm, I rode bareback on his draft horse. Old Joe was broad. My short legs stuck out. I didn't have any reins, just held on to his mane."

Pauline laughed. "You must have looked silly."

"Maybe so, but I had fun."

Pauline patted the horse's neck. "Hank, do all horses have the same color eyes?"

He said, "Well, they all look black from a distance, but if you look close you'll see the vertical pupil is purplish, or a deep red, blue or green."

Pauline rubbed Dixie's velvet nose and looked into her eyes. "You have beautiful eyes, Dixie. I think they're purple, and you have a good name, too. Why is her mane so short? It feels like a brush."

"She runs from us sometimes, hides and thrashes around in the bushes. A long mane gets tangled with twigs and seeds. It's a job combing it out."

Dixie snorted, stamped her feet and swished her tail back and forth.

Hank gave a last tug on the strap. "Come around on this side, Pauline, and I'll give you a step up. Always mount a horse on its left side."

"Why?"

"Oh, I guess it started way back when men wore swords. They put their left leg into the stirrup and then lifted their right leg over the saddle. Horses seem to like it better, too."

"You sure know a lot about horses."

"I've always loved them. Used to read about them when I was a kid. Looks like your legs aren't long enough."

Hank cupped his hands. "Here step up with your left foot." He gave her a boost. She grabbed the saddle horn, swung her right leg over and sat in the seat.

She looked down at Hank, "I'm sitting up pretty high."

After Hank adjusted the length of the stirrups, he showed her how to hold the reins. The hand-tooled decorative leather saddle squeaked as Dixie stepped from side to side. "Gev hasn't ridden her for a while, but she'll calm down when we get going."

Chris and Kelly rode up on their brown and white pintos,

Silver and Scout. Chris led a beautiful chestnut named Royal King. "I put the saddle on best I could, Dad, but you better check it."

Hank gave the girth a hard tug. "It's tight. Good job, son." King, a spirited horse, chafing at the bit, stepped up and down and sideways, anxious to be on the way. Hank mounted him and clicked his tongue. The horses started moving.

Pauline said, "Your horse does look like a king the way he prances and arches his neck."

Hank turned in his saddle. "He's an American Saddlebred, a thoroughbred, very smart and proud. Pauline, you don't need to hold the saddle horn. Press your knees into her sides, sit back, and relax, let Dixie take you for a nice ride."

They walked the horses from the barnyard and as they passed the house, Gev waved and called from her porch, "Have a good ride. I'll have lunch ready."

Pauline called back, "I'll wash the dishes."

Dixie followed King, her nose almost against the tall horse's rear. Pauline relaxed. Her body moved from side to side in the smooth leather saddle as Dixie stepped along. The sun had not yet burned through the fog and a light breeze blew from the west. Pauline felt cool moisture on her face, and as they rode toward the beach, caught the scent of the wild roses on each side of the lane. They crossed the culvert over the lagoon. She called to Hank, "How deep is the water?"

"It's eight, maybe ten feet deep in some spots."

The riders reined in their horses at the end of the lane. Water-soaked logs and stumps left by high tides lay in jumbled piles. Dense fog walled off the view of the water.

Pauline looked up and down the driftwood-littered beach. She watched a seagull swoop up a clam from the wet sand and drop it onto a pile of rocks. A second gull flew down, but lost the fight over the small mollusk.

"Hey, Dad! Kelly and I are going on ahead."

"Okay, son. We'll be on the sandbars."

The boys nudged their horses forward, stepped over and around the logs and onto the smooth sand, then galloped away. Hank laughed. "They like to play Cowboys and Indians in the sand dunes by Cranberry Lake."

Fred brought Peanuts up to stand by Dixie and King. He said, "I like the deep tone of the buoy bell. We hear it on still nights. It carries a long way."

Hank said, "Yes, there are two out there, one by Smith Island and another on the point to the south."

"I can't see anyone, but I hear voices and horns," said Pauline.

Hank said, "There's a lot going on out there in the fog. The men on their purse seiners toot horns as they chug around to claim a spot to put out their nets." He explained how men in a small boat would row away from the seiner pulling nets out of the stern and forming a circle. "When it's completed, they pull a line that closes the bottom of the net making a pocket called a purse to trap the fish. After the sun breaks through the fog, you'll see the men setting the nets."

King was moving about, full of energy and ready to get going. Hank pursed his lips, "Pssst!" King walked forward and picked his way around the piles of wood. Peanuts followed, but Dixie hung back. Hank said, "She's stubborn, kick her belly."

Pauline kicked and kicked and said "get-up." Finally Dixie walked down through the driftwood. The horse's hooves dug into the wet sand and made crunching sounds when stepping on mounds of gravel.

Hank used the reins on King's neck to direct him onto a sandbar. Steam rose from the bars as the sun's rays shone through the dissipating fog. Water squirted up through the rippled sand as clams felt the weight of the horses.

Pauline felt at ease as Dixie walked between King and Peanuts on a long stretch of sandbar. Waves broke on the outer bars, their white foam beautiful against the blue sky. Now visible, seiners tooted and chugged a few hundred yards away. The riders pulled-up their horses and watched the men set their nets. They heard the high-pitched calls of seagulls as the birds swarmed in the air above the seiners' nets. They saw salmon jump and splash as they fell back into the water.

Chris and Kelly came at a full gallop. The boys shouted, "Dad! Dad!" Their horses' hooves dug deep into the sand as they reined them to a stop. "There's a boat stuck on a bar in front of Uncle Ted's beach!"

Hank said, "Let's go have a look." He and the boys urged their horses off the sandbar into knee-deep water and over to the beach. Dixie and Peanuts followed.

Pauline stuck her legs out as water splashed on her trousers. "Do you think she can swim?"

"I'm sure she can," said Fred, "but the water isn't deep, not even up to her belly."

Out of the water and on the beach again, Chris and Kelly trotted their horses. Hank held King back until Pauline and Fred caught up to him. Anxious to follow the Pintos, King walked at a faster pace. Dixie and Peanuts trotted after him.

Pauline bounced up and down in the saddle, grabbed the saddle horn and yelled, "Stop! Stop!"

Hank looked back over his shoulder and slowed King. Fred called, "Tell Dixie to whoa and pull back on her reins."

Pauline yelled, "Whoa, Dixie! Whoa!" She pulled hard on the leather reins. The horse stopped so fast her feet dug into the sand. Pauline let go of the reins and grabbed for the pommel, but slipped out of the saddle and plopped onto a pile of gravel. "Rats!"

Dixie snorted, shook her head and stepped a few feet away.

Fred looked at Pauline sitting on the gravel. "What are you doing down there? Are you okay? Are you hurt?"

"I'm fine, and I know, when you fall off a horse, you get right back on."

He laughed. "But you didn't fall."

"Yeah, I slid down her side." Pauline got up and brushed sand from her trousers, then took Dixie's reins and patted her soft muzzle.

Fred asked, "Do you want help getting into the saddle?"

"My bottom's sore from bouncing up and down. I'm going to walk for a while."

"Okay, we'll walk together." He dismounted and took one of Dixie's reins.

They stopped on a sandbank and watched as Hank and the boys rode their horses through ankle-deep water to an old wooden tugboat. It listed to one side in the shallow water. Hank handed King's reins to Chris and climbed onto the stubby, weathered tug. In its prime, it had probably been a sturdy boat pulling rafts of logs through Deception Pass.

Pauline said it needed new paint, but Fred said, "Ah, it's just worn-out. It'd be a shame to waste good paint."

They saw Hank walk from one end of the old boat to the other and then disappear into the wheelhouse. He came back up to the deck followed by a grizzle-faced older man shouting and gesturing with his arms. They talked for a few minutes, and then Hank got on King. He and the boys rode back to the beach.

Hank nodded toward the man. "He didn't know about the sandbars and anchored the boat last night to get some sleep. When he woke up the tide had gone out and left him stuck. He figures he'll just wait it out until the tide comes in." Hank checked his pocket watch. "I think it's time we head home. Gev probably has lunch ready."

Fred helped Pauline onto Dixie and he mounted Peanuts.

"Want to race?" asked Chris.

"Not me," answered Pauline.

"You go on, boys," said Hank. "Tell Mom we'll be along shortly."

Chris and Kelly spurred their horses and raced up the beach.

At Gev's lunch table, Pauline watched the boys, their eyes shining with excitement as they bubbled over with the news about the man on the boat stuck on the sandbar. She smiled to herself. *What fun it is to be included in this family.* She reached under the table for Fred's right hand, gave it a little squeeze and he squeezed back.

Chapter Twenty-Four... Frustration

Pauline enjoyed spending the afternoon ironing sheets. She thought of her aunts who had embroidered the pillow-cases and edged them with lace they had crocheted. She thought about Fred. *What could be bothering him? He has always been so considerate and gentle.*

Fred came home later than usual. He said he would bring Billy and Nanny in, and then left.

Over supper, Pauline asked how the work was coming along.

He said, "McCleary changed his mind and wants more shelves, so we used my truck to go out to the mill to pick up more boards." Fred leaned back in his chair and looked at Pauline.

She frowned and said, "Why are you staring at me like that?"

"I'd like to start taking my lunch to work with me. It would save time and gas."

"I can make lunches for you, Fred, but I'll miss our time together."

"Yes, well, I'll miss you too, but I should have started

taking my lunch a long time ago. Gas jumped up to fourteen cents yesterday. I've been doing some figuring. It's about eighteen miles round trip into town, the truck gets about twenty miles per gallon and at fourteen cents a gallon, that's how much it costs every trip. Coming home for lunch makes it twenty-eight cents for gas every day. Otto always wants me to take my truck to pick up supplies, and if we go out to the mill, that's another twelve miles. It takes quite a chunk out of my pay when I'm only getting seventy cents an hour."

Pauline started to say something when Fred said, "I haven't wanted to worry you, but Otto has only one more job lined up for me. I could be out of work anytime."

"Well, remember we still have some of my dad's savings."

"How much? We went kind of wild there for a while when we fixed-up the house and bought the truck."

"I'll get the box," she said, going to the dresser.

Pauline inserted the key into the lock. The wooden box lid popped open. She took out a roll of bills and laid them on the table in stacks of denominations. "We started with five hundred fifty-two dollars."

Fred counted, "One hundred, one twenty, three fives and two ones. $137. Where did it all go?"

"You know I'm a careful bookkeeper and I have it all right here," said Pauline, taking out a small booklet filled with her notes and figures. "The truck, of course, was the big expense, two hundred sixty-two dollars."

"The truck was a good buy."

"I know, dear, and we certainly had to have one, but you bought lumber to make the cupboards and cabinets around the sink, door pulls, nails and…"

"Yes, and you bought curtain material."

Pauline looked at the figures. "That cost forty-seven cents and the oilcloth for the table a bit more, sixty-five cents. And I bought overalls and trousers, and we both had to have boots."

"Our food and the chicken feed," Fred continued. "Yes, it all adds up."

"But, Fred, I do have my tea money." She rose from her chair to get her childhood piggybank.

"Never mind, dear, if we're careful…"

Pauline sat down. "I suppose I could sell the hens' eggs, instead of giving them to Alice and Marian."

"No, they've been good to us and are having hard times, too. Will's monthly check is pretty small. He said the farmers are not getting a decent price for milk, even after the big milk-dumping strike the dairymen had last year."

"They dumped the milk?"

"Hank Martin sold cream to the creamery, but fed the milk to his pigs. Milk prices were so low it wasn't worth shipping it to the factory and the farmers went on strike." Fred sighed. "Well, tomorrow's another day, time to turn in."

Pauline's eyes filled with tears as she made Fred's lunch the next morning. Hearing his boots scrape on the door mat, she dabbed her tears away with a corner of her apron. She felt the cold air as the door opened, and asked, "How are Nanny and Billy? Is it foggy?"

"Not a lot, but the boards are slippery. Walk carefully when you go out to check the hens." He pulled his chair from the table and sat down, sprinkled brown sugar and poured rich, yellow cream over his oatmeal. He sat hunched over, elbows on the table, and spooned the hot cereal to his mouth. Pauline sat across from him, sipping her coffee, trying to think of something to cheer him.

After he left for work, Pauline dawdled through her chores. She did breakfast dishes, made the bed, and then shrugged into a warm sweater and went out. She walked on the board path to the chicken coop and scolded the hens when she didn't find many eggs. She poured the last of the water into their jar, noticed another empty bucket and decided to surprise Fred. She walked up the hillside, her shoes sinking into the soft, muddy ground. "Oh, nerts! I should have worn my boots."

Crystal clear water bubbled up into the small rock-edged pool, spilling over onto the marshy slope. She tucked her skirt under her, sat on a flat, granite rock, and enjoyed the warm sun. Delighted to see a little green frog hopping from one small rock to another, she asked, "Are you Jimmy?" She remembered lying in the grass on a warm summer's day beside her dad, looking for four-leafed clovers. She had found a small green frog. Her dad said, "Oh, that's Jimmy." Afterwards, every time they heard a croak, they would say, "Oh, that's Jimmy." They often heard his croak in the damp basement by the washing machine and sometimes they found him in the tulip bed.

She sat with her elbows on her knees, and resting her chin in her hands, thought of her dad. She smiled thinking about how every spring he tricked her. *I ran from one window to the next trying to see the Easter Bunny dressed in purple pants and a pink polka-dot shirt. I called "yikkity-yikkity" out the door to tell the bunny to bring eggs to my grass nest. Will spoiled my fun, telling me Dad put the eggs in the nest.*

The frog disappeared into the grass. *Time for me to go, too. I should be baking bread.* She dipped the two buckets into the pool of water, filled each half-full and carried them back to the hen house.

Pauline enjoyed kneading the bread, pushing the heels of her hands into the warm dough, turning it over and over until it felt spongy. She put it in a yellow Pyrex bowl, covered it with a pretty, but worn, linen towel, and set it on top of the warming oven to rise. She washed the dishes and then, sitting at the table, wrote in her journal.

As she sat lost in thought, the good smell of the rising bread brought her to her senses. She punched the dough down to rise again, and then went out to walk in the fresh air. Her thoughts went back to Fred. *What will we do if Otto doesn't have more work? If I learn to drive I might be able to do housework for someone. I could sew clothes.* Back in the house, she formed the dough into loaves and set them to a third rising. She picked up one of the magazines Alice had given her. Thumbing through it, she found a Dolly Dingle paper doll. *I could frame this and hang it between the south windows.*

At supper Pauline told Fred about her morning and her idea of sewing clothes. "I really want to learn to drive your truck so I can go to town." She took her dishes to the sink and then stood behind him and put her arms around his shoulders. She felt his annoyance when he shrugged away from her, stood up and went to his easy chair.

Fred said, "After last night's talk about money, I thought you'd forget about learning to drive the truck."

"No, Fred, I'm serious. I want to help out and you know I'm a good seamstress. Mrs. O'Dell can probably give me names of ladies who need someone to sew for them. I could visit the ladies in their homes."

"You'd have to take me to work, come home, go back into town…"

"Well, I could go to work with you and stay in town. I could visit Thea."

"Fred said, "And then come home with me? It would make a long day for you."

Pauline pleaded, "It's what I want to do, and I really do want to learn to drive your truck. Will you teach me to drive this evening?"

"Otto and I hope to finish the cabinets in McCleary's hardware store tomorrow. I need a good night's sleep." He started unbuttoning his shirt. "We'll wait for Saturday."

Chapter Twenty-Five... Pauline Learns to Drive Fred's Truck

Saturday finally came. Pauline, wide-eyed and eager for the day to begin, decided she would make Fred's favorite apple fritters. She got out of bed and stoked the fire back to life. Waiting patiently for her sleeping husband to wake up, she sat down with her journal.

She heard Fred stirring. "Good morning, dear."

"Why are you up so early?"

"The moonlight makes it seem like day so I got up and built up the fire. This is the day you're going to teach me how to drive our truck."

Fred climbed out of bed and padded over to her. He put his arms about her shoulders. She turned in her chair, and then stood facing him.

"I'll see," he said, nuzzling her neck.

"Fred, this is Saturday. You said…"

"Is it raining?"

"No, it's going to be a perfectly nice day."

"The day is young," he said, loosening her robe from her shoulders. "Come." He led her to their bed.

Pauline playfully submitted to his request.

Later, she whispered, "Now, can we have breakfast? I'll make apple fritters."

Fred gave her rear a pat as she moved from the bed.

He enjoyed fritters with his coffee. "I love you, Pauline, as much," he said, his blue eyes twinkling, "maybe a bit more, than the first time I told you."

"I love you, too, darling." She planted a kiss on the top of his head, and then turned back to the stove to flip another fritter.

"Would you like me to take care of your hens?"

"Thank you, dear. It won't take me long to clean up the dishes, and then, you can show me how to start our truck."

Fred took a last gulp of coffee. "So, my truck has suddenly become our truck."

"Of course! If I'm going to be driving it, it's my truck, too."

Fred laughed, took his hat and went out. Pauline cleaned up the dishes, got dressed and joined him. He had finished feeding the chickens and held up an egg. "Only one this morning."

Pauline frowned. "I found two yesterday and the hens are losing their feathers. Look at Candy. The feathers on her head are coming off and the other hens pick on her."

"They're probably going into a molt."

"A molt?" she asked.

"Yes, when chickens lose their feathers and they don't lay as many eggs. New feathers will grow back and they start laying again. Something else I learned from Uncle Jack was that he left a light on when the days were short in the winter. The hens thought it was still day time and they laid more eggs."

"That was a mean trick."

"Well, it worked." He grabbed two buckets. "I'm going up to the spring."

Pauline trudged behind him carrying an extra bucket. *I just have to learn to drive our truck. If I'm a good helper maybe Fred will be patient.*

They walked back to the animals. Fred filled Billy's and Nanny's water pan and used the pitch fork to fluff their bedding.

"Okay, we've done the chores, now I'll show you how to start *my* truck," Fred teased. He helped her into the driver's side of the truck. "First of all, Pauline, you have to know my truck is different than Will's Willy's truck or his Model T car. His truck, remember, was a car made into a truck and doesn't have as much power as mine. My Double A is meant for real work. That's why I'm not so keen on you driving it."

"But I won't be driving it often."

"That's right. Now, this has a four-speed transmission. A transmission is a box of gears that transfers the power from the engine to the rear wheels. My truck has four gears. When you drove Marian's car you only had three gears." He leaned over and put his hand on two levers. "One is a brake and one for the gears." He took her hand and said, "Feel the gear-shift knob. It has a lock-out so you don't accidentally put it in reverse while moving." Pauline felt the little knob. Fred continued, "This lever with the silver button on top is the parking brake. To put the brake on, push the button down and pull the stick back. To release the brake, push the button down and push the stick forward."

"It sounds complicated."

"It is at first, but no more than Marian's car, just different. If you really want to drive, you have to know how everything works."

"Okay, I'll be a good student."

Fred told her to move over. He got in and said, "Watch closely." He started the motor and showed her the throttle and the choke, and named all the buttons on the dashboard, the pedals on the floor, and explained how they were used.

Pauline said, "Whew! There is a lot to learn." She watched as Fred pushed the button to start the motor and maneuvered all the levers making the truck move forward. While driving down their driveway and back to the house, he told her everything he was doing. He stopped and turned off the motor and said, "Okay, your turn. Let's trade seats."

Pauline got settled behind the steering wheel. "Tell me again how to start." After several attempts, the motor started. The truck started jerking forward, and then jerked to a stop. The motor died.

"What did I do wrong?"

"The motor dies if you just push on the brake. The clutch and brake have to work together. Start the motor and drive a little. Now push in the brake pedal and as the truck slows down, gradually push in the clutch and take your foot off the brake. You have to work them together."

After two more attempts, the truck rolled forward without jerking. Pauline held tightly to the steering wheel as it moved down their driveway. "We're going too fast! How do I stop?"

"Push in the brake a little to slow down. When we're almost to the end of the road, push the brake all the way in while pushing in the clutch."

Pauline followed every word he said and stopped at the end of their road. She asked, "Should I put on the parking brake?"

"An excellent idea. We don't want to roll down Ducken Road."

"It takes a lot of practice to drive your truck."

"Oh, so now it's my truck."

She laughed. "Yes, it's your truck, but after I have more practice, it will be our truck."

"Have you done enough for today or do you want to try it again?"

"Let's do it again."

"Okay, start her up and you can drive uphill to the house."

After Pauline practiced driving up and down their driveway two more times, Fred told her to drive on Ducken Road to Will's house. She drove slowly and made a successful turn into Will's yard, worked the clutch and brake together and stopped. She set the parking brake and turned off the motor. Fred tooted the horn.

Will came out onto the porch and saw Pauline behind the steering wheel. "Marian, we have visitors!"

Pauline called out the window, "Surprise!"

After passing the day for a bit, she drove back home. As they walked to the house, she said, "You're a good teacher, Fred. Was I a good student?"

"Umm…I'll think about it."

She put her hand on his arm and pulled him to a stop. She

looked up into his eyes, "I was, wasn't I?"

He put one arm around her as they continued to the house, and laughing, said, "I have to admit you actually were a good student. I want you to remember, though, you're not going to be driving at night or in the rain."

"What if I'm caught in a rainstorm, or get delayed and have to come home in the dark?"

"Not a chance. You're going to be a fair-weather driver for a while. And that's final."

"But…"

Chapter Twenty-Six... A Garden

As Fred left for work Monday, he saw Pauline had sorted the darks from the whites. "You might want to put off the wash for a day. It looks like rain."

"I'm going to take my chances," she said.

Sparks flew up as she poked a few more sticks of wood into the stove. She carried water from the porch and poured it into the big copper canner on the stove. It would take a while for the water to heat. She thumbed through a magazine and read the second part of a romance serial story. *It's so sad, I hope Alice gave me the next issue so I can read the ending.*

Pauline wrung the water from the last of the wash. Wind from the Strait of Juan de Fuca blew her hair as she hung the wet sheets on the line. The jingle of a horse's harness caught her attention. She turned to see Will coming into the yard with his work horses. Taking the clothespin from her mouth she finished pinning a pillowcase to the line.

"Hey, Will," she called to her brother who was sitting up on the box-wagon.

"I told Fred I'd bring Maud and Buster to break up the sod for your garden. It needs to be plowed to give the grass and weeds time to rot over the winter."

She watched Will unload the plow from the wagon. "I don't know much about growing vegetables."

"Don't worry, I'll help you. In no time you'll get the hang of it." He switched the double-tree from the wagon to the plow. "Show me where you want the garden."

"I did find an area where an old garden may have been between the house and that old, rusty wire fence."

Will agreed it had once been a garden and said it would be easier working the soil there than trying out a new area. He whistled a little tune and walked over the ground looking through the weeds. "I wouldn't want them stepping on broken glass or nails in an old board," he said. Satisfied, he put his horses to work. With a whistle and a flick of the leather reins on Maud's big rear, they moved forward pulling the plow, turning the ground over. Will walked in the furrow behind them. After several trips in the large area, he asked Pauline if it was big enough.

"Big enough? It's huge. Back home Fred and I had a small backyard with a lilac bush and a few flowers against the fence."

"Oh, you'll fill it up. You'll have fun choosing seed packets at the Co-op. Once you get started it's hard to stop planting."

"How come you know so much about farming?"

"Paulie, when I was in Future Farmers of America in high school, I decided I wanted to be farmer. Remember, I lived two years on Uncle Jack's farm in Wisconsin."

He stooped and picked up a handful of dirt letting it run through his fingers. "This ground hasn't been worked for a while, but it seems to be good soil, which surprises me, judging from all the clay and rocks on most of the hillside. Someone must have picked a lot of rocks and worked humus and rotted manure into it."

"I have no idea what you're talking about. What's humus?"

"Oh, dead grass, old hay—rotted stuff. When it's mixed in with the dirt it adds nutrients. You'll learn. When you clean out your chicken coop spread the manure here. Next spring I'll bring cow manure and work it in with my cultivator."

Standing beside Buster and patting the Percheron's shiny, black neck, Pauline asked, "How old is he?"

"He's ten, Maud's son. Maud's fifteen."

"They're nice, so gentle. Do you ever ride them?"

"Sometimes. I take them into Oak Harbor for the Holland Days pulling contests. Farmers take their draft horses to Freund's Field by City Beach and take turns having their horses pull a sled loaded with sacks of grain. They pull hundreds of pounds, sometimes over a ton. Maud and Buster won blue ribbons twice."

"Before you go home would you like to have lunch with Fred? He'll be home any minute. I made chocolate cake for him yesterday."

"I can't turn that down."

They heard Fred's truck drive up.

Pauline hurried over and opened his door. "Hi dear, come look at the work Will has done with Maud and Buster."

Fred walked around the plowed area. He grinned at Will. "Pauline's going to have a big garden. It'll keep her busy."

"I'll give her starts of raspberry and loganberry bushes from my garden patch."

"She'll like those," said Fred. They knocked dirt from their shoes before going into the house.

After the men finished their stew, Pauline set generous pieces of cake on the table and poured coffee.

Will took a mouthful of cake. "Very good, Paulie," he said, returning her smile.

Fred said, "A garden needs water. I think I'll be making a lot of trips to the spring. By golly, I do need to dig a well. Why the people who lived here didn't, is beyond me."

Will picked up his cup. "Like I said before, Fred, wait and let the ground soak up the rain." He took a gulp of coffee. "Hey, tell me about this Rupert fellow."

"We had a nice visit a few weeks ago. We've been curious why his father abandoned this property. Turns out he joined the army soon after taking Rupert to Pennsylvania. He was killed in France a bit before the Armistice." Fred finished his coffee. "He could have been in my regiment."

"I feel sorry for Rupert," said Pauline. "His mother died when he was so little, and then his father nine months later. He grew up with his father's folks. I'm going to find his mother's family."

"How do you plan to do that?"

"Well Rupert's last name is Long. His father was Ralph Long. His mother was Ruby."

"I've never heard anything about the people who

lived here, but it seems like Alice would know about them since they were neighbors."

"I've asked her. She was young and doesn't remember them, but I can ask around town. Someone must have known Rupert's father."

Will grinned at her and said, "Fred, I know that face, she's determined."

"I am. I'm sure glad I know how to drive our truck now."

"I told Marian she was foolish to teach you to drive." He turned to Fred. "Sometimes women don't know what's best for them."

"Have to agree with you, Will," said Fred, shaking his head.

"Wait a minute. Who taught Marian to drive?" asked Pauline.

"She learned before I met her. She drove her own car, a 1912 Model T when she was teaching in the little country schools in Wisconsin. We sold it before moving here."

Pauline said, "I'm learning more about Marian every day."

"Marian doesn't talk about herself," Will said. "She was a very independent gal when I met her. And now our Jenny is going to be a teacher, too, and says she needs a car, but that's not going to happen. She'll have to room and board with a family and walk to school." Will stood up from the table. "Time for me to head home."

"I'll give you a hand loading the plow," said Fred.

After supper Fred got comfortable in his easy chair. Pauline relaxed in her chair, rocking back and forth, thinking about finding Rupert's family. "Dear, I wonder if Rupert remembers his mother's maiden name. I'll need to know that before I ask around town. I could ask Mr. Gilbert at the Co-op."

"You might be biting off more than you can chew, Pauline. I think you should be careful talking with Rupert about this idea. It could lead to disappointment."

Chapter Twenty-Seven... Making Sauerkraut

Pauline heard Will's truck door slam and, wiping her hands on a dish towel, went out to greet him. "Hi. What are you doing up here so early? I can hardly see you through the fog."

"Better get used to it. There's usually fog in the morning 'til the sun breaks through about noon." He met her at the porch. "The heads on my cabbage are starting to split. Marian could use an extra hand making sauerkraut and I don't want to take time away from my work. I need to plow up the back field today so I can plant winter oats."

Pauline teased, "If I get to have some."

Will laughed. "Sure, you can have more than you can eat. I know you'll like it. Dad said all us good Germans like sauerkraut. Remember him waking us up singing, *Guten Morgen ruft die Sonne?*"

Pauline joined him singing the children's song and then reminded him, "We had the best dad, always so loving."

"We did, Paulie, and thanks for helping Marian today. I better get going and put Maud and Buster to work. See ya!"

"Tell Marian I'll be down shortly."

As he went to his truck, Will called back, "Ich liebe dich!"

"I love you, too!" Pauline waved and went inside. She gave the soup pot on the stove a last stir and moved it away from the heat. She changed from her housedress to her overalls and an old shirt, pulled on her red sweater, tied a scarf around her head and started down to Marian's.

The little song Pauline and Will had sung came back to her as she walked along the gravel road. She turned onto the path leading to Marian's house and heard singing. *I think Marian is feeling happy, too.*

As Pauline stepped up onto the porch, Marian called out, "Hey, there, I'm so glad you've come to help. It's going to be fun. Come on in for a second while I get a couple aprons."

Pauline closed the door behind her. Marian came from her bedroom. "We have another crock so you and Fred can keep kraut at your house. I've got the cabbage loaded in the truck. We'll stop and pick up Alice."

"Wait! Will didn't tell me we were going somewhere. I thought we would make it here in your kitchen."

"Oh no. We're going out to Mildred's for a kraut-making party with Alice, Gev and Thea."

Pauline looked down at her overalls. "I should have worn something better."

"Hey, you're fine. Nobody pays attention to what we wear around here, especially when we're making sauerkraut. Okay, I guess I've remembered everything. Let's go."

Pauline admired how Marian skillfully backed the truck and turned onto the road.

Alice lugged a large crock as she came down her porch steps.

Marian called, "Jump in, Alice." She set her crock in the back of the truck, and then stepped up on the running board and sat next to Pauline. With Alice settled, they were on their way.

Chatting and laughing together, it seemed they arrived at Mildred's in no time. Walking into the yard, Thea and Gev waved as Marian parked the truck on the gravel between Ted's barn and the green lawn. Ted's little black spaniel scampered over to them, wagging his tail. Alice stooped and gave Pepper a few pats on his head. "You're a good dog, aren't you, boy? He's smart, too. He brings Ted's slippers to him."

"Here Pauline, help me with these cabbages," said Marian, reaching into the back of the truck. "I'll bring the crocks." Gev and Thea came to the truck and helped take everything to Mildred's porch.

Mildred waved them into her kitchen and after exchanging hugs said, "Have a chair and I'll bring coffee and cinnamon rolls." Sitting at the large, oilcloth-covered dining room table, Pauline enjoyed listening to the women's lively conversation about their children. When the last cinnamon roll had disappeared, Mildred said, "We better get to work. By the looks of all these cabbage heads, it will be an all-day job."

Pauline watched as the five women, Mildred, Alice, Thea, Gev and Marian all seemed to have a particular job setting out the equipment. They bustled around, chatting and laughing when they sometimes bumped into each other.

"Okay Pauline, here's a job for you, but first let me help you with an apron." Pauline bent forward as Marian lifted the red and white checked apron loop over Pauline's head and tied a bow around her waist.

Noticing the red rickrack sewn on the hem of the ruffled apron, Pauline commented, "This is too nice for a work apron." She looked at the other women and realized they had all put on pretty aprons. It seemed like a dress-up occasion.

Standing beside Marian at the counter, she listened to her explain, "We have to core all the cabbages and give any damaged leaves to the pigs. The heads are so large it's hard to cut them unless you hold the knife in one hand and use your other hand to press the blade down. Cut the cabbage down the middle like this." Marian demonstrated, pressing the knife firmly into the cabbage and with a rocking motion cut through the round cabbage. The halves fell apart and she cut each half again. "Be careful to keep your fingers up and away from the blade. Cut out the core using the tip of the knife like this."

Pauline held the knife handle with her right hand and pushed hard on the blade with her left hand. "Careful," cautioned Marian. "These heads roll around. Here, I'll put this towel under it. Now try."

Pauline pushed the knife down. "Ugh," she let out a big breath. The cabbage head fell apart. She continued as Marian had shown her and put the cored cabbages into a tub. Alice, Thea and Gev each had a cabbage shredder, a board about twenty inches long and fifteen inches wide with a sharp knife blade set diagonally. They slid chunks of cabbage back and forth against it slicing off thin shreds. If a finger got nicked, a drop of blood was wiped away with a damp cloth.

Mildred and Marian took the bowls of shredded cabbage,

and grabbing handfuls at a time, packed the cabbage firmly into crocks, pressing it down with big wooden mallets. They sprinkled each layer of cabbage with three tablespoons of salt. The women traded jobs every few minutes as their hands tired of cutting the heads and shredding the cabbage.

As they worked, Pauline thought about the relationships of the good-natured ladies. *Alice and her sister, Thea, are Hank and Ted Martin's sisters. Gev is married to Hank and Mildred is Ted's wife. They all seem devoted to each other. It's so nice to see such harmony in a family. I hope Marian and Will and Fred and I will always be close. I'm really fond of Marian and I love my brother even though he is a big tease.*

After all the cabbage had been shredded and packed into crocks, the women covered it with clean cloths of flour sacking. Mildred placed a large dinner plate on top of the cloth on each of her crocks. She brought glass gallon jars filled with water and placed them on the plates to weigh them down. She explained to Pauline that as the salt "worked" with the cabbage it would make brine. The weight would help the brine come up to cover the cabbage. "That's what you should do with your crock when you take it to your kitchen," said Mildred. "You might like to keep it on the porch."

Pauline said, "I think making sauerkraut is hard work and the men better appreciate it."

"Yes," said Thea with a little laugh, "the men get off easy, and they do love their kraut. Sometimes I cook it with chopped apple and brown sugar."

Clean-up began and the women started chatting again as they enjoyed a cup of chicken soup and little egg salad sandwiches Mildred had prepared.

Pauline greeted Fred home from work. "Look, dear! I learned how to make sauerkraut today. Will came and asked me to help Marian. We took all the cabbage from Will's garden out to Mildred's house. Alice went with us and Gev and Thea helped, too. Marian gave me one of her old glass gallon vinegar jugs."

Pauline removed the plate and cloth so Fred could see the cabbage. "Mildred said it would take nine to fourteen days to ferment and I can keep it in my kitchen or outside on the porch. Scum has to be skimmed off every day. The cloth and plate have to be rinsed before putting them back on the cabbage."

"The porch would be cooler. Where did you get the crock?"

"Marian had an extra one." Pauline put everything back together over the cabbage and said she would make a quick supper.

When supper dishes were put away, Pauline remembered to tell Fred, "Next Saturday there'll be a party to make apple cider at a farm by Ala Spit and we're invited. Isn't it nice they include us when they have all these parties?"

"Yes, we have many new friends. And it'll be another new experience for you. I remember pressing apples at Uncle Jack's farm. My aunt put those little cinnamon sticks in the cider while it was warming on the stove."

"And you liked it!"

"I sure did. Are you tired tonight after being on your feet and working all day?"

"Actually, I am tired. Will came just as I getting ready to iron the sheets and pillowcases I washed yesterday. Now, I'm a day behind."

"Well, I think it's early to bed for you. I'm tired, too. A little snuggle time will do us both good."

"I bet I'll be the first one in bed." Pauline began stripping off her clothes on the way to the bedroom.

Chapter Twenty-Eight... The Cider Press Party

Dressed in warm trousers, sweater and coat, Pauline carried a pot of baked beans out to the truck. She had wrapped it in a terry cloth towel to keep it warm. She noticed Fred had loaded two boxes of apples picked from the old trees. The small Gravensteins would add flavor to the cider.

They drove down Ducken Road. "Hey! There's Rupert. Let's ask him to go with us."

"Sure. Hank says everyone is welcome." Fred stopped the truck, rolled down the window and called, "Hi, Rupert! Were you coming up to see us?"

"Yes, I thought I'd drop by for a few minutes."

"We're on our way to make cider. Would you like to go?"

Standing with hands in his pockets, Rupert looked up and down the road, "Uh…well…"

Leaning forward against Fred, Pauline called, "Come on, you'll have a good time."

Fred said, "Jump in by Pauline."

Rupert adjusted his cap, grinned and said, "Okay."

Pauline moved closer to Fred and Rupert squeezed in

beside her. She asked, "Did you want to tell us something?"

"Yeah, I was thinking last night about you trying to find my ma's folks and I remembered my gramma has a box of letters and old things on a shelf in my pa's old bedroom. She said someday I might want to look at them. I kinda forgot all about them."

"I wouldn't have forgotten them," said Pauline.

"No," Fred laughed. "You're as curious as a cat."

Rupert chuckled. Pauline turned to him. "There's a good chance you can learn a lot from those letters. Do you remember your mother's family name?"

"You mean her ma and pa's last names? No, I didn't ever know them."

"Can you ask your gramma to send the letters and box to you?"

"Yeah, I can do that."

As Fred drove around the bend toward Ala Spit, he said, "Help me find the Troxell farm, Pauline."

She saw the water through the trees. "There." She pointed to a white house on the hillside. "That's the Troxell house. Marian told me it's made of old fish-trap huts."

Fred said, "That's interesting. I'd like to have a look." He parked the truck near the apple orchard, and as they got out Hank and his dog, Shep, a German Shepherd and Collie mix, came to greet them. Pauline patted the dog and ran her hands through his long shaggy hair.

"Hank, we brought a friend, Rupert Long," said Fred. "He's one of the C's."

Hank shook Rupert's calloused hand. "Good, we can always use some help."

Children had climbed trees and were tossing apples to men and women below who filled boxes and buckets. A young girl held a long pole with a wire basket on one end. She pushed it up into the tree and collected apples from high limbs. Two boys struggled with a three-legged ladder trying to put it up into a tree.

Pauline found Thea and Alice on their knees by a large galvanized tub washing red and yellow apples. After greetings were exchanged, she asked, "What kinds of apples do you have?"

Thea said, "Kings, Jonathans, Winesap…"

Alice held up a huge apple. "See this? It's a Twenty-Ounce. Two will make a pie." She cut a slice. "Try it."

"Mmm, tart, just the way I like them," said Pauline.

"Take a few home. Make an apple cake with cinnamon."

Pauline heard the noisy whirring of an electric motor starting. She watched a teenage boy dump washed apples into the hopper at the top of the press. The apples bounced up and down as sharp blades shredded and dropped them into a slatted barrel below. When it was full, the boy pushed it forward and replaced it with a second barrel. Another boy placed a lid, made of a round flat board with a big iron screw, on top of the apples. Then he turned a wheel on top of the press to squeeze the apples into pulp. Juice ran down a large board funneling into a galvanized bucket.

Will took the brim-full bucket away and Marian replaced it with an empty one. Will carried the full bucket to a long plank table. Gev held a funnel lined with cheesecloth above an empty glass vinegar jug, and Will poured the apple juice into the funnel. As soon as a jug was almost full, Gev moved the funnel to a new jug. It was a well-coordinated operation.

Pauline asked if she could help. Gev said, "Take my place and I'll help wash the apples."

Happy to have a job, Pauline smiled when she saw Rupert turning the iron wheel. Fred had taken over Will's job and brought a bucket of juice to her. "Hi! Are you having fun?"

"Yes. I love all the activity." Fred left and then Pauline heard, "Aunt Paulie!"

She turned to see Jenny running toward her. She gave her niece a big hug and kissed her cheek. "Oh, it's wonderful to see you!"

Just then Alice came over. "I know you haven't seen your Aunt Pauline since the Grange picnic, Jenny. You two go sit by the fire." She smiled at Pauline. "I'm sure this young lady has lots to tell you. I'll help fill the jugs."

"Thanks, Alice." Pauline put her arm around Jenny, and they walked over to the fire and sat on a large log. Jenny poked the fire with a stick and told about her summer classes at college in Bellingham.

"How long before you finish?"

"Next June. Dad says the new high school should be finished by fall and I'm going to try to get the Home Ec job."

Pauline said, "Better say hello to your Uncle Fred." She watched as Jenny walked up behind Fred and put her arms around his waist. He laughed, turned, and gave her a bear hug. He ruffled her curly hair and told her it was about time she came home for a visit.

She asked, "How are Billy and Nanny?"

"They're not kids any more. You better come up and see them, and Pauline's hens."

Jenny saw Rupert and asked, "Who's the guy turning the press wheel?"

Pauline said, "He's our friend, Rupert. Come meet him." They walked to the press and Pauline introduced them. He wiped a wet hand on his pants and shyly shook Jenny's hand. She gave him a big smile.

Someone announced the last apple had been squeezed. Women gathered around the picnic tables, setting out lunch. The men dismantled and washed the cider press and put it in the shed for the next year. Ted whittled points on branches from an alder tree so the kids could roast hot dogs. Mothers cautioned children to hold their crooked sticks up from the exposed hot embers. Folks filled their plates with baked beans and other picnic food.

Standing in line beside Hank, Pauline asked him, "I noticed you put the apple peelings in your truck. What you do with them?"

Hank quipped, "My pigs will hog 'em down."

Jenny wrinkled her nose at Pauline and they all laughed.

With much merriment and joking, everyone enjoyed their food. Pauline looked up when she heard Jenny laughing. She saw her fill Rupert's tin cup with cider. They walked away from the group. *That Jenny. It didn't take her long to make friends with him.*

The grown-ups folded the chairs and tables and put them in the shed. They rounded up the children and took jugs of amber-colored juice to their cars or trucks. It had been another good cider press year with plenty for all.

Will reminded his daughter, still talking with Rupert, "Jenny, we better get moving if you're going to take the ferry tonight and catch your ride to Bellingham."

"Okay, Dad." She said something to Rupert.

He laughed and said, "Yeah, see you again."

Jenny walked backwards from him and called, "Maybe at Thanksgiving!" She hugged Pauline and Fred and then followed her dad to his car.

Pauline thanked Gev and Hank for inviting them. "We always enjoy being with your family."

Hank said, "We're glad to have you any time."

Gev put her arm around Pauline. "We would like you and Fred to come some evening and play cards."

"We'll do that. We love card games."

On the way to take Rupert back to the C's camp, Pauline teased, "I think Jenny likes you."

He grinned and looked out the side window. "Yeah, she's nice."

Fred laughed. "Jenny likes everybody." He parked the truck by the main camp building.

Rupert got out and as he closed the door said, "Making cider was fun. It tasted good, too."

Pauline said, "Remember to ask your gramma about the letters and box."

"Yes, I'll write to her." He waved his hand and loped down the trail toward camp.

Chapter Twenty-Nine... The Cranberry Bog

Pauline heard footsteps on the porch and opened the door to find Marian.

"Hey, kiddo, get your trousers on and come with me."

Pauline laughed and asked, "What are we going to do?"

"It's a gorgeous day to go to the bog and pick cranberries. You'll need your boots."

"Well, goodness sakes, Marian, you certainly don't give a person any warning. I guess I can go. I haven't any reason to stay home and it sounds like fun. Fred and I like cranberries."

Marian drove her car down Ducken Road and parked at the Dirken's farm. "I called earlier and asked Rachel if she would like to come with us, but she said not this time. She doesn't mind if we park here and walk through the pasture. Here's a pail for you."

Pauline took the gold pail with the words James Henry Lard painted in bold red letters. They walked through a gate into a pasture where several Guernsey cows paid no attention to them as they continued down toward the bog. At the edge of the field, Marian held apart the barbed wire fence strands while Pauline bent down and stepped between them, then she held the wires for Marian. After walking several hundred yards through the next field, they climbed over a board fence.

Marian led the way on a muddy path through scrub brush to a boardwalk over marshy ground. "We have to be careful. These old rotted boards were put down many years ago. You could step into a foot or more of water if you break through them. The water level is low now compared to what it will be in a few months. The winter snowmelt and spring rains flood this area. Cranberry Lake is in front of us a few hundred feet."

They came to waist-high bushes laden with dark red berries. Surprised birds flew up and away to secluded spots. "Alice brought me here the first fall Will and I moved to the farm. She told me she and Hank used to come here with their grandmother to pick cranberries for Thanksgiving dinner."

The board path forked. Marian went to the left and Pauline to the right. They dropped berries into their empty pails, ping, ping, ping. Soon the pings were muffled as the buckets filled with the ripe fruit.

Pauline ducked under a low-hanging wild cherry branch, trying not to spill her half-full pail. She began to slide and grabbed for a branch. It broke and she slid off the wet board into the bog. "Nerts!" She caught at the berry branches to keep her balance and stood with knee-deep murky water pouring into her boots. "Marian!"

"What did you do?"

"I fell off the board."

"Hold on, I'm coming!" Marian made her way over

the boards.

"I didn't spill my berries." Pauline handed up her berry pail and Marian set it with hers on the board behind her. She took hold of Pauline's hands, but lost her balance and tumbled down, knocking Pauline back into the thicket of bushes. The thick tangled mass kept Pauline above the water. She began to laugh, "Oh, Marian…"

"Golly, Pauline," said Marian as she untangled herself from the brush.

"Here I am again, a dummkopf," said Pauline.

Marian said, "I think we've had enough berry picking for one day." They slogged through the water and slowly made their way along the boards. When they reached the beginning of the path they took turns supporting each other to empty the water from their boots.

Marian walked back on the boards and picked up the pails. "We have plenty for Thanksgiving dinner." They walked through the fields, wet socks squishing in their boots.

Pauline said, "When we get to my house, we'll have coffee. I made bread this morning."

"Oh, that will be wonderful!" said Marian. "I smelled the bread when you opened your door." She looked down at her boots. "I should have worn my wool socks." She joked, "Of course, I didn't plan on rescuing you. I could have left you there."

Pauline gave her a playful shove. "I don't think I'll give you any of my precious blackberry jam." They were laughing when they got to Marian's truck.

"Oh, let's not tell Fred and Will we fell into the bushes. I can hear them making fun of us," said Pauline. "Would you and Will like to have Thanksgiving dinner at our house?"

"I would like you and Fred to come to our house. Jenny will be home. I'm thinking it would be nice to invite one or two of the C's like many of the families in the community do."

"Can I invite Rupert?"

"Yes, that'd be fine."

At the supper table, Pauline told Fred about the day's events. "I knew you would laugh, Fred. I almost didn't tell you."

"But I would have wondered where you got the cranberries."

"I can't keep secrets from you anyway," she said. They both laughed.

Fred helped clear away the dishes. "Chalk it up to another new experience, dear. You've certainly had many since we came to Whidbey."

Chapter Thirty... Thanksgiving

During the day before Thanksgiving, temperatures dropped to below freezing. Wind whistled through cracks in the old house. Pauline stoked the fire, added more wood and opened the damper to keep a hot fire. She went out on the porch for more sticks and found Will with an arm load of wood.

"Hi, Paulie." He set the wood in the box by the stove and gave her a hug. "Looks like Fred's been busy. That's quite a pile of rounds out there."

"Fred's at work, but he's been coming home early this week trying to a cut a big supply for winter. Have coffee with me."

Will pulled a chair from the table and sat down. "I can't stay long."

Pauline filled two cups with the steaming brew. "Did you see Fred's wheelbarrow? He bought a wheel and used some of his scrap wood to make it."

"I did. Fred's pretty good with a saw and hammer." Will stirred a heaping teaspoon of sugar into his coffee and added rich cream.

Pauline pushed a plate of oatmeal cookies to her brother. "Fred had to break ice on the goats' water this morning."

Will set his cup down. "Old man Jorgens is predicting a cold winter, and he's usually right on target." After taking a big bite of cookie, Will said, "Marian's really busy butchering out the turkey I killed for tomorrow's dinner and she wondered if you'd bake a pie."

"Of course I will. I'd sure rather bake a pie than clean a turkey. Do you want cherry or apple?"

"Well, it's Thanksgiving. I've got a pumpkin in the truck and brought milk with extra cream."

"Oh, sure. How silly of me."

After Will left, Pauline put on a coat and went out. She saw that he had set the pumpkin on the chopping block. She got Fred's double-bladed axe from the shed. After admiring the large orange pumpkin, she raised the axe above her head and brought it down hard. Kerplunk! The pumpkin split open and small chunks flew every which way. Her hens, out of their pen for the day, cackled and rushed to peck at them. "Shoo, go on, shoo!" she said, clapping her hands to scare them away. She gathered the pumpkin pieces into her apron and carried them to the house.

Pauline scooped out the seeds and spread them on a large cookie sheet to dry. She would roast some for Fred and save a few to plant in her garden next year. She mixed pie dough while the pumpkin steam-cooked in the oven. When it had cooled, she removed the skin and threw it to the chickens. Pauline laughed as they scurried to get it.

She mashed the pumpkin pulp with a fork, mixed it with the milk, eggs, cinnamon, and ginger and completed making the pie. She licked the remnants of the tasty filling from the spoon. "Mmm, so good."

Thanksgiving Day arrived bright and clear, but cold. "I'll help bring water, Fred. It's so pretty out, it'll be a nice change after being in the house so much the past few days." Their boots left footprints in the frosted grass. Ice crystals sparkled on twigs and the sides of rocks. Fred filled the buckets. Pauline asked if the spring would freeze.

Fred said, "No, the water coming out of the ground and flowing down the stream is close to fifty degrees. You'll always have water," and joked, "as long as I keep carrying it," and after a pause, "of course that will stop as soon as I dig my well."

She rubbed her hands together. "I'm cold."

He took her hand. "Where are your mittens, kitten?"

Pauline laughed. "You're funny, Fred. Yes, I do need to make mittens or gloves."

They carried the water to the house. He said, "I'll take care of the goats and chickens and make another trip to the spring."

At noon on his way to pick up Rupert at the C's Camp, Fred dropped Pauline off at Marian's. She carried the pie and a bowl of cranberry sauce to the door and heard Marian call to come on in. She stepped into the steamy, warm kitchen filled with the smell of cinnamon and cloves. "Jenny, I'm glad you're home for the holiday. What are you cooking?"

Jenny piped up, "I'm making Mrs. Shubert's recipe for orange-spiced cider."

Pauline hung her coat on a hook by the door. "What can

I do to help?"

Marian dried her hands on a terry towel, opened the oven door, wiggled a turkey leg and smiled with satisfaction. "Good, it feels ready. Jenny has the table set and as soon as Fred and Rupert get here, we can fill the serving dishes. Will carves the turkey at the table."

With everyone seated, Marian looked across the table at her husband. "Well, here we are. A real Thanksgiving with Pauline and Fred." She looked at them. "Will and I are so happy you decided to come live near us."

Fred said, "It took Pauline a while to make up her mind, but once she did, there was no stopping her."

Marian smiled at her daughter. "And Jenny, you've had another successful year at school. We're so proud of you."

Jenny said, "Thanks, Mom."

Marian looked at Rupert. "It's nice to have you with us today, too, Rupert."

Will said, "Yep, it's been a good year. Now let's cut into the turkey."

Jenny said, "Remember to save the wishbone, Dad."

"You can't break it until it dries," said Rupert.

"I know. I'll put it on top of the warming oven."

"I wonder what you'll wish," he teased.

She gazed at his blue eyes and said, "I'll never tell."

They passed the turkey, stuffing, riced potatoes and gravy, brown-sugared yams, cranberry sauce and Marian's home-canned pickles around the table. They enjoyed seconds of their favorites, and finished the feast with Pauline's pumpkin pie topped with dollops of thick whipped cream.

Patting their full bellies, the men complimented the

cooks and retired to the living room. The women cleared the table and busied themselves in the kitchen.

After the clean-up, Jenny suggested they play a card game called Pounce.

"Do we have enough decks of cards?" asked Will.

Jenny said, "Yep, we do. Come on everyone."

Seated around the table, they all shuffled their cards. "Three times," said Jenny. And then she instructed them, "Count out thirteen cards in a pile and put four face-up like this. Now it's just like Solitaire, but we can play on anyone's cards in the middle after I say go, and remember the person who uses all the cards in his pile first, wins the game." The fun began. They slapped their hands on the table as they raced to put cards down.

Pauline chided Rupert, "You've won three games."

He grinned, put his hands in the air and looked at Jenny. "Beginner's luck."

She suggested they go for a walk to see her cow, Betsy. As they went out, Jenny called, "Okay if Rupert wears your boots, Dad?"

"Yeah, he'll need them," said Will. "I'm going to switch games. I like to play Rook."

Pauline asked, "Does Betsy really belong to Jenny?"

Marian answered, "Well, Jenny likes to thinks so because the cow was born on her birthday."

A good hour had gone by when they heard laughter. Rupert and Jenny came in. He stuffed his stocking cap in a coat pocket and rubbed his hands together. Rosy-cheeked Jenny took off her cap and mittens. Pauline watched Rupert help Jenny with her coat and kneel to pull off her boots. *She's already got him wrapped around her little finger.*

Jenny said, "It's freezing, Dad. The cows were standing around their water tank, so Rupert broke the ice for them."

"Glad you checked on them," said Will.

"Rupert used to be in a 4-H Club. He won blue ribbons with his chickens at the county fair." She turned to him and with a big smile told him, "Rupert, tell them the 4-H pledge."

"Oh, they don't want to hear that."

"Sure we do," said Pauline.

Reluctantly, he gave in.

Jenny said, "Do the hands, too."

Reciting the pledge, Rupert put one hand to his head, then one to his heart and then held out both hands for the last two lines.

> *I pledge my head to clearer thinking,*
> *my heart to greater loyalty,*
> *my hands to greater service and*
> *my health to better living,*
> *for my club, my community and my country.*

They all clapped and Rupert, his face flushed, sat on the couch.

Jenny collapsed beside him. "I wish we'd had 4-H when I was in high school. It would have been fun showing my heifers at the fairs."

"We didn't have 4-H clubs on the island back then, Jenny," said Marian. "But Alice said the county extension agent is working to get them started and is looking for men and women to be leaders."

"Well, maybe I can be a leader," said Jenny.

"First you better concentrate on getting a teaching job," said Will.

Rupert said, "I think I should be going."

"Dad, I'll drive Rupert back to camp. Okay?"

"Yes, but be careful," he cautioned. "The roads might be icy."

Rupert thanked Marian and Pauline for a great dinner.

When Jenny came home, she bounced through the door, all smiles and flashing eyes. "I invited Rupert to the dance Saturday night."

"Dance?" asked Fred.

"It's a Cornet Community tradition at the old schoolhouse on Monkey Hill Road," said Will.

Pauline's eyes lit up. "Fred! What fun! We haven't danced in ages."

Fred asked, "What kind of music do they have?"

Marian looked at Will for help, and he said, "Well, let's see, Tommy Jones brings his bass fiddle, his wife pounds the key boards, Hank and Ted play their harmonicas. Never know who's going to bring an instrument. Those who do, take turns playing and dancing. A couple of the ladies have pretty good voices, and then there's Mrs. Brockton, who trills like a nightingale."

"Now don't make fun of Annie," scolded Marian. "She's a sweet soul and enjoys singing."

Chapter Thirty-One... The Dance

Friday morning Fred announced he and Will were going duck hunting at Hank Martin's lagoon. After he left, Pauline pulled the table closer to the stove, and with her journal open and pen in hand, reflected on the past few days. She began writing: *Marian made a fine dinner and everyone complimented me on my pie. Jenny is really putting on the dog for Rupert, and the way he looks at her, it's obvious he's entranced with her.*

Pauline put the pen down, leaned back in her chair and smiled remembering Rupert saying the pledge. Picking up her pen again, she wrote: *When Rupert recited the 4-H pledge, Fred and Will chuckled a bit, but he was a good sport. When we clapped, his freckled face turned almost the color of his hair.*

She continued writing: *Tomorrow night we'll go dancing. Rupert said he didn't have the right shoes, but Jenny told him it was okay to dance in his socks.*

Pauline leaned back in her chair again. "Hmm...what'll I wear?"

She went to her closet. "Housedresses! I'm so tired

of them. I have to find something better." She rummaged through her red trunk and found her only store-bought dress, a rayon blue skirt with a white ruffled bodice and large blue bow at the neck. *Can I still get into it?*

She had just slipped it on when the door opened. "Oh, Fred, look! It still fits." She did a little dance for him, he held out his arms, hummed a bit of a tune and twirled her around. She laughed and said, "Do it again."

He took her in his arms and they laughed as he twirled her again and again.

When he let her go, she flopped down in her chair, breathless. "That's so much fun." And then she asked, "Should I wear this to the dance tomorrow night? It's not fancy and styles have changed, but at least it's not a boring housedress."

"Dear, I doubt any of the ladies will be wearing fancy dresses."

"That's true, but I'm going to drive the truck down and ask Marian."

"I'll go with you."

"It's not dark. I would like to drive by myself."

"It's almost dark."

"I won't stay long. I didn't make any mistakes last time we practiced."

"Well, just remember to go easy."

She did a little quick step as she went out to the truck.

"Oh, Aunt Paulie," Jenny said when she saw her standing in the door. "Your dress is beautiful."

"But the styles have changed. Is it too old-fashioned, Marian?"

Marian shook her head. "The women in our community don't worry much about new fashions these days. Many of the ladies will be wearing their best housedress."

"Oh, maybe this is too fancy."

Jenny retied the bow. "No, it's perfect."

As Pauline drove out of Will's yard she started humming, *Come along with me Lucille, in my merry Oldsmobile.* She arrived home and threw her arms around Fred. "I did it! My solo trip. Now I'm ready to drive anywhere. Right?"

"We'll see." He saw her frown. "Yes, on a nice day."

Saturday evening Fred and Pauline arrived to hear loud piano music coming from the old schoolhouse. Fred held her elbow as they walked up the creaky wooden steps and entered the vestibule.

Marian, Jenny, Rupert and Will, carrying his guitar, came in through the door after them. They hung their coats on hooks on the wall. Rupert took off his shoes and set them in a row of leather work shoes lined up under the coats. He showed Jenny his grey wool socks. "I'll be sliding around in these. Hope you can keep up."

"You won't have to worry about Jenny, she's fast on her feet," said Will looking fondly at his daughter.

They turned to watch the dancers and waved to Hank and Gev doing a fox trot.

"What do you think, Fred?" asked Will. "Is the music up to your standards? It's a bit different for you city folks," he teased.

Fred looked around at the crowd. "Seems like everyone's having a good time. Come on, Pauline, let's show Will we're not too citified." They joined the fun on the dance floor, Fred holding up his arm and twirling Pauline underneath. They laughed and Fred said, "Just like old times, you never miss a beat."

"I love it, Fred, you've always been the best dance partner." She looked around at the dancers. *Marian was right, the women are not wearing new styles. I guess they haven't had money to buy new material for dresses either.*

A group of young men with hands in their pockets leaned against one wall, talking and watching the dancers. "Those guys over there," Fred motioned with his head, "are probably from the C's camp."

Several girls quietly slipped in through the open door, attracting the men's attention. Fred spoke softly into Pauline's ear, "Will said young ladies come from Anacortes and Mount Vernon to meet the C's."

She watched over Fred's shoulder and saw the girls walk toward the guys. One fellow reached out to a gal, gave her a hug, and led her onto the dance floor. Pauline whispered, "I think the blonde girl has met a friend." Soon all the girls had partners and were dancing, leaving a few men by the wall.

Jenny laughed as she danced by with Rupert, who nodded and made comments to his fellow C's. Mildred and Marian sat chatting on a bench against the wall. Ted, playing his harmonica, and Will, strumming his guitar, stood on the small stage. A petite gray-haired lady played a small accordion. A tall skinny man, dressed in a red shirt and overalls, blew his coronet.

Fred made Pauline giggle as he pushed her back and around and around and joked that the lady at the piano must be Will's nightingale.

She wondered to him, "Do you think anyone dances the Lindy or even knows how? We danced it a lot at the Pavilion."

The music stopped and a pudgy fellow wearing red suspenders spun his big bass fiddle and called out, "All right folks, everyone on the floor in a big circle." He motioned to the group of single fellas. "Come on boys, no need to hold up the wall."

The musicians started out with "Ballin' the Jack." The dancers followed instructions as the words were sung. "First you put your two knees close up tight, then you sway 'em to the left, and then to the right, step around the floor kinda nice and light," and so on to the end of the song.

"All right folks, we're going to play a little jazz now. Get a partner and if you don't have one, when the music stops, step right in and get one." The music began with the lively, "If You Knew Susie." Dancers joined in singing the chorus, having a hilarious time and changing partners when the music stopped and started up again.

Fred laughed and said, "Goodbye, dear." He danced off with Marian.

Pauline turned when she felt an arm go around her waist. "Well, Rupert! Are you enjoying the dancing?"

"Yeah, it's fun. I danced a lot in high school."

He twirled her around. She laughed and said, "This is fun. You're a good dancer."

"Yeah, I'm having a nice time."

"Did you have a favorite girlfriend?"

"Not one in particular. I liked them all."

The music stopped and Hank Martin stepped up claiming Pauline for a dance. He held her a bit tight, weaving in and out of the other dancers. She thought it fun, but was relieved when he danced her over to the refreshment table.

The merriment continued for several more dances. When the musicians played "Good Night Ladies" everyone joined in, making a circle with their arms around each other's waists and swaying back and forth. They laughed and collected their coats.

Pauline and Fred walked out with Marian and Will. "And we get to do this again on New Year's Eve?" asked Pauline.

"You bet!" exclaimed Will. "We'll ring in the new year together for the first time in fourteen years." He called, "Come on, Jenny. We'll take Rupert back to camp."

Chapter Thirty-Two... A Stressful Time

Fred came home from work early and said he had a belly ache. He brushed it off as a touch of food poisoning. He and Otto had eaten lunch at The Good Eats. "I'll be all right. I just want to lie down for a while. Maybe you could get the hot water bottle for me."

Pauline filled the red rubber bottle from the tea kettle on the stove. He cradled it over his stomach and Pauline went back to her cooking. She scraped carrots to add to the stew.

When she heard Fred groan, she went into the bedroom. Fred's face was flushed. She felt his forehead. *Oh dear he has a fever. I have to get Will.*

She pulled on her boots, slipped on her coat, tied her red scarf around her head, and stepped out into the cold, blustery night. The crescent moon shed light onto the yard. She looked at the truck. *No, I promised Fred I wouldn't drive in the dark, but I need Will quick. No, I promised Fred.*

She hurried down the rough gravel driveway. The wind whipped the ends of her scarf onto her face. She tightened it under her chin. *We should have spent the money and had the phone line brought into the house.*

Pauline found it easier once on the road as she half-walked and ran the mile to Will's driveway. Light shone from the barn windows. Wind rushed through the breezeway between the barn door and the milk house. She struggled to keep her balance. She found the door handle and pulled. It didn't open. "Nerts!" It didn't push in. Pauline beat her fists against the rough boards. "Will! Marian!" Then she remembered the door hung from an iron rod. She slid it to the side just enough so she could squeeze in sideways. The wind blew straw along the limed floorboards. She was greeted by the pleasant smell of warm milk, the sound of the cows munching and their contented low murmurs. "Will? Marian?" Pauline hurried along the line of cows.

Marian sat on a three-legged stool, her head pushed against a cow's soft, warm belly. She pulled milk from the cow's teats into a shiny steel pail held between her legs. She noticed Pauline and asked, "What is it?"

"Fred's sick! His stomach hurts and he has a fever."

Will poked his head around the rear end of the cow he was milking and called, "Marian, go call Doctor Carlyle. I'll finish up."

Pauline followed Marian into the milk house and watched her pour white foamy milk into the large stainless steel receptacle at the top of the cooling pipes. The milk ran over corrugated pipes and funneled into a ten-gallon milk can. Marian wiped her hands on a towel hanging by the door and grabbed her denim work jacket. "All right, let's go." They went out into the gusty wind. In the house, Marian turned on a light and reached for the telephone. She cranked the phone handle one long turn. "Operator, this is Marian Ansbach. I need Dr. Carlyle."

Pauline said, "Tell him to hurry."

Marian held her hand over the mouth piece and said, "Everyone on our party line will know we're calling the doctor." She spoke into the phone, "Tell him to come to the Gunther home on Ducken Road."

"How many are on your line?"

"Seven, maybe eight…Oh, June, did you reach him?" She listened. "Okay. Thanks." She hung the receiver on the hook. "Doctor will come to your house. I'll take you home in the car."

As Marian drove, Pauline sat forward, peering through the windshield. "I didn't want to leave him, but he's in so much pain I just had to get help."

When they reached the driveway she ran to the house. She found Fred bent over the stove, holding his belly. "Fred! You should be in bed."

"Where have you been? Something's burning."

"Oh dear, I forgot to take the stew off the stove. I went to Will's to call the doctor."

Marian looked at Fred's ashen face. "Get him back to bed. I'll take care of the stew."

Pauline helped Fred into bed and pulled the quilt up to his neck. "Do you still hurt?"

"I hurt like hell."

"Oh, Fred, I'm sorry. I'll fill the hot water bottle again. Would you like a cup of tea?"

"No. Nothing." Pauline fussed over him, wrung a wash-cloth with cool water and wiped his forehead.

When Dr. Carlyle's auto lights shone through the window,

she held open the door and called, "Fred's in so much pain and he has a fever."

Kneeling beside the bed, Dr. Carlyle put a thermometer in Fred's mouth, and with a light touch pushed on his abdomen and asked where it hurt. Fred put his hand on the lower left side of his abdomen and mumbled, "Here, right here."

The doctor said, "He has appendicitis. Call the *Cup and Saucer* and tell them to be ready. I'll take him to the hospital in Mount Vernon."

Marian grabbed her coat. "I'll go."

Fred lay on his side with his knees pulled up. Pauline, near tears, asked the doctor what she should do. He said it would be best for her to stay home. He would call her. Marian came with news that the ferry wasn't running because of the incoming tide and strong wind.

Dr. Carlyle looked at the women. "We'll do it right here."

Pauline protested, "How…?"

He gave her a stern look. "Just do as I say. We need hot water and towels."

Marian put her hand on Pauline's arm. "I'll stay and help. We'll get this done together." She put a kettle of water on the stove and Pauline brought towels.

The doctor looked up at the light bulb hanging from the ceiling. "I'll need more light."

Pauline got out two kerosene lamps and set them on the table. "It's all I have."

Dr. Carlyle moved the table closer to the bed, took instruments from his black bag and spread them on a towel on the table. When all the preparations had been made, he said, "Close your eyes, Fred, relax. You're not going to feel a thing." Then he unscrewed the cap on a small brown bottle, poured the liquid on a cotton ball and held it to Fred's nose. Soon Fred was asleep.

The doctor reached for a sharp scalpel.

Pauline said, "Marian…"

"It's okay, Pauline. Step out on the porch."

The next day Pauline sat in her rocking chair beside their bed listening to Fred's even breathing. She dozed off, but awoke when she felt cold. The fire had died down so she poked the coals together and added sticks of wood. Steam came from the tea kettle and water collected on the kitchen windows. Pauline dried them with a towel and read her magazines.

Fred opened his eyes in mid-morning, groggy and asking questions.

"No," Pauline assured him, "the appendix did not rupture."

"Did you watch? Did the doctor do everything right?"

"Dear, I couldn't watch when he started cutting your tummy, but Marian was right there. Nothing seems to phase her. I'm sure the doctor did everything right. You have sixteen stitches on your belly. Doctor said as the wound heals, it might itch. He gave me ointment to rub on it."

Fred reached for her hand. "You're a good wife."

She stooped over him, brushed his hair back and kissed his forehead. "You had a strange dream last night. You talked in your sleep."

"What did I say?"

"You kept talking about rolly-pollies, whatever they are."

"You don't know what a rolly-polly is? You haven't lived."

"What is it?"

"My grandmother used to make real thin hotcakes and smear them with butter. She sprinkled cinnamon sugar on and rolled them up like logs. She would give me three on a plate. I picked them up with my fingers. Sometimes the butter would drip out and I'd lick my plate."

"Sounds like you were a little pig. Would you like me to make rolly-pollies?"

"No, nothing to eat, just some water."

"Okay. I'll make them another time." She held a glass to him. "The doctor is coming this afternoon, dear." She fluffed his pillow and straightened his quilt.

Fred lay back and dozed off.

Will popped in at noon. "Have you taken care of your chickens and goats?"

Pauline put a hand to her mouth.

"I'll look after them, Paulie, you take care of Fred." He hesitated before going out. "You should get some sleep." Later, he returned with a few eggs and two buckets of spring water.

For the next week, Pauline took care of Nanny and Billy. The light in the coop had fooled her hens and she was pleased they were laying more eggs. She busied herself knitting stockings for Will and Fred for Christmas and made Lebkucken, Fred's favorite German molasses cookie.

Pauline didn't tell Fred the wood pile was getting low. One afternoon when he was asleep, she turned the radio on low, put on her overalls and Fred's mackintosh, and went out. She looked at the pile of wood to be split. She had watched Fred put rounds of wood on the chopping block and cut them smaller to fit in the stove. "Rats! It's too heavy," she muttered as she tried to lift one round up to the chopping block. She left it on the ground, but turned it on end. Then she picked up the axe, raised it above her head, and swung it down hard. The blade lodged in the wood. She rocked it back and forth, pulled it out and tried again and again, but the round kept bouncing on the soft pile of chips.

"Mrs. Gunther, I'll split the wood."

She turned. "Rupert?"

"I got a letter from Jenny telling me about Fred. I came as soon as I could to see if you need help, and I think you do."

"Thank you, Rupert." She saw a few cedar sticks lying on the ground. "I can cut the old shakes for kindling, but I'm not good at splitting the big stuff."

"Does Fred have a splitting maul?"

"There might be one in the shed."

Rupert went to the shed and came back with a maul and a splitting wedge. He put the round on the chopping block and placed the wedge in one of the cuts Pauline had made. When he hit the wedge with the blunt end of the maul, the wood fell apart. As he split the chunks in smaller pieces, Pauline gathered them in her arms and carried them into the house. One fell to the floor.

Fred opened his eyes. "Pauline, do I hear someone by the wood pile?"

"Yes. Jenny told Rupert about your operation and he came to help. Isn't that thoughtful?"

Fred sat up. "It isn't right. I should've split those

rounds myself."

"Dear, Rupert likes to help. It won't be long until you're back on your feet, but until Dr. Carlyle says it's okay, don't even think about chopping wood. You might pull out the stitches."

Rupert stacked the wood on the porch. Pauline told him to come in and have a bowl of chicken soup. He visited with Fred, telling him about the work he'd been doing. "No more blasting. I'm working with a crew building a road bridge over a trail from the Cornet Bay Camp to the park on the west side of the road." After lunch, Rupert pulled a brown paper packet from his coat pocket. "Mrs. Gunther..."

"Please call me Pauline."

"Okay. Uhh...Pauline, my gramma sent my pa's letters. I thought you and Fred might like to read them." He set the packet on the table.

"Yes, we would. It was swell of you to come today. I certainly did need help with the wood."

"I'll stop by again when I can." He walked to the door and looked back. "Hope you're feeling better, Fred." He closed the door and went on his way.

Chapter Thirty-Three... Letters

Rupert was hardly out the door when Pauline picked up the packet. She sat in her rocking chair next to Fred and studied the address.

Rupert Long, Camp Deception SP-3 #266, Whidbey Island, Washington

As she opened the packet, torn envelopes spilled onto her lap. "Listen to this, Fred. Here's a letter from Rupert's grandmother that he got last week."

Dear Rupert,

I got your letter and am happy to hear you are doing okay with the CCC. You've traveled a long way, clear across the country. You say the work is hard, but you're getting in good shape. I'm glad you get lots to eat. Uncle Jess told Grampa that cousin Joe is at a CCC camp in Darrington, not too far from you. Maybe you will have time off to see him.

Your pa left us in 1906 when he was only fifteen years old. His friends were quitting school to work in the mines. There wasn't any other kind of work, and one day he just up and left. We worried about him.

Once in a while we had a postcard or letter. In your last letter you wrote that you have made friends with the people who live where you used to live. Since you're wondering if your ma's folks live on Whidbey Island, I'll send your pa's letters to you. Maybe they will help you find her relatives.

I'm sorry we didn't ever meet your ma. I think she must have been a very good person. When your pa brought you to us, he said she loved you and had taken good care of you. He said she was kind and gentle. Your pa said she got real sick, but there was a bad snowstorm and he couldn't get her to a doctor. A few days later she died. She probably had pneumonia. I'm so sorry. Before your ma married your pa, her last name was Roberts.

Grampa misses fishing with you and I miss cooking for you. Please write soon.

Love, Gramma

"That's sad. Here's an envelope dated March 3, 1907 with a two-cent stamp and addressed to Mr. and Mrs. Owen Long, Lynch, Pennsylvania." Pauline looked at the bottom of the letter. "Rupert's father wrote this to his folks."

Dear Ma and Pa,

I guess you are wondering where I've been for the past year. I'm sorry if I worried you, but I didn't want to work in the coal and just wanted to get on my own. I hooked up with another guy from Pennsylvania who didn't want to work in the mines. Me and Charlie find work here and there, but don't stay in one place for long. We were on a cattle ranch in Texas for a while but now we are headed over to the coast. Charlie wants to see the big ocean. Don't worry about me. Just think of me exploring the world.

Your son, Ralph

Pauline continued reading to Fred.

May 1907

Dear Ma and Pa,
    Me and Charlie heard about the big earthquake so we headed up to San Francisco. Guess you read about that in the paper. The city was a mess, so we didn't want to stick around. We decided to keep going north. We've been working pretty steady in the straw-berry fields but we're getting pretty sick of them. We heard there is good work in the woods cutting trees in Oregon, so that's where we're headed as soon as we pick up our pay. Seems my feet don't want to stay in one place.

Your son, Ralph

The next letter was dated 1909. "Two years between let-ters? That's a long time not to write."

"Maybe the poor guy didn't have any paper," Fred chuckled softly.

"Well, maybe she didn't send them all, or maybe some

were lost."

Dear Ma and Pa,

Well, you might say my wanderings have paid off. Since I last wrote, Charlie and me worked in the forests for a year or so and then came up to Washington with a couple other guys, and I'm sawing down trees again. Some of these trees are really big. Charlie and me and a couple other guys put our arms around one of them, but our hands couldn't touch. I'm working for a man who owns a lot of acres all in trees that are being cut for lumber. There's a lot of young guys here who are working for a piece of land like me. My piece is about three acres. It's kind of rocky and covered with blackberries and what they call Oregon grape and a couple acres is trees. It's got lots of water from a spring. I'm going to build a house, but first I have to clear a lot of brush.

Well, I hope everyone back home is doing okay. I'd sure like to get a letter from you. It's been a long time, but I finally have a place to get mail. Send it to me at Oak Harbor, Washington. They'll keep it for me until I can to pick it up. Oh yeah, I'm on an island called Whidbey. The only way to get here is by a little ferryboat, unless you want to swim. Ha Ha.

Your son, Ralph

"So, Fred, he got our land in 1909."

"Yeah, it wasn't much then, and it isn't now. You can't grow much in rocks."

"But Will says we can have a nice garden."

"It'll take a lot of time and work, Pauline."

"I have plenty of time and I like to work. The garden will be fun. Here's a letter from 1911."

Dear Ma,

I got your letter about Pa. I sure hope he's going to be okay. I hope he won't go down in the mines again. I worked enough to pay for my land and I'll send some money for you when I get my next pay. Ma, so much has happened to me since I wrote you. Guess that was back in the summer. First off, when I wasn't working in the woods or at the saw mill for my boss, I kept clearing land and working on my house. I met a girl. Her name is Ruby. Boy, she's some gal. You might say we liked each other as soon we met at a social. They have dances here every Saturday night and after a few Saturdays I asked Ruby if she wanted to get married and we got set on that idea, but first I wanted to get my house built. When it turned out Ruby was going to have a baby, her step-father kicked her out of the house, so she moved in with me even when my house wasn't done. But she didn't mind, and together we got the house so it's nice. It's not real big, but I added a lean-to where Ruby has a few chickens and I'm going to get a cow. I don't work in the woods on Sunday, so that's my day to work on our place. Come spring I'll make a garden for Ruby. Before you know it you're going to be Gramma and Grampa.

Your son, Ralph

Oh yeah, I have a mailbox on the road by my place and you can send letters to Rt. 1 Box 39, Oak Harbor, Washington.

"So, Ruby got pregnant. I wonder if they ever got married. I wonder if Rupert knows."

"I don't think you should ask him."

"No, of course I won't. Here's one from August 1911."

Dear Gramma and Grampa,

Yep, that's what you are now, Gramma and Grampa. We have a fine little boy we call Rupert. He was born on July 4. That's how we celebrated the Fourth of July! So he's almost two months already. Ruby is a good mama. I bought a cow so we have milk and lots of eggs. Ruby grew up on a little farm and she takes care of the chickens and milks Clara. I'm still working in the woods cutting trees. Someday I'll bring Ruby and Rupert home so you can see my family.

Your son, Ralph

Pauline started to take out another letter.

"Wait, Pauline, I'm cold. Can you fix the fire?"

"Dear, I'm sorry. Yes, and I'll start supper, too." She put the letters aside. "Oh, my sakes! I haven't even cleaned up the lunch dishes."

Pauline stoked the fire, watched the flames jump up and added a few sticks of wood. Fred came to the table when the chicken soup was hot, ate and then said he would lie down. "You read the letters and tell me about them later."

The next letter, dated 1914, had a dark ring like a coffee

cup stain on it.

Dear Ma and Pa,

Ma, that's too bad about Uncle Bob dying. I guess he was my favorite of all your brothers. Wish you could see little Rupe. He's growing like a weed, almost three years old. I'm still working in the woods and he wants to come with me so bad, but the woods isn't a place for a little tyke. Besides he's got his own woods and he's a little trooper when I go out to cut wood for our stove. I made a wheelbarrow and he tries to help fill it up, then I put him on top for the ride to the house. I've got a big stack in the lean-to where it can dry. Rupe has plenty to do helping his ma with our cow and chickens and two goats a man gave me. Ruby takes Rupe up to the spring and he plays in the water. He likes to count the eggs when he and Ruby feed the chickens. He's a good little boy and has red hair like his ma.

Your son, Ralph

Pauline noticed the postage on the next envelope had gone up to three cents by March 1917.

Dear Ma and Pa,

I have sad news. My Ruby died. I feel so bad like my whole world is coming to an end and I don't know how I can take care of Rupert. I want to bring him home to you. I have enough money saved up so we can take a train. I might see you before you get this letter.

Your son, Ralph

Pauline looked over at Fred. "Oh, poor Ralph."

"What did you say?" asked Fred, pulling the quilt up to his chin.

She picked up an envelope dated July 1918. "This is from Ralph when he was in France."

Dear Ma,

I sure like getting your letters. Some of the guys don't get letters. Guess I'm one of the lucky ones. I sure miss Rupe. I hope he's being a good boy for you. Ma, I've been thinking about if something happens to me. I know you'll take good care of him, but I've thought that someday he might want to know about his ma. Ruby was a great gal and she loved me and Rupert. It isn't fair that his mother died when he was so little. I'm thinking he might want to find her kinfolk someday. But Ma, I don't remember their last names. Ruby's last name was Roberts, but her mother had a different last name. I never met her. She lived over in Anacortes. We didn't ever go on the ferry. Ruby was afraid to go home.

Before I left for overseas, I put Ruby's things in a box on a shelf in the bedroom closet. I figured someday Rupert might like to have something of his mama's. I know there's a pocket knife that belonged to her pa and a picture of her ma.

When I get home I want to take my son fishing

*and do all the fun things Pa and I did. Give Rupert a
big dose of hugs from me.*

Your son, Ralph

Pauline found another letter in the envelope. "Oh, here's one to Rupert."

Dear Rupert,

*I sure was happy to get your pictures. You are
learning to draw real good. Your gramma said you
are being a good boy. She says she will have a birthday party for you and Uncle Jess will bring Skip and
Rachel. You take a big deep breath and blow out all
your candles. Seven candles already! Grampa said
he's going to take you fishing at the lake. You catch
a fish for me. I love you, son, and I'll be home soon.*

Love, Pa

Pauline put the letters into the packet. "Well, maybe the picture in the locket will help me find his grandmother. I wonder if she's here on the island."

Fred squirmed in bed and nestled down under the quilt. "I wouldn't get your hopes up. She must be old by now."

Rocking back and forth, Pauline remembered Rupert had put the locket in his pocket. She would have to ask him to let her see the picture, maybe let her take it to town to show people.

Chapter Thirty-Four... Recovery

While Fred felt better each day, Pauline insisted on doing the chores. Will came to check on the animals and kept the milk can on the porch filled with water.

Their friends stopped by. Gev and Hank Martin came one evening, Alice brought homemade doughnuts one afternoon, Thea and Bert Van Zef drove out from town bringing ice cream, and Otto visited to let Fred know he had a new job for him. That pleased Fred so much he said he was ready to go to work, but Pauline said, "No, absolutely not until Dr. Carlyle gives his okay."

One day Fred said, "I feel better, Pauline. I don't hurt. No reason for me to stay cooped up in the house when I should go back to work."

Over and over she had said, "You must wait until Doctor says it's okay," but tired of arguing with him, she gave in. "Go on then."

"All right, I will." He put on his overalls and padded around in his stockings. "I can't find my boots."

"You'll find them in the shed along with your shoes."

"What? You put them out there?"

"I figured it was the only way I could keep you down. Going to the outhouse in your slippers is enough of a walk for you."

"I didn't know you could be so mean."

"Well, I didn't know you could be so stubborn."

"Okay, fine. You win." He plopped down in his rocker and moped.

Pauline didn't let Fred's grumbling bother her. She dug through her small trunk for the box of ornaments packed between linens brought from Bay City. "Fred, remember our first Christmas? We didn't have money so I strung beads and pieces of old jewelry to decorate a little tree."

He sighed. "Yes, how could I forget after having them on our trees for thirteen years?"

"When you sawed up the big alder that fell in the May wind storm, you found a little fir that would make a perfect Christmas tree. I'll string rose hips and make a paper angel for the top. We have my mother's pink bird and the gold acorn balls from your mother."

Hearing no response, she noticed he had fallen asleep.

Dr. Carlyle came in the afternoon. His jovial manner of making jokes while taking out the stitches made Fred laugh. "Well, you've healed nicely. A bit of laughter won't hurt you, but take it easy for a while. No heavy lifting."

After the doctor had gone, Fred put his arms around Pauline and held her close. He whispered, "I'm sorry for being a grouch."

"I know it's been hard on you, dear. I'll get your boots and shoes in the morning so you can do the chores. You won't need to go to the spring. Will brought one of his ten-gallon milk cans full of water for me to use in the house and he filled all the water buckets for the animals."

On her way from the outhouse, the next morning, Pauline stopped by the chicken nests and reached under the hens warm, downy bodies to get their eggs. The hens cackled, flew out of their nests and strutted around making soft murmurs. She called, "Here chick, chick, chick" and threw a few handfuls of grain and grit to them. The hens scratched in the hardpan dirt floor.

Pauline carried the eggs in her apron and walked on the wet boards toward the house. One boot caught on the edge of a plank and down she plopped onto the icy board. "Nerts!" She took off her apron, now covered with broken eggs, and set it on the ground. She stood up and the back of her wet dress clung to her legs. "Yuck!" She picked up the apron and shook it over the chickens' pen. The hens clucked noisily and pecked at the scrambled eggs.

Pauline saw Fred standing on the porch watching her while waiting for his boots. She thought he might laugh. "It's not funny, Fred."

"Are you hurt?"

"Not a bit," she said. "I just need to change my dress and then I'll get your boots."

"It's okay, I'll wear my slippers to the shed. No need for you to go out again."

When he returned, she asked, "Did you enjoy puttering in the shed?"

"Yep, got my tools ready for work tomorrow."

Pauline went about doing her house chores and Fred rested in his chair.

A little while later, he said, "I hear something outside." He peeked out the window and saw Rupert splitting wood. "I think he's taken a liking to you. He comes around kind of often."

"He's become a good friend...to both of us."

Fred put on his coat and boots and went to talk with Rupert. Pauline grabbed her coat and stepped out onto the porch

She heard Fred tell Rupert, "We appreciate your help, but I'm ready to get back to work. You won't need to come chop wood again."

Oh, I hope Fred hasn't hurt Rupert's feelings, Pauline worried.

Rupert replied, "I'm happy to help. Pauline wasn't having much luck chopping these big rounds and I enjoy time away from camp. There's not much to do on rainy Sundays. Lots of guys sit around playing checkers and cards. I'd rather help you."

Pauline called, "Guys, I'll have lunch ready in a few minutes. You come on in."

She felt relieved when she heard them laughing as they came up onto the porch.

Fred said, "Yep, I've got a new job remodeling kitchen cabinets. I start tomorrow."

Pauline brought sandwiches to the table. Fred and Rupert sat down and each took one.

Fred said, "We learned a lot about your father when Pauline read your letters to me. Your father was quite a traveler, but settled down once he got his land. It took a lot of work to clear the scrub brush. Maybe he felled trees here to build the house. I don't suppose he'd had work in construction before he left home. He was a smart young man."

Rupert sat up. "I never thought about that, but I guess you're right."

Pauline joined them at the table. "You can be proud of your father, Rupert, and you know from the letters he wrote to your gramma, he loved your mother very much, and they loved you."

"Yes, they did, but I still don't know anything about my ma's folks."

"You know her name was Ruby Roberts," said Pauline. "I'm wondering if there are names on the back of the picture in the locket. Have you looked?"

"No, I haven't, but that's a good idea."

"I'd like to help you find your mother's family."

"Yeah, that'd be nice. Of course, I don't know if they live here. Gramma told me my ma, Ruby, grew up in Sedro Woolley. When her pa died, her ma married another man and they moved to Anacortes. In Pa's letters, he said the man kicked my ma out of his house."

"Perhaps if I took the locket into town, I could show it to a few people. They may recognize the people in the picture."

"Yeah, that might work. I'll bring it up next time I come."

A west wind pelted rain against the windows during the night. Pauline turned over and over in a restless sleep. She got up several times to stoke the fire. Fred, anxious to see Otto, woke before daylight. He lit a kerosene lantern and said he would feed the animals. "No sense in both of us getting wet."

Pauline had troubles in the house. Since it was impossible to dry anything outside, she decided to wash only the necessary garments. As Fred was about to leave for work, she told him, "I don't know how I'll get the washing dry today. I need another clothes rack. Can you buy one at the Co-op for me?"

He said he would and kissed her on his way out.

Pauline kept a hot fire going and hung clothes on her old rack near the stove. She opened the oven door for more heat. The windows fogged and she wiped them down so water wouldn't puddle on the sills. The house was warm and humid. She stepped out and listened to the rain pound on the porch roof. The cold air felt refreshing.

Remembering she needed to make cookies to take to the children at the schoolhouse Christmas Party, she went back to her kitchen. *Kids always like cut-out sugar cookies, and decorating trees, Santas and angels will be fun.* She mixed the dough and put it in the cooler to stiffen overnight.

Fred came home late to find a frazzled, tired wife who wanted to know if he bought a clothes rack. He ignored her, sat in a chair by the table, pushed his hat back and started talking. "This morning I turned left onto Monkey Hill, drove a few yards and realized the truck had a flat tire. Luckily, I had the spare. I changed the tire, in the rain mind you, and by the time I got to Otto's shop he'd gone, so I went to his house."

Pauline took cups of coffee to the table and sat with him.

"His wife said he'd gone to the lumber yard. I waited a few minutes and when he showed, we drove over to the house where I'll be working. Otto reminded me that although the country is in a depression, there are a few families in town that still have money. Turns out this is a remodeling job in one of the older homes." Fred stirred sugar into his coffee. "It's a white house with green ornate trim on the roof eaves and lattice porches."

"I probably saw it when I went to Sewing Circle. Most of the houses on Thea's street have bric-a-brac."

"The man wants it finished by Christmas as a surprise for his wife who is out of town for a couple weeks. Otto said I'll get to know the guy because he'll be checking my work and might want to make last minute changes." Fred fiddled with the sugar spoon, filling it and watching the sugar spill back into the bowl. "I don't like someone hanging around."

"I'm sorry, dear, but we should be thankful you have work."

"Yeah, I know." He bent down to take off his grey wool socks.

Pauline carried the empty cups to the sink. "I'll have supper ready soon. And, Fred, I still want another clothes rack."

Chapter Thirty-Five... Pauline's Day in Town

Pauline opened the door. "I'm surprised to see you, Rupert. Come in."

"I can't stay long. It's been raining so much everything is mud so we have the day off. The guys are all lined up to get haircuts." Rupert smiled. "I want to get back while Oscar's scissors are still sharp."

She noticed the shaggy red hair over his ears. "You're funny. Hang your jacket on the rack by the stove and have a cup of coffee." She sat with him at the table.

He took a tiny box from his pocket and gave it to Pauline.

She opened it to find the oval locket engraved with a rose. She felt the softness of the gold and opened the latch. "No names, just a date, 1898. Perhaps these are your grandparents, maybe their wedding picture."

"Do I look like them?"

"Well, let's see." She held the locket close to Rupert's face and looked back and forth from his face to the picture. "Not the woman, but his eyes... hmm..." She paused and looked again. "It's possible he's your grandfather." She closed the locket. "It would be nice if we knew when your mother was born. From your pa's letters, she was young, maybe fifteen or sixteen when you were born."

"I wish I remembered more. I'd like to know my ma's folks."

"Well, I'll try to get into town this week. I might meet someone who knew your father." She got up and offered more coffee and a second cinnamon roll. He held his hand over his cup and said he ought to go.

It rained steady for the next two days. Fred said a stream ran down the driveway and washed dirt away from the rocks. "I get a bouncy ride in the truck all the way to the bottom where the water runs into the ditch."

Pauline held the locket for him to see. "Dear, now that I have the locket, I want to go to town and find someone who remembers Rupert's grandparents. I could ride in with you tomorrow."

"What'll you do all day? Walking from store to store in the rain won't be much fun."

"I like to shop. I don't mean buy. I know I can't do that, but I can talk to people about Ralph and show the picture. There are older folks who might have known him."

"I wouldn't be able to pick you up until after five."

"It's only a few blocks to Thea's house. I could wait for you there."

"I suppose I could drop you off at the Co-op. Bernie always opens at eight. We'll need to get an early start, so you better set the alarm."

Pauline had a restless night and woke often to see the time on her clock.

When the alarm went off, Fred mumbled, "Time to get up already?"

She pushed the quilt away and padded over to the stove. The fire came to life as she poked the charred sticks. "I'll make oatmeal while you do the chores."

Pauline cooked breakfast and then dressed in her wool trousers and a warm sweater. She laid her tweed coat, hand-knit hat and gloves on a chair. *What's taking him so long?* She looked out the windows at the rain, and then stepped out onto the porch. "Fred, where are you?" she called. "Nerts! It's so wet," she muttered to herself. She changed into her boots, put on her coat and scarf and walked to the shed, careful not to fall on the board path. "Fred! Fred! Where are you? You-hoo! Fred!"

Nanny and Billy, bleating as they ran around the corner of the house, darted past her and into their pen. She closed their gate.

"I found them in the woods." Fred bent over, hands on his knees, to catch his breath. "I guess I forgot to hook the gate last night. They were asleep in a hole by a big cedar stump."

"Come, get out of the rain, breakfast is ready." Fred followed her to the porch and they took off their boots. He brushed at his overalls and went into the house in his stockings.

"I'm going to be late."

"Well, surely Otto will understand. Eat."

"I don't like being late the first day of a new job."

Pauline laughed as the truck jolted down the driveway. "This really is a bumpy ride." The windshield wipers squeaked the raindrops away. She kept up a steady stream of chatter. The glass got foggy. Fred used his red bandana to wipe it clear.

She got after him, "Why do you do that? Don't you have an old rag to use?"

"If you'd stop talking, the window wouldn't fog up."

She sat back in her seat and stared out the window.

"I'm going to drop you off at the Co-op loading area rather than drive through town."

"That will be fine, dear."

Fred stopped the truck. "Here you are. Have fun. I'll pick you up at five."

"I'll be at Thea's."

"You watch for me so I won't have to come in."

"Okay." She leaned toward him. He gave her a quick kiss.

"Take care, Pauline."

"You're sweet, Fred, I'll be fine." She smiled and waved him away.

She put her purse over her arm and walked to the Co-op's back door. She stepped aside as two men dressed in work overalls and high-top leather shoes came out. They tipped their hats to her and one held the door. She smiled a thank you and entered the big room. A whiff of oil reminded her of the old wood floors in her school in Bay City.

She went to the dark brown counter where Bernie Gilbert stood with his back to her as he examined pages of the black receipt book. "Good morning, Mr. Gilbert."

He turned and peered over his glasses at her. "Mrs. Gunther, nice to see you. Not many folks come into town on a rainy day."

"Fred dropped me off on his way to work. I wanted to get

out of the house for a day." She set her purse on the counter. "I wonder if you remember Ralph Long. He lived out by Ducken Road about twenty-five years ago."

Bernie said, "That's a while back, but I vaguely remember someone named Long charging groceries. He always paid his bill on time, a scruffy young man in work clothes. He probably worked in the woods."

"Yes, that might be Ralph." Pauline fumbled through her purse and found the locket. "Do you recognize this couple?"

Bernie adjusted his glasses, held the locket close to his face and scrutinized the picture. "No, I don't know those faces."

"Well, I'm going to ask around, maybe someone will remember them. I'll see you later when I come back to pick up a few groceries."

"Don't get wet."

"I have my umbrella."

Pauline stepped out onto the wet sidewalk, took a few steps and looked through the Ford showroom window at a new car. *Rupert's father had a truck. Maybe he bought it here.* She went in and walked directly to the black car. She slid her finger tips across the shiny front fender. The 1934 two-door Ford convertible sported a canvas top and rumble seat.

An elderly man came from a small office. "Do you like her? Just came in last week." He opened the door on the driver's side and motioned for Pauline to get in.

She stepped up onto the running board, climbed in and sat up tall to look over the hood. The steering wheel felt smooth. She ran her hand over the leather-cushioned seat.

"It's beautiful."

"Deluxe Model A."

"My husband calls our truck a Double A."

"I know that truck. Fellow named Gunther bought it from me, must be your husband."

"Yes, I'm Pauline Gunther."

"Nice to meet you. I'm Dick Sanders."

"Have you lived here many years, Mr. Sanders?"

"Well, pretty close to thirty-six years now."

"That's long enough for a question I have. I wonder if you knew Ralph Long? He might have bought a truck from you."

"Can't say I ever knew him."

Pauline drew the locket from her coat pocket and held it out. "Maybe you remember these people."

"No, can't say as I do."

"Well, I'm going to find someone who will remember Ralph. I like your car, Mr. Sanders." She turned and walked toward the door.

The salesman followed her. "Come in again. Bring your husband along."

"Oh, we'll just have to be happy with our truck for now. Goodbye."

She wandered down the street to the shoe store and looked at the display in the window. *Oh, purple shoes. Wouldn't I love to have those!*

A dapper young salesman opened the door and ushered her in. "Did you see a pair you like?"

Before she knew it, she was seated with her shoes off, and then standing with one foot on the metal measure. "Size eight and a half," he announced.

"Oh, but I don't plan to buy any today."

"No, of course, but let me show you a few of our latest styles."

Just because I try them on doesn't mean I have to buy. It'll be fun.

When Pauline left the store, she carried a box tied with a string. Inside the box, nestled in tissue, there was a pair of purple one-inch, high-heeled shoes. *I've not had new shoes for a long time, and we do have the New Year's dance. I bet there's enough tea money to pay for them.* She bent to the sidewalk and picked up a penny.

Whiffs of freshly baked bread drew her into the bakery. Pauline counted out change for two doughnuts and coffee and asked that one doughnut be put in a bag. She shared a table with an older woman. Pauline took out the locket and asked the woman if she knew the Long family.

Each store she visited, she chatted with the clerk about the weather or merchandise, showed the picture in the locket and asked about Ralph Long. No one remembered him.

Ralph must have cashed his work checks at the bank. She walked between two tall white pillars and pulled the door open. She saw two teller windows, one closed. She waited in line behind a heavy man in a business suit. When he turned, he tipped his hat and walked out of the bank. Pauline stepped up to the window.

The short bald man behind the counter asked, "Can I help you, lady?"

"I hope so." She opened the locket and held it out to him. "I wonder if you recognize the couple in this picture."

The teller took the locket and studied the picture. "No, I'm sorry, I've never seen them. You might want to talk with some of the old-timers."

Pauline put the locket in her purse. "Of course, thank you."

"You could ask the woman at the Fabric Shoppe."

"Thank you, I'll do that." She went out into the rain. *Thea said Mrs. O'Dell had been living here a long time. Surely she would know.* The little bell tinkled as she entered the shop.

A young woman greeted her with a smile and extended her hand. "I'm Hazel."

"Hello, I'm Pauline Gunther." She shook Hazel's hand. "Is Mrs. O'Dell here?"

"No, she's not feeling well. I'm helping out this week."

"Oh, I'm sorry. I hoped to talk with her, but I do need to get yarn."

Hazel led the way to the next aisle.

Pauline chose three skeins, blue, red and green. Hazel wrapped them in brown paper, pulled string from the spool above her head and tied a bow around the package.

"Hazel, my friend, Thea Van Eck, said Mrs. O'Dell might be able to help me, or perhaps you can. I'm trying to find the family of Rupert Long. His father's name was Ralph."

Hazel hesitated. "I can't help you, but I'll mention it to Mrs. O'Dell."

"Thank you. It was nice to meet you." Pauline left the shop. She felt let down, but crossed the street, walked another block and ducked under the dripping awning and into The Good Eats Café.

She dawdled over a cup of steaming vegetable soup and

watched people come in, order, anxiously wait and leave with brown bags. *They seem to be in a hurry, maybe it's their lunch hour. I won't bother them with the locket.*

The drug store down another block featured a picture of a young couple sipping a soda and the inviting words "Refreshingly Good. Try a Green River Float." *Oh, yummy.* She climbed onto a round green-cushioned stool at the counter and ordered a "Green River." She pushed the penny she'd found on the sidewalk into a slot on the gray punch-board. The small round disc fell out and on the back had a five-cent symbol. The cashier smiled and gave her a nickel. While enjoying the tasty ice cream drink, Pauline asked about Rupert's family. She heard another, "I'm sorry, but I don't know them."

Weary and not making any progress learning about Ralph and Ruby, she decided to stop at the Co-op for the groceries and go to Thea's.

Bernie Gilbert asked if she'd had any luck with the picture. "No, no luck so far, but I'll keep trying." She gave him the list of food and watched as he used the long-handled grabber to reach the higher shelves.

The rain had stopped when Pauline left the Co-op with her packages and groceries. She smiled at passers-by on the street, the men doffed their hats.

By the time she got to Thea's, her coat felt heavy and her arms were tired. She climbed the steps and knocked on the front door. No answer. She knocked again. "Rats! She's not home." *Oh that's right, Thea spends Wednesdays with her mother. I'll just wait here for Fred.* She sat on a step and looked over the bay at the gray water, then let her eyes close slowly.

When she heard, "Ahooga-ahooga!" she jumped up and saw their truck.

Fred helped her get settled with the groceries tucked in around her feet. He asked if she'd had a nice time.

She sighed. "I'm disappointed. Nobody could tell me anything about Rupert's family. I'll tell you all about it over supper." She slumped down on the seat. *What will he say when he sees my new shoes?*

"I met Van Staat today. He wanted to make sure I understand that he wants to use the old cabinets in his hardware store. He's worried I might damage them. I spent the day using a pry bar to pull them from the walls, a bigger job than I figured."

Pauline sat up as the truck started on their bumpy driveway. "It won't take long to fix supper, dear. I bought a can of Dinty Moore Stew."

They took everything into the house. Fred built up the fire before going out to do chores.

Pauline went directly to the bedroom with her packages. She put the shoe box on the floor in a corner of the closet.

Chapter Thirty-Six... A Visit with Jenny

Pauline had finished knitting stockings for Fred and Will, potholders for Marian and mittens for Jenny. Fred had brought the little tree from the woods, and put it in a bucket filled with water and gravel to hold it upright. Decorating the tree and cut-out cookies were next on Pauline's list.

Jenny, home for Christmas vacation, came one afternoon and found her sitting at the table making ornaments. "That looks like fun." She pulled out a chair and sat down. "Where did you get all these necklaces?"

"They're mostly old beads I had when I was a kid."

Jenny reached into the jewelry box and picked up a pin. "This is pretty."

"That belonged to your grandmother."

Jenny held the pin, an ivory silhouette of a woman's head on a pink background set in a gold band.

"If you like it, it's yours."

"Thank you. I'll wear it on my white ruffled blouse." She threaded a needle with green yarn and began stringing beads while answering Pauline's questions about her studies. "I'm doing my student teaching in Home Economics at Fairhaven

High. It's a freshman class and most of the girls have never done any sewing. Miss Francis said I'm doing a swell job helping them use the sewing machines."

"I think you'll be a great teacher, Jenny."

"We have one Singer that's been converted to electricity."

"I didn't know they could do that. Do you like using it?"

"Yeah, I told Mom we should do that with ours."

They worked quietly, and then, "Aunt Paulie, I was only five years old when you got married. I remember you wore a white dress."

"Yes, my mother's wedding dress."

"Where did you and Uncle Fred go on your honeymoon?"

"Your uncle planned it all. We took the Lady of the Lake ferry to Goderich, a pretty little town in Canada. It was my first ferry ride."

"The only ferry I've been on is the *Cup and Saucer* when we go to Anacortes or Bellingham." Jenny held up a string of beads. "What do you think of this?"

"Nice! Adding the silver with the red and green gives it a festive touch."

Pauline stood up from her rocker. "It's time we have some lunch. Are peanut butter with jam sandwiches okay?"

"I love peanut butter and dill pickles."

"I haven't tried that, but why not?"

"It's good. You'll like it. Can we have hot cocoa?"

"All right, you make the sandwiches and I'll heat up the milk. Peanut butter on the right top shelf, pickles in the cooler."

Sitting at the table, Jenny took a bite of her sandwich. "I love your bread. Do you like your sandwich?"

Pauline swallowed. "It's okay, but next time I'll try the sweet pickles."

Jenny placed a bead ornament on the tree and turned to her aunt. "Do you think you and Uncle Fred will ever have children?"

"We'd love to have children. I've dreamed of making dresses for a little girl." She put her hands in her lap and looked down. "Our doctor back home didn't give us any encouragement. Maybe it's just not meant to be." She reached for a handkerchief in her apron pocket, dabbed at her eyes and wiped her nose.

Jenny put a hand on Pauline's arm. "Oh, I've made you cry. I'm sorry, Aunt Paulie."

"It's all right that you asked. It would be wonderful for you to have cousins."

"I hope to have children someday, a boy and a girl."

"I hope you do." Pauline smiled. "I would be a great-aunt and make cookies for them."

Jenny laughed. "You'd spoil them."

"That's what aunts do. Have you met any nice boys at college?"

"I've dated a couple, but no one special."

Pauline looked up from her sewing and glanced at her niece. "Do you like Rupert?"

"Do I like Rupert?" Jenny put a finger up to her chin and cocked her head. "Hmm, well he is kinda cute with his red hair and freckles. He tells funny jokes and makes me laugh. He's a good dancer."

Pauline raised her eyebrows and said, "Yes, I could see you enjoyed dancing with him."

With a mischievous smile, Jenny said, "I did. We had fun. I guess you could say I like him."

"Did he tell you about his parents?"

"I felt sad when he told me they died when he was little. His dad was in the war. He grew up with his gramma and grampa."

"Yes, that's what he told us." *I don't think I'll show her the letters.* Pauline took the lunch dishes to the sink. "Would you like to decorate cut-out cookies for the Christmas Party?"

And so went the afternoon. Jenny left before Fred came home. Pauline fell asleep in her rocker.

Chapter Thirty-Seven... Fred Finds the Shoes

"Pauline?"

Startled, she opened her eyes. Fred stood over her.

"Are you okay, dear?"

"Oh, Fred. I dozed off after Jenny left. We had a nice visit. She wanted to know all about our honeymoon. I loved every minute of it. I couldn't have asked for a nicer one."

"I'd do it all over again," he said with a smile.

"Where shall we go this time?"

He laughed. "Can we have supper first?"

"It'll take just a few minutes to warm the chili."

Later, Pauline sat at the table stringing popcorn. "Dear, tell me about your new work."

Fred walked around the room, stretched and swung his arms back and forth. "Van Staat came again today to check up on me. He seems pleased with my work. I should be finished on time." He rubbed a hand up and down one arm. "My shoulders ache."

Pauline got up from the table. "Take off your shirt and I'll rub liniment on them." She reached high in a cupboard for a brown bottle. She took off the cap and held it up to

Fred's nose. "Does this remind you of anything?"

"Yeah, the mothballs in my grandmother's closet."

She massaged his shoulders with the clear liquid. "Feel good?"

He hunched his shoulders up and down under her hands. "Ah, yes. Wonderful."

She laughed and squeezed the muscles by his neck.

"Jenny frosted the cut-out cookies while I wrapped my gifts."

"Sounds like you're ready. I'll have to go shopping."

"You won't need to shop for me. I can't think of anything I want or need."

"Pauline, it wouldn't be fun for me if I didn't shop a bit for you. That's part of Christmas."

"No, I don't need anything. Having you well and working again is enough Christmas for me." She planted a kiss on his bald spot. "Do your shoulders feel better?"

"You've always had a magic touch. I'll go to bed now. Are you coming?"

"In a bit," she said as she put the liniment back in the cupboard. "I'm almost finished with the popcorn." She sat at the table and threaded her needle with red yarn.

Fred patted her on the shoulder and went to the bedroom. She knew he was changing into his worn nightshirt, one she had made from flour sacking, and that he would fall to sleep and give her time to finish his gift, a new nightgown.

"Pauline, what's in this box?"

She turned in her chair and popcorn spilled onto the floor as she jumped up and went to the bedroom door. He sat on the bed holding the box still wrapped in brown paper with the white string bow. "Oh, Fred, it's a surprise. It's my Christmas present from you to me."

"What? You bought your own present?"

"It was an accident."

"How can buying your own present be an accident? What is it?" He shook the box.

She put a hand up to her mouth and mumbled, "I couldn't help it."

Fred untied the string.

"No! Don't look now or it won't be a surprise." Pauline reached for the box.

He held it back. "I heard you say you weren't going to buy anything."

"I know, but he was so persuasive, and they are so pretty. I couldn't say no."

"Who is he?"

"The young man in the store. Please don't open the box."

"How much did you spend?"

Pauline sat on the edge of the bed. "I paid fifty cents and charged the rest."

Fred looked at her, disbelief in his eyes. "Charged? Wait now. What happened to our agreement? In fact, it was your idea, your dad's advice to always pay cash or do without."

Pauline lowered her head and fingered a button on her dress, afraid to see his face.

"How much did you charge?"

"Two dollars and forty-five cents plus two tax tokens."

He held the box out to her. "Are you going to tell me what's in this box?"

She let out a big sigh, dropped her hands to her lap and

said, "Oh, go ahead and open it. I'll take them back."

Fred took off the brown wrapping and opened the box. "Shoes? Purple shoes?"

"Yes, I love the little purple bows." She got up and reached for the box. "I'll take them back next time I'm in town."

"No, I will, tomorrow after work."

Pauline walked slowly from the bedroom. She swept the popcorn into a dustpan, and with a heavy sigh, sat in her rocker. Later, when she heard his snores, she sneaked into bed and lay awake with her back to him.

After a fitful night, she got up early and made the usual oatmeal with raisins.

Neither spoke until he left for work with the box under his arm. "I'll see you tonight."

Pauline took a step forward, but stopped. He closed the door. She wiped tears from her eyes. She cleaned up the breakfast dishes thinking about Fred taking the shoes back to the store. "Nerts!" she scolded herself out loud. "Why did I let that young man convince me to buy those shoes?"

After she made the bed, she went out. Her boots left prints in the crusty frost-coated grass as she walked to the chicken coop. She heard a boasting cackle, threw corn kernels to the hens and laughed as they clucked and rushed to scratch in the dirt. She collected blue, green and brown eggs from the sturdy nests Fred had built.

Nanny and Billy weren't babies anymore and they playfully rubbed against Pauline's legs when she petted their backs. She had learned that if she petted them on their heads, they would butt her. Fred kept them in their little barn on rainy or cold days. Today, since the sun shone on their fenced pen, she let them out. They ran, kicked up their heels, butted heads, stopped and looked at her as if to ask, *Aren't we cute?* Pauline laughed at them, picked up the egg basket and carried it to the house.

She kept busy and emptied the ash box and rubbed the iron top of the cook stove with newspaper to make it shine. She still thought about Fred though, taking the shoes back to the store. *What will the young man think of me? How will Fred feel when he comes home?*

Bread pudding! Fred will like that with lots of raisins. I'll make meat loaf, scalloped potatoes and green beans. She took special care to set a nice supper table.

When she heard the truck door close, she opened the door and saw him walk to the goats and heard him laugh at their frolics. He put them in their barn, then turned and with hands in his pockets, whistled as he came toward the house.

She smiled. "You're in high spirits."

"Yep, I got you an early Christmas present. Something you've wanted for a long time. Can you guess?"

"A toilet."

"Nope, you have to wait for that."

She saw the glint in his eyes and a broad smile. He paused a minute while she thought. "Well, you'll never guess so I'll tell you. You must decide on which wall you would like your new telephone."

"Oh Fred, really?"

"Yep, it'll be installed tomorrow. The men will come first thing in the morning."

The Whidbey Telephone Company men arrived shortly after Fred left for work. Pauline fed the chickens and then watched from the porch. An older man told a young fellow what to do. By noon the men had strung a wire from Ducken Road to a pole a few feet from her house. They attached a wire to a box on the porch and then came into the house and mounted the telephone between the door and Pauline's coat rack.

They showed her how to use the phone. She had to reach up to turn the handle. "Can I call my sister-in-law?"

They told her Marian's number would be two long rings and two short rings.

"And what is mine, if she wants to call me?"

"She'll turn the handle one long ring and two short. Here's a list of the nine people on your line. When you want to call someone on a different line, you'll turn the handle to make one long ring to get the operator to ring them for you. You can tell people your number is 2F7, but the operator will know that when someone tells her your name."

"I think I should try it."

"Okay, go ahead."

Pauline stepped up to the phone, turned the handle two long times and then the short ones. She held the receiver to her left ear and a woman said, "Hello."

Pauline said, "Hello, Marian. Guess who this is?"

The woman replied, "Pauline, I recognize your voice. I'm Alice."

"Oh Alice, I made a mistake. I just got my phone."

"That's okay. You just ring two long rings and two short ones for Marian. Mine is two long rings and three short ones."

Pauline looked at the two men. "I guess it takes practice."

"Not much. You'll learn fast," said the older man.

She offered them coffee and cookies, but the older man said they needed to install another phone on Monkey Hill. "Have fun calling your neighbors," he said. "Remember, everyone can pick up their phone and hear you. This isn't a private line."

"Thank you. I'll be careful what I say."

After they left, she rang two longs and two shorts. When Marian answered Pauline said, "Guess who this is?"

"Pauline, I'd know your voice anytime. When did you get your telephone?"

"This morning. The men just left."

"What's your ring?"

"One long ring and two shorts. You call me so I can practice."

She hung up and in a minute she heard her new black telephone ring and she answered Marian's call. She heard Alice say, "I'm here, too, Pauline. I thought you would be making a call." They all laughed and Pauline told them she would call them again soon.

And she did.

Chapter Thirty-Eight... Christmas

"Merry Christmas!" "Merry Christmas!" "See you for the New Year's dance!" Good cheer filled the night air as party goers departed from the schoolhouse. Children dressed in Christmas Pageant costumes carried red net stockings filled with oranges, nuts and candy. It had been a fun-spirited evening with the children's program, carol singing and sharing favorite Christmas goodies. Fred carried the empty plates that had held Pauline's Lebkucken and cut-out cookies.

Jenny caught up with Pauline. "Rupert is coming to dinner tomorrow and Mom told him to invite some of his friends. We don't know how many we'll have, but Dad said he can always bring in sawhorses and boards to make the table bigger."

"I'm glad you told me. I'll bake an extra pie."

"See you tomorrow." Jenny hugged her and left to join Marian and Will.

Fred hummed a favorite carol, "Deck the Halls," as he drove home. He helped Pauline from the truck, and they gazed in awe at the bright stars in the clear sky. He put an arm around her and they walked to the house. "Our first

Christmas in our new home. Are you happy, dear?"

"Yes, I'm happy. Have I done something to make you think I'm not?"

"No, not at all. It's been quite a change for us, especially for you. You've done a great job making this old house feel homey, but I want more for you. If I could give you one thing, what would it be?"

That's easy, an indoor bathroom."

"Actually, that's not so easy. I have to dig a well first and that won't be until spring."

"I know, everything takes time." She went to the cooler for the tin pail of milk. "Let's have hot cocoa before bed."

On Christmas morning, Pauline opened a jar of wild blackberries she had picked and canned in August. The small berries floated on the top two-thirds of the jar leaving a cup or more of juice. *What to do?* She paged through her mother's old recipe book. Fruit juice pudding was marked with a handwritten comment, "Family Favorite." *I remember this. Mom made pudding with loganberry juice and sago tapioca.*

Fred came with an arm load of wood to find Pauline singing an old nursery rhyme about blackbirds baked in a pie. He looked in the yellow Pyrex bowl. "I'm glad those are black*berries*."

"I had to open three jars to get enough for two pies." She told him how the berries floated to the top and she would use the juice for pudding.

Fred snitched a berry and popped it in his mouth. "Use lots of sugar."

He turned on the radio. The announcer said, "And here's a

new Christmas recording by the Paul Whiteman Orchestra." Bing Crosby began singing "Silent Night."

Fred said, "I'm going to take a nap. Shall I leave the radio on?"

She licked juice from the spoon. "Please do. I like the company."

Pauline had taken the pies out of the oven when Fred came from the bedroom dressed for Christmas dinner. He pulled up his trousers to show off new red stockings. "See here?"

"Do you like them, dear?"

"They're soft and fit just right."

"I think that's a yes. I made them with lamb's wool. I'll change my dress and fix my hair, and then we can go."

Fred sat down and turned his rocking chair toward the bedroom door. He called to her, "I think Santa was here last night, Pauline."

She came from the bedroom brushing her hair, mumbling through the hairpins in her mouth, "What did you say?"

"Santa must have been here last night." He pointed to the little tree.

She stepped over to the tree. "Oh Fred, you rascal. You didn't take them back to the store? All this time you've hidden them away?" She untied the red yarn Fred had used to tie the purple pumps with the cute bows to the branches. Tears came to her eyes as she stroked the soft leather.

"Merry Christmas, darling," said Fred.

She kissed his cheek and whispered in his ear, "Thank you, dear. I love you."

He gently pushed her back. "Why do you whisper?

Shout it out!"

She laughed and shouted, "I love you, Fred Gunther!"

"Now that that's settled, I think it's time to go down to dinner. We don't want to keep Marian and Will waiting."

"Yes, as soon as I put on my new shoes and get my coat."

Fred added wood to the stove, closed the damper and called, "You'll want to wear your scarf and gloves."

"Okay. Will you carry the pies? They're in the picnic basket. I'll bring the pudding."

Fred held Pauline's arm as they climbed the wet slippery steps to Will's porch. They heard laughter from within the house. "Sounds like Jenny's at it again."

"That girl sure knows how to entertain the boys."

Will met them at the door and ushered them into the living room. "We've got Rupert and two of his friends with us. Jenny has enjoyed being the center of attention for the past half-hour."

During the festive dinner, Will and Fred questioned Rupert's two friends. John was from a small town in upstate New York and Marvin grew up in Detroit. Lean and muscular like Rupert, they agreed the work with the CCC's was hard, but they liked it and were proud of what they had accomplished. Yes, they liked Whidbey Island and might settle here someday.

Marian smiled when they praised her for a fine dinner. She gave credit to Pauline for the pies and pudding. The men carried their dishes to the kitchen and then retired to the living room. Marian and Pauline, with no help from Jenny, were left to do the dishes.

"New shoes, Pauline?"

"Do you like them, Marian? They're a present from Fred. He tied them to our Christmas tree. Wasn't that sweet?"

"What a romantic. There aren't many men who would choose purple shoes for their wife. Yes, I think they're beautiful."

"Me, too." Pauline danced a few steps. "I'll wear them to the New Year's Dance."

"Murder!" someone shouted, and "That's not fair, Rupert!" exclaimed Jenny. Everyone laughed.

Pauline asked Marian, "What are they playing?"

"Murder is the name of a board game like Parcheesi, but played with marbles. A fellow in Oak Harbor makes them. Will bought this for Jenny a few years ago for a dollar. It's one of her favorite games, and she usually wins."

Pauline dried the last dinner plate. "It was nice to invite Rupert's friends."

Marian pulled up the sink drain plug and watched the murky water disappear, then turned to Pauline. "I had a reason for asking Rupert to bring them. I think Jenny needs to meet more boys. She's only known Rupert since we made cider, and she's always talking about him: Rupert this and Rupert that." She wiped the counter. "How old were you when you and Fred met?"

"Well, I was sixteen, a sophomore, and he a senior, but he joined the army and we didn't marry until he came home from France after the war. We wanted to get married, but Dad told us to wait until Fred had a job. So we did. I was nineteen, but turned twenty a few days later. How old were you when you and Will got serious?"

"I met Will when he worked on your uncle's farm, but I

went away to school for two years, and then taught school for two years before we got married. I was twenty-two."

"Marian, Jenny's a smart girl. She wants to teach next year and I don't think she's in any rush to settle down. She's having too much fun."

"I suppose you're right. What do you think of Rupert?"

Pauline hung the damp dishtowel on a rack. "I like him. He's polite and considerate. He chopped wood for the stove when Fred had appendicitis." She leaned against the counter and watched Marian put the pots in the cupboard. "You know, his mother died when he was very young and his father was killed in the war. His gramma and grampa in Pennsylvania raised him."

"Yes, Jenny told me, but what about his mother's family?"

"He knows only that Ruby's mother lived in Anacortes. He doesn't know her name. I'd like to find her. He really is a nice young man."

"Who's a nice young man?"

"Jenny, I was telling your mother I think Rupert is a nice fellow. Do you like his friends?"

"Sure, they're all fun guys. They're going back to camp now."

Marian and Pauline took off their aprons, went to the living room and said goodbye to the three men. Merry Christmas wishes were exchanged as the four young people went out into the chilly dark night. Pauline heard more laughter and Jenny calling, "See you at the New Year's Dance, Rupert."

Marian pointed to the kitchen. Pauline followed her. Marian picked up the dishrag and wiped the stove. "Pauline, have you been to the courthouse? There must be a record of

Rupert's birth. It would have his mother's name."

Pauline sat on the kitchen stool and said, "I'm not sure his parents were married."

"Really? Oh, my."

Pauline continued, "His father didn't mention it in the letters he wrote to his folks."

"Oh, dear." Marian scrubbed hard at the splashes of turkey gravy on the stove. "Well, if they weren't, her maiden name would be on the birth records. I'd like to know before Jenny gets too interested in him. Let's take a little jaunt over to Coupeville after the holidays."

"We'd have to take your car Marian, Fred needs his truck for work. I haven't been to Coupeville. How long would we be gone?"

"Most of the day. It's a nice town with pretty houses built by sea captains. We can have lunch at a little café that sits over the water with a beautiful view of Penn's Cove."

"Let's not tell Fred and Will what we're doing. Fred thinks it's a waste of time to look for Rupert's family."

Chapter Thirty-Nine... A Busy Time

"Let's see." Pauline wiggled a pencil between her fingers as she checked the calendar, and talking out loud to herself, said, "We'll go to Hank and Gev's Wednesday to play cards, Will and Marian come for supper Friday night, and the New Year's Dance is Monday."

"Are you talking to me?" asked Fred.

"No, just to myself."

"Seems you like to talk to yourself."

"It helps me sort things out. Did I tell you I asked Marian and Will to come to supper Friday?"

"That's fine with me. Will can bring up an extra chair for Jenny."

"Jenny won't be with us. She's spending a couple days in Mount Vernon with a friend. She told Rupert she'll be back for the New Year's Eve Dance."

Otto and Fred took the days off between Christmas and New Year's, and now Pauline, used to having the house to herself during the day, felt crowded. "Fred, dear, don't you have a project in your shop?"

"It's too cold out there. It's nice in the house with you."

"I was just wondering. Maybe Will needs help."

"Are you trying to get rid of me?"

"I'm not used to you being in the house all the time. I get distracted from my work."

"Maybe I can help you."

"Will you help me make over a dress for the dance?"

He saw her amused smile. "Okay, I'll go see Will. I'm sure he has something I can do."

After Fred changed to his work clothes and left, Pauline took out the blue dress she had worn to the Thanksgiving Dance. *Oh, dear, I can't wear this with my new shoes. I wish I could buy material to make a new dress.* She sat at the table, her fingers smoothing out the skirt. *I wonder...*

She slipped into her coat and went out to Fred's workshop. Looking in the old wardrobe, she found the box containing Ruby's dresses. Back in the house, she opened it and took out the print dresses. *These are just simple housedresses, but this one has lavender and purple flowers. Maybe I could...but, oh dear, I don't know if I should use this, would it be right to wear Ruby's dress? What if Rupert remembered it? I could alter the bodice a bit, change the neckline. I like the flared skirt, but it would be much too short. I could put a white ruffle around the bottom.* She sat still thinking, then looked at the dress again. *I could use those white buttons on the dress I wore to the Thanksgiving Dance. No, they're too big.* She dug down into her trunk. *Oh, here's some lace I saved from the pillowcases Grandmother made for me. I'll sew it around the collar.*

She found several small pearl buttons, sewed them in a row down the bodice of the dress, and then attached the white lace to the collar. She tried on the dress and used her hand mirror. *Yep, it's nice, a whole new look. I wonder what Marian will think?*

After supper that evening, she sat at the table and planned for Friday night's supper. "Dear, I'd like to take the truck into town tomorrow to get groceries." *And maybe I can pop down to the Fabric Shoppe to talk with Mrs. O'Dell.*

He frowned and said, "I don't think so, the roads are…"

"I would be home before dark."

"Are we going to Hank's tomorrow night?"

"Yes, that's the plan."

"Okay, we'll go to town in the afternoon, catch a bite of supper at The Good Eats, and then go to Hank's. It'll save some gas."

Bundled up against the winter cold, Pauline stepped across the crunchy ice puddles and into the truck. The windshield wipers squeaked across frost on the glass as Fred drove down the driveway. He steered around the potholes on Monkey Hill Road.

"Will said keeping up these county roads out our way is the farmers' job. They plan to have a "fix the roads" day soon after New Year's. Everyone who has a truck is expected to go to Moran's Beach and haul gravel. Men who don't have a truck will bring shovels and buckets to help with loading."

"Will you help them with our truck?"

"What do you think?"

"If I know you, you will."

"You know me."

In town Fred drove down Telephone Hill to the Co-op

and parked. He helped Pauline from the truck and to the store door. "I'll leave you here while I go on down to Al's garage, get the oil checked and fill up the gas tank. I'll be back in twenty minutes or so."

Pauline watched him drive away and then, rather than go into the Co-op, walked to the Fabric Shoppe. She read the scribbled sign on the door, "Closed for the Holidays."

"Nerts." She stamped her foot. Cold water splashed onto her ankle. "Oh, Nerts!" She trudged back to the Co-op and stood to the side while Bernie helped another customer. *Is that her?* Pauline walked over to the next counter and down the aisle. "Mrs. O'Dell?"

The woman turned. Pauline said, "Oh, I'm sorry. I mistook you for…"

"For my sister? I'm Alma, Olga's sister. It's confusing, we look so much alike. I've come to spend the holidays with her."

"I've been hoping to see her, but it seems she's been ill or the shop is closed each time I get into town." Pauline felt in one coat pocket and then the other. "Nerts!"

"What did you say, dear?"

"Oh, just talking to myself, looking for something in my pocket, but I guess I left it at home." She glanced up at the sound of the Co-op door closing. "Oh, there's my husband. I've enjoyed talking you…"

"Alma, Alma Strump."

"I'm Pauline Gunther. Tell your sister Happy New Year. Goodbye now." She smiled and walked away to join Fred and give her list to Bernie.

Fred took off his hat as they walked into The Good Eats. He looked around and nodded to the men sitting at a nearby table. The window in a wood heater glowed with an orange flame. Fred helped Pauline with her coat and held a chair for her.

"This is cozy by the stove," she said and studied the chalkboard above the cashier's counter. Soup and Bread: ten cents, Meat Loaf or Fried Chicken with coffee: thirty-five cents.

Fred rubbed his hands together. "Mmm, would you like fried chicken or meat loaf?"

"I'm not very hungry, the daily soup and bread will be fine."

"Well, the meatloaf sounds good to me."

When they had finished eating, Fred paid for the meal with a dollar and held out his hand for his fifty-five cents change. He left three pennies on the table.

As they left the café, the town clock struck seven. "Are we going too early?" asked Pauline.

"No, by the time we get there, Hank will probably have his chores finished."

Chapter Forty... An Evening with the Martin Family

The smell of fried potatoes and onions greeted them when Gev opened the door, a dishtowel draped on her shoulder. "I'm just finishing the supper dishes," she said. "Hank was late getting home from work. We had a quick supper and then he and the boys went out to milk the cows. They're in the basement now changing their clothes."

They heard the boys laughing as they came up the steps and Hank's husky voice telling them to slow down. Pauline smiled when she saw Kelly fall on his knees as Chris pushed him through the door. They looked at Pauline and Fred, got up giggling and came into the kitchen.

Gev said, "Boys, wash up," and then, "Chris, I told Mrs. Gunther you would show her your collection of fishing floats. Will you bring them to the table?"

"Sure! Be right back." He scurried from the warm kitchen.

Kelly, his brown eyes sparkling, smiled at Pauline and asked, "Would you like to see my arrowheads?"

"I'd love to see them." She heard the boys racing up the

wooden steps to their bedrooms.

Pauline and Fred, sitting on the high-backed wood chairs at the checkered oilcloth-covered table, watched Hank wash his hands at the kitchen sink. Fred said, "Last time I checked the work on the bridge, I noticed stacks of wood planks.

Hank turned his head to him. "Yeah, those will be used in the next few days. We had a little trouble today near the bridge. Loose rock sloughed down onto the road overnight." He dried his hands and then sat at the table. "It took us two hours to clear it so a truck loaded with steel girders could get through."

Fred said, "Otto and I drove down a while back and snooped around. Seems to me those hard rubber tires on the chain-driven dump trucks wouldn't have much traction."

"That's right. They don't. We had to work fast before the road thawed. We've cleared and graded a big area for the Puget Construction work crew."

"That bridge is going to take a lot of steel. How do they bring it here?"

"Wallace Bridge and Structural Steel fabricators in Seattle barge it into Cornet Bay and from there our trucks haul it up to the work area.

They heard the boys bounding down the stairs. Chris came in with a cardboard box and Kelly with an old cotton salt sack tied at the top with a red string, both eager to show their treasures. Gev came to the table and said, "Chris, you go first."

"Ah shoot! I wanted to be first," said Kelly. He slumped back in his chair.

"No, I'm the oldest," said Chris. He set floats on the table and proceeded to explain that glass balls break loose from the Japanese fish nets. "They just wash up on shore. I look for them after a storm. Most of mine are green. Here's one still wrapped in the net."

Fred took it. "Heavy rope. It must've caught on something."

Pauline held a large brown ball up to the light. "It's beautiful."

"Yeah, it's my favorite," said Chris.

Pauline said, "Okay, Kelly, let's see your treasures."

Kelly opened his sack, dumped arrowheads and spear points onto the table, and said, "Now these are neat. Dad finds them for me, but I found this one myself when I was digging around an old tree stump." He held up a spear point. "I bet it killed a deer."

Fred and Pauline picked through the collection, commenting on this one and that one. Kelly said, "I didn't ever see an Indian, but Dad played with the kids."

"Dad had two dogs, too," chimed in Chris.

Pauline looked at Hank.

Hank winked and chuckled, "Well…"

"The dogs names were Snoop and Kiya," broke in Chris. "He tells us stories about when he was an Indian."

Gev said, "Boys, it's time you take your things away. Mr. and Mrs. Gunther came to play cards. You can come back for cookies and milk."

"Can't we hear just one story?"

Hank shook his head yes to Gev and she said, "All right, just one."

"Tell when the Indian ladies came to see Gramma," said Kelly.

Hank rested his arms on the table and got right into the story. "I was only a little kid, about five or six. I played with the Indian boys when their mothers came to visit my mother. Johnny was the oldest, probably nine or ten and pretty tall. Billy was seven or eight. We had lots of fun. See, I had this big red ball." Hank held his hands to show the size. "They thought that was just the best ball. So Johnny said, 'If I kick this ball over that chicken coop I get to take it home.' I didn't think he could do it, so I said okay."

"Johnny kicked it and it went over the roof, but rolled down and stopped on the gutter on the other side and stayed there. He said, 'I'm gonna get that ball and take it home. It's mine. It went over the roof.' I told him it was too high but he climbed a tree thinking he could jump over to the roof. Billy kept egging him on yelling, 'Do it, Johnny. Do it!' And Johnny jumped."

Chris blurted out, "And he landed in a pile of chicken manure!"

Hank said, "He was a sorry sight and when his mother saw him, she was mad as a wet hen. I don't know what she said. I spoke some of their jargon, but she talked so fast the spit just flew out of her mouth." Hank grinned at Pauline. "That was the last time we played that game."

"And Dad didn't have to give the kid the ball," Kelly beamed.

Gev said, "Okay boys, you had a good laugh, now go play for a bit before bedtime."

Pauline watched the boys leave the kitchen. "They're

such nice boys, Gev."

Gev smiled and said, "Most of the time. I'll get the cards."

Fred asked Hank, "Were there many Indians living here?"

"Not many, maybe five or six families. My mother was a bit afraid of them. Three or four squaws would come at a time and sit on the kitchen floor. They wouldn't leave until she gave them needles from her sewing basket. Mother didn't understand their language and they didn't know German."

"German?"

"That's what my mother and father spoke until Alice went to school. Dad wouldn't let us talk German anymore because he and mother wanted to learn English."

Fred asked, "How about the Indian boys? Did they know English?"

"Oh, yes. They learned. They went to the regular school." Hank took a deck of cards from a box, shuffled and said, "Time to play Swedish rummy."

"We don't know that game, Hank, you'll have to teach us," said Pauline.

Hank dealt nine cards to everyone. "You want to try to make runs in suits…like four, five, six in hearts. You put those down, see, and that's a run and it counts fifteen points. It's your turn first, Fred. You draw from the stack or take the turned-up card."

Fred drew a card and laid down a queen, king and ace. "How much does that count?"

"No, you can't play the ace. It's low in this game."

Fred picked up his cards.

"Now you have to discard something that doesn't fit in

your run."

Hank explained again as they all had a turn, laying down runs, picking up the discards and playing on the others' runs. Gev kept a tally of the scores. When Fred won the first hand, he said, "This is a good game."

Hank handed the deck to Pauline. "It's your turn to shuffle and deal."

She took the deck and split it in halves. "Whoops!" The cards jumped out of her hands and some scattered on the linoleum floor.

They all laughed and Fred said, "Fifty-two card pick-up, dear."

Pauline collected the cards. "I know how to shuffle, they just slipped."

Hank won the next two hands and then Gev won a hand. When Hank's score reached 300, Gev said, "I think it's time for coffee."

Pauline sat quietly on the way home. She slipped her cold hands into her coat pockets.

Fred broke the silence. "While Gev was showing you the quilt she's making, Hank told me they started building their house in 1928, but the upstairs isn't finished. He asked me if I would be interested in finishing it. Of course I said yes. Otto doesn't have that much work for me."

Pauline moved a bit closer to him. "When will you start?"

"Not sure. I don't think Hank has the money to pay me right now."

"I hope it's soon. It will make Gev very happy."

Fred parked near the porch and helped Pauline from

the truck. The frosted steps sparkled in the light reflected from the full moon. "Careful," he cautioned, his arms loaded with the groceries. "The steps are slippery." He set the bags on the table and said he would tuck the animals in for the night.

Chapter Forty-One... Marian and Will Come to Supper

Temperatures had dropped to the thirties during the day and twenties at night. Pauline peeked from under the quilt and watched Fred. He put cedar kindling in the firebox and lit a wood match with his thumbnail. Flames leaped up. He added fir and adjusted the damper, and then went out dressed in his heavy mackintosh and rubber boots. She heard him talking to the goats. The chickens clucked when he put grain in their feeder. He filled the wood box by the stove and set the water can inside by the door.

"Thank you, dear."

"Have you been spying on me when I was trying to surprise you with a warm house?"

She laughed. "Just a little. I'll get up now."

"I'm going out to check the truck, be back in a few minutes."

"I'll have oatmeal ready."

The house wasn't cozy, but warm enough that steam from the tea kettle condensed and froze on the cold, thin-glass window panes. Fred came in, his cheeks and nose red, and found Pauline leaning over the sink drawing on the glass with her fingernail. "At it again?"

"It's like an artist's palette."

Fred looked at her drawing. "A heart?"

"Yes, for you."

He dropped his wet gloves on the counter. "I spilled water inside them when I dumped the hens' jar over. My fingers are numb."

Pauline filled a bowl with cool water and Fred soaked his hands. "Your hens aren't laying many eggs these days."

"I know, but we have enough for the lemon meringue pie I'm baking for tonight's supper."

Pauline had the table set and supper ready to serve when headlights shone through the window. Fred waited until he heard Marian and Will's footsteps on the porch, and then opened the door. "Come in, come in. Don't want to let any heat out."

Talk at the table centered on the cold weather. Will said it kept him busy thawing pipes for the cows' water trough.

Marian said, "But we get to go skating. Gev and Hank have an open invitation to anyone who would like to skate on their lagoon."

"Oh, we didn't bring our skates," lamented Pauline.

"What size shoe do you wear?"

"Eight and a half."

"With a pair of heavy socks mine should fit you, and I'll wear Jenny's if she didn't take them to school. Will has extra skates that will fit Fred."

Pauline said, "Oh good. We had such fun every winter

back home."

Will patted his stomach. "You're a great cook, Paulie. Your lemon pie would have won grand prize at the county fair."

"Mom was a wonderful teacher." She leaned toward him. "Do you remember how Dad liked to stop at roadside stands and buy boxes of fruit? We canned peaches, pears and applesauce. Mom let me write on the fruit room wall how many jars of each we canned. Remember the pickle crock in the basement? It took eight days to make bread and butter pickles, but I had to come to Whidbey to learn how to make sauerkraut."

"Yeah, Mom got kraut from the meat market," said Will.

Marian saw Fred cover a yawn with his hand. "Well, I think we should be on our way home."

Will got up. "Yeah, morning comes early. Hey, would you like a ride to the dance Monday?"

Marian put her hand on Will's arm. "Jenny will be home Sunday night. She told Rupert we'd pick him up."

Fred said, "We can go in our truck."

"Should be a fun dance," Will said. "The Roseland Five Band is coming from Oak Harbor."

Pauline asked, "What kind of music do they play?"

"Let's just say you won't be disappointed." Will took Marian's arm and they left.

Fred closed the door behind them. "You out did yourself, Pauline. Best pot roast we've had in a long time."

Chapter Forty-Two... Dancing into January

"Hurry, dear, we don't want to be late."

"Can't," he said, his voice muffled through foam. "Wouldn't look good going to the dance with bloody nicks on my face."

She watched him sharpen the straight razor on the leather strap and finish shaving. She smiled when he unscrewed the cap on his aftershave and patted some on his cheeks.

She sniffed. "I never tire of Old Spice."

He winked at her and said, "My birthday is coming up soon."

"I'll remember that."

"I'll get my shirt and tie."

"I polished your shoes for you."

"You're a good wife, Pauline."

"I know." She fussed with her hair and satisfied with it, slipped into her new shoes and twirled around. "Oh, it's going to be so much fun."

Fred took Pauline's arm to guide her around the frozen puddles in the old schoolhouse yard. They heard strains of music as the Roseland Five warmed up their instruments.

"Fred, look, Ted and Mildred brought Hank and Gev

in Ted's new car."

"It looks new, but it's a 1919 Hudson. He bought it second-hand from Gus Olson."

Pauline called, "Hello, Gev! Hello, Mildred!"

They returned her greeting and the three couples climbed the steps to join other excited party goers. As they entered, a young man handed out pieces of paper. "Ladies, write your name on the paper and put it in the glass fish bowl on the table."

"What's this all about?" asked Fred.

"You'll find out in a bit. Have fun now."

The Roseland Five got everyone dancing with a lively fox trot, then a waltz and another fox trot. A drum roll called them to attention. The young man stood beside the band. "Time to play *Fish for a Partner*. Men, line up and come on over and draw a name from the fish bowl."

When Pauline asked Fred whose name he had drawn, he said, "I'll be dancing with Mildred."

Pauline waited anxiously to see who might claim her, and when she heard a voice say her name, she turned. "Rupert?"

"Yep, it's me. I traded with my friend since I haven't seen you for a while."

"That's right, not since Thanksgiving."

They heard a few notes played on an accordion.

Pauline said, "A Schottische! Oh, this will be fun. Do you know it?"

"Guess you'll have to teach me."

"You put your arm around my back. See how the others are doing it." Rupert looked at Hank in front of him. "We start with our left foot and then step with our right.

One, two, three, hop, one, two, three, hop, then you raise your arm and twirl me around and then we step again. Shall we try it?"

"Okay." Rupert put his right arm across Pauline's back. She clasped his hand with her right hand and his left hand with her left.

"Here we go." They stepped together...one, two, three, hop, one, two, three... Pauline let go of his left hand and tried to turn, but Rupert let go of her right hand. "No, you have to hold my hand up and let me go under your arm."

Rupert caught on and they danced around and around the floor with the other dancers, everyone having a grand time.

The music stopped and Jenny came up to them. "Oh, here you are. Hi, Aunt Paulie."

Pauline gave her niece a hug. The music started. Jenny took Rupert by the arm. "My turn." And off they went. Pauline sat on the hard bench and watched couples dance by, but she wasn't a wallflower for long.

Hank held his hand out to her. "Our dance, Pauline."

"Oh, Hank, I believe you're right."

She laughed when he twirled her around. Hank was fun and she felt sorry when another fellow tapped him on his shoulder and she had a new partner. Fred soon tapped the shoulder of the large boisterous man. "You saved me, dear. I don't enjoy dancing with some of the men."

"Why?"

"They hold me too close."

He held her tight. "Like this?"

"Yes. It isn't proper."

Fred laughed. "I saw you doing the Schottische with Rupert."

"Yes, he caught on quickly."

"That was quite a coincidence, him drawing your name."

"He didn't. He traded with one of his friends. He started to tell me about a letter he received, but Jenny came and said it was her turn and took him away."

"Can't blame her for wanting to dance. Here's a good jazzy piece." Fred swung Pauline onto the floor to the tune of "Sweet Georgia Brown."

"Wow!" she said at the end of the dance. "That leaves me breathless. Oh, my. Look at Jenny. She's maneuvered Rupert to dance right under the mistletoe."

"She's a smart girl, but how do you know it wasn't Rupert who did the maneuvering?"

"Marian's not so pleased. She doesn't know enough about Rupert."

"He likes Jenny."

"Marian thinks they're too young."

"Pauline, remember how we felt? You were younger than Jenny."

The school clock struck midnight.

Someone called out, "Goodbye '34! Hello '35!"

"It's here!" Pauline exclaimed, smiling up at Fred.

He said, "Happy New Year, darling." He held her close for a long kiss.

"I love you so much, Fred."

"And I love you." He kissed her again and they laughed.

People clapped and yelled, "Happy New Year!" over

and over and shook hands. Whistles blew. Will rang an old cow bell.

Pauline put her head on Fred's chest, and he wrapped his arms around her as they rocked back and forth a bit with the music as the band played "Auld Lang Sang." "I wonder what this year will bring," she said.

Fred replied, "This past year has seen a lot of changes for us. Has it been good?"

"It's a whole new life. It's been hard, especially when you had appendicitis." She kissed his cheek. "I'm so glad I have you."

Joining hands in a circle, the dancers swayed left and right and sang, "May auld acquaintance be forgot and ne'er brought to mind..." As they left the schoolhouse, "Happy New Year" could be heard again and again.

Going down the slippery steps, Fred took Pauline's hand. "Wouldn't want those purple shoes to slip."

As he guided her to the truck she said, "The air is so still. It smells like snow." She tilted her head back. "I feel tiny flakes on my face."

"Yep, maybe Old Man Winter will bring some. Would you like that?"

She laughed. "It doesn't matter who brings it, I'd like it."

The sun shone bright on New Year's Day. There was no trace of snow. Fred said it would be nice to have a quiet day at home.

Pauline said, "I hoped for a day of fun in the snow."

"Another day, dear. Will said the almanac claims it will come."

I need to do something fun. I'll bake cookies. She combed through her recipe books. *Here's one I haven't made. It will be nice to try something new.* While the cookies baked, she wrote to her friend, Marie, telling all about the dance.

Chapter Forty-Three... The Beginning of a New Year

The house shuddered from a blast of wind. "Did you hear that, dear?" When he didn't answer, she turned over and felt for him on his side of the bed. She went out to find him. He stood close to a window with his hands cupped to his face as he peered out the glass. "Is it snowing? It sounds like a wild wind storm."

Pauline stood beside him and pressed her nose to the cold glass. She ran to the door, turned on the porch light and stood barefoot looking out. "Yes, it is snowing!" Snow swirled around the corner of the house. The wind whooshed through her nightgown. Snow blew in her face. "It's really snowing!" she shouted gleefully.

Fred added wood to the stove. "I'm going back to bed. Are you coming?"

"I'll stay up for a while and watch out the window."

"You better come to bed. It'll be there in the morning."

"I'll be in."

Twice during the night, she heard the clank of the stove lid when Fred added wood to the firebox.

In the morning, she threw back the quilt, eager to see if it was still snowing. Wrapped in her robe, she padded barefoot to the door and opened it. An inch or two of snow covered the porch floor. Small flakes drifted from the apple tree branches.

"What? No slippers on?" Fred took her arm. "Let's keep the door closed so the house will stay warm."

"You sound like a grouch."

"Well, I was up and down all night to keep the fire."

"You go back to bed, I'll take care of the fire." She gave him a little push toward the bed, and then poked at the smoldering coals.

"No, I'm up now. Here, let me do that while you get dressed and then we can have some oatmeal. I'm hungry," said Fred.

When they'd finished eating, she said, "I need to go out for a few minutes." She went to the bedroom to put on warmer clothes.

He called, "You can wear a pair of my long johns under your overalls."

Pauline finished dressing and handed her shoes and socks to Fred. "I need help."

He looked at her and began to laugh. "Yes, you certainly do. Here, sit down." She perched on the edge of a chair. He bent down on one knee and slipped the heavy wool socks and shoes on her feet. She stood up.

"How many sweaters do you have on?"

"Only two."

"You look like a big bear that needs a hug." He hugged her and they laughed together.

"Better take off one sweater. You'll burn up. I should get to work. See you tonight."

"Okay, dear."

The wind swirled the dry snow against the house and shed. She kicked it away from the outhouse door. Peeling off her clothes down to Fred's long johns took a while. *When Fred digs the well, I'm going to insist on an indoor toilet.*

While getting her clothes back on, she heard tires crunch on the ice and snow. *I wonder who that could be.* The zipper on her coat stuck. "Rats!" She put on her hat and went out.

"Hey, Paulie," Will called as he got out of his truck. "Fred stopped by on his way to work. I told him I'd look in on you."

"He and Otto are starting a new job today."

"Fred said snow had blown in on the chickens and goats. I brought a few bales of straw to make a windbreak for them."

"Would you come here and help me, Will?" Pauline asked. "My zipper's stuck."

Will stepped up close to her, fiddled with the zipper and zipped up her coat. He gave her a brotherly chuck on her chin. She pushed him aside and said, "Oh, go on with you."

They spread straw over the floor of the pens. The hens cackled and scratched through it as they pecked for seeds. Will stacked bales along the walls. "This makes good insulation. Weather report said we're in for a long cold spell. How're you doing for water?"

"The ground is covered with thick ice near the spring, but water keeps gurgling out in a steady stream. Fred keeps the milk cans full and I'm careful not to waste it."

The goats bleated for attention. Pauline rubbed their

heads and held their chins up to look in their blue eyes. "Poor Nanny, poor Billy. It's so cold for you. Do you think I should take them in the house?"

"No, you don't want to mess with that. Their thick fur coats keep them warm." He opened his truck door.

"Wait, Will. My hens aren't laying many eggs, but I've got enough to share with Marian. Take these." She handed the egg basket to her brother.

"Thanks, Paulie, she'll be glad to have them. You better go in the house and get warmed up. See you later."

"Big brother, always looking after me." She laughed and waved him away, took one last look at the animals and went back to the house.

Pauline played with the radio dial and stopped when she heard the jingle telling about Ovaltine, the sponsor for the *Little Orphan Annie* program. The simple tune reminded her of the hot chocolate her mother had frequently made for Sunday breakfast. Turning the dial again, she heard the ad for Oxydol—*the laundry soap for cleaning your husband's soiled overalls. Buy today! Always another drinking glass hidden in the box. Buy Oxydol today!* "Okay," Pauline said, "I'll see what *Ma Perkins* is up to today." The soap opera kept her company while she kneaded bread dough.

With three loaves set to rise, she sat at the table with her journal. She began to write about poor Nanny and Billy, but was interrupted by a loud knock. She opened the door to find Rupert, black stocking cap in his hand. "Why Rupert, what a surprise to see you. Come in."

He kicked off his boots and stepped in on the rug. "I won't stay long. We didn't have a chance to talk at the dance."

"No, but did you like doing the Schottische?"

"Yeah, it was fun. Jenny kept me busy the rest of the time."

"I noticed that. I think she likes you."

His cheeks flushed a bit red. "Well, I like her, too. She's a lot of fun."

He stood by the side of the stove and held his hands over it to feel the heat while Pauline put the bread loaves in the oven. She added wood to the firebox. "Would you like coffee?"

"That'd be great. I should have worn a sweater under my coat."

Pauline filled two cups and sat across the table from him. "Did you come to tell me something?"

"Yeah, I got a letter from my Aunt Esther. My gramma died after Thanksgiving."

Pauline set her cup on its saucer, reached out and put her hand on his arm. "I'm so sorry, Rupert."

"I guess she wasn't feeling good for a while. It was her heart." He sipped his coffee and stared at the little Christmas tree. "Nice tree."

"Thank you. Jenny helped decorate it. I should take it out, the needles are falling off."

"When my gramma moved in to live with Aunt Esther, she put her house up for sale. That was a few months back. I guess there's a man who will buy it, but my aunt wants to know if she should keep it for me."

Pauline pushed her cup aside and asked, "Do you want to go back home to Pennsylvania?"

"Not really." He picked at his hat. "I don't want to work

in the mines."

"Just a minute." She went to the stove. "It smells like the oven is too hot." She peeked in at the brown loaves and held the door open for a minute to cool the oven, closed it, and then sat down again. "It's something you'll have to think about. Maybe you should write to your aunt and ask for her advice."

"Yeah, I'll do that." The chair scraped the plank floor as he pushed it from the table. "I guess she'll know what's best. That bread sure smells good."

"It will be done soon. Stick around a bit and have a slice with blackberry jam."

"Thanks, but I really need to go. I just wanted you to know about my gramma."

Chapter Forty-Four... Cutting Wood in the Snow

Pauline awoke to a quiet stillness about the house. "It's freezing. Did you keep the fire going last night, Fred?" He didn't answer. She shook his shoulder. "Well, obviously you didn't."

"Uh, no," he muttered. "I guess I slept straight through."

She flung the quilt over him and got up. "I'll build the fire, and then come snuggle until the house warms up." She put the quilt back to keep her side warm.

"Pauline, you come back to bed. I'll get up."

"No, stay there. The lights are out, but the sun's coming up. It's so cold I can see my breath." She tied the belt of her flannel robe and pulled on a pair of Fred's wool socks.

The kindling came to life with snaps and crackles. She added a few dry sticks of fir and put the stove lid in place. She rubbed her fingertips on the frosted glass to melt a peek hole in the sink window. Snow sparkled in the morning sun. "Fred! It's beautiful out. The sky is all pink and yellow. Come see the snow."

"You just tell me how much there is," he mumbled.

"At least five or six inches."

"Then I won't be going to work. After I eat, I'm going to work in the shed. Come back to bed."

"No, I'll make oatmeal."

Later, Fred came in from the shed and asked, "Would you like to play in the snow with me?"

"Do you want to play Pie Tag?"

He laughed and said, "That could be fun, but actually, there's a small tree down across the trail Will and I made last fall. I need to cut more wood and I'd like to see if we can saw it up with that old saw in the shed rafters."

"Okay, give me a few minutes. I'll put your overalls on and come out."

Snow covered the board path to the shed. Whoops! Pauline's feet went out from under her and she sat on her rump. "Nerts! Fred!"

He stuck his head out of the shed door. "Pauline, are you hurt?"

"I slipped, I need help," Pauline said, reaching up for Fred's hand.

"The snow's melting a bit, but the ground is frozen and everything's icy. I should have warned you." He helped her stand. "Are you okay?"

"Yes," she said, "I've got so many clothes on, I'm well-padded."

"All right, come with me," he said, taking her hand again. Fred reached up, pulled the saw down from the rafters and used his glove to dust off the cobwebs. "It's a bit rusty, but the teeth are still sharp." He squirted oil from a small can and wiped it over the saw blade. "It has two handles, one for you and one for me."

"Do you think Ralph used it?"

"Probably. What do you think, want to try it?"

"I'll try anything once," Pauline said, but looked at the long saw a bit dubiously.

"Okay, let's cut some wood."

Fred carried the cross-cut saw on his shoulder, the teeth facing away from his neck. Pauline followed and with a little boost in each step, she could put her boot in his footprints. Fir boughs, heavy with snow, sagged to the ground at the edge of the woods. Fred held back branches from brushing against Pauline as they made their way through the undergrowth. It was silent but for an occasional squeaky sound. Pauline looked up. She saw two trees swaying in the light breeze. The eerie noise was made by their two trunks rubbing together. Snowflakes filtered through the air as globs of snow fell from one branch to another. Blackcap chickadees and sparrows left their tracks as they hopped about in search of seeds amongst the Oregon grape and snowberry bushes.

Fred stopped, put a finger to his lips and pointed. Pauline looked through the sparsely wooded area. Two alert deer stood a short distance away watching them. One doe turned, flicked her black tail and stepped delicately over snow-covered branches and twigs. The other stood and gazed at Pauline and Fred.

Pauline held her breath. The older doe looked back and raised her head as if to call the other one to follow. Then they bounded effortlessly over fallen branches through the trees and out of sight.

"Oh, Fred, they were beautiful! It was worth coming out just to see them."

They walked on to the fallen tree. The trunk had splintered from its base, and was held off the ground a little by tangled branches on each side of the trail. Fred stepped over the fir, brushed snow off the bark with his gloves and set the saw's teeth against it.

"You take hold of that handle, and as I pull the saw, you push on it." Pauline held the handle with both hands. After several tries the saw scratched through the bark. Fred said, "We have to work together and get into a back and forth rhythm." They pushed and pulled. The saw buckled and stuck in the bark. Fred pulled it up and then realigned it in the cut. "Pauline, I guess we can't push it so hard. Let's try again. I'll pull and after it cuts through on my side, you pull."

"This is work." Pauline flexed her hands to ease some of the stiffness.

"That's why they call it a misery whip. Get down on your knees like I am, so your back won't get tired."

She knelt in the snow, gripped the handle and they started again. Slowly they got into a rhythm—back and forth, back and forth. Sawdust fell onto the snow at their knees as the saw sank farther into the wood.

"Let's take a short rest." Fred stood, loosened his red neckerchief, threw his mackintosh onto a pile of branches and sat on the tree trunk. Pauline lay backwards in the snow and looked up through the firs to the sky. Gray clouds hid the sun. They enjoyed the quietness of the forest.

A few minutes later, Fred stood up. "Ready to have another go at it?" They soon found their rhythm again and quickly cut through the rest of the twelve-inch trunk. "That wasn't so hard once we got started. Let's move the saw up about ten inches and do another round."

The second cut went easier and faster. "We did it!" Pauline called out as the round broke loose and rolled toward her. They sawed several more.

"My arms are tired, Fred," Pauline groaned.

"I'm surprised you held out this long. You've gotten stronger since we came to the farm."

"It's all the work I do. Hauling water and scrubbing clothes hasn't been easy. I miss my washing machine."

"Maybe we can buy one. I know you've been putting money aside."

"How do you know?"

"I remember your way with saving when we were back home."

"Well, I have to admit, I do put away some every time Otto pays you, but I don't know if it's enough to buy a washing machine." She took off her wet gloves. "My fingers are numb." She held her red hands up to him and rubbed them together.

Fred pulled his gloves off. "Here, wear mine, they have a warm lining. Let's go back to the shed. I have a surprise for you." He shouldered the saw. Pauline trudged through the soft drifts behind him.

"I hope we get more snow. Remember the fun we had sledding down Grant's Hill?"

"I do. Those were good times. Dark clouds are blowing in. If the temperature doesn't drop too low tonight, we might have snow in the morning."

When they reached the shed, Fred opened the door and brought out his surprise. "What do you think of this?"

"A sled. You made this?"

"Yep, and you can pull it with this rope. It'll be easier to use than the old wheelbarrow."

She took off his gloves and ran a hand over the steel he had nailed to the hand-hewn runners under the thick plywood deck.

"Here, get on, I'll pull you."

Pauline sat on the sled, her knees up to her chin. Fred pulled the sled a few feet and stopped.

"Maybe you're too heavy."

"I don't weigh as much as I did back home." She rolled off the sled and stood up, but quickly bent down, made a snowball and threw it at him.

"Are you sure you want to play that game?" He gathered snow in his bare hands.

Pauline giggled and hurried to the house.

Chapter Forty-Five... Paulie-Alls

Blasts of wind whistled through cracks around the windows. Pauline said, "I sure hope the electricity comes back on soon."

Fred stood, hands in his pockets, and looked out at the small swirling snowflakes. "It might take a few days before the crew can get it fixed. I'm going to take the sled and get more wood cut. Good thing we have a wood stove."

As Pauline put the last lunch dishes in the cupboard, she heard Will's voice. She looked out the sink window and saw him holding a sheet of plywood. He said, "Yeah, Fred, it's going to be cold the next week or so."

She tapped on the glass. "What are you guys doing?"

Fred called back, "Keeping the wind out."

"But then I can't see. It will be dark in here."

"Too bad," said Fred, "You'll have to use the lamps."

Pauline checked the coffee pot, added more wood to the firebox, and when she heard boots being stamped on the porch, opened the door. Will held a gallon of milk. "I figured you might need this."

"Thanks, I can use it. Come on in. I made coffee cake."

She set the glass jug on the counter. "Look at all that cream. Guess what I'm going to make?"

"Chocolate pudding with whipped cream."

"Nope. Ice cream if we get lots of snow."

"I wanted to come while I could get the truck up the hill," said Will. "There must be six or so inches of snow, but it's blowing off the road and filling in the ditches to the top wire of the fences. Trees fell across power lines on Monkey Hill. Electricity's been knocked out all over the north-end of the island leaving everyone in the dark. Telephones are out, too." He sat down and fiddled with the kerosene lamp on the table. "Do you need any more lamps?"

Pauline said, "No, I have candles and another lamp. We use our lantern to get to the outhouse at night." She put big pieces of coffee cake in front of Will and Fred. They dug right in and the three of them chatted while the men ate. Will picked up a last raisin from the table and put it in his mouth. "That was good cake, lots of raisins, just like Mom's, Paulie."

"Thanks. It's her recipe."

Will stood and slapped his hat onto his head. "I better get down home while we still have some light. Marian will be anxious to get the cows milked. I just hope the milk truck can get through or we'll have to dump the milk." He walked toward the door. "Oh, I brought a couple cans of water for you. Want to come out and help me bring them in, Fred?"

"Sure thing," said Fred, getting up from the table.

Pauline put a hand on her brother's arm. "How's Marian today?"

"She has a bit of a cold and doesn't feel like milking the

cows, but she doesn't complain."

The men went out.

Pauline wiped the windows and put towels on the ledges to catch the condensation. *I'm glad they boarded up just the north windows. It's like a cave in here.*

When Fred came in from shoveling snow, he found Pauline bending over an open trunk. He stood with his back to the stove and soaked up the warmth. "I see you put your yellow Pyrex bowl out to catch the snow. Maybe you can open a jar of your peaches."

"Sure, peaches in the ice cream," she replied softly.

"What are you looking for?"

"I'm tired of wearing men's overalls. I want some that fit me. I know I brought the material leftover when I made work trousers for you. Aha, found it!" She untied the blue yarn around the brown twill and held it up. "I think this is enough." She spread the wrinkled cloth on the table. "Are you sure you have enough light to work?"

"Yes, I have good eyes, remember. The light from the lamps will be enough if you move my Singer over by the window, and you can get the ironing board down."

Fred went to the wall, opened a door, and eased the board down. Then he got on his hands and knees.

"What are you doing down there?"

"Just want to see how Ralph made this for Ruby. He did a nice job."

"I'm surprised you didn't take a closer look before this. I'll need both flat irons."

Fred put the irons on the stove and added sticks of wood. "Well, I'll let you be. I'm going back out."

After she ironed away the wrinkles, Pauline adjusted the pattern for Fred's trousers to her size. She hummed a little tune. *This feels good, to be sewing again. I'll get material next time I'm in town and make a new shirt for Fred.*

The cold continued with snow flurries off and on for three days. Pauline finished her sewing project and modeled it for Fred and Will.

"First time I've seen brown overalls," said Will.

"They're not really overalls," said Pauline.

"They sure look like brown overalls to me."

She put her thumbs under the shoulder straps and pulled them out. "See, I sewed a piece of cloth across the front, sort of like an apron, and made three pockets, easy to carry all my stuff."

"Guess you'll have to call them Paulie-alls," he teased.

Pauline screwed up her face.

Fred said, "Paulie-alls."

Pauline said it and they all laughed.

"I'll tell Marian about your Paulie-alls," Will said. "By the way, I saw the C's helping clear the roads. Rupert's probably out there with them."

Pauline said, "He got some news from his aunt back in Pennsylvania. I'm wondering if he'll stay here when he finishes with the C's. His mother died and he has inherited her house and land."

"In Pennsylvania?" asked Will.

"Yep," said Fred.

"Well, I sure don't want Jenny getting any ideas about moving there," said Will.

Pauline said, "He likes Whidbey Island, I doubt he'll leave. He likes Jenny, too."

Will said, "Marian and I should get to know him better. Jenny's all set to teach come June. Married women aren't allowed to teach here."

"That's about the dumbest rule I've ever heard," said Pauline. "Aunt Ethel was married and taught school for several years until Richie was born."

"Guess the folks out here are old-fashioned," said Will.

Fred said, "It's best if Jenny teaches for a while anyway, before getting married. Rupert doesn't have any money."

Pauline said, "He'll have his inheritance."

"The way the economy is now, it probably won't be much," said Fred.

Chapter Forty-Six... Winter Fun

"I feel like a shut-in, Fred. Let's walk down and visit Alice and Joe. I haven't seen Alice since the New Year's Dance." Fred agreed he'd enjoy a walk in the sunshine. They put on their boots and went out on the porch. Water dripped from the icicles hanging from the eaves. They walked through slush the half mile to the Andrew's farm.

When Alice opened the door, she invited them in and said, "Joe will be coming from the barn soon. You're just in time for coffee."

Fred said, "I'll go on down to the barn."

Pauline took off her boots and coat and stood by the wood stove. She watched Alice brush frosting on warm cinnamon rolls. "I love coming to your home. Your kitchen is always cozy and smells of baked bread."

"I like to bake. What are you wearing, Pauline, something new?"

"Yes, they're not especially pretty, but I got antsy in the house, so I made these. They're like overalls, but Will calls them Paulie-alls."

"Paulie-alls?" Alice fingered the brown twill and

examined the stitching. "You do nice work."

The men came in, rubbing their cold hands.

"Come sit down, Fred." Alice poured coffee and set out plates and napkins.

"Joe's been telling me about the big snow they had back in 1916," said Fred. "Reminds me of our winter storms in Bay City."

Pauline licked frosting from her fingers and wiped her mouth with her cloth napkin. "I wished for snow, but after these past days, I'm tired of it. I don't need any more."

Alice's brown eyes twinkled. "You haven't seen the last of winter yet, Pauline."

Alice's prediction came true. The snow melted away over the next few days. Will complained that his cows were ankle-deep in stinky muck. When he brought them to the barn, the mud sucked at his boots and gripped one so tight, he lost his balance. "My foot came out of the boot and I had to put my foot down into the cold slop to keep from falling. Then my wool sock was wet and muddy and I had a devil of a time putting it into my boot."

A few days later, he complained again when the mud froze. His barnyard, pock marked with holes and ridges from the cows' hooves, made it dangerous for them to walk. One cow fell and broke her hip when her foot sank so deep in a hole she couldn't pull it up. She had to be slaughtered. "Joe helped me skin the carcass and I've got it hanging in the shed. I'm hoping you'll come down and help us butcher it out, Fred."

"Sure. I've never done it, but I'll give it a try."

Will turned to Pauline. "There's work for you, too. We'll share the meat with the neighbors, but Marian wants to can a lot of it."

"Tell Marian, I'd like to help."

"Great. It will need to hang for a few days. I'll let you know when it's ready. We got a call from Hank last night. He said their lagoon has good ice and I should tell you to come over and skate. Marian and I'll go this afternoon after I finish work, but you go anytime.

"Sounds like fun."

The lagoon, about a quarter mile long, varied in width from twenty to eighty feet across. Snowberry, wild rose bushes, crabapple and alder grew along the banks. Clumps of bushes, some several feet tall, stuck up here and there through the ice. Youngsters raced around the bushes as they played tag and called out to one another, some playing hockey with homemade sticks.

Fred put a foot on the ice to test it. "How thick is it?" Not waiting for an answer, he stepped onto it and jumped up and down.

Hank said, "It's three or four inches thick out in the open, but don't skate close to the bushes as the ice doesn't freeze as thick." He laughed and teased, "I don't know that I could rescue you."

"Gev is over there by the bonfire." He pointed to a big pile of stumps and brush. "I'm clearing an area to make an arena for the Cattle Club Shows and Posse Drills. Gev has cider and doughnuts."

The bonfire, built on a sandy bank beside the lagoon,

snapped and crackled sending sparks into the air. After greeting Gev, they sat on logs and put on their skates. Fred skated a few feet onto the ice. He made a few turns and went back to Pauline. "Do Marian's skates fit you okay?"

"With these wool socks they should be fine. I can wiggle my toes." She finished double knotting the laces. "I'm ready."

"Here, take my hand."

She pulled her stocking cap over her ears, put a mittened hand into his and stood. "I'm a bit wobbly. You know it's been a few years since I've been on ice."

"You were good. I remember your figure eights and races with your girlfriends."

"Now that was a long time ago." She let go his hand. Her arms flailed about as she tried to keep her balance. "Whoops!" Down she went onto the hard ice. Fred helped her up, stood behind her and put his hands on her waist.

"I'm okay, Fred. Just a bit wobbly. I want to go by myself." Her feet teetered side to side. She moved her right foot forward, then her left, her right again, and coasted a few feet. It was all coming back. She began to relax and feel comfortable. She practiced by herself.

Fred said, "You're doing great." She skated away, her confidence renewed, and made a wide circle around a group of bushes.

"Hey, Paulie!" Pauline looked back. One skate hit a tuft of grass sticking up out of the ice. She fell on her hands and knees.

"Nerts! You shouldn't surprise me like that, Will!"

"Marian's over by the fire. Come have some cider."

"Okay, in a few minutes. I'm going to skate up to the end

of the lagoon."

She found Fred listening to folks reminiscing about incidents in past winters.

One fellow reminded them, "The winter of 1916 was so cold Penn's Cove froze over."

Someone asked, "How can that be? I thought salt water didn't freeze."

Several men started talking to explain. The loudest voice was heard to say, "You're right, salt water doesn't freeze, but they had so much rain and snowmelt in the mountains that year the Skagit River flooded. The fresh water floated on top of the salt water and froze."

A voice added, "I heard my pop say the ice was thick enough people could walk out several hundred feet."

Another old-timer interjected, "That same year, two men drove their Model A out on Cranberry Lake and drowned when the car went through the ice."

Someone commented, "Sounds like they were a couple of fools."

After another half-hour skating, Fred asked rosy-cheeked Pauline if she'd had enough for the day. "One more fast skate to the end." And off she went.

Chris came up beside her. "Want to race?"

"Okay." They skated side by side and then she pulled ahead to circle around a small alder. Suddenly the ice gave out and she stood knee deep in cold water.

Chris called, "Don't try to get out, it'll only keep breaking. I'll be right back," and he skated away.

Pauline held on to a sturdy alder branch and looked at the jagged ice. *He's right, the ice would just keep breaking.*

Within a minute Chris and Kelly were there with a sled. They pushed it toward her and told her to ease onto it. Pauline took hold of the sides of the sled, laid her chest on it and inched her way forward. The boys pulled. Edges of the ice broke off, but they pulled the sled onto thicker ice.

"Stay on the sled," Chris said. "We can pull you down to the fire."

Pauline held on, her skates dragging on the ice. *What a fool. I must look ridiculous.* They came to the fire where several men and women had gathered. Everyone started asking what happened and if she was all right. *Oh, this is so embarrassing.* She put her head down on the sled. Fred and Hank came over to her.

Fred helped her up and to sit on a log, and then started taking off her skates. "Are you hurt, dear?"

"Just feel like a fool in front of everybody."

Gev wrapped a blanket around her. "Let's go up to the house and get you into dry clothes."

On their way home, Fred said, "Hank and Ted are going to kill a pig a week from Saturday, and wanted to know if I'd like to come over. I told him I will. It should be interesting."

"I want to go too. Gosh, between helping Marian and Will cut up their beef and now a pig, we sure are going to learn a lot about butchering."

Chapter Forty-Seven... The Butchering

Steam rose from the large, cast-iron black pot set over red-hot coals in the fire hole. Pauline, Fred and Gev stood close to it, warming their hands. They watched Hank load his thirty-caliber hunting rifle. He called to his brother, "Okay, Ted, everything's ready."

Ted held a rope tied around a pig's right hind leg. He pushed on the pig's rump with his knees. Hank's dog, Buddy, tied to a nearby tree, pulled on his leash, yelped and danced with excitement. The pig squealed in a high-pitched voice, jerked the rope from Ted's hand, and scooted away. Hank leaned his rifle against a fence post and he and Ted ran after the pig. Fred joined the chase crouching down and spreading his arms out to head it off.

"Run, pig, run!" called Pauline.

Gev laughed as they watched the commotion. The pig's ears flapped up and down as it came their way. Pauline backed up, but Gev put her arms out and shouted, "Shoo! Shoo!" The pig ran past her toward a grove of wild rose bushes. The rope snagged on a tree root and the pig flipped over backwards, squealed, and kicked its legs in the air.

Ted picked up the end of the rope as the pig scrambled to stand up.

Ted coaxed the panting pig to a water spigot, rubbed its back with water and a brush. It made grunting noises and moved back and forth under the brush.

Pauline laughed. "Look at him! He likes his bath."

Fred playfully asked, "How do you know it's a he, Pauline?"

Hank joined in the banter. "It's actually a she."

"Well, does she have a name?" asked Pauline.

"Yep. Miss Tootsie."

"That's quite a name for a pig."

Fred asked, "How much does Miss Tootsie weigh?"

"Oh, about one hundred sixty pounds. She's one of Old Sheba's. Right, Ted?"

"Yep, the runt of the litter."

Ted nudged the pig to a large piece of plywood on the ground near the fire pit. It snuffled and smelled the board. Hank picked up his rifle, walked slowly up to the pig, put the gun to its forehead and pulled the trigger. Pauline flinched at the sharp crack of the shot. The pig collapsed. Ted rolled it onto the plywood, took a long, sharp-pointed knife from the sheath on his belt and slit the animal's throat. Dark red blood spilled onto the board.

Hank put the gun aside and stood beside his brother. He asked, "Okay?

"Okay," said Ted. Together they lifted the pig by its hind legs, counted one, two, and on three, swung it back and forth, and heaved it head-first into the iron pot. Water splashed out onto the sizzling coals. They jostled the animal around in the hot water, and then, so the meat wouldn't cook, pulled it from the pot and plopped it onto the plywood.

They used tools called cups to remove the hair from the pig's hide. The cups were made of three-quarter-inch wide, five-inch long doweling with shallow metal cups on each end. The brothers bent over and worked fast scraping the hair from the pig's skin, shaking hair off the cups and scraping again and again. Pauline pinched her nose at the smell of the singed hair that fell into the fire pit.

The men rolled the carcass over to do the other side. When they were finished, they stood and each man reached into the back pocket of his overalls to pull out a red handkerchief. Pushing their hats back, they wiped their brows and blew their noses, then stuffed the bandanas back into their pockets. Pauline thought it was amusing how they had done this almost simultaneously.

Ted slit the skin and tendons of the pig's hind ankles and put a hook in each while Hank sawed off the head and tossed it into a five-gallon bucket.

Gev explained they would make head cheese with the jowls, ears and lips.

"Yuck! That sounds horrible," said Pauline.

"It makes a good sandwich with a little mustard."

Hank and Ted, one on each end of the plywood, carried the carcass a short distance to an open shed and set the board down on sawhorses. They fastened the hooks to ropes on pulleys hung from rafters and pulled the pig up with the neck hanging down a few inches from the ground.

The onlookers watched Ted cut the body open from its tail down to its throat. He held the entrails aside with one hand, careful not to knick them with his knife, as he cut the membrane that held them to the fat in the body cavity. The glistening mass fell down onto the plywood.

Steam rose from the messy heap of entrails. Fred and Pauline stepped over for a closer look. She wrinkled her nose at the warm smell. "They look like a slimy, gray snake all curled up."

"That's about the only part we don't keep. We use almost everything but the squeal," Ted joked. "Some people use the intestines as casing for sausage, but we don't like to mess around cleaning them." Ted pointed out the different organs in the pig's body. He cut out the heart and liver and threw them into a shiny galvanized bucket.

"I'll take those to the house and wash them. Would you like to take some liver for your supper?"

Fred said, "You bet! I love liver and onions."

Hank brought a water hose and clean rags. The men washed the carcass inside and out and threw buckets of water over it to rinse it off.

Pauline asked Gev, "Do you watch every time they butcher?"

"No, I just came out to be with you. My work will start tomorrow. They'll leave the carcass hanging here for the night to cool and in the morning bring it to our basement to cut it up."

They watched as Hank used the handsaw to cut down the pig's spine. Gev explained, "The hams and bacon slabs will be salted down for several days."

Fred shifted his weight from one foot to the other and looked at Gev. "I read a bit about this in one of Will's farm magazines. The brine was mixed in a five-gallon bucket. They put enough salt in the water to float an egg."

"Hank does the same. He'll put the hams and bacon into a fifty-gallon oak barrel and cover them with brine for two to three weeks, then take the bacon slabs to the smokehouse. Hams need to be salted down a bit longer."

Gev pointed across the orchard. "Hank and Ted dug a hole seven or eight feet down the hillside from that little building. In the hole they'll keep an alder wood fire burning night and day. Smoke goes up through a pipe into the bottom of the smokehouse."

"Ted said nothing goes to waste," said Pauline.

Gev laughed. "That's about right."

Fred said, "I like pickled pig's feet."

"You never told me that," Pauline said.

"Mom got them at the meat market, boiled them in spices and fixed them with onions and vinegar."

"I fix them that way, too," said Gev.

Pauline asked, "How do you make head cheese?"

Gev explained, "We grind the meat from the head, mix spices and salt into it, put it in a salt sack, and press it flat into my large cake pan. We pour some of the rendered fat over the sack."

"What is rendered fat?"

"We take the fat off the pig, cut it into small cubes, and roast it in the oven. Rendering the fat takes nearly all night. I save some of the fat in a tin bucket that I keep above the warming oven on my stove."

"Is it a gold James Henry bucket? I found a bucket like that in my house, but I threw it away. It smelled horrible," said Pauline.

"Yes, it would after sitting around so many years."

Pauline asked, "What do you do with the melted fat?"

"We call it lard after it hardens and use it for frying or to make pie crust."

"Does Alice use lard? I love the flaky crust on her cherry pies."

"Yes, we all use lard. I'll give you some."

"I'd like that. I've been using shortening."

Pauline and Gev looked up the road when they heard, "Hello, ladies!" Mildred wore trousers and a wool jacket with a stocking hat pulled low on her head.

Pauline said, "You've missed the fun!"

Mildred's blue eyes twinkled. "I think I timed it just right."

Gev said, "I think you did, too. Let's go to the house and I'll make coffee." She called, "Come to the house, boys, Pauline brought an apple crisp."

"We'll be along after we get cleaned up," Hank called back.

Mildred slipped her arms around Gev and Pauline's waists. "It's good to see you again, Pauline." The women began the walk to Gev's house.

Chapter Forty-Eight... A Trip
to the Courthouse

Patches of snow lingered along the roads and the ground turned to slippery mud. Pauline volunteered to do the morning chores. She liked taking the responsibility and did the chores often before Fred came home in the evening. One morning while in the hen house, she heard the motor of a car and looked out to see Marian.

"I'm over here," she called as she closed the hens' door. She saw Marian wearing her blue wool coat and blue felt hat and asked, "Where are you going all dressed-up?"

"Are you terribly busy today? I thought we could take a trip to Coupeville. I'd like to go to the courthouse and have lunch at a little café on the waterfront where you can look across the cove."

Pauline thought for a moment. "Well sure, I know you want to get information about Rupert's family history. What I planned to do can wait until tomorrow. Come on in." She changed from her Paulie-alls to a rayon print dress and put on her good shoes. She wore her black wool coat and pinned a hat over her blonde curls.

Marian, thumbing through a *Pictorial Review*, looked up. "New hat?"

"Oh, I was fiddling with this old one the other day. I found a couple of blue feathers from a Bantam hen. Do you think it's silly?"

"Indeed not. It's very smart looking."

"How long do you think we'll be gone?"

"It's pretty much an all-day trip, about twenty miles to Coupeville."

"Just a minute, I'll get my purse and leave a note for Fred."

Pauline closed the door as they went out. They tip-toed over the muddy path to Marian's car.

"I don't know much about the island. I get as far as Oak Harbor for groceries and to Hank and Gev's, but that's about it. I've got lots to learn and I want you to tell me everything."

"Did Gev tell you she was born in Coupeville?"

"No, she doesn't talk much about herself."

"She has an interesting family history. Her grandfather's family came here from Michigan in covered wagons in the early 1850's. I read about it when her great aunt's diary was printed in the *Farm Bureau News*. Her grandfather, John Kellogg, was called the "Canoe Doctor" because he hired local Indians to paddle him to and from the little towns in the Puget Sound area where he helped sick or injured people. Lucky for him he was on one of those trips when Indians came from the north to kill him."

"Really? Why did they want to kill him?"

"Oh, one of their chiefs was killed and they wanted to kill the doctor in retaliation. Since he wasn't here, they killed

Colonel Ebey instead. Ask Gev about it someday."

Marian slowed the car to a stop and they watched a farmer herd his cows across the road. She rolled down the window. "Good morning, Jake."

"Hello, Marian. On your way to Coupeville?"

"Yes, I'm giving my sister-in-law a tour."

Jake told them to have a good day, waved and followed his cows.

On their way again, Marian said, "We'll have new neighbors in a year or so. Thea and her husband are going to build a house on property down the road from Alice. They ordered house plans from Sears and Roebuck. Bert's been hauling the maple flooring lumber and tongue and groove siding from the buildings being razed at Fort Casey."

"Where's Fort Casey?"

"It's west of Coupeville on a steep bank above the water. It was built around the turn of the century in order to protect Puget Sound. Luckily, they never had to fire the big guns. During the war it was used for training troops."

"It'll be wonderful to have Thea living near us, although I always enjoy going into town for the Sewing Circle."

Marian laughed. "Yes, an excuse to go shopping." She drove down Telephone Hill, through Oak Harbor and up the hill past Freund's Marsh. Trees hid the view of the water, except for an occasional opening where a house rested on the side of the steep bank.

They saw a herd of Jersey dairy cows in an open field, and then the road took them down a hill to Penn's Cove. "Oh, look at the beach. The tide's out. I bet we could dig for clams," said Pauline.

Marian pointed across the water. "That's Coupeville. It would almost be faster to take a boat. You can see the Methodist Church steeple. And just below this hill there used to be an Indian Longhouse. The winter high tides eventually washed it away."

"I've read about the Indian Potlatches when the chief gave away lots of his stuff."

"Quick! Look up in that tall fir. A white head just landed."

Pauline leaned forward to look up through the windshield. "An eagle. It's so majestic the way it sits there surveying the cove. There's another one on a lower branch."

"They probably have a nest around here. Now we're coming into San de Fuca. That's the Benson Hotel where Will and I stayed overnight so we could get up early to take the steamer to Seattle. Years ago there was talk of putting a railroad through here and other talk to build a canal from here out to the beach on the west side. At one time, the state considered having a college here, but instead they built it in Bellingham—where Jenny goes now."

Pauline craned her neck to see the white San de Fuca schoolhouse on the hill. "Maybe Jenny can teach there."

"No, it closed in 1933. The kids go to Coupeville. Here's the saw mill. Lots of big timbers have been shipped from the island, some to California to be used for spars for the rigging on ships." As they rounded a corner, Marian pointed to a red two-story building. "That's the old courthouse. I heard someone say an Indian was hanged there. I don't know the whole story."

"Are there many Indians living on the island?"

"I don't think so," Marian replied. "Some died of diseases

and many moved to the reservations on the mainland."

Pauline said, "Hank told us when he was a boy, he played with a couple of Indian boys. Of course, he's about forty now, so that was some time ago. Look at the lake. Wouldn't it be fun to live on that tiny island?"

"It's really a little peninsula on Kennedy's Lagoon, but it does look like a fun place to have a rowboat and go for a swim." They went around a long curve. "On the left is the Whid-Isle Inn. It's made of logs. I've never been there. I love the red bark on the madrone trees."

Pauline enjoyed the wonderful scenery. The blue water sparkled in the sun with the snowy Cascade foothills in the background. Marian drove along the curves and up and down the hilly road, and down into Coupeville. "This is the second oldest city in our state." She drove up the hill and parked the car in front a large square building. "Captain Lovejoy, a sea captain, built this ornate courthouse and many of the homes."

"It's a beautiful building."

"Well, shall we see if we can find out about Rupert's family?"

As Pauline stepped out of the car, she bumped her head and her hat fell to the ground. "Nerts!" She picked it up, brushed off specks of mud and put it on her head. "Is it on straight?"

"Uh, yes, just move it a little to one side."

Men tipped their hats to them as they climbed the steps. Marian said, "Let's try the clerk's office." She led the way to a tall door with a glass window inscribed, *County Clerk*.

Marian told the woman behind the desk they were looking

for the birth record of Rupert Long. The middle-aged woman took a large ledger from a shelf and laid it on the counter. "What year did you say he was born?" She adjusted her glasses, leafed through the pages and ran her finger down the list dated 1911. "No, I don't see a Rupert Long."

"Maybe that's the wrong year," said Marian.

The clerk paged back to 1910 and then checked 1912. "There are several Longs. Is Rupert his full name, maybe a different first name?"

Pauline said, "He just said Rupert Long."

Marian asked, "Do you have a marriage record for Ralph Long?"

Again, there was nothing.

As they got into Marian's car, she said, "What a waste of time. Can you imagine, no record of a baby being born? Isn't that against the law? And no marriage record? Wouldn't a minister have to record it? Wouldn't they have to have a license?" She started the car and drove down the hill. "I don't want Jenny getting mixed-up with Rupert."

"Jenny's just having fun. She's not thinking of marrying anyone yet. Remember how she flirted with all the boys at Thanksgiving?"

"I remember how she danced with Rupert at the New Year's dance."

Pauline said, "Oh, there's the café. Are we going to lunch?"

"Yes, of course, I promised you a lunch out."

They chose a table by a corner window and shrugged off their coats. Pauline leaned toward the window, looked down to the water where seagulls floated around the pier, and then out at Penn's Cove. "There's the school, straight across from us."

Marian handed her a menu. Pauline studied the soiled paper. "What will you have, Marian?"

"I'm not even hungry, but you go ahead and get anything that looks good to you."

Pauline ordered clam chowder. She tried to think of something to say to bring Marian out of her angry mood.

Marian fumed, "Ruby must've had him at home all by herself. What was Ralph thinking? You'd think she would have had a doctor or a midwife and they would have recorded the birth. I don't want Jenny to see Rupert anymore."

"Really Marian, maybe it's just a passing fancy with Jenny. She told me she's excited to teach. Yum, this chowder is delicious. You better have some."

"You're right. I should eat something, it's a long time until supper." She motioned to the waitress to take her order. "No, Jenny shouldn't see Rupert. We don't know anything about him."

Pauline insisted, "Fred and I know Rupert. He's a fine young man. We just don't know his family."

"It's terrible," Marian complained. "They weren't even married. I can't imagine what Will's going to say."

"Rupert's a good person. You can't hold it against him for what his parents did or didn't do."

"Someone must have known them. Did Ruby stay home all the time? Never go to town?"

As Pauline was about to take a sip of coffee, she saw a dark spot come up out of the water. "Marian, is that a seal?"

"Yes, a harbor seal. There are lots of them around the

island. We see them at Cornet Bay." She wiped her mouth with a napkin. "Guess I was hungry."

Pauline pointed. "A boat is coming in." A wooden steamer moored at the dock.

"That's the *Atalanta*. It's one of the boats in the Mosquito Fleet. They pick up farm produce and take it to market in Seattle. It stops at docks along the island and takes passengers, too."

"Have you been on it?"

"Not that boat. Will and I went to Seattle on the Calista for our anniversary in 1922. It sank a couple months later when it collided with another boat in a dense fog.

"Did anyone drown?"

"No, they were all rescued. Gev's sister was one of the passengers." Marian pushed her chair back. "Shall we go?" She paid for their lunch and they went out to the car.

Chapter 49... Home from the Courthouse

As Marian dropped Pauline off at her house and drove away, Pauline saw the glow of Fred's lantern coming from the hens' coop. She called to him, "Hi dear, I'm home."

He answered, "Did you and Marian have a swell time?"

"I did, but Marian's in a tizzy."

"And why is that?"

"Let's go in and I'll tell you about it over supper."

Pauline changed her clothes while Fred built up the fire. Together they got supper on the table, and then she told him about not finding any records of Rupert's birth or Ralph and Ruby's marriage.

"Well, maybe they never did marry, maybe they never told anyone about Rupert."

"I asked Alice if she had known Ruby and Ralph. She said being a teenager, she didn't pay attention to the folks living in the woods."

"That's strange. The people in this community seem to know everyone and help one another."

"Alice said they saw him go by in a rickety truck once in a while, and he might have worked in the hay field for her dad."

Fred reminded her, "Rupert said when they went to Pennsylvania, Ralph gave his cow and truck to a friend. I wonder if that was the Charlie who Ralph wrote about in his letters."

"We should ask Rupert if he remembers Charlie. Anyway, Marian said she'll never let Jenny marry Rupert."

Pauline put the butter dish and milk jug in the cooler. Fred carried heated water to the sink and poured it into the wash tub.

"I loved the trip to Coupeville. Marian told me a lot of island history. We should take Sunday drives to explore. You might like to see Fort Casey."

"With gasoline at fifteen cents a gallon, it's a bit expensive to go sight-seeing."

Will came by the next day. He told Pauline that Marian was on her high-horse and he felt like he was caught in the middle. "I like Rupert. Don't know much about him, but he seems like a regular fella. Of course, I'd just as soon Jenny not get married until she's at least twenty-two."

"Will, Jenny isn't interested in getting married. She's young and wants to teach. Marian shouldn't worry so. I wonder if it would help if you and Marian read the letters that Rupert's father wrote."

"Should we read them without asking him?"

"I don't think he'd mind." Pauline went to the bedroom and brought out the letters. "You and Marian will know his father better. Rupert's a good person." She turned to Fred, "Isn't he, Fred?"

"He seems to be all right. He's been very helpful to us."

"Well, I feel sorry for Jenny when Marian lights into her," said Will. He opened the door to leave, but paused and said, "Paulie, it's time to start thinking about your garden. I follow the *Old Farmer's Almanac* and plant my peas on George Washington's birthday."

"That's more than a month away."

"True, but you can think about what you want to plant and as soon as the ground is ready to work I'll bring up Buster and Maud."

Gray Whidbey skies broke up with short periods of sun the next two weeks. Will stopped by with Rupert's letters. "These are interesting, but Marian still isn't ready to hand her daughter over to Rupert, or to anyone for that matter."

"When will Jenny be coming home?"

"Probably when the quarter ends the last of March."

"That gives Marian time to cool down."

"I doubt it," said Will. Pauline followed him out.

He walked around the porch and over to the patch of ground he had plowed in the fall. "It's dried out enough to be worked. I'll bring Maud and Buster up tomorrow."

"Will, I promised Alice I'd spend the day with her. She's not been feeling well and needs help washing their clothes."

"What's wrong with her?"

"Something men don't understand."

"Oh. Well, tell you what. You don't need to be here. I'll bring the horses up and get it done."

"I did what you said and spread the chicken manure over the ground, and Fred dumped the wood ashes in one corner."

He looked where she pointed. "That's good. You can work the ashes into the soil. I like to plant my potatoes in a trench."

"Are you sure I shouldn't be here to help?"

"Nothing for you to do except watch me. There'll be plenty for you to do later, rocks to pick and raking. I'll buy a gunny sack of seed potatoes and give you some." He fumbled in his pocket and took out a tattered paper. "This is a plan of how I plant my garden. Some vegetables don't like each other and shouldn't be planted side by side."

Pauline studied the paper.

Will said, "I listed the plants that do well when they're planted in rows next to each other. It helps keep insects away."

"Gardening seems complicated. There's so much to do."

With twinkling eyes he looked at his sister. "It'll keep you out of mischief."

Pauline had a pleasant day helping Alice, for although she wasn't feeling well, she never complained. While they were working, Pauline told her about the trip to the courthouse. "We were disappointed. We couldn't find any information."

Alice said, "Maybe the midwife helped Ruby. We used to see her drive by every so often." Alice laughed a little. "My brother, Ted, would say, 'There goes that old lady in her rattle-trap car.' She was a nice lady, though. Her name was Mrs. Hannegan or something like that, who helped the women. We didn't have a hospital, so babies were born at home. Everyone called her Auntie. I remember my mother saying, 'Auntie helped Mrs. So and So and there's a new baby in their house.' Until I learned better, I thought Auntie brought the baby."

"I'll ask Rupert if he remembers her." Pauline swished the water in the rinse tub and put a towel through the wringer. "Your Water Witch does a good job. I love using the wringer! I had a Maytag back home, but we couldn't bring it with us so I gave it to Fred's niece. I don't wash Fred's work clothes as often as I used to, and sheets don't get washed every Monday either. It's just too hard to wring them out by hand and they get so wrinkled."

Alice said, "Maybe you should tell Fred you want a Water Witch."

"He doesn't like to spend any unnecessary money."

"Pauline, you need a washing machine. You tell Fred I said so."

After they hung the clothes on the lines strung across the porch, Pauline looked at pictures of washing machines in Alice's Sears and Roebuck catalog. Alice, standing by Pauline's shoulder, pointed and said, "That's it. Joe bought it for me in 1929. He had to pay almost eighty dollars."

Pauline turned the page. "Look here at the Toperator. It's newer and only costs sixty-four dollars and ninety-five cents. Isn't it grand?"

"Yes, it's so modern."

Pauline left Alice's with the catalog under one arm, anxious to show Fred and check their bank account. When she reached the house, she found that Will had finished the garden and gone home. The soil still had a few dips and humps with rocks and roots sticking up. She took care of the animals before going into the house. When Fred came home, he found her humming a little tune and peeling potatoes for supper. "You're extra happy tonight," he said.

"I had a real nice time with Alice today. We did all her washing. Fred, it was so easy with her washing machine. And I loved using the wringer. I'll show you."

She wiped her hands on her apron, brought the catalog to the table and opened it to the page with one corner folded down. "See, here's Alice's electric Water Witch and on the next page is a Toperator."

Fred read the descriptions of the two machines.

Pauline said, "The Toperator is the newest."

"And that's the one you want, the newest one."

"Don't you think that's best? It doesn't cost as much either. I really do think I should have it, my old wringer doesn't do a good job and my hands are tired of wringing out wet clothes."

"Do we have enough to pay for it?"

She snuggled her arm around his shoulders and showed him the savings book. "I think you'll be surprised. I've been very careful, and put money in the bank almost every time we go into town. Look, one-hundred sixty-eight dollars and fourteen cents."

"Yes, don't forget the cents," he teased, and pulled her onto his lap. "I think your hands need a rest. Go ahead and put in the order. Otto and I have a couple jobs lined up that should keep us working for a few months."

Chapter Fifty... Gardening

Pauline stepped out onto the porch. Redwing blackbirds chirped their musical hellos in the big old Gravenstein apple tree. *Do they think it's spring?* Brown birds with speckled feathers pecked for larva in the yard. She clapped her hands. The starlings rose together and flew in a half circle, and then the short distance to the wooded area.

A gunny sack lay on the porch with a note attached. She unfolded the paper and read, *Paulie, Here are a few spuds. I'll let you know when I plant mine. Cut them into chunks so there will be at least one or two eyes on each. Dig your holes about eight to ten inches deep and drop the spuds in them with the eyes on top. Cover them with about six inches of dirt. After they start growing all you have to do is push more dirt around them. I'll check on them next time I'm up. Remember, peas on George's birthday.*

She untied the string, reached into the sack and took out a shriveled brown potato with white nubs growing out of its eyes. She carried the sack to the shed. "Fred, look what Will left on the porch."

"Yes, we talked for a just a minute. He was in a hurry to get back home, but said you should plant your peas tomorrow."

"I'd like to drive into town this afternoon to buy seeds and a few groceries."

"Okay, I'll go too. It's been a long time since you've driven the truck."

Pauline had no trouble starting the motor and drove down the rocky driveway. The trip to Oak Harbor was uneventful. Fred told her she had done a good job shifting gears, and teased, "You didn't even go off the road and get stuck in the ditch."

"No, but I sure had to navigate around a lot of puddles."

"Yes, it's time to fill in the pot holes with gravel. Another trip to the beach."

"I'd like to go with you."

"Wouldn't think of going without you."

"You're silly, Fred. You always say that."

He laughed and said, "I think it's what you want to hear."

Pauline parked at the back of the Co-op. They greeted Bernie at the long, brown counter where he and Fred struck up a conversation. Pauline went to the seed racks and stood beside a woman who was picking out seed packets.

"Golly, how do you choose?" asked Pauline. "There are so many and they're so pretty. I'm new at gardening. It's my first time to plant anything."

"I usually buy Burpee seeds," the woman advised. "You can get good results from Ferry-Morse, too."

"Peas. My brother said I should plant peas tomorrow."

"Oh, yes. Washington's Day. Here's a packet for a bush variety, but you might want the others, though you do have to string them up."

"How do you do that?"

"Well, I dig a little trench by my fence, lay a board down and tie string to the board every few inches and attach the string to the top wire. The peas will just naturally cling to the string. They're easier to pick than the bush type. I don't like to stoop over much."

Pauline read the instructions on the back of the package and checked Will's list... peas, carrots, beets, radishes, lettuce, turnips, spinach, beans.

The woman handed her a packet of pea seeds. "To get an early start, soak the seeds overnight."

Pauline said, "I'll do that. My husband likes squash. Do you have a favorite?"

"Hubbard. No question about that. They get big - fifteen to twenty pounds - but they keep into the winter. Of course, they take up a lot of garden space."

"My brother, Will, made a big garden for me."

"Will Ansbach?"

"Yes."

"Marian's husband."

"Yes. I'm Pauline Gunther."

"My sakes, your husband works with my Otto."

Pauline extended her hand. "Mrs. Van Eck, I'm pleased to meet you. Fred enjoys working with Otto."

"And Otto tells me Fred is a fine carpenter."

"Fred will be happy when I tell him. He loves working with wood." Pauline looked at Will's list again. "Will said spinach and leaf lettuce are good early crops." She searched the rack for the packets.

Mrs. Van Eck said, "Chard is another. I prefer the Swiss.

Here it is." She handed it to Pauline, and then looked at the seed packets in her basket. "Well, I think I have all I need, I better be running along."

"Thank you for your help, Mrs. Van Eck. Perhaps you and Otto would like to come by for coffee sometime."

"That would be nice, dear."

"I'll tell Fred."

Pauline watched as the older woman walked away using a cane for support. Pauline turned to the rack and looked at the array of flower pictures. *Let's see, asters and cosmos were Mom's favorites, and I like snapdragons.*

Fred stepped beside her. "That's a good many seeds you have there, Pauline."

"Oh, Fred, it's going to be such fun. What do you have there?"

"You've been using that old rake with the broken handle, much too short for you. I bought a new one and a hoe. You'll need both."

Pauline smiled when she saw the new tools. "Oh, thank you."

"Well, it's going to be more work than you've ever done. You need the right tools."

Dressed in her Paulie-alls, down on hands and knees in the dirt trying to move a rock, she heard Rupert's voice. "Here, let me help you with that."

Pauline looked up into his smiling face. "What brings you up here this morning?"

"I've got a day off and nothing much to do, so I thought I'd see what you and Fred are doing." He took her shovel and pulled dirt away from the rock. "Where would you like it?"

"How about in that corner by the porch?"

Rupert carried the rock to where she pointed. "Would you like me to bring over more rocks, make a border for a flower garden?"

"A flower garden, I'd like that. It won't be hard to find more rocks. We have all sizes." She took the packets from her pocket. "I bought lots of seeds."

"You sure did, but I don't see any marigolds. Gramma always planted them with her vegetables."

"Well, I'll get some next time I'm at the Co-op. Fred's in the shed working, but I think he's ready for coffee. Want to get him and come in the house?"

When the men came in, Pauline had cookies and coffee ready and they all sat at the table. Fred asked, "What have the C's been working on lately?"

"Yesterday, a couple of other guys and I were delegated to carry steel reinforcing rods for the roadbed on the bridge. It about broke our backs."

"Yes, those rods are heavy," said Fred. "Sounds like they're ready to pour concrete."

"The planks are laid on the girders now. Looking over the side is sure a thrill, but I wouldn't want to fall into those whirlpools. It will be safer when the sidewalks and railings are there."

Pauline said, "Rupert, you know I've been trying to find anyone who knows your mother's family. Alice told me she used to see a woman, I think she said, Mrs. Hannegan, drive up to your place. Do you remember her?"

He coughed and put his cup down, coffee spilled into the saucer. "You mean Auntie? She was nice to me. She and my ma would talk and have coffee. She always brought me something, a book or those malt balls. Sure, I remember her."

"Do you remember going to town?"

"No, Ma and I stayed home. We used to play games in the woods. There was a big old tree with a long trunk that grew close to the ground before it went up. It must have gotten knocked over when it was little, but it kept growing. Ma sat on it and wrote in her book. In the fall we'd pile up the big leaves and then I'd jump around in them and fall down." He looked at his cap resting on his knee, and then up at Pauline. "My ma told me about the fairies and little men that lived in the mossy logs. She'd tell me to be quiet and listen. I never did see any, but it was fun thinking they were hiding from me."

"You have nice memories of your ma."

"Yeah, I do." He looked around the room and at the mantel clock. "Guess I better get going. I'll come again and help you make a garden for your flowers."

"Thanks, Rupert."

As he stepped out onto the porch he said, "Don't forget the marigolds."

Chapter Fifty-One... An Exciting Day

Pauline raked the clods of sod to smooth out a place for the peas. She found an old board about six feet long in the lean-to and laid it on the ground near the side of the house and then dug a two-inch deep trench beside it. She tied strings from the board on the ground five feet up to one that Fred had nailed to the side of the house. Then she planted the wet, swollen pea seeds two inches apart in the trench, crumbled the fine damp soil in her hands, sprinkled it evenly over the seeds, and patted it down. "There, that's done." She stood back and admired her work. Hearing the honk of a car horn, she rubbed the dirt from her hands and walked to the porch.

"Pauline, good news!" Marian called. "Sears phoned. Your washing machine is at the dock warehouse."

"Already?" Putting her hands together and up to her chin, she said with a big smile, "I didn't think it would come so soon. I'll ask Fred to bring it home after work tomorrow. I can't wait to see it!"

"I'm going into town. We'll take Will's truck and bring it home."

"Really? Oh, my! Let's do it, but first come see my pea

patch real quick."

Marian came over and looked at Pauline's work. "I have a suggestion. Move the board forward so the peas will grow up under the strings."

Pauline thought for a moment. "Oh, I see what you mean." She repositioned the board. "Yes, that makes sense. Come in while I change my clothes. I have something to tell you."

Marian plopped down in one of the rocking chairs, and from her bedroom Pauline said, "I visited Alice the other day and she told me about Mrs. Hannegan—well, she thinks that was the woman's name. From what Alice remembers, this woman was a midwife who might have helped Ruby when Rupert was born."

"Maybe, but she should have had his birth recorded," Marian called back. She rocked and listened to Pauline.

"Rupert came up yesterday and I asked him if he remembered the lady and his exact words were, 'Sure, I remember her.' He told us she used to come for coffee visits with his ma and brought him treats." Pauline came from the bedroom, sat at the table, and bent down to put on her shoes. "You know, they could have been married. Maybe they went on the ferry and to the courthouse in Mount Vernon."

Marian said, "In Rupert's letters Ralph wrote that Ruby didn't like to go on the ferry. I doubt they were married and I don't want my Jenny to marry Rupert."

Pauline stood up and adjusted her belt. "Marian, wait 'til Jenny's home. You can talk with her then and get an inkling how she feels. You worry too much."

"It wears me out thinking about her so much."

"Then don't think about it. Okay, I'm ready."

Marian got up, Pauline picked up her purse and they went out to Will's truck.

As Marian drove, Pauline talked about her garden. She said that Fred had suggested she draw a plan, a kind of map, where she would plant everything. "That was a project all by itself. I laid the packets out on the table and grouped them together, those that could be planted by each other and so on." She sighed and leaned back. "I'm so anxious to plant everything."

"It doesn't pay to plant too early. The ground needs to warm up for the seeds to germinate. You can get the potatoes in soon and then radishes, spinach and lettuce. The lettuce seeds are so small I use my tweezers to pick them up, otherwise they fall too close together, and it's a waste to thin them."

Marian turned down Telephone Hill and drove through Oak Harbor. Pauline sat up as they turned onto Maylor's dock. The tools Will kept behind the seat rattled as the truck bumped over the wood planks of the dock. Pauline wrinkled her nose. "What's that bad smell?"

"The tide's out."

"It doesn't smell like this at West Beach."

"The sea creatures collect on the pilings and dirty water comes down the bank from homes and businesses. The bay doesn't get flushed out with the tide like the beaches on the west side of the island."

"I love West Beach. It would be a dream to live out there."

"You might not like the wind."

"There's a truck coming. Is there enough room for us?"

Marian pulled over at the "T" in the middle to let it pass. She honked and waved as the truck went by. "That's Jens Meyer, the chicken man."

"He gave me my hens. I told him to come for coffee and cookies, but he hasn't so far."

Marian drove on out to the wharf and parked. They went to the little office building and soon Pauline's Toperator was loaded onto Will's truck. Pauline looked through the wooden slatted crate at the green tub with white speckles. "Isn't it beautiful?"

Marian peeked through the slates. "Yes, it is," she said."

"Here you are ladies, the wringer came in a separate box." The jolly man laughed and set it in the truck. "You'll need help putting that together. The directions are probably inside the tub."

Pauline thanked him and said, "It's going to be fun when my husband sees it."

"He doesn't know about this?"

"Oh, he knows I ordered it, but he'll be surprised to see it when he comes home."

The man said, "You're a lucky lady to get it."

Back in the truck, Marian said, "I'm going to stop at the Co-op. Do you need anything?"

"Yes, I should get soap. What kind do you use in your machine?"

"I use bars of Fels Naptha. It's a chore shaving it, but it does a good job. I rub it on the tough spots on Will's overalls. Sometimes I need to use the scrub board."

"I've been using Borax. Fred doesn't get his overalls very dirty."

"Well, that's the difference between a farmer and a carpenter."

They came out of the Co-op, their arms filled with groceries, and got in the truck. Pauline turned and looked out the back window at the crate. "I'm going to be so glad to throw out that old plunger and hand-crank wringer."

"You could ask around. Someone might like to have your old wringer."

"That's a good idea."

Marian parked the truck close to the house. "We'll need Fred's help to unload."

Pauline said, "It's almost five-thirty. He should be home any minute. I'm getting lots of eggs these days, Marian. You go on in and I'll gather some for you."

"All right, I'll take in your groceries."

Marian sat in Pauline's rocker with her eyes closed. The door opened and Fred came in. He took off his hat and set his lunch pail on the sink counter. "Hello, Marian."

"Hi Fred. Are you still working at Jefferson's house?"

"Yes, we should wrap it up in a couple more days. Where's my wife?"

"She's getting eggs for me."

He hung his coat and hat on a peg and sat in his rocker. "I see you have a crate in the truck. I suppose Pauline's pretty excited."

"Oh yes, she is indeed."

Pauline came in with her basket. "Oh, hi dear. Did you see what's in Will's truck?"

Fred winked at Marian. "Didn't notice anything."

"You didn't see my Toperator? Marian and I brought it

home. Come on, let's bring it in."

Marian and Fred followed her out the door.

Fred did most of the lifting, and with Pauline and Marian each holding a corner of the slatted box, they carried it to the porch. Fred used his tools to dismantle the crate. They lifted the machine over the door threshold and stood it near the sink.

Marian said, "It's beautiful, Pauline. I'm a bit jealous, but I guess my old one will have to last a few more years." She went home leaving Pauline to ooh and aah over her wonderful Toperator.

Pauline read the directions to Fred while he attached the wringer. She ran her hand over the smooth inside of the tub. She inspected the wringer. "Where can we plug it in?"

Fred squinted at the light bulb hanging above the stove and said, "Since we don't have any electrical outlets, you'll have to take out the bulb and screw in an adapter. I'll pick one up at the Co-op tomorrow."

Pauline hurried with her chores the next morning, and then read the pamphlet to learn everything about the Toperator. She was delighted when Fred came home early, but then disappointed when he said, "I didn't get to the store to buy an adapter, didn't think you'd wash today anyway. It started raining so hard we decided to quit for the day." He hung his coat on a peg and turned to her. "Do I smell cinnamon rolls?"

She said, "Yes, I wanted to surprise you."

"That's good, because I asked Otto and his wife to come over this afternoon."

"Oh, but we're going to Gev and Hank's for cards this

evening, and I want to take rolls."

"I'm sure you'll have enough." He gave her a playful look. "Tell you what, I won't eat any while the Van Ecks are here."

Pauline laughed and brushed him off with her hand, "Oh, there'll be plenty." She scurried around clearing a counter and stacking the newspapers and magazines.

Otto and Ellen Van Eck arrived shortly after two. Pauline showed off her Toperator and beamed when Mrs. Van Eck thought it beautiful.

They all sat at the table enjoying coffee and rolls. Conversation centered on changes coming to Oak Harbor with the anticipation of the completion of the bridge. Fred said, "Will and other farmers are looking forward to shipping their milk and produce by truck."

Otto said, "Yes, Darigold has already agreed to a contract with the farmers. There'll be more trucks and cars on the road and less business for the Mosquito fleet."

Pauline said, "When my sister-in-law and I went to the dock to get my washing machine, she said once a team of horses went over the edge of the dock."

Otto straightened in his chair, cleared his throat and said, "That was about thirty years ago. John Lang had finished unloading a wagonload of potatoes at the wharf on the end of the dock. He had turned his team around when he saw Arnold Freund drive on the dock with his horses pulling a wagon load of hay. John drove his team alongside Arnold's wagon. They talked for a few minutes, and then rolled a few bales onto John's wagon. John started up the dock, and when he saw two teams pulling wagonloads of wood coming toward him he stopped and tried to back up to let them pass him at the T."

Pauline said, "That's what Marian did yesterday. She stopped at the T to let Mr. Jensen pass."

Otto looked at Fred and continued, "Well, John's horses backed in the wrong direction. The wagon's back wheels went over the edge of the other side of the dock. The wagon kinda hung there for a few seconds. John jumped off and tried to get his horses to pull the wagon up, but they were excited, stepped backwards, and then the whole wagon went down pulling the horses with it."

Pauline put her hands to her face. "Oh no, did they drown?"

"John got down into the water in minutes alongside them, but it was too late. It seemed they didn't make any effort to swim. John figured the horses died at once when they hit the water. He took the harnesses from them and let their bodies float out with the tide. People came running from all over downtown to see what was making all the commotion."

Fred said, "Must have been a real loss to him."

"That's true, not every farmer had a team of horses back then. John got them from Alfred Maylor when they were colts and trained them himself, a beautiful pair of black Percherons. He earned his living working the fields and hauling produce to the dock for his neighbors."

Pauline asked, "What happened to the wagon?"

"It was all broken up. John salvaged the wheels and what boards he could."

Fred held his cup up to Pauline. "Is there more coffee, dear?"

Pauline brought the coffee pot to the table and filled the cups. She noticed that Mrs. Van Eck held out her little finger when she took a sip. *Reminds me of my grandmother.* Without staring, Pauline studied Otto's face and then his wife's. *They must be over sixty. Maybe she remembers Rupert's Auntie.*

"Mrs. Van Eck, did you know Mrs. Hannegan?"

"Edith? Why of course, dear. She was my sister. She died in the 1916 flu epidemic."

"Oh, I'm sorry."

"Yes, we lost quite a few folks on the island."

"Was your sister a midwife?"

"I guess you could call her that. She had a bit of training with one of the old doctors on the island. She helped many a good baby come into this world, and made special friends with some of the families, always on the road visiting. One family in particular she visited often. The young mother had a little boy Edith took a liking to. I think she felt sorry for them because they lived off in the woods."

"Do you remember their names?"

"Hmm... that was many years ago." Mrs. Van Eck looked down at her cup and thought for a moment. "No, I don't recall their names."

Otto looked at his watch, cleared his throat and stood up. "We better get on the road, Ellen."

Mrs. Van Eck rose from the table and tugged her flowery rayon dress down to smooth the skirt. Otto helped her with her coat. She took her cane and gave Pauline a twinkly smile. "Have fun with your new Toperator."

After Fred and Otto shook hands and Pauline invited them to come again, the Van Ecks drove away in their old Reo.

Pauline closed the door. "Bit by bit, I'm learning more about Ruby and Rupert."

Chapter Fifty-Two... Hank's Bear Story

Fred drove down Ducken Road and turned onto the main road toward Oak Harbor. Pauline looked west to the water. "Smith Island looks like a big boat. I wonder if anyone lives on it."

"Guess Hank can tell you," he said as he turned down the hill toward West Beach.

Pauline caught her breath, "Oh, my! The sun looks like a great red ball sinking into the water. I'd love to live on the beach, Fred. Wouldn't that be a dream?"

Hank's dog, Sport, greeted them as Fred parked the truck on the graveled driveway. Chris came out on the porch and told the dog to quiet down. He called hello to Fred and Pauline as they got out of the truck and walked on the wide wood planks to the house.

Chris said, "If you're still and quiet, you can hear the frogs croaking." They stopped and listened. Soon the frogs started up their spring song. "My mom said the frogs are in love and sing to each other."

Pauline laughed. "They sound like a choir, a very loud choir."

"They're laying their eggs in the lagoon."

Gev opened the door. "Come in, come in."

Pauline said, "Gev, we saw the most remarkable sunset."

"Yes, we should have a good day tomorrow."

After they hung their coats on pegs in the wall behind the door, Pauline and Fred sat at the old oak table in the warm kitchen. Steam came from the spout of the aluminum tea kettle on the wood stove. Pauline watched Gev take the kettle to the sink and pour the hot water over the dishes in the rack. *I must remember to do that.*

Kelly came in carrying a gallon-size jar. "Want to see our frog eggs?" He set the jar on the table. Pauline and Fred looked at the jelly mass in the jar.

The boys leaned on the table with their chins in their hands. Kelly pointed. "See, the dark spots in the eggs. There's sure gonna be a whole lot of frogs."

Fred asked, "How did you get these?"

"We took our raft out on the lagoon," said Chris. "Just dipped the jar in the water by the weeds and the big lump of eggs floated in."

Kelly piped up, "When they start growing legs and tails we'll call them polliwogs, and then we have to take them down and put them back in the water."

"Well, I do like frogs," said Pauline. "I find them on the rocks by our spring."

Hank came in, tousled his sons' heads, shook hands with Fred and asked Pauline how she'd been, and not waiting for an answer, said, "You put the jar away now, boys." Chris grabbed the jar before Kelly and they left the kitchen. Hank pulled out a chair. Gev joined them at the table and grown-up talk began.

Soon the boys were back. Chris stood behind his mother, hands in his overalls pockets, listening to the talk, and Kelly stood by Hank with an arm around his father's shoulders.

Pauline smiled seeing how the boys hung onto every word Hank said about the day's work on the road to the bridge. When he had finished, Gev said, "Okay, off to bed."

Kelly said, "Mom, our story."

Gev turned to Pauline. "A nightly ritual."

"We always like hearing Hank's stories," said Pauline.

Hank asked, "What's it going to be tonight, Chris? Your turn."

"Tell about the bear."

"Okay, take a seat." Hank winked at Pauline. "This is one of their favorites."

With the boys settled, chins resting on their folded arms on the table, he began. *One late September, Ted and I took our horses up to Heather Meadows for a few days.*

Pauline asked, "Where is Heather Meadows?"

"It's in the Mount Baker National Forest, about a three-hour drive."

Gev said, "Pauline, you would love it. That time of year the meadows and hills are filled with purple heather and wild blueberries. The heather leaves are iridescent in the sun when you walk on a path one way, and then when you turn and walk back, they change color." Hank put his hand over his wife's hand. "I'm sorry, Hank, go on with your story."

"Gev's right. It's a beautiful time of year," he said, and then continued telling the story. *Well, we loaded the horses, our sleeping bags, a sack of oats, saddles, and a few other supplies into my Dodge truck. It has high sides and a tailgate. We took off about ten in the morning. Got to Heather Meadows about one, and found a new shelter built by the CCC last summer.*

Hank pushed his chair back, stood up and raised his arms and hands to describe the shelter.

It was probably twenty feet across and had a three-foot high rock wall around the edge of a concrete floor. Six or eight poles held up a sloped shake roof about fifteen feet above the wall. It was like being in the open air with a bit of protection from the rain if the wind wasn't blowing too hard. It was a cool, shady place for picnickers in the summer. There was a table built around a center support log, and a fireplace set off to one side with a grill used for cooking.

Anxious to ride, we ate sandwiches Gev had sent along, saddled up and rode the trail down to Reflection Lake. That was a pretty sight with red sumac on some of the lower slopes and the white glaciers on Mount Shuksan. We met a few tourists having picnics and hiking. After about four hours we headed back to set up our camp for the night. The horses sniffed the air and acted excited. When we got to the camp site, we found a black bear on the truck with his nose in the sack of grain.

Hank looked at his sons. "What should we do with a bear?"

The boys looked at each other, giggled and said in unison, "Take him for a ride!"

We tied the horses to the support poles of the shelter, closed the tailgate, drove a couple miles, stopped and let down the ramp. The bear walked down the planks, and without a glance our way ran off into the heather.

We woke with the sun the next morning, fed the horses and had some hotcakes. I'd made a big box hinged with a lid to keep our food. We tied a rope around it and hoisted it to the rafters of the shelter, saddled up and took off toward Austin Pass. We stopped now and then to rest the horses and snack on blueberries.

We rode back into camp late in the afternoon. Ted pointed and said, "Looks like we've had company." We found the box still hanging from the rafters, but the lid was open and all the food stuffs lay scattered on the table and floor. We saved what we could and decided to stay one more night.

Kelly said, "This is the scary part, isn't it Dad?"

Hank smiled at him. "Yes, son, it was scary."

Ted and I always kept a fire going during the night, and slept in our sleeping bags with our feet to the fire. About four in the morning, the horses woke us with their whinnying and snorts. I shined my flashlight around and saw a bear walking around their legs. I put my fingers to my lips, whistled and he ran away. We pulled on our boots, got up and found the bear had left paw prints around our heads.

Pauline put a hand to her mouth. "Oh, my."

Kelly looked at her. "Do you think that was scary?"

"Yes, very scary."

Ted started frying bacon and hotcakes while I fed the horses.

Hank looked around at everyone. "Nothing smells better than bacon frying over a fire, and I guess that bear thought so, too."

We were just about ready to eat when the horses started up again, stomping their feet and snorting. We backed away from the fire and watched that bear run over to the grill. There was a loud clatter. With one big swipe of his paw, he knocked the fry pan onto the concrete floor, grabbed the bacon and ran out into the brush a few feet from the shelter. The horses were nervous, stomping side to side and neighing. We waved our arms and shouted, but that didn't faze the bear. Ted asked me what I thought we should do. I knew the bear would come back and keep bothering us and the horses, so I said, "Let's try to tie him up to one of the support poles, and then we can load the horses."

Hank looked at Fred. "See, I was afraid once we untied the horses to load them in the truck, they might get more excited." *Ted asked me how I thought I'd get a rope around him. I told him my idea and he went along with it. He brought a long rope from the truck. I laid a garbage can on its side and looped the rope around the opening of it. All this time the bear walked back and forth sniffing the ground.*

Chris said, "Dad wasn't even afraid of him."

Kelly said, "That's because the bear was used to people."

Hank continued, *He'd been getting fat off the food left behind by the summer picnickers. He wasn't afraid of us. Ted threw a hotcake close to him, and then another one closer to the garbage can. Those cakes got gobbled up and I told Ted, "Throw one in the can." He did. The bear sniffed around the can and then went head first into it. I flicked the rope. It caught him around his middle and I pulled it tight. He backed out of there, stood on his hind legs, let out a roar and pawed the air. I climbed up on the table and took the rope around the center post.*

Chris turned to Pauline and Fred. "This is the real

scariest part."

"Yeah," agreed Kelly.

I pulled on the rope to tie it to the pole, but before I could, he came up on the table after me. We were eye to eye. I jumped down, and pulled the rope around him and the pole. He growled and fought the rope all the time, but I kept going around the table snugging him tighter to the pole. Ted asked me what I was going to do with him. I said to give me the axe.

I got back up on the table. The bear snarled with his mouth open and showed his fangs. He had one paw loose from the rope and lashed out at me.

Kelly said, "Show them your scar, Dad."

Hank turned his head to the side. Pauline and Fred saw a short scar on Hank's neck. He said, "It just bled a little, but those claws were long and sharp." He pulled the collar of his shirt up and went back to his story.

So, I raised the axe, but he grabbed at me and the axe flew out of my hand. Ted handed it back to me. I raised my arms and with a forceful swing, I brought the blunt end down on his head. I heard his skull crack. He slumped and hung limply to the pole.

Chris raised an arm up and brought it down on the table. "Dead!"

Hank continued, *Ted wanted to drag the bear about twenty feet and hide it behind some bushes, but I said, "No, let's take him home and I'll get the hide tanned for a rug." So we loaded the horses, and then hoisted the bear into the truck, covered it with a tarp, put the tailgate up and came home.*

Fred asked, "How much do you think he weighed?"

"Oh, he must've been about two hundred pounds, about all we could do to throw him up into the truck, and boy, did he stink."

"And they didn't even bring home their box," said Kelly.

"Nope," Hank laughed, "for all I know, it's still hanging from the rafters."

The boys looked at each other mischievously and started giggling."

"Shall we?" asked Chris.

Kelly scooted out of his chair and started toward the door to the hall. "I'll do it."

"No," said Chris. "It was my idea."

"Wasn't either. We thought it at the same time."

"Okay, we'll both do it."

Pauline heard a door open and then close, then giggles and a growling noise. Gev and Hank laughed. Pauline and Fred looked toward the hall. Chris came in on his hands and knees with the bear rug draped over his back. Kelly lashed at him with a Lincoln Log stick to make him move.

Pauline and Fred laughed. She asked, "Is the fur soft?"

Chris crawled over to her and rubbed against her leg making growling noises. She laughed again and put her hand out. "Feel it Fred, it's really coarse."

"My turn," said Kelly.

Pauline laughed as Kelly pulled the rug over his back, and on his hands and knees and growling like a bear, he and Chris disappeared down the hallway.

Gev put her hands on her knees and got up. "I'll bring coffee and Pauline's rolls."

Hank opened the drawer under the table top and brought

out the cards. They passed a pleasant evening playing and chatting. Around ten o'clock Fred said, "Well, we'd best be going, Pauline. Hank and I both have to get up for work tomorrow and we still have to drive home."

Pauline hugged Gev while Hank and Fred shook hands. "Next time you come to our house," Pauline said as they walked out to the truck.

"Sounds great," Hank replied, and they waved goodbye as Fred drove down the driveway.

Chapter Fifty-Three... Water Witching

Pauline put the last dish in the cupboard, gave the counter a final swipe, hung her apron on the towel rack, and then sat in her rocker beside Fred in his chair. "I had a nice talk with Jenny this morning. We sat on the rocks by the spring. I was surprised you didn't tell me about the daffodils."

"I meant to surprise you with a bouquet."

They heard a loud knock on the door and Will came in.

Pauline asked, "Is everything all right? How's Marian?"

"Oh, I think she's feeling better. She and Jenny made supper together and I heard them laughing when they did the dishes. I brought your goats back."

"Back?" asked Fred. "I didn't know they were gone."

"Yep, I found them in the ditch by the road." He sat at the table, crossed his legs and leaned back in the chair.

"Wow. Thanks, Will. I must have forgotten to latch their gate. I've got a lot on my mind."

"Is something bothering you?"

"I've decided to do it."

"Do what?" asked Will.

"Dig my well."

"I think it's a crazy idea. Why not just pipe water down from the spring?"

"No, I don't want to dig a ditch to bury it," Fred countered. "I want a well."

Will asked, "Where do you think you'll start digging? If you're really serious, you should ask Bert Van Zef to witch it."

"To witch it?" asked Pauline.

"Yeah, the idea of water witching is old, but seems to work. Some people have a knack for finding water underground by holding a stick as they walk back and forth over the ground. The stick twitches if it detects water."

Pauline said, "Will, that sounds ridiculous. Are you serious?"

"Sure am. You should get Bert out here. He's been witching for years."

Bert Van Zef came Saturday morning and after pleasantries were exchanged, Pauline followed the men out. Bert walked to a sapling willow tree and cut a thin Y-shaped branch. She watched Fred and Will walk beside him over the ground. *How silly they look, three grown men walking around with a stick.*

Bert said, "Here, do you see it twitching?"

Fred and Will said in unison, "Nope."

"I feel it in my hands," said Bert.

Will asked, "How many feet deep?"

"Twenty, maybe thirty or so."

Amused, Pauline continued listening to the men standing with hands in their pockets, looking down at the ground, bantering ideas around.

Fred shuffled his feet, kicked a rock, and they watched it hop down the driveway. "I'm going to do it."

Will shook his head. "You're going to hit hardpan clay at about six inches after you get down through the sod and gravel. All I can say is good luck. I'll leave you to it." He patted Fred on the shoulder. "I've got chores to do." He walked to his truck, and called, "See ya, Bert."

Pauline put her hand on Fred's arm, and when there was a break in their conversation said, "Come in and have coffee, Bert."

His face broke out in a big grin. "That will be nice."

Seated at the table, stirring sugar and cream into his coffee, Bert said, "Will is right, Fred. Digging in this hardpan, why, it'll take more work than it's worth. You wouldn't have to bury a pipe very deep, maybe nine, ten inches."

Fred was quiet, twiddling his thumbs and thinking. Then he answered, "I don't know, it would just be convenient to have a well with an electric pump."

Pauline offered more coffee and cookies, but Bert put his hand up. "No, no. Best I be on my way home."

Fred walked Bert out to his Model T. Pauline rushed out of the house with a green Pyrex bowl filled with eggs nestled in a linen napkin, and called, "Wait, Bert, here are some eggs for Thea."

Bert smiled as he took the bowl of eight colorful eggs. "I think the Easter Bunny's come already. Thea will be pleased." He waved and called, "Hope you find water, Fred."

Fred went to his shop, brought out tools and started to work. Pauline watched him swing a pickaxe at the turf and dirt to clear a space to start digging the hole. She heard a thump when it hit a rock. Fred let go of the handle and shook his hands. "That stung!" Using a rock as a fulcrum, he pried the boulder loose. Then down on his hands and knees, he muscled it out of the hole, and rolled it to aside.

When rocks and dirt lay in loose piles, he shoveled them into the wheelbarrow, and then dumped it into a low area behind a stand of brush. He pushed back his hat. "Can you bring me some water, Pauline?"

"Yes, dear."

Fred wiped his brow with his red bandana, leaned on his shovel and waited.

She brought water and a cookie, which he ate in two bites. "Thanks, I thought after all the rain the ground would be softer."

"How big a hole do you have to dig?"

He thought for a minute and then reasoned, "It will have to be roomy enough to swing a pick- axe and use a shovel."

"That makes sense," said Pauline. "Come in and rest before supper."

"I'll give it another go."

The next day Fred swung his pickaxe and shoveled until his muscles ached. At bedtime he suggested, "Pauline, maybe you could rub on some of that liniment."

She massaged his shoulders and back. With a final pat, she said, "Okay, off to bed with you. Tomorrow you work with Otto."

After a restless night, Fred told Pauline he was concerned about how many feet he'd have to dig to reach water.

"Maybe Will's right, dear. Would it be terribly hard to pipe the water from the spring?"

"I'd still have to dig to bury the pipe so it wouldn't freeze in the winter, and I'd have to dig out a lot of Oregon grape, snowberry and rosebushes. That's no easy job."

Longer April days gave Fred time to dig for a couple of hours after he came home from work, and bit by bit he stood deeper in the hole. Eventually he could only throw the dirt to the top edge, and as it piled up, some dirt rolled back down.

He called to Pauline, "Can you help me? Could you pull the dirt away from the edge?"

Pauline used a hoe, and then a rake. Not used to that kind of work, her arms and shoulders got sore, but, still, every night when Fred came home and dug in his hole, she went out and helped. She tried not to complain, and occasionally lay down in the grass and pulled her knees up to her chest to get the kinks out of her back.

The time came when Fred couldn't throw the dirt up to the top of the hole. He told Pauline that he would tie a rope to the handles of two buckets, and when one was full, she could pull it up, dump it into the wheelbarrow and take it away while he filled the other bucket. "Just half-full so they won't be too heavy."

After several trips with the wheelbarrow, Pauline said, "Fred, it's too much for me."

He crawled up out of the hole. "We're both tired. Let's go in." After supper Fred said, "Tomorrow I'm going to the Co-op to get a ladder."

The next morning he wasn't surprised when Pauline jumped into the truck. "I need a few groceries," she said.

While Fred looked at ladders, Pauline gave Bernie her

list and cruised the candy case. "Bernie, I'll have three sticks of licorice and a few white pop-ins for Fred."

She moved aside when Fred brought a ladder, leaned it against the counter and pulled out his wallet.

Bernie said, "You know you have to be careful with ladders, Fred. Have you heard the story about old Gus Volker?

"No, that's one I haven't heard. Let's hear it."

"Yes," said Pauline. "We're always ready for a good story."

Chapter-Fifty-Four... Bernie Tells a Story

Bernie sat on his stool, folded his arms on the counter and began, *Old Gus and his wife, Hilda, came from Germany and settled here on the island back in the twenties. They bought a little house on a few acres near the Tea and Coffee Road.*

"That's such a funny name for a road," said Pauline.

"Yeah, the county renamed it Troxell Road, but some folks out your way still call the road west of Monkey Hill, Tea and Coffee." Bernie continued, *So, Gus started raising chickens and Hilda made friends with the neighbor ladies. Gus decided he had to have a well. He had Van Eck witch one and he got started, digging through rocks and clay, much like you're doing. He had Hilda help him and every day they made some progress to the point where Gus couldn't get in and out of the hole so he used a ladder. Once Gus was down there, Hilda would take the ladder up. He had dug down about fifteen feet. Hilda thought she needed a day off. She wanted to invite the neighbor ladies for afternoon coffee. Gus told her okay, he'd take a few hours off and go to town. That evening Hilda made phone calls to her neighbor ladies.*

One Friday, Gus climbed down into the hole, Hilda pulled up the ladder, set it to the side, and then hauled up a bucket of dirt. Suddenly, she cried out, "Oh, mien Gott! mien Gott! The ladies are coming today! Gus, the ladies are coming!"

She let the bucket down to Gus and rushed into the house to bake a cake. After putting the cake in the oven, she ran out and hauled up a bucket of dirt. Back and forth she went, checking the cake, tidying up the house, hauling up a filled bucket, emptying out the dirt, letting the bucket down to Gus, back to the house to make coffee and change her dress, then out again.

"Gosh," said Pauline, "she must have gotten tired."

Bernie laughed and continued his story, *Well, when she heard a car coming up the hill, she let an empty bucket down to Gus, rushed into the house, took off her apron and greeted her company.*

The ladies started talking gossip the way women do when they get together. Poor Gus, forgotten in the well, yelled and yelled to no avail. He turned the bucket upside down, sat on it and waited. The afternoon slipped away. Down in the well, Gus heard the starting welcome of a car motor. He called again and again, but they didn't hear him.

In the house, Hilda carried her pretty china teacups and cake plates to the sink and thought about the tidbits of gossip she would tell Gus.

"Gus...Oh, mein Gott! Oh, mein Gott! Poor Gus, I left him in the well!" She rushed out the door and ran to the well. Looking down, she called, "Gus! Gustave, are you down there?"

Gus stood up from his overturned bucket, put his hands on his hips and declared, "Woman! Where do you think I am? Do you think I sprouted wings?"

Bernie laughed. "I can hear her now asking him if he would be good to her. It was a couple of days before he would even talk to her. She promised all kinds of favors."

Fred said, "That's quite a story." He looked at Pauline and teased, "Would you forget me?"

"Dear, how could I forget *you*?" She turned to Bernie and asked, "Did they finish digging the well?"

"No, Gus gave up on the well, and a few weeks later he sold the place and they moved off the island."

Back home, Fred lowered the ladder into the hole and climbed down. Pauline pulled the ladder up and out of the way to give Fred room to work. She let the bucket down, pulled it up when Fred called, "Ready!" and then dumped it into the wheelbarrow. Up and down, up and down. Finally, she called down to him, "Fred, I'm tired. My back hurts."

"All right, now don't be a Hilda, put the ladder down and I'll come up. Maybe," he smiled up at her, "you have some cookies?"

"Do you promise to be good to me?" she teased, and then she put down the ladder. They both chuckled remembering the story about Gus and Hilda.

"Pauline, I feel stronger than ever." He held his arm out and she felt his muscles, tight under his shirt.

"Feel *my* muscles." She held out her arm.

He squeezed it gently. "Yep, you're a real work-horse."

"You're making fun of me."

"Well, just a little," he laughed. "Hey, come down in the well and I'll show you something interesting. I know you can climb ladders."

"How deep is it?"

"About twelve feet."

She climbed down, and jumped off the last rung. "It smells musty."

"Yeah, but look at the walls."

They marveled at the layers of tan clay, sand, pockets of gravel, and bands of damp blue-clay. Water trickled down the sides and puddled at their feet.

"Hey, down there!"

Pauline and Fred looked up to see a fellow sporting a red beard.

"Do we know you?" kidded Fred.

"It's Rupert!" exclaimed Pauline.

"So it is," said Fred. "Pauline's just coming up."

As she reached the top, Rupert helped her step off the ladder and asked, "When did you start this project?"

"About ten days ago." She gave him a mischievous look. "What's all that red stuff on your face?"

Rupert stroked his beard. "Everyone on our team is growing one for good luck."

"What team is this?" asked Fred, as he stepped off the ladder.

"Baseball. Next Sunday we play a team of C's in Anacortes."

"Remember, Fred, we saw his picture on the bulletin board." She looked at Rupert. "Your team was holding a trophy."

"Yeah, we were pretty good last year." He turned to Fred. "Do you want help with your digging?"

Pauline had an impish grin. "Say yes, Fred."

"Sounds like Pauline wants me to help," said Rupert.

Fred scratched his head. "Well, I need a better way to get the dirt up."

"You mean like a windlass?"

"Yeah, I guess that's what I'm thinking."

Pauline listened while Fred and Rupert discussed how they could make a windlass.

"Let's go to the woods and cut the right size log," said Rupert. "First, though, I want to tell you my news. You know I told you a man wanted to buy my property?"

"Yes, I remember," said Pauline.

"Well, my aunt sold Gramma's house and land for six hundred dollars. She put it in a bank for me."

"That's wonderful, Rupert!"

"It's not as much as Grampa paid for it, but I guess now days that's all it's worth."

"That's a good chunk of money," said Fred. "What are you going to do with it?"

"I guess just leave it in the bank until I get out of the C's. I have a couple months to think about it."

"That sounds like a smart plan. I'll get the axe and saw from the shed and then let's go find a log for a windlass."

Chapter-Fifty-Five... It Happened So Fast

Pauline followed the men into the woods and listened to them debate about which tree would be the right size. Tired of waiting for them, she called, "I'm going back, Fred. I'll make some lunch." As she weaved around brush and stepped over moss-covered branches that littered the ground, she broke off twigs of wild red flowering currant. *These will be colorful on the table.* She stopped at the edge of the clearing and sniffed. *It smells like smoke.* She looked toward the house and saw flames coming out of the chimney. "Fred! Fred! The house! Fire!" Frantically, she ran toward the house and through the garden.

Fred and Rupert ran past her. Fred yelled, "Chimney fire! I'll get the ladder from the well!"

Pauline watched as Fred leaned the ladder against the house and then started to climb. He carried a bucket of water that Rupert had handed to him. Reaching the top of the roof, he threw the water on a smoking spot.

Pauline saw smoke coming out from under the eaves. "Oh, no! The house is on fire, Fred!" Flames spewed out from the eaves and up around the roof. "My quilt!" She ran into the house.

She heard Rupert call, "It's useless, Fred! Come down!"

Fred scrambled down the ladder and rushed into the house. "Pauline, get out!"

"I have to get my grandmother's quilt! And Grandpa's clock!" She yanked the quilt off the bed and grabbed the clock from the dresser.

Rupert shouted, "Get out, Pauline and stay out! The ceiling will fall!"

"My Singer, Fred!" she screamed as she hurried down the porch steps, ran to the apple tree and dropped her load on the grass.

Coming out of the house with the sewing machine, Fred called, "Pauline, let the chickens and goats out of their pens."

"Save my Toperator!" she yelled.

Rupert carried out a rocking chair. Fred pulled the washing machine off the porch and dragged it away.

Pauline opened the coop and chased the cackling chickens out. The goats ran to the grass when she opened their door. She heard glass popping. Smoke and flames poured out of the shattered windows and into the lean-to.

She heard the brakes of Will's truck screech and ran to him. He pushed her aside. "Back Fred's truck out of the way," he ordered. "Fred, let's get water on the shed!"

Rupert and Fred grabbed water buckets from the porch and rushed to the shed. The water sizzled as it hit the walls. Steam rose from the roof.

Alice and Joe Andrews drove up in their truck. Alice hurried to Pauline and pulled her back from the heat. Joe took buckets from his truck and dashed water onto the shed.

"It's too late," said Fred.

"No, keep the water coming, let's save the shed and the outhouse," said Will.

Two more neighbors drove up and joined in. One brought a bucket of water from the spring and handed it off to another and he to another who then splashed the water onto the scorching boards.

The fire roared, the heat intense. The roof and walls of the house collapsed. Ash and sparks filled the air. Pauline held her hands to shield her face. The fire crackled. Flames leaped into the air, reaching out like arms to torch anything within reach. Everyone stood back in awe as flames consumed the old house.

"Oh, Fred, our house. Why?"

He put an arm around her waist and she leaned into him.

Marian drove up in her car, hurried to Pauline and Fred, embraced them, and then said, "Come, Pauline, you don't have to watch this."

"No. I can't leave."

Fred said, "Yes, go with Marian."

"Come, Pauline." said Marian, taking her arm. "You, too, Alice."

"Wait," said Pauline. "I want to get my things."

They put everything Pauline had snatched out of the house onto the quilt, and carried the bundle to Marian's car.

At Marian's house, Pauline laid the saved things on the floor and looked down at them. "I didn't know what I was doing," she said. "I just grabbed anything I could. I couldn't go back into the bedroom. Rupert pushed me out. I lost all my clothes and my good shoes." She started laughing hysterically and put a hand to her mouth. "My purple shoes."

"Yes," said Marian. "Your beautiful shoes, but they can be replaced."

Pauline said, "Here I am in my dirty Paulie-alls, sitting on your floor with my quilt and my clock. And I saved my journal." She held it to her chest. "It was on the table." She paused and looked at Marian. "It seems like I should cry."

Alice helped her to sit on the couch, held her, and with a soothing, comforting voice said, "You're in shock. You'll cry later." Pauline rested her head on Alice's shoulder. Alice hummed and rocked her back and forth. Pauline closed her eyes.

They heard voices and footsteps as Will, Joe, Rupert and Fred came onto the porch and into the house. Fred went to Pauline, reached into his pocket and brought out her childhood piggy bank. "I grabbed it from the windowsill." Pauline started to cry. Fred held her tight.

Marian gathered everyone to her large oak table. "Come and eat. You must be starving. You had no lunch, and it's way past supper time." She served sandwiches and coffee. Pauline sat by Fred, his arm about her. The men talked about creosote in the chimney, and said the fire spread through the cracks where the mortar had burned out from between the bricks.

In a daze, Pauline listened and heard them say that the shed had lost part of the roof and one wall charred.

Will pushed back his chair. "The cows are calling me."

Rupert stood and said, "I'll give you a hand."

Joe said, "Come Alice, we have cows waiting for us, too."

Chapter Fifty-Six... After the Fire

The next morning Fred and Pauline drove up to their place. Here and there smoke rose from the smoldering ashes on the ground. The stove, covered with fallen bricks and ash, stood alone with more bricks scattered around it.

Pauline saw the rocker and her Toperator, the kitchen table and four chairs near the apple tree, coats and boots helter-skelter about them.

Fred said, "This is all we could carry out before the smoke and heat were too great."

"Oh, but you saved the flat top trunk."

"Yes, that's the last thing we got, couldn't go back for the other two."

"Your tools, Fred, they were saved?"

"Yes, everything in the shed is fine. The outhouse is fine, too." Fred picked up a stick and poked through the ashes, turning charred pieces of wood over. He bent down and picked up a small object. "Looky here," he brushed the ash from the vase and handed it to her.

She held the blackened Hull vase. "It was my mother's."

They turned at the sound of a car. "It's Hank and

Gev," said Fred.

Gev and Pauline hugged. Hank shook Fred's hand. "News travels fast, Fred."

The men walked around and talked. Pauline told Gev about the few things they had saved and then the four friends sat in the four yellow chairs at the table under the old apple tree.

Fred put one hand over Pauline's. "Dear, Hank and Gev have made us a proposition. Remember I told you they've never finished the second floor of their house, but when they have the money would hire me to do the work?"

"Yes, I remember that Gev wants cupboards like you built for me."

Gev agreed, "That's right, I do."

Fred said, "Hank has offered to trade a piece of his beach property for my work."

Pauline's eyes got big, and she looked at Hank. "Are you kidding?"

Hank laughed. "Nope."

"Oh, my! A house near the beach. That's been my dream."

Once again Marian and Will opened their home to Pauline and Fred. Wearing her sister-in-law's blue robe, Pauline sat hunched over the kitchen table. With one finger, she absent-mindedly traced the flowers on the oil-cloth cover. She looked at Marian mixing batter for hotcakes. "I don't know what we'd do without you and Will."

"You and Fred would do the same for us, dear. Fred said you tossed and turned all night and finally settled down about four. We decided you should sleep, so he had a cup of coffee and left for work. He said he'll have lunch with Otto."

"His overalls must have been filthy."

"They were. Will gave him a pair of his and a clean shirt. I hear Will on the porch now. After breakfast you and I will rummage through my closet and find something for you."

Will came in with a large cardboard box and set it on the table. "Look what I found on the porch, and with your name on it."

Pauline asked, "What is it? Who brought it?"

"That, is something you'll probably never know. Someone in the community wants to help."

Pauline opened the box.

Marian said, "Let's eat before you look through it. Will, can you take it to the bedroom?"

Pauline followed him into the bedroom. "I can't wait, Will. You go eat. I'll come in a minute." A folded, faded housedress was on top. She laid it on the bed and then took out a long-sleeved, black wool sweater with frayed cuffs. She found a sauce pan with a lid, and then four cups and saucers wrapped in two used bath towels.

She put on the cotton print dress and went back to the kitchen. "I think someone gave up one of her dear possessions to help me."

"That's what neighbors do in our community; share what they have," said Will.

"How can I thank her?"

"You won't likely get the chance," he said. "People are proud and don't expect to be thanked." He got up and put on his hat. "I'll see you gals later. I've got work to do."

After helping Marian with the dishes, Pauline went to

the bedroom.

Marian found her sitting on the floor, taking things from her trunk. Pauline said, "I'm so glad Fred saved the flat-top trunk. It has our birth certificates, marriage license, and a few pictures." She held up the framed pictures of her mother and father and one of Fred's father and mother." She wiped away tears with the back of her hand. "Here's the pocket watch that belonged to Fred's father." She wound it and listened to the steady ticking.

Marian said, "Fred should use it. It's silly to leave it in the trunk."

"He's afraid he'll lose it."

Marian got up. "I'm going out to the garden and pull weeds. They love these warm days."

Pauline said, "I'll put this stuff away, and then I'm going to walk up to my place."

"You sure?"

"Yes, I want to find Billy and Nanny and look at my garden."

Marian said, "Rupert found the goats lying near the spring and brought them down last night."

"He did?"

"They're with the cows in the pasture."

"Oh, I'm so glad. I'll go up anyway. Maybe I can find my chickens."

"Okay, see you for lunch."

Pauline walked up to the old home. The apple tree in full bloom and the lilac just starting to show a bit of purple were both dusted with ash. She poked around the cold, gray ashes with a stick, picked up pieces of broken pottery, and let them fall from her hands. They raised puffs of dust where they landed. She found a hunk of twisted metal. *It's my favorite pie pan, and here's my cast iron skillet. I bet I can clean it up.* She looked at the garden and thought of the days spent working in the soil. Dusty green leaves poked up through the ash that covered the potato patch.

She walked to the shed, opened the door and saw the four chairs stacked on top of the yellow table. The door on the old wardrobe was ajar. Pauline smiled when she saw Ruby's sewing basket, glad they had stored it here for Rupert. *Someday he will want it.* She filled a can with grain, went out and called, "Here chick, chick, chick." A few hens hurried skiddle-skaddle as she scattered the wheat around the yard. She laughed and felt a heaviness leave her chest.

Making her way around the rose brambles up to the spring, she kneeled on the rocks that lined the pool and saw her reflection in the clear water. *Oh, my hair. I should ask Marian to cut it.* She dipped her hands in the water and patted some on her warm face. When she looked up, two fawns stood a short distance away watching her. She sat back, took off her shoes and Marian's borrowed socks and put her feet into the pool. The fawns darted into the underbrush.

Walking down Ducken Road, she thought about the beach property. *Everything's going to be all right, it will just take time.* She smiled at the fluffy clouds and began humming. She walked with a little bounce in her steps to her brother's house.

Will was coming from the barn. "Do I hear you singing?"

"Yes, Will. Everything's going be all right."

They heard Marian call, "Come on you two. The soup's hot."

Will held the screen door.

Pauline said, "It always smells good in your kitchen, Marian, and I've worked up a bit of an appetite."

"What kind of work have you been doing?" asked Will.

"Well, not so much, just walked up to have a look around. My crock of sauerkraut is just sitting there black on the outside and the top is covered with ash. Do you think it's still okay?"

Will grinned at his sister. "It might be well-cooked, but no, I wouldn't mess with it. The crock is probably cracked."

"A few of the hens came when I threw out grain. I hope I can catch them."

"Sure you can. Just hook them with your pole and put them in a gunny sack. We'll add them to Marian's flock."

"I'll wait until Fred can go up with me."

Will scraped the last bit of pea soup from his bowl. "Good as usual, Marian." He gave his wife a playful pat on her rear as she cleared the table. "Fred told me about Hank's offer."

Pauline said, "When he comes home, maybe we can go look at the property."

Fred returned early and said he'd like go out to Hank's.

Pauline took his arm. "Will and Marian would like to go too, dear."

The four settled into Will's car. Pauline sat with Marian in the back and listened to the men.

Fred said, "I told Otto about the property. He got excited and suggested we might like to build a cabin."

Pauline leaned forward and asked, "What? Not a house?"

Fred looked back at her. "It would be a house, but built with logs."

Pauline relaxed in her seat. "What do you think of that idea, Marian?"

"I like it. Gev's brother has a beautiful log cabin near the beach. Hank's proposition to you isn't the first one he's made. He has a way of trading his property for what others do for him."

They found Gev gathering clothes from her wire lines. "Here, let us help," said Pauline. She and Marian unpinned sheets, folded and put them in Gev's wicker basket. "Nothing smells as good as fresh laundry," said Pauline.

"You're wrong there, Pauline," said Fred. "Bread, just out of the oven, is better."

"I'm with Fred on that," said Will.

Fred carried the large basket of dried wash to the house. "We think it would be nice to look at the beach property, Gev."

She said, "Let's walk and find Hank. He's working on a fence on the other side of the lagoon."

They followed her, single-file, on a path down a bank to the gravel road that went to the beach. They crossed a bridge over the lagoon and walked past the sandy area where Hank had built an arena for showing cattle. Gev cupped her hands to her mouth and called, "Hank! Come walk with us."

He waved, put his hammer in the loop sewn on one leg of his overalls and came over to them. The men shook hands. Hank said, "We can take a short-cut over here." He led the way on a narrow path through wind-blown crabapple trees past the picnic grounds.

"Marian and Will brought us to the Grange picnic here," said Pauline.

"That's right," said Gev, "when we first met, and we've had some swell times since then."

"Yes, we have, and I'm going to love being your neighbor, Gev." She took a deep breath. "Mmm, that fresh salty air. I love it."

Hank stopped and pointed. "Gev's brother built the log cabin just up the beach from here. We pipe water down this way from our well, and we can hook into that for you."

"You mean I won't have to dig a well?" asked Fred.

"Nope," said Hank. "We've got lots of water to share. I've picked out a spot I think you'll like on the top of a knoll. You'd have a great view."

They reached the high spot, and Fred asked, "It's not far from the beach, does the high tide ever come in this far?"

"There's enough berm to keep the water from reaching here. It would have to be a giant storm to flood," said Hank.

The women walked a few hundred feet through tall blue-green beach grass and sat on a big log. They watched waves rush over mounds of gravel, and then recede again and again pulling the little stones back and forth. Pauline said, "It sounds like music."

She heard Hank say, "No, Fred, you need to get the logs for the cabin before you start the work in my house. This is the best time to peel logs. Ted and I will cut and pull the logs from the woods with my team, but it'll be up to you to skin the bark off." He winked at Gev, grinned and looked at Pauline. "That will be a good job for you."

"What will I do?"

"Peel the logs. I have a spud you can use."

"Oh, I get to use the spud? Just like the C's at the park?"

Hank said, "Yep, you'll learn pretty fast."

Later at Marian's house, Fred sketched a floor plan and showed it to Pauline. "I think we'd like a large window in the living room with a view."

She said, "Yes, and it would be nice to see the beach from the kitchen window. I'd like morning sun in the kitchen, too."

"The beach is on the west side. I don't know if you can have both. I'll play around with this and talk with Otto." Fred penciled in a kitchen window. "I think one bedroom will be enough."

"Two would be nice," she said.

"Well, we need to keep it small. Hank is being generous to give us the logs and do so much work."

"Yes, that's certainly true."

He drew built-in benches on each side of the fireplace and asked, "How do you like this?"

"That's a good idea," she said. "Then we'll have space for Marie and Glenn when they visit."

"When's that? You haven't told me."

"I'm hoping they'll come sometime."

"Well, I'm going to stop by Hank's on my way home from work tomorrow and show him the plan. I've got a lot to learn about building a cabin, but Otto will take charge in exchange for some of my work." Fred folded the paper.

They looked up when a car door slammed. Pauline went to a window and pulled back the lace curtain. "It's Jenny!

And there's Rupert kissing her and she's kissing him back. Now Rupert's getting into the car, but here comes Jenny."

She opened the door. "Jenny, I didn't know you were coming home."

"Neither does Mom." She gave her aunt a big hug. "I got a ride to the ferry with my friends who live in Anacortes, and Rupert and one of his friends met me on this side." She came in and greeted her uncle.

"I didn't know Rupert had a car," said Fred.

"He doesn't. He and some of the C's are friends with a couple of the local guys and one of them brought Rupert to meet me. I wanted to come home for Easter."

Fred, his blue eyes twinkling, said, "Seems like you had another reason, too."

Pauline sat on the couch and patted it for Jenny to sit beside her. "Your folks are at the barn. They'll be surprised to see you."

Jenny sat beside Pauline. "I know."

"Not just that you're home, but that you're getting on so well with Rupert."

Color rose in Jenny's cheeks. "Oh, you saw him kiss me. You better not tell Mom."

Amused by their conversation, Fred said, "How long do you think your aunt can keep a secret?"

"Are you in love, Jenny?" asked Pauline.

"Promise not to tell Mom, but I think I am."

"Dear, I won't, but you should tell her, and your father."

"I hope Mom's changed her mind about Rupert," said Jenny. "She wrote in her letters what a big help he was when your house burned, and that he's been helping Dad with chores."

Fred said, "If it hadn't been for Rupert, we'd have lost almost everything."

They heard Marian and Will come up on the porch. "Surprise!" Jenny exclaimed when her parents came in. After she hugged them, they wanted to know how she'd gotten home. Fred cleared his throat. Pauline nodded her head in Marian's direction.

Jenny hesitated, but then blurted out, "Rupert and his friend met me at the ferry. I wanted to surprise you."

"You did," said her father. He smiled and hugged her again.

Marian looked at Jenny. "I didn't know Easter mattered to you anymore."

"Well, I won't call "yikkity-yikkity" out the door for the bunny to come, but I do like to be with you."

"With us, or with Rupert?" asked Marian.

Jenny blushed. "Oh, Mom, with you and Dad, Aunt Paulie and Uncle Fred."

Fred added, "And Rupert."

"Uncle Fred, stop teasing."

Marian said, "Come in my bedroom while I change my clothes, Jenny."

Will said, "Now, Marian, we've talked about this, don't be too hard on her."

Jenny followed her mother and closed the door.

Pauline cocked her head toward the bedroom door and put a finger to her lips.

When Marian came out a few minutes later, she shrugged her shoulders. "What can I do? She says she's in love. She says they've been writing letters almost every day."

Jenny walked up behind Marian and put her arms around her mother's waist. "Mom, you just have to get to know him."

Pauline said, "I agree with Jenny."

Fred piped up, "He's not afraid of work."

"You're right, Fred," said Will. "He comes up on his days off and milks cows, shovels manure, anything that needs to be done. He doesn't run from work. He's a fine fellow and if Jenny likes him, that's okay by me."

Marian said, "But what about his folks? What about your teaching, Jenny?"

"Mom, I told you, I want to teach. Golly sakes, Rupert and I haven't even talked about getting married. He's just a good friend."

"But you said you love him."

"Yes, I do, but even if we were to marry, it wouldn't be for a year or two."

Will said, "Let it go, Marian. Jenny seems to know what she wants."

"Thanks, Dad." She turned to Marian. "It's going to be okay, Mom. You'll see."

Chapter Fifty-Seven... Sparkle

"Paulie! Paulie!"

She opened the door and saw Will rushing up the porch steps. "What is it?"

"Come on, you wanted to watch a calf being born."

"Oh, sure!" She tugged on her black sweater and hurried after him.

He held a gate open and pointed to a Guernsey cow lying a short distance away. "She's been in labor about an hour."

The cow got up and walked a few steps, sniffing the grass and swishing her tail back and forth. She plopped herself down onto the weedy pasture. Elsie's body moved up and down as her muscles contracted and relaxed. She mooed, and then got up, smelled the ground, walked a few feet, and went down again. She turned her head and looked backward.

"It won't be long now," said Will.

Pauline saw two white feet protruding from the cow's rear.

"Looks like the calf is coming just right," he said.

"How can you tell?"

"The hooves are pointing upward. If they were pointing

down, the calf would be coming breach, backward, and that could mean trouble. A few more heaves and we should be able to see the calf's nose."

The cow heaved and pushed with another contraction.

"Look! There's its pink nose," said Pauline."

The cow rested, and then with a few more contractions, the calf's head appeared. With a final big push, the calf, encased in slimy placenta, slipped out of Elsie's body.

Pauline heard a small whimper from the calf. The cow hauled herself up and mooed. She turned, looked at the calf and mooed again. The calf answered with a tiny m-a-a.

"That's a weak little noise," said Pauline.

"It's enough," said Will. "The mother will always know her calf and the calf will recognize its mother's moo."

The cow began licking her baby with her rough tongue.

"Yuck!" said Pauline.

"All part of the process," said Will.

The calf shook its head and blinked its eyes. Elsie kept licking and murmuring softly.

Will lifted one of the calf's hind legs.

Pauline saw four little pink teats in the white hair. "It's a girl!"

"Yep, a good-sized heifer. Just what I was hoping for." He stood with his hands in his pockets looking a little like a proud papa.

They heard a screech and looked up into a tall nearby fir tree where a large bird sat on a limb staring down at them.

"An eagle," said Pauline.

Will said, "Yeah, just waiting for a chance to swoop down and clean up the afterbirth. The cow usually eats most of it. It helps start the milk flowing."

The calf's head, now licked clean, had a white mark on its brown forehead. Pauline reached down and patted it. The cow stopped licking and shook her head. Pauline stepped back away from the calf.

"Well, Paulie, I guess you've had a show. I'll give the calf a vitamin shot, put a tag in her ear, and think of a name for her."

The calf started moving and kicking its legs.

"It's trying to get up, and it's only a few minutes old," said Pauline.

"It wants to nurse. It'll be running around the pasture before you know it."

Pauline watched the calf struggle a bit and then stand on wobbly legs. It walked a few steps. Elsie reached back and licked the hair on her calf's hip, encouraging it to find a teat. After several tries, and butting its head against Elsie's udder, the calf began sucking. Soon white foamy milk dripped from its mouth.

Pauline reached out, stroked the calf's soft damp hair, and asked, "Can I name her?"

"Sure, pick a good one."

"She's so sweet. Her brown eyes shine so bright. Let's call her Sparkle."

"Sparkle it is."

That evening, Fred walked with Pauline to the pasture and heard every detail about the calf's birth. They found her lying in a grassy spot. Elsie was grazing nearby. Pauline knelt by the calf and petted her, but she got up and took a few steps closer to her mother.

Fred said, "Stand still and maybe she'll come to you."

Pauline held out her hand. "Come, Sparkle. Come see me." Sparkle took hesitant steps, put her nose to the ground, and then walked to Pauline and licked one leg of her Paulie-alls. Pauline put her hand down to pet the calf, but she backed away and went to her mother.

On their way to the house, Fred said, "Okay, now it's my turn to talk. I stopped at Hank's on the way home. He and Ted have a pile of logs ready to be peeled. He said he'll help you get started tomorrow. I can drop you off on my way to work."

"I thought he was kidding," said Pauline.

Fred took her hand. "Hank will show you how and his oldest boy will help. Otto and I will come in the afternoon and stake out the site."

Pauline looked at the piece of iron on the end of the long handle. "So this is a spud. It looks like a big chisel."

"Yep. Watch me." Chris jabbed the sharp iron blade into the bark on a Douglas fir log. "Now I push it under and the bark starts to peel off. Here, you try."

Pauline pushed the spud down into the log, too deep to go under the bark. She tried again and learned to angle the spud just right under the edge of the bark.

Hank said, "That's right. Chris, you watch and make sure she doesn't get too wild with it." He laughed, and then said, "I'll leave you two now. I'm going to help Ted saw down more trees."

Chris taught her how to turn the logs.

"What did you say this thing is called?"

"A peevee."

She looked at the iron hook at the end of the wood handle, put it under the log and with a tug pulled up, the log rolled over.

"When you lift and push so hard, the log rolls too far. Ease up on it." They laughed and Pauline tried again. She got the hang of it and then grabbed the spud again and started peeling. Beneath the bark, the wood felt wet, a bit slimy.

"Look Chris, I peeled a strip of bark almost the whole length of the log and it's all curled up."

"Yep, it's fun to try."

Although Chris was just nine years old, he was strong and chided her when she said her arms ached.

Hank and Ted arrived with Hank's team of horses. Buster and Maud were dragging more logs. Then Gev and Kelly came with lunch packed in James Henry lard buckets.

Fred found them sitting on driftwood logs.

"Here, Fred," said Gev, handing him a sandwich.

"Thanks, I didn't take time to get lunch today." He chomped into the beef and mustard sandwich, swallowed and said, "Otto has recruited two men who've been out of work for several months to come help build the forms for the concrete floor. They should be here any minute."

Hank said, "Otto had Wayne Smith build the fireplaces and chimneys in my house. He's a good worker, and doesn't charge an arm and a leg." Hank looked over at Fred. "Are you going to use bricks or rocks for the fireplace?"

Pauline broke in, "I'd like rocks from the beach, Fred."

"I'm thinking the same," he said.

Pauline put her hands on her knees and pushed herself up. "Well, Chris, I guess it's time for us to get more logs peeled." They headed back to the log pile.

Otto drove up and watched Pauline for a minute. "How's it going?"

"We've got six logs peeled. It's work. I feel it in my back."

Chris laughed and leaned on his spud. He grinned at Otto. "A while ago it was her arms that ached."

Otto said, "Yah, well, I've got a couple men coming tomorrow." He looked at Pauline. "I have another job for you. The men will bring their wives to gather moss in Hank's woods for chinking. You can help them."

"Chinking?"

"We pound moss between the logs to make the walls airtight."

Later at Marian's supper table, Fred announced, "Pauline and I are going to live in a tent at the beach while working on the cabin."

"We are?"

"Yep! Hank has a tent we can use and old army cots we can sleep on. You'll have to cook over a fire pit. We'll be camping. You'll be right there so you can help with our cabin, and I won't have to drive so far," said Fred.

"I've never cooked over a fire and I've never been camping."

"Well, Paulie, there's always a first time," teased her brother.

"It'll be fun, Pauline," said Marian. "I'll help you get things together. I have blankets and pots and dishes you can use. When Will and I first came to Whidbey, we lived in an old chicken coop for three months while we got our house fixed up."

The next few weeks were filled with activity. Hank used his big draft horses to pull a wood platform built on skids to the building site. The platform had three-foot high walls and a pole frame supported the canvas tent.

Fred and Hank dug a deep hole in the sand and lined it with rocks to make a fire pit, and with more rocks built up the sides to support a large iron plate for a stove.

Pauline gathered dried reeds and sticks from the beach to start fires. Gev loaned her a Dutch oven for cooking stews and soups on the iron plate. Marian brought loaves of bread and cookies.

Pauline never tired of watching all the activity. Fred brought cement from the Columbia Lumber Company for the men to mix with sand and gravel from the beach for the floor. Logs were measured and notches cut into the ends.

A fireplace would be at one end of the cabin and a brick chimney for the kitchen stove at the other end. Bill and Pauline talked about rock for the fireplace. She walked the beach looking for granite rocks the right size, and collected rocks that had a layer of white quartz. She showed them to Bill and told him, "I'd like to help make a design."

He put his hand under his hat and scratched his head. "Okay, I'll keep that in mind."

When the workmen had gone home for the day, Fred and Pauline walked over the hardened concrete floor. She said, "It looks so small."

"It seems that way, but you'll see when the cabin is finished, it'll be large enough."

Water and sewer pipes had been laid out before the concrete had been poured. Fred explained, "These pipes are for the kitchen sink on this side of the wall and for a bathroom on the other side."

"Oh, Fred, I didn't know we would have a real bathroom in a cabin."

"When Hank suggested it, I jumped on the idea."

Pauline put her arms around his waist and leaned her head against his chest. "Thank you, dear."

He pulled her chin up and gave her a big smooch. They laughed and held hands while he continued telling her details about the cabin. "We'll have a built-in bed in our bedroom like I'm going to do for Hank's upstairs bedrooms, but ours will be a double bed. I'll make the benches on each side of the fireplace like we talked about."

Pauline said, "Make them wide enough for a person to sleep on. I can sew covers for the bench mattresses. Maybe I'll use material to match the curtains at this end of the cabin."

"I'll build the kitchen cabinets and bedroom closets and dressers. You'll see. Everything will be built-in. You won't have to dust under beds and dressers."

"I'd love to have storage space under the beds for my quilts."

"Okay, I can do that."

They walked to the beach, sat together on a log, and watched the sun go to sleep behind Smith Island. The blue sky held golden clouds. Gulls swam in the still water at slack tide. Fred broke the silence. "I'll talk with Bill about pine lumber."

Pauline said, "I was hoping you'd use pine again. I liked the cabinets you built in our house." With a sad face, she looked at Fred.

He put an arm around her. "I know, dear, I miss our house, too."

Chapter Fifty-Eight... Working on the Cabin

Pauline took one of the yellow chairs from the tent and placed it near the makeshift rock stove she used for cooking. She sat with her feet resting on the rocks and watched the men build the log cabin walls. When a wall of logs reached too high for them to lift another log up, they leaned two poles against the highest log in place, looped ropes around the ends of a new log, and then men on the inside wall pulled on the tops of the ropes making the log roll up the sloping poles. Men on ladders put the new log in place at the top.

Pauline gave Otto a cheery hello when he came to see her. "You need to get to work, young lady, instead of watching the men. Go collect moss for the chinking."

She frowned. "I don't know where to go."

He walked away. "Talk to Hank. He'll tell you where to find it."

Pauline complained to Fred that she didn't like Otto's attitude. "He's grumpy and bossy."

"Don't mind Otto."

"He's treating me like a child."

Fred's eyes twinkled when he laughed. "To him, you are

a child. He's anxious to help us and we need to show our appreciation and be cooperative. Do anything it takes to get the cabin built."

That afternoon two men who had been peeling and notching logs, brought their wives to help gather moss. Pauline liked Betty and Martha from the start. They were her age and good-natured.

Betty said, "Okay, grab a sack and follow me. I know where the best stuff is. I helped gather moss and chink the logs for Gev's brother's cabin."

They walked single file on a deer trail, skirted around blooming wild rose bushes and ducked under hanging twigs. Betty held back blackberry vines for Martha who did the same for Pauline. They stepped over and around roots. "It's a bit marshy up ahead," said Betty. "Pauline, you should be wearing boots."

"I haven't taken time to buy new ones since the fire."

Pauline sloshed through muddy water in her old brown shoes. Red-winged blackbirds rested on tall cattails. She said, "They're my favorite birds." She tried to imitate their call. "Kongaree-kongaree-kongaree." She giggled when Martha and Betty laughed.

Gray-green moss hung from the branches of dead Ocean Spray bushes. Martha grabbed a long strand and held it to her face. "Old Man's Beard."

Pauline pulled a chunk from a low hanging branch. "It's lacey and pretty."

"But it's not the moss we want," said Betty. The trail led them to a grove of second growth fir where tree roots grew over and around stumps of trees that had been logged years ago. Sword ferns stood tall around moss-covered logs lying helter-skelter on the forest floor. Salal grew from tops of huge old stumps. Betty scooped a hand-full of moss from a log and held it out. "This is what we need."

As Pauline gathered the soft green moss, she thought of Rupert's story of when he played in the woods with his mother. She smiled thinking about little men hiding in the nooks and crannies of the old logs and stumps. She asked about the beetles and millipedes. "I hope I won't have these critters in my house."

Betty told her, "Never mind, the moss will be mixed with clay for chinking and the creatures won't live to bother you in the cabin."

When her gunny sack was full, Betty slung it over her shoulder. "Well, let's go. This is enough for one day."

Following her example, Pauline and Martha carried the heavy sacks over their shoulders. Tracing their way back on the trail, the women rested on the trunk of a fallen maple. Pollen glistened in the filtered sunlight through swaying branches. They watched sparrows pick seeds from the ground and flit from bush to bush. Pauline enjoyed the peaceful moments and the companionship of Betty and Martha.

Martha stood, stretched and said, "Wish I'd thought to bring water."

When the women got in sight of the cabin, Betty said, "Looks like the men are wrapping-up work for the day. Tomorrow we'll start chinking." She and Martha got into their cars with their husbands. Betty waved and called, "See you in the morning."

Pauline stood beside Fred and waved back. "They're

nice. We had a good time, but look at my shoes. I need to get new boots."

"The cabin's coming right along," said Fred. "It's becoming a community project. How can we ever thank them all?"

"I know one thing we can do. We can have a big beach party when the cabin is finished."

"Well, it's a start, but maybe we can do more."

"We will, dear. When someone needs help, we'll help them." She put her arm through his and they walked towards the tent. "Would you be happy with a sandwich for supper?"

"Yes, and coffee. I'll bring up more wood for the fire."

The chirping birds woke Pauline early the next morning. She dressed and went to the beach. A lone grey heron waded in a tide pool. Seagulls screamed at one another as they fought over the mussels and clams they dropped on the gravel. Along the water line of the last high tide, she found tiny red crab shells among bits of sticks and seaweed. She collected them in a large clam shell and took them back to show Fred. He had coffee brewing over the fire. Pauline fried bacon and pancakes. They had just finished eating when Otto drove up in his truck.

Fred held out a tin cup full of steaming coffee.

Otto sipped the hot brew. "Now that all the logs are in place, we'll get the roof started. I'll get the women filling in the chinks, and later you can start the daubing."

"This is all new to me, Otto. You'll have to teach me."

"Well, Fred, we don't want bare wood laying on bare wood. Chinks allow for expanding and warping. The women can stuff the chinks with moss. You can follow them and daub clay over it. I had Joe French dig out clay from the cliffs down by Partridge Point. It makes a tight seal on the outside. Keeps the wind and rain out."

Pauline joined Betty and Martha when they arrived with their husbands. The women chatted until Otto called them over and started to explain the process of chinking. Betty reminded him that she had worked on the Kellogg cabin. He said, "I guess you can teach Pauline." He looked at Pauline with a wry smile.

Pauline wasn't sure how to take it, but said, "I know Betty will be a good teacher."

"Okay, let's get to work. Here's what we're going to do." Betty grabbed a handful of moss from a gunny sack and started stuffing it in the cracks between the logs. She used a piece of shingle to jam it in. Martha and Pauline followed her example.

"If you press it in too far, it might go out the other side," said Betty. "Pauline, will you go work from the inside?"

"All right." She took her sack of moss and a shingle and worked opposite Betty and Martha.

Fred found her and approved of her work.

"I hope Otto will think so. He's so critical of me."

"He probably thinks you're still a city girl. You aren't built like these other women. You don't look sturdy and strong."

"I am strong. I showed you my muscles."

Fred laughed. "Maybe you better show Otto your burly muscles."

Later, after everyone had gone home with a promise to come back on Monday, they went to their tent. Pauline stretched out on her cot. "I'll just take a little nap."

She woke up at the sound of voices and looked out to see Fred talking with Chris and Kelly who had come riding bareback on their horses.

"Hi," the boys said in unison when they saw her.

"Well, hello," said Pauline. "We haven't seen you for a while. Is school out for the summer?"

"Yep," said Chris. "School ended the Friday before Memorial Day."

"Where are your shoes?" asked Pauline.

"Mom said it's okay. We go barefoot most the summer."

"You must have tough feet."

Chris laughed. "It takes a while."

Pauline patted the horse's neck. "What's his name?"

"Silver."

"And my horse is Scout, like Tonto's," said Kelly.

Chris teased, "But your horse is really a girl."

"I don't care. Scout's a good name for a girl, too."

Fred said, "Sounds like you boys know about the Lone Ranger."

"Yeah, we listen to it on the radio in the barn when Dad's milking the cows," said Kelly.

Chris remembered, "Dad said to tell you we're digging clams tomorrow morning. Tides gonna be real low 'bout seven. Just bring a shovel and a bucket down in front of our place."

"I think we'll do that," said Fred. "I like clam chowder."

Kelly said, "Come on, let's ride up to the dunes." They turned their horses.

Chris yelled, "Hi-ho Silver, away!" They trotted their

Pintos up the beach.

Pauline called, "Have fun!"

The sun had not broken through the fog when Pauline awoke the next morning. Fred, holding a cup of coffee, looked down at her. "Wake up sleepy-head."

"It's so cold. What time is it, Fred?"

"Six-thirty."

"I'm warm and cozy here. I don't want to get up."

"But we're going clam digging."

"You go." She snuggled down into her blankets.

"Okay, but you're going to miss out on all the fun with Gev." He left the tent.

Pauline thought, *Oh dear, Gev.* She threw back the covers and dressed in her Paulie-alls, a flannel shirt borrowed from Marian, and put on her old brown shoes. "Wait, Fred. I'm coming." She ran and caught up with him, grabbing his arm.

Almost losing his balance, he said, "Hey! Take it easy."

Their shoes sank into wet sand leaving deep footprints. Pauline took a big breath. "Oh, I just love the smell of the beach."

"I've heard you say that often."

"Well, I do. I'll never tire of it. I like to be quiet and listen to the beach sounds, the bubbles popping from the sea creatures in the algae and shallow pools."

Good morning greetings were called back and forth as they approached Hank and Gev, busy with their shovels and their buckets already half-full of clams. Fred and Pauline picked their way over slippery rocks to a sandy area where they found Chris and Kelly on their knees digging for geo-ducks with their hands. Chris said, "See what I found?" He gave a green glass globe the size of a baseball to Pauline. "You can have it."

"Thank you, Chris, but you should add it to your collection."

"Naw, I've got lots."

Fred started digging with his shovel where clams squirt-ed water up through the sand. Water quickly filled the hole. "Pauline, I'll dig and you pick up the clams."

She held up a big blue-black clam. "Wow! Look at this, Fred."

Hank said, "That's a horse clam. Leave it and go for the butter clams."

With their buckets filled, Gev suggested they come for supper. "We'll take the clams home and soak them in water with cornmeal."

Pauline frowned. "That's a funny thing to feed clams."

"They take it in and spit it out along with the sand. Come up this afternoon and we'll clean them together."

After lunch, Pauline walked to Gev's for her lesson in cleaning clams. Fred came later and they all enjoyed clam fritters.

Chapter Fifty-Nine... Jenny's Graduation

"Fred, I have to go to town today, or tomorrow at the latest."

"What's the rush? I thought you were going to help me with the daubing."

"I need a dress and new shoes. I haven't been shopping for any clothes since the fire."

"Are you going someplace?"

"Have you forgotten? We're going to Jenny's graduation and you need a new suit."

"Maybe I'll stay home. I've got a lot of work to do right here."

"And disappoint Jenny? No siree. We're both going."

"Pauline, there's no sense in my going. It'll be a big crowd of people and we won't even see Jenny. Otto has a schedule all worked out."

"Oh, forget Otto! It's our cabin. What will one day mean?"

"No, you go and have a good time. I'll stay and work."

Marian scowled when she learned Fred would not be going to the graduation. Will said he understood Fred's decision. "The only reason I'm going is if I don't, I'll never hear the end of it from Jenny and Marian."

Marian took an envelope from her purse. "Look, four tickets. It's a shame to let one go to waste." She put them back into the envelope. "Who can we invite to take Fred's place?"

"Maybe Jenny can give it to one of her friends."

"Yes, I'll call her tonight. By the way, you probably need something decent to wear. Have you a dress?"

"No, I wish I could make one, Marian, but there isn't time. I told Fred I want to go shopping and I think that's the main reason he doesn't want to go. He would need to buy a new suit. Want to go shopping with me?"

"All right. When can you go?" asked Marian.

"Tomorrow, but can I come take a bath first? I feel so grubby. Taking sponge baths in my tent isn't all that great."

Pauline faced an upset Marian the next morning. "What's the matter?"

"I called Jenny last night. Of course she's disappointed her Uncle Fred isn't coming to her graduation, but she's also delighted, because now she can ask Rupert. Can't you make Fred change his mind?"

"No, Marian, Fred and Otto have made their plans. Why not take Rupert?"

"You know how I feel about him, but you really like him, don't you?"

"Yes. Fred and I think he's a fine young man."

"Jenny will call him tonight, and if he doesn't have a ball game on Saturday, I'll have to call and ask him to ride with us."

"It'll be fun to have Rupert with us. He's probably never been to a college graduation."

"I suppose. Okay, take your bath, towels are under the sink. Come into my bedroom when you're finished."

After her bath, Pauline put on the clean housedress someone had left for her in the box the day after the fire. She saw her reflection in the mirror. *Who is that woman?* She leaned forward to study the lines on her face, grimaced, and using Marian's hand mirror, turned her head from side to side. *Old, that's how I look, just old.*

She heard Marian's tap on the door and said, "I'll be right out."

Marian had laid out two dresses on her bed. She handed Pauline a slip and helped her into a two-piece blue rayon. "No, not for me." Pauline shook her head. "Makes me look old. Have you noticed all my wrinkles?"

"Umm, no, not really." She held up a yellow floral print dress.

Pauline said, "Oh, I like this one. Looks like summer." She slipped the dress over her head and fastened the belt.

Marian said, "It pretty on you, and I have a hat that'll be nice with it."

"I feel terrible going to a shoe store with these messy shoes."

Marian brought a pair of shoes from her closet. "Try these on. I know they'll be a bit big, but we'll put cotton in the toes."

Pauline stuffed wads of cotton into the shoes. She stood and tried to wiggle her toes. "I guess I can keep them on. I'm ready." She followed Marian out to her car.

"The Co-op doesn't have much for fashion," said Marian, leading the way into the store.

Pauline said, "It'll be nice to see Bernie."

He greeted them with a big smile. "Hello, ladies. Haven't seen you for a while."

Pauline said, "I've been busy filling the chinks between the logs for our cabin."

"Fred was in yesterday and told me the roof is going on today. Work goes fast when you have lots of help."

"Yes, many folks have been so good to us."

Bernie said, "That's the way it is in our community, we help each other."

Marian asked, "Bernie, do you know our Jenny is graduating from college?"

"How can that be? Seems that young lady has grown up awfully fast."

"She hopes to find a job teaching home economics."

"The High School's going to need a teacher. Edith Wilson's getting married."

Marian's eyes lit up. "Oh, I'm going to tell Jenny to apply right away. It will make her so happy."

"I know someone else it will make happy," said Pauline.

Marian said, "Yes, I will love having Jenny home."

"I wasn't really thinking of you, Marian."

Marian frowned and said, "Oh, I suppose you're thinking of Rupert. Shall we go find shoes for you?"

They walked down the street toward the shoe store. Pauline saw the Fabric Shoppe sign and thought of Mrs. O'Dell. She hesitated, but then took a step toward the shop. *I gave up looking for Rupert's family after going to the courthouse, but maybe...*

"Give it up, Pauline." Marian took her arm and led her into the shoe store.

After trying on several pair, Pauline chose black, low-heel pumps. "These are pretty with the fringe flap over the ties."

"And practical," added Marian.

The sun peeked through pink clouds early Saturday morning when Fred drove Pauline to Will and Marian's house. They were waiting on their porch. Fred helped Pauline from the truck, gave her a hug and a kiss, and told her to have a good time.

She straightened her hat over her blond curls. "We will, Fred, but I wish you were coming with us."

"Give Jenny a hug for me, and tell Rupert to come see our cabin."

"Goodbye, dear. Don't work too hard."

Will drove down to the C's camp. Marian said, "I hope he's ready."

As Will parked the car, they saw Rupert come around the corner of the large log building. He called, "Good morning!"

Marian opened her door and got out. "Rupert, you ride in front with Will and I'll sit with Pauline."

He smiled, opened the back door for her, and after she got comfortable, closed it and got in with Will.

"You clean-up pretty good," Will teased.

Rupert grinned. "And so do you." He adjusted his tie and white shirt collar under his blue and red argyle sweater.

"We're right on time," said Will, as he drove his Model A onto the ferry. "This'll probably be our last trip using the

Cup and Saucer."

"Let's get out so we can look up at the bridge," said Pauline.

"We better stay in the car and watch out the window," cautioned Marian. "It's windy. We might lose our hats."

The little ferry rocked from side to side as it made its way through mist across the churning water. Pauline leaned close to the window. "The men look like ants crawling around on the steel girders. Has anyone fallen?"

Rupert said, "No, not yet. It'd be a long fall. One hundred eighty feet."

Will asked, "Have you heard if the bridge will be ready for the grand opening?"

"It seems to be right on schedule for the end of July."

At the Swinomish Slough drawbridge they had to wait for several seiners and a barge to go through. Marian looked at her watch. "Nuts, eight thirty already. I hope this won't make us late."

Will said, "We have plenty of time."

Marian slumped back in her seat, and then she sat forward and rested a hand on the back of the front seat. "Rupert, tell us about your family."

"There isn't much to tell. My mama died when I was a little boy and my daddy died in the war." He looked out the side window.

"Who took care of you?"

"I was living in Pennsylvania with my gramma and grampa."

"What did your grandfather do?"

Pauline puckered her brow, hit her knee against Marian's

and shook her head no.

Marian frowned at her. "I'm sure Rupert doesn't mind telling me about his family."

Rupert turned to her. "Grampa worked in the coal mine until he got that disease, and then he stayed home and started raising chickens."

"Did you go to high school?"

"Sure did. Played on the baseball team all four years."

Will asked, "What position?"

Rupert grinned and said, "I pitched most of the games. We had a good team."

Pauline piped up, "And now he pitches on the C's team. Did you win the game in Anacortes last Sunday?"

"Yep! Nine to three."

Much to Pauline's dismay, Marian continued asking Rupert about his family, and he patiently answered her. "After Grampa got real sick and died, it was too much for Gramma and me. We decided I should join the C's. Gramma sold all the chickens and moved in with my Aunt Esther."

Marian said, "Are you're going back to Pennsylvania after you leave the C's?"

"Probably not. Gramma died just after Thanksgiving. I don't like it there and now that my property sold, I don't have any reason to go back."

"How about your aunt and the rest of your family, don't you want to be with them?"

"Aunt Esther moved to Texas to live with her daughter."

"So you want to stay here?"

"I like it here."

"And you like Jenny?"

Pauline pulled on Marian's arm. "Look, Marian, the last boat went through. The bridge is closing and we can be on our way."

Will started the engine. Marian leaned back, rested her head on the back of the seat and closed her eyes. Pauline let her be and enjoyed looking at the scenery.

When they arrived at the college, Will parked in a designated visitor area.

"Jenny will meet us after the ceremony," said Marian, leading the way as they walked under the canopy of chestnut trees to the ivy-covered Main Building.

Pauline, walking beside Rupert, put her hand on his arm and stopped him. "Just look, isn't this splendid?"

He scanned the well-kept lawns, trees and brick buildings. "Yeah, it's all really green and lush."

Marian urged, "Come along, Pauline."

When they reached the building's entrance at the top of the stairs, Rupert held the tall, narrow door open. They stepped into the dimly lit hall. Will took off his hat. Rupert ran his hand through his red hair and stood with hands in his pockets.

Lights on long chains hung from the ceiling. Dark wood framed the doors to classrooms and offices. "Sort of a dreary place," said Will.

They joined other proud families as they walked to the auditorium. Their footsteps echoed on the wood floor. Rupert stood back to let Will, Marian and Pauline seat themselves and then he sat in the aisle seat. People talked in whispery voices.

A man walked on stage, tested the microphone, and

satisfied with the squeaks, he left. There was a hush when the heavy maroon curtains opened. Professors, dressed in their alma mater's caps and gowns, sat in a half-circle on the stage. Organ music played "Pomp and Circumstance."The parade of students, in their dark blue gowns and hats with gold tassels swinging on the right side, entered from the rear of the auditorium and paraded down to the sectioned-off front seats. People craned their heads to see the graduates. Rupert whispered to Pauline, "There's Jenny." They waved and she gave them a big smile.

Marian put her hand to her mouth with surprise and excitement when she saw Jenny wearing a gold cord over her gown. She nudged Will, "Look, Jenny's an honor student."

President Fisher welcomed the graduates, parents and friends. The ceremony commenced with speeches and honor awards. As their names were called, the graduates crossed the stage, shook hands with the president, received a rolled-up, ribbon-tied diploma, and then returned to their seats. President Fisher made one last congratulatory speech wishing the graduates a purposeful, successful and happy future. Then with arms spread wide announced, "I give you the Class of 1935."

The audience clapped and cheered. The graduates rose and walked up the aisle, laughing and waving to their parents and friends.

People moved from the auditorium to the hall to meet their daughters and sons amid cheers, hugs and laughter. Jenny found them, reached up and tousled Rupert's red hair, and said, "It wasn't hard to find you!" He gave her a big hug. Marian, Will and Pauline hugged and kissed her, and told her they felt proud.

Rupert asked, "Aren't you supposed to put your tassel to the other side?"

"I did, but it keeps falling over when I move my head. Are you hungry? There's a luncheon for graduates and their families." She put her arm through his and looked at her mother. "Come on. I'm famished."

Jenny took them through the long hall, past many closed doors and out a door that led up the concrete path to Eden's Hall, the women's dorm. They sat at round tables covered with white linen.

Will looked around at other families being seated. "Is the college paying for all this?"

"No, Dad. I did. I've been saving my allowance."

Pauline and Rupert thanked her and said they appreciated being treated so special. Marian put an arm around her daughter. "Jenny, I'm sure proud of you."

After an extra helping of dessert, Will patted his tummy and said, "I'm stuffed. Do you eat here every day?"

Jenny laughed. "No, Dad, I usually bring an apple or peanut butter sandwich."

"You better come home so we can fatten you up."

Rupert's eyes shone as he asked, "When will you be coming home, Jenny?"

"I'm going on a camping trip with my girlfriends to Sinclair Island this week, and then I'll be home for the summer unless I can get a job."

Marian asked, "Have you any prospects?"

"I've applied to be a counselor at Whatcom Parks Summer Camp. It's only six weeks, but I think it would be fun, and I can still live with Doctor Shubert's family. I'll come home for a week before it starts."

As they left Edens Hall, Jenny asked, "Are you in a hurry to get home, Dad?"

"No, Andrew and Old Man Jorgen told me to take a day off. They're doing my chores for me tonight."

"Oh good, come this way then, I want you to walk on Memory Lane." They followed Jenny past the ivy-covered Main Building.

On the sidewalk, Rupert stepped over the cement squares with the numbers imprinted on them. "Why the years?"

"That's to mark the year we graduated. We put our ASB cards in a vault. My friend and I put a picture of us in it. A hundred years from now, when they dig it out of the sidewalk, they can see how we dressed, the songs we sang and the games the Vikings ball teams won." Jenny led them around the campus telling them the names of the buildings and where she had taken classes.

Pauline felt relieved when Will said they should start for home. Her new shoes pinched her toes.

At the car, Will pulled Marian away from Jenny. "Come on, Mom, we'll see her soon."

After getting in, Marian looked back and saw Jenny throw her arms around Rupert. "Oh, dear me," she said softly to Pauline. "What am I going to do?"

"I think you're going to let Jenny and Rupert work it out."

Will drove out of the parking lot. "We can take Highway 99 home or go back the way we came. What will it be?"

Rupert said, "I'd like to treat you to supper at the

Oyster Creek Inn."

"Oh, that's too much," said Marian.

"Not at all," he said. "Do you like oysters, Pauline?"

"I don't know, but I'm willing to try them."

"Sounds good to me," said Will. "Marian?"

"Okay, that's fine."

Rupert said, "It's settled then."

Will drove south through Fairhaven on the way to Chuckanut Drive.

Pauline sat on the right side and looked through the trees down the steep bluff. "Look, there's the train down there. Can you see it, Marian?"

"I don't like to look down. These narrow, winding roads are scary enough. I wish you wouldn't drive so fast, Will."

"Only going twenty-five, Marian. The Inn is on the bluff just around the next curve."

Will parked his Model A and they went into the dark, cave-like restaurant. Rupert ordered oysters for appetizers. Pauline decided she didn't want to try them. "They look so disgusting. You can have my share, Rupert. I'll be happy with a small salad."

Will asked, "Rupert, how did you hear about this restaurant?"

"Oh, our baseball team played against the Fairhaven C's team. We came home this way and stopped here to celebrate. It was the first time I ever had oysters and I like them."

They enjoyed their meal and the view of the creek. Marian reminded Will that it was getting dark and he checked his watch. "Yep, we better hit the road."

Marian and Pauline dozed in the back seat, but opened

their eyes when they heard humming.

"Sing the words," said Pauline.

In a rich baritone, Rupert started singing, "In the Good Old Summertime." Will and Pauline joined in. They laughed and started another song. Soon Marian sang along with them and suggested, "How about "Bye, Bye Blackbird?" They sang song after song, taking turns suggesting new ones.

After dropping Rupert at the camp, they found Fred waiting at home. Pauline and Marian laughed as he helped them from the car. "I guess I don't have to ask if you had a fun time."

Will said, "Fred, you'd think these two were still teenagers."

"Oh Will, you had fun, too," said Marian. "Rupert started it. He got us all laughing and singing."

Fred asked, "Well, how was my favorite niece?"

"Jenny said she forgives you. She'll come home after a short holiday with her girlfriends."

"We stopped at the Oyster Creek Inn, a restaurant on Chuckanut Drive," said Will.

"Rupert bought our suppers," said Pauline. "Wasn't that nice of him, Marian?"

"Yes, it was."

Will said, "He's a thoughtful, generous guy. Too bad you couldn't get away, Fred."

"Well, I had a good day, too. Let's go home, dear."

Chapter Sixty... Home Again

As Fred drove toward the beach, he said, "I have a surprise for you."

"Oh good! Will you give me a hint?"

He laughed. "Nope, you have to wait." Rather than stopping near the tent, he drove to the cabin's back door. He helped her out of the truck and they walked to the door. He reached inside and flipped a switch.

Pauline gasped. "Lights!"

"Whidbey Electric came out and connected a wire from the pole that carries electricity to the Kellogg cabin."

She stepped inside and saw the yellow table and chairs and their cots. "My goodness. You moved everything from the tent to the cabin."

"Yep! I figure we can live here while I finish the walls and build the cabinets. I had a bit of help. Betty and Martha came this morning to see you. I told them my plan to surprise you and Martha said to let them do it. Pretty soon they had brought the cots and carried the table and chairs over. And your bed is all made up for you, clean sheets and all."

"They did all that? What wonderful friends." She walked

over to the kitchen area. "You already put in a sink?"

"Yep, I sure did. I bought it a couple days ago. Come try it out." He pointed to the faucet. "It'll just be cold water until we get the hot water tank installed."

To Pauline's delight, water splashed out when she turned the handle.

"There's room for your Toperator in the corner. Now look over here." Fred pointed through the two by four studs. "The hot water tank will be near the stove, but in the bathroom on the other side of the wall. Otto is going to bring it and the stove tomorrow and we'll get everything hooked up. The bathroom sink, toilet and tub will come next week. Bernie had to order them from a place in Seattle."

She ran her hand over the ribbed drain board on the white sink. "I love it. So this is the real reason you didn't want to go to Bellingham today."

"That's right. I didn't forget Jenny's graduation; I just wanted to surprise you."

"Thank you, dear!" She put her arms around his waist.

He held her tight and nuzzled her neck. "You've had a long day and I'm tired," he said. "Let's get into the cots and you can tell me all about your trip."

It didn't take long before she heard Fred's soft snoring. She snuggled deep into her new flannel sheets and fell asleep.

Before sunrise, Pauline woke up. Wearing Fred's mackintosh, she went barefoot out the front door. Lighted by a crescent moon, she picked her way over small sticks and stones. Sticky sand verbena clung to her feet. At the water's edge, she let her feet sink into the cold wet sand as waves advanced and receded, their froth shining white in the moonlight. The forlorn sound of the buoy bell sounded in the distance. *I wonder if every seventh wave is a big one, as Gev said.* She counted, and counted again. *I think Gev was teasing me.*

She turned when she heard Fred whistling and walking toward her. After a warm embrace, he said, "I'll make coffee on the cook stove by the tent. After tomorrow you can make it on your new stove."

Everything seemed to be happening so fast. Workers came in and out, calling back and forth. They sawed and nailed boards. A truck delivered glass panes for the windows. Feeling in the way, Pauline went to the beach.

The tide was out. She poked around in little pools making shore crabs scurry under the green algae. Barnacles and limpets clung tight to rocks. She wiggled her finger gently across anemones to make them close.

"Aunt Paulie!" Jenny caught up with her.

She gave her niece a hug. "When did you get home?"

"Last night."

"Are you home now for the summer?"

"Just a week, then I'll take the job with the Whatcom Parks Department. I've wanted to talk with you."

"About Rupert?"

"Yes."

"Okay, let's walk out on the sandbar."

They high-stepped over the little pools and onto the rippled sand, jumping aside and laughing when clams squirted water up from below the sand.

"It's so hard to talk with Mom about Rupert."

"She doesn't want to lose you, Jenny."

"How can she lose me? I'll always be her daughter."

"True, but you would belong to Rupert."

Jenny picked up a stick and drew a heart in the sand. "When did you know you were in love with Uncle Fred?"

Pauline laughed. "Goodness, I don't know *exactly* when, but I couldn't stop thinking about him after our first date."

"How old were you?"

"Sixteen, a sophomore, and he asked me to the Prom. He wouldn't have if it hadn't been for my friend, Marie. He asked her first, but she had a date with Glenn, so she told him to ask me."

Jenny stooped and picked up a round rock. Pauline watched her turn the smooth rock over and over in her hand, and then Jenny said, "When I came home for Mother's Day, Rupert and I climbed Goose Rock. The trail was quite steep. I walked in front and when I turned to look at a mossy stump, I stumbled over a tree root. Rupert caught me and held me, and then we kissed and kissed again. We looked at each other and started laughing. I get so excited when I hear his voice on the phone. I think about him during my classes and doodle his name in my notebook."

"I remember that feeling and writing Mrs. Fred Gunther again and again in the margins of my notes. I guess we women are all rather silly when we're in love. Do you think Rupert loves you?"

"I think so. I hope so. We've been writing letters and when I get one from him, I can hardly wait to get to my room to read it."

"So, has he told you about his mother and father, about his childhood?"

"Yes, I think I know everything about him. I love him." She stopped walking and put a hand on Pauline's arm. "I'm not going to tell Mom and Dad, but I just had to tell someone. Please don't say anything."

"I won't, Jenny, but you should. Your mother needs to know how you feel. Rupert's enlistment in the C's ends at the end of July, and he told your mother he doesn't want to go back to Pennsylvania. He'll have to find work and a place to stay."

"This morning I drove Mom's car into town and applied for the Home Economics job at the high school. If I get it, I'll have to find a place to room and board in town."

"It will be wonderful to have you back home." Pauline put an arm around her niece and looked up at the sky. "That sun tells me it's time I get back and make lunch."

"And I should go back home. Mom picked strawberries yesterday and I told her I'd make jam."

After lunch, Fred went to Christopherson's Mill and brought home knotty pine lumber for the cabinets. He stacked it in the middle of the cabin and suggested to Pauline, "Let's go out to the old place for fun."

As they drove up the driveway, Pauline dabbed at her eyes. "We had good times here."

"Yes, all but two times I'd like to forget."

"When you had appendicitis, and then the fire."

"That's right." He stopped by the shed.

Pauline got out of the truck and walked over the ashes of

the old house.

"No use looking, Pauline. We sifted through everything pretty well." He went into the shed and opened the old closet. "What shall we do with this?" He picked up the box with Ruby's sewing basket.

"Let's take it home. I'll ask Rupert what he wants to do with it."

She looked at the chimney, half gone now, and bricks scattered. She walked toward the old apple tree and turned to her husband. "What are we going to do with this old place?"

"I've been thinking about that. The county doesn't want it, but they'd expect us to pay taxes every year." He pushed the box toward the front of the truck bed.

Pauline asked, "Do you think Rupert would want it?"

"He has money. I guess we could sell it to him."

She said, "We could just give it to him. After all, it really would have been his if the taxes had been paid all those years after his father took him away. He could build a new house."

"Yeah, he could live in the shed for a while."

"It's not very big."

"It's just as big as the tent," Fred said.

"True, but it would be cold in the winter. Of course, he could live somewhere else while he builds a house."

"Seems we're doing a lot of speculating when we don't even know if he's interested. We can ask him. Let him figure out what he wants." Fred took a last look inside the shed. "Ah, the misery whip. Don't suppose I'll have any use for that old saw."

"I know," said Pauline. "Let's mount it above the

fireplace mantel."

Fred pulled the saw down from the rafters. "Maybe Rupert will want it."

"Dear, do you think I could take some of the lilac shoots with us?"

"Bring a bucket and show me where they are," Fred said as he got a shovel from the truck.

They stopped by Will and Marian's. Will looked in the truck. "You've got quite a load there, Fred."

"Yeah, all my tools. We emptied out the shed. I'm ready to start building cabinets. You know, we miss Nanny and Billy. I've got brush they can clear."

Will said, "Tell me when you're ready and I'll take them away from the cows."

"I'm going to get chickens again, too," piped up Pauline.

"Fred can build you a new coop."

Fred started the truck motor and told Will, "The projects just keep piling up."

"Hank and Gev came by last night for a game of cards," said Will. "Jenny told them how she had learned to bake fish in the sand. Hank said he'd get a salmon and we should all come over for a picnic."

"That sounds like fun," said Fred.

"Yeah, Paulie, you be sure and make your rhubarb cobbler."

Pauline laughed. "Okay, and tell Marian to bring her blackberry pie. We'll see you soon."

Chapter Sixty-One... The Salmon Bake

Hank knocked on the cabin door early Saturday morning and asked, "Would you like to go for a boat ride? I'm rowing out to a seiner to buy a fish. Jenny's going to show us how she learned to bake one in the sand."

Fred looked at Pauline, still wearing her robe. "Hurry up and get dressed. Better bring a jacket. I'll help Hank with the boat." The men carried the row boat from Hank's truck to the beach.

Pauline sat on a tiny seat in the bow, Hank in the middle with the oars and Fred in the stern. "Easy rowing with the tide on the way out," said Hank. Pauline held on to the sides as the boat skimmed over the smooth-as-glass, clear water. Drops of salty water splashed onto her face as Hank dipped the oars down and up, down and up, water dripping from them.

Several seiners had let out their nets. Hank headed toward the nearest one where men worked hauling up their net full of lively fish, their silver backs flashing in the sun. Gulls screamed and dived above the catch.

Hank let the rowboat drift up beside the seiner. He

called, "Hello there!"

A grizzled fisherman looked over the side. They talked back and forth.

"Yeah, we got a good catch this morning, time to take 'em in."

"La Conner?"

"Yep."

"Got a fish for me today?"

"How big?"

Hank laughed. "Enough to feed twenty." He held up a five dollar bill.

The man disappeared when he bent down. After a minute he reappeared and held up a large fish by its gills. "This one okay?"

"Looks good to me," said Hank. He reached up, took the fish, and handed over the money. "It's a beauty. Thanks. We'll see you again."

Hank laid the King in the bottom of the boat. It thrashed about a bit, then lay still. The fisherman waved as Hank started rowing away. Pauline waved back. Fred ran his hands over a silvery side of the salmon. "That's a lotta fish, Hank."

"Yep, about forty pounds. Pauline is going to help me clean it," he teased.

She said, "Oh, no. That's Jenny's job."

Jenny and Rupert came in the early afternoon. Rupert carried a shovel. They cleared a space away from the driftwood and Rupert dug a hole in the sand. Pauline sat on a favorite log and watched. Jenny stood with her hands on her hips. "That should be big enough. Now we need to get some big rocks."

Pauline said, "I'll help. I know the best rocks are along the edge of the sandbars, but don't take any from the tide pools. You might hurt the animals."

With the pit lined to Jenny's satisfaction, she gathered dry reeds and seaweed. "You can bring small sticks, Aunt Paulie. Rupert, will you get some big dry firewood?"

"And just how big is big, Miss Jenny?"

"About as big as you can carry, Mister," retorted Jenny, getting down on her hands and knees. She scratched a match on a rock and started a fire. Smoke from the dry reeds rose and made her cough. She stood up holding her hand over her mouth, rubbing her eyes, tears running down her cheeks.

Rupert pounded her on the back. "Are you okay?"

"Hey, not so hard." She coughed again. "Let's build up the fire."

As flames licked their way through the small wood, they added larger sticks and driftwood. Soon they had a blazing fire. "Let's go for a walk, Rupert. Want to come, Aunt Paulie?"

"No, you go ahead, I'll see what Fred's doing." Pauline watched them hold hands, walking barefoot on the sandbars. She turned, skirted around logs and beach grass to a path she had cleared to the cabin, and taking one last glance at the two figures, smiled.

She found Fred checking each piece of pine for the cabinets. He nodded when she said, "It's time for me to make the cobbler."

"Hi, guys," called Marian. "We came a bit early. Hope

that's all right."

"Naw, you better go home and come back later," teased Fred, as he took a pencil from behind his ear to mark a board.

"That's quite a pile of lumber you've got here," said Will. "For the kitchen cabinets?"

"Yep." Fred unrolled the sketch he'd made of the inside of the cabin, showing the details for the cabinets and bunk beds. "Pauline wants everything knotty pine."

Pauline, wiping her floury hands on her apron, came from the kitchen, took Marian's arm, led her onto the porch, and pointed to the sandbars.

Marian watched her daughter and Rupert out on the farthest bar and smiled at the lovely sight, two young people chasing each other, and falling into each other's arms.

"Oh my, they do look like they're having fun. I suppose my Jenny is in love."

Pauline said, "That would be my guess. Oh, I better finish my cobbler. Come see my stove."

Marian eyed the Hotpoint electric range. "You have an electric stove?"

"Fred bought it second hand. Look at the buttons, one for each burner and two for the oven. It has a broiler. Isn't it wonderful?"

Marian traced the words *Hot Point* on the oven door of the sleek white range. "Yes, it's wonderful and so modern standing on those four skinny legs."

Pauline turned a dial. "I need the oven at three hundred seventy five degrees. I better get busy with the cobbler. Gev told me to help myself from her garden."

Marian watched as Pauline mixed flour, sugar and cinnamon into the diced rhubarb, and then mixed oatmeal, brown sugar and melted butter together. "So the oatmeal makes your cobbler crunchy."

"Yep, the way my mom taught me."

Jenny came in, breathless, her eyes shining, "We had a wonderful time." She saw Marian and stopped. "Oh, hi Mom. Did you see us?"

"It looked like you were having a great time."

Jenny walked to the table. "What's this?" She touched the red tassel on the brown straw basket.

Pauline came from the kitchen. "That sewing basket belonged to Rupert's mother. Luckily, it was stored in the old closet in the shed and didn't get damaged in the fire."

"Can I peek inside?"

"I don't think Rupert would mind."

Jenny unfastened the reed hook and lifted the hinged lid. "These are pretty." She handed a set of embroidered pillowcases to her mother.

Marian said, "It's nice stitching. Pink and red roses, but the green leaves aren't finished."

Jenny laid a packet of needles, scissors and several skeins of colorful embroidery cotton on the table. "It's just her sewing stuff. I can look at it later. I'm going to put on my swimsuit. I'll change in your bathroom, Aunt Paulie, and then Rupert and I are going to swim in the big pools between the bars."

Not paying attention to Jenny, Marian pulled on a piece of paper stuck in the bottom of the basket. "What do we have here?" She lifted a corner of a cloth-covered board that matched the lining. "Look, Pauline, it has a false bottom."

"Marian, maybe we shouldn't..."

Marian unfolded a creased paper. "It's about Rupert." She read out loud.

Ruby Rose Long gave birth to a healthy baby boy today, July 4, 1911. He has red hair and weighs about nine pounds. He was named Rupert Ralph Long after his father, Ralph Long, and his grandfather, Rupert Long.

"It's signed Edith Hannegan, midwife." She handed it to Pauline.

"Well, that answers some questions," said Pauline. "They were married, and before Rupert was born."

Marian picked up another paper. "Here's a letter." She began to read the ink stained paper.

Dear Mother,

I know you are disappointed in me, but I love Ralph. He is a good man and works hard. I know Ralph loves me. He said we will get married the next time the preacher comes through. I was sick for a while with that morning stuff, but now I feel good. I think the baby will be born in June or July. Maybe your husband will let you come to the island. I know Ralph will be a good father. Please...

Marian slumped back in her chair, laid the paper on the table, and folded her arms. "That's all. Ruby didn't finish it."

Pauline picked up the letter, read it to herself and looked

on the back. "Here's a name and an address scribbled in pencil. *Mrs. Olga O'Dell Rte 2 Anacortes.*" Pauline put her hand to her mouth. "Oh my word, that's the lady in the Fabric Shoppe. I met her sister at the Co-op a while back. I wonder... Marian, I want to tell Rupert that we've found his grandmother." She folded the letter. "Yes, I have to tell Rupert. I told him I would try to find his relatives. I think I asked everyone in town if they knew Ralph Long, but I never got a chance to ask Mrs. O'Dell."

Marian picked up a small blue book embossed with gold letters, RRR, in fancy script. She opened the cover and read to herself, *To My Ruby Rose, Love, Mother.* "It looks like a diary. I'd like to read it."

"No, Marian, I should give it to Rupert," Pauline said. She heard Jenny on the porch, took the book from Marian and put it in her apron pocket. "I'll give it to him later."

Jenny opened the door and called, "Hank and Gev are here. We're going to put the fish in the pit to bake. Want to come watch?"

"Oh, the cobbler." Pauline hurried to the kitchen and took the browned dessert from the oven. She hung her apron on a hook behind the kitchen door. "Fred. Will. Are you coming?"

"You go ahead. I'll be along." Fred continued measuring.

Hank had cleaned the salmon at his house and brought it laid on a board with a flour sack cloth covering it. "All right, Jenny, it's all yours."

The women sat together on logs around the fire and the men stood with their hands in their pockets watching as Jenny took over. "First we have to take the fire apart."

The fire had burned down to red and gray coals. Rupert used a shovel to take out a few large chunks of blackened burning wood, and set them on the sand to the side of the pit. Jenny took newspapers from a box and spread them onto a piece of chicken wire. She tried to move the slippery fish from the board to the wire, but it got away from her, landing in the sand. "Help me Rupert, it's heavy. We'll have to wash it off."

The men chuckled as Rupert grabbed the salmon by its gills and carried it down to the water. Jenny splashed water over it, and they brought the dripping fish back and wrapped it in several layers of paper.

"Now we're going to wrap it in seaweed to keep the paper from burning," said Jenny as she and Rupert pulled gobs of wet seaweed from a bucket and put it around the fish.

"Jenny, will it taste like seaweed?" asked Pauline.

"Maybe just a tad."

Rupert took one side of the wire, and together they lowered the fish into the pit. Satisfied that the wire was secure on the rocks, Jenny said, "Now we have to build a big fire on top of it."

"How long will it take to cook?" asked Marian.

"It's bigger than the one we baked on Sinclair Island. We'll check it in about three hours."

"Jenny, that's a long time for us to wait for supper," said Will. "I'm hungry."

"You were supposed to eat a big lunch, Dad."

Hank grabbed a shovel. "Bring that bucket, Will, we'll dig us some clams."

Pauline looked up the beach. "Is that Ted and Mildred coming? I wonder if she baked her chocolate cake. Let's go meet them."

Gev took off her shoes and socks. "I like to walk barefoot in the sand, good for the calluses."

Marian took off her shoes and stockings. "Good idea."

"I walk barefoot a lot," said Pauline, "my feet are getting tough."

"Hello, new neighbor." Mildred gave Pauline a hug. When the four friends started catching up on their gardening and canning, Ted left them and joined the men.

Hank and Will laid a couple dozen or so clams in the bowl of the shovel and held it over the hot coals. Within ten minutes the small butter clams popped open.

"Delicious," said Will. He ate a second and then a third. "Try one, Paulie."

"No, that's okay. You guys enjoy them."

"I think she's squeamish. She didn't want to try the oysters either."

Pauline got up. "I'll be right back," she said and went up to the cabin.

She found Fred sawing a board. She put a hand on his back. He jumped and almost dropped the saw.

"Don't do that," he said.

"I'm sorry, but come to the beach. Ted and Mildred are here. You can carry the pitcher of lemonade."

As they stood on the beach, the women chatted together, but turned to the men when they heard Will say, "So you're a risk taker, Hank, the first to drive on the bridge over the Pass."

Hank laughed. "I guess someone had to be first."

When asked if it was scary, Hank said, "Naw, not at all. It's twenty-eight feet wide, lots of room. The railings haven't been put up yet. I could see the water through the planks and girders, but there wasn't any danger, just a rough ride in the truck."

"How long is the bridge, Hank?" asked Fred.

"From Whidbey to Pass Island it's nine hundred seventy-five feet, over Canoe Pass from the little island to Fidalgo, it's five hundred eleven."

"How high is it above the water?"

"About one hundred eighty feet," said Hank.

Someone asked, "Will it be ready for us to drive on by the dedication?"

"Should be." And then Hank changed the subject by asking Will if he was still interested in buying a heifer.

The women talked about the picnic plans for the dedication. "We'll have to get there early to reserve a table," said Gev. "It would be great to have one of the new picnic shelters."

"We've been too busy with our haying to go over," said Mildred. "Thea said she and Bert took their family for a picnic last week. Bert was impressed with the C's rock work for the restrooms. She said the kids had fun swimming in Cranberry Lake."

Jenny and Rupert, their wet swimsuits and legs covered with sand, joined them. Will said, "You've got a lot of skin showing there, Jenny."

"Oh, Dad." She pulled the thin straps up over her shoulders. "All the girls wear suits like this. It's the new style."

Pauline said, "I think it's adorable."

Marian handed her daughter a large towel. "Wrap this around you." Jenny fastened the towel like a sarong around her slim figure. Marian turned to Rupert. "Was the water cold?"

"Only on the outer bar where the waves are breaking." He smiled at her. "The pools between the bars are warm though after the water comes over the hot sand."

Marian smiled back. "Yes, I remember that."

Hank said, "Jenny, I bet that fish is well-cooked."

The fire had burned down leaving just a few coals and ashes covering the wrapped salmon. Jenny looked at Rupert. "Let's take it out."

He grabbed the shovel. "Let me get some of the burned wood and ash off first."

Jenny watched him and then said, "Okay, I'll take this side and you get on the other. We'll lift the fish out together." As she bent over to take hold of the wire, her left foot slid in the sand toward the coals. She jumped back.

Will got up and went to Jenny. "Here, let me do that." He helped Rupert pull up the wire holding the fish. They laid it on the makeshift driftwood table.

"Thanks, Dad. Rupert and I can peel off the dried seaweed and newspaper." They brushed the ashes off and unwrapped the fish. "Ouch!" She put her fingers to her mouth. "It's so hot, it must be done."

Rupert used a butcher knife to cut the salmon open in two long filets showing thick pink meat.

The women brought baked beans and salads from their picnic baskets. Jenny served large portions of salmon to everyone, reminding them, "Watch for the bones."

"It's delicious, Jenny."

"It doesn't taste at all like seaweed."

"Good job, Jenny."

She beamed from all the compliments.

As Marian and Will left to go home, Marian whispered to Pauline, "Do you want me to go with you to see Mrs. O'Dell?"

"No, I'll do it, but I'll let you know what she says."

Chapter Sixty-Two... The Sewing Basket Treasures

Pauline, anxious to get Rupert by himself, got up from the log where she had been sitting beside Gev, and picked up the empty casserole dish and the lemonade pitcher. "Can you help me with these, Rupert?" He took them and followed her to the cabin.

"Remember when I told you I'd try to find your relatives?"

"Yeah, I do. It was nice of you and I'm sorry you didn't have any luck."

"Well, I want to show you something. Come sit down." Rupert sat at the table and Pauline brought the sewing basket to him. "Remember this? Open it."

"Yeah," he laughed. "I didn't want to take it down to camp." He lifted the lid.

"Your mother did beautiful embroidery on the pillow-cases, but take them out. Look what else she left."

Rupert picked up the small book with his mother's initials printed on it. "I remember this. My ma used to write poems for me. We sat in the woods by her favorite tree."

"Let me guess, that big maple tree with the long trunk growing on the ground?"

"Yeah, that's right."

Pauline smiled. "I like that tree, too. Last fall the leaves turned golden."

"I played with my trucks and Ma told me about little elves living in the woods."

"That's a wonderful memory, Rupert."

He picked up Ruby's unfinished letter. "This is the first time I've seen her handwriting. It's nice." He read what his ma had written and looked at Pauline. "So, I guess Ma got pregnant and couldn't live at home anymore because of her step-pa."

Rupert quietly read aloud the paper signed by Edith Hannegan. "My ma and pa got married before I was born. I guess that was good."

"Yes, it was."

"I always wondered where I got my name. Now I know I was named after my pa's father. I don't much care for it. I'd rather have a name like John or Bill."

"I like your name. It's distinctive. I've never known anyone named Rupert."

"My dad called me Rupe."

"I like that too."

"I'll take the book back to camp with me. Okay if I leave the basket here? I'll show it to Jenny someday." He started to get up.

"Rupert, one more thing, I know who your grandmother is."

"You do?"

"Yes. Would you like to meet her?"

"Well, sure, of course. Do you know where she lives?"

"She has the Fabric Shoppe in Oak Harbor. I met her when I bought material, but I didn't know then that she was your grandmother. I can take you into town to meet her."

"That would be a big surprise to her, just walk in and say, 'Hi, I'm your grandson.' No, I wouldn't want to shock her."

"Would you like me to talk with her before you meet her?"

Rupert got up, put one hand on the back of his neck, looked down, and walked around the room. "I think that's a good idea."

"All right, that's what I'll do."

Fred sat at the table watching Pauline, still in her robe, flipping hotcakes. "We had quite a party yesterday." He stirred sugar and cream into his coffee. "I noticed Marian seemed to enjoy something Rupert said to her."

"I think she liked his attentions, and since we found the paper about his birth and know his parents were married before he was born, her feelings toward him have softened."

"Have you read the diary?"

"No. I'd like to, but it wouldn't be right unless Rupert offers it to me." She brought blackberry syrup to the table. "Rupert put the diary in his pocket and said he'd read it at camp." Pauline sat down and sipped her coffee. "He's excited to meet his grandmother, but wants me to talk with her first. I'd like to drive into town today and visit with her." She glanced at the clock. "The shop should be open in an hour. Do you need the truck?"

"You go ahead. I don't think we'll get any rest until you talk with her."

"Thank you, dear. I'll wash the dishes when I get back."

"I hope you won't be disappointed."

As she came from the bedroom, she said, "I'll be going now." She picked up her purse, patted Fred on his shoulder and hurried out to the truck.

He followed her to the porch. She had become a skillful driver but he still cautioned her, "Keep it down under thirty." She waved goodbye and honked the horn.

As Pauline drove to town, she thought about the discovery of Rupert's family history in the basket. *I should have taken everything out of that basket when I first found it. Oh, well, they say good things happen... I wonder what Mrs. O'Dell will say?*

She parked in the usual spot behind the Co-op and went in the back door. "Hello, Bernie."

The grocer, on his ladder arranging cans on high shelves, stepped down. "Nice to see you, Pauline."

"Remember a while back when I tried to find the family of my friend, Rupert Long?"

"You asked all around town with no luck."

"Well, I finally got lucky. The answer was right under my nose all the time."

"You don't say." He pushed several cans on the counter aside and sat on his stool.

"I do say. And now I'm on my way to the Fabric Shoppe to talk with Mrs. O'Dell."

Bernie said, "Oh, but I doubt you'll find her there. She's been out of town for some time."

"But I need to talk with her."

"Far as I know, she's living with her sister."

"I met Mrs. Strump once. Do you know where she lives?"

"Perhaps the young lady taking care of the shop can tell you."

Pauline moved toward the door. "I hope so. I'll pick up a few groceries later."

"Okay, good luck."

She left the Co-op and marched down the street to the Fabric Shoppe. A red paper dangled from a string in the window, *Everything on SALE*. The little bell tinkled as she opened the door and a young woman came forward to meet her.

Pauline smiled. "Hi. If I remember right, your name is Hazel."

"Yes, I'm Hazel."

"I understand Mrs. O'Dell is out of town."

"That's right. She was in St. Joseph Hospital in Bellingham for a while, but she's living with her sister now. I'm managing the store until it sells. Everything is fifty percent off."

"That's a wonderful bargain, but I can't buy anything today. Do you have an address or phone number for Mrs. Strump?"

"I have an address. Hmm, now where did I put it?" Hazel muttered. "Oh, of course, it's in the cash register." She pulled a lever on the old register, the drawer clanged opened and she took out an envelope. "Here it is. I'll write it down for you." She wrote Alma Strump, 1315 J Street, Bellingham, Washington on a small piece of paper and handed it to Pauline.

"Thank you, Hazel. I'll write to her." She started toward the door, hesitated at a table of rayon material and felt the smooth fabric. *Fifty percent off. No, maybe later.* The bell tinkled as she closed the door.

While Bernie filled Pauline's grocery list, she told him about her visit with Hazel. He said he hadn't heard about the sale. He chuckled, "I imagine that will make a lot of women happy. A sale seems to bring them into town."

Pauline said, "Well, if I weren't in a hurry, I could spend hours looking at material." They laughed and she followed him as he carried her box out to the truck. "Thanks, Bernie."

He said, "Not at all, have a good day now."

When she drove up to the cabin, Fred met her at the door and took the groceries. She dropped into an easy chair. "Whew! I'm so disgusted with myself."

"What's wrong?"

"I just wish I had found the letter in the basket when we first took it out of that old closet. Rupert could have known his grandmother a year ago. And, guess what? The Fabric Shoppe is for sale. Hazel said Mrs. O'Dell lives with her sister in Bellingham." Pauline wiped her nose. "I have an address. Do you want to go with me to talk with her?"

"Bellingham? That's a far way to go. Can't you just write to her?"

"I guess I could. I need to go for a walk, want to come?"

"No, you go ahead. I'm almost finished with the bathroom cabinets. Think you could varnish them?"

"Yes, I'll do it tomorrow."

Chapter Sixty-Three... Gev Brings a Letter

In the morning, Pauline wrote to Alma Strump, explained about Rupert and asked for her advice. She used Gev's phone to call Marian and told her what she had learned about Olga.

Days went by without a word from Alma. Pauline kept busy by sanding and varnishing cabinets. She baked bread and cookies in the Hot Point, washed clothes in the Toperator and hung them on a new clothes rack. Fred, busy working for Otto and on the cabin, said yes, he would make a clothes line, but never seemed to get around to it. There was always one more thing to do first. She helped him hold boards when he sawed, and then swept up the sawdust.

On the beach one morning, she heard her name.

"Pauline."

"Why Gev, I didn't expect to see you on the beach this early."

"I have a bit of time to myself this morning."

"Come sit down. I've been watching my friend, that grey heron. Henry is here almost every morning, always by himself." Pauline put an arm around Gev's shoulder and kissed her cheek. "How have you been this past week?"

"Busy canning and tired. Hank's been working overtime in the rush to get the road and bridge parking area finished before the dedication. I've been milking morning and night. We'll both be glad when it's over." Gev took an envelope from her sweater pocket. "This came in the mail yesterday."

Pauline read the return address on the blue envelope. "It's from Mrs. Strump." She tore it open, removed the flowery note paper and read aloud.

Dear Pauline,

Yes, I do remember meeting you at the Co-op before New Year's. You have interesting news. I didn't know I had a grandnephew. Olga has not been well, but she has been smiling ever since I read your letter to her. She keeps it nearby and I see her reading it over and over.

I don't know if Olga will go back to the store, even if she's strong enough. She was not a good manager and didn't take care of it. You can see it needs painting and the plumbing went out. She owed the suppliers of the material and such. I suppose she will have to sell it.

I knew Ruby as a child and often had her for a few days during the summer. She enjoyed coming to our farm. I have a grandson and a granddaughter just a bit younger. Phillip and Carol live out in the county on our family farm with my son and his wife. We would all like to meet Rupert.

May I suggest that we meet you and Rupert, and your husband, when we come to the island for the dedication of the bridge? We've been planning the trip ever since we knew the date. July 31st is just a couple weeks away.

I think Olga is feeling better by the day. What a grand meeting it will be.

You can call me at BHM 6958 to set a time and place.

Sincerely, Alma Strump

"Oh, this is wonderful news. Olga is feeling better, and they're coming to the dedication."

"You're talking about Olga, who has the Fabric Shoppe?"

"Yes, and won't Rupert be surprised to learn he has two cousins? When we first came to the island, I found his mother's sewing basket in the old house. Rupert didn't want to take it to the camp, and we've had it ever since. Several days ago Marian opened it. There was a pair of pillowcases and some sewing things, but under them we found a diary and a letter written by Ruby with Mrs. O'Dell's name on it. When I learned Olga is living with her sister, Alma, in Bellingham, I wrote to Alma about Rupert."

Gev said, "I didn't know Olga had a sister."

Pauline frowned. "But where can we meet them?"

"Maybe at the park and have a picnic."

"Do you think we could find them?"

Gev took Pauline's hand. "I'll help you make plans.

Coming from Bellingham, they'll be on the Fidalgo side of the bridge until after the ceremonies. I'll ask Hank. He'll know a good place to meet."

"Thanks, Gev, I'll come up and use your telephone to call Mrs. Strump and Marian. I know Marian is anxious to meet Rupert's grandmother and she'll want to help with the picnic. Gosh, that's only two weeks away. Jenny will be coming for the dedication, too."

Pauline sat with her elbows on the table and hands on her forehead. Fred stopped his work and asked, "Are you going to make lunch? It's almost one-thirty. You've been sitting there for almost an hour. Aren't you feeling well?"

She got up and went to the kitchen. "I've just been thinking about Rupert. Finally he'll have family. Gev found me on the beach and brought a letter from Alma Strump, his aunt."

Fred leaned back against the new sink counter and watched Pauline slice wheat bread. "So what does the aunt say?"

"I'll read it to you while you eat." She cut thin slices of leftover roast beef, smeared mustard on the bread and put the sandwich on a plate. "Here you go." She walked to her rocker. "There are dill pickles in the cooler if you want."

Fred poured himself a glass of milk, picked up his lunch and sat at the table.

Pauline read Alma's letter to him. "What do you think of that?" She got up, put her arms around Fred's shoulders and kissed the top of his head.

"Well, I'd say Rupert's in for a surprise. He's going

to meet his grandmother, an aunt and cousins all in one day." Finished with his lunch, Fred took his plate and glass to the sink, and reached into the Red Riding Hood cookie jar. "I like these," he said, as he took a big bite of a molasses cookie, "but maybe next time you could put in some raisins."

Chapter-Sixty-Four... Rupert's Grandmother

Fred pulled on his Levi jacket. "It'll be good working with Otto again." He put his arms around Pauline and nuzzled her neck. "Maybe you'll miss me today."

She kissed his cheek. "Oh, maybe not too much. I'm going to walk up to Gev's and call Marian to tell her about Mrs. O'Dell."

"Okay, see you about five."

Pauline left the cabin soon after Fred had gone. She stepped over piles of wet seaweed left by the night high tide. Remembering how the boys at the summer picnics used bull nose kelp as whips, she picked one up and tried to fling it out. "Ugh! It's too heavy. Nerts." She threw it onto the sand and brushed her sticky hands on the legs of her Paulie-alls.

Beds of small rocks gleamed in the morning sun. She stooped now and then to pick up what might be an agate. Holding one up to the sun, she saw her finger's shadow. She put the amber rock in her sweater pocket.

She crawled over the driftwood and rocks that lined the parking area, and then walked up the gravel road to Hank and Gev's yard.

Kelly, carrying a bucket of fresh milk from the barn, greeted her. "Hi, Mrs. Gunther."

"Ah, Kelly, you can call me Pauline."

"All right, if that's okay with Mom."

"I'll tell her it is. Is she in the house?"

"She and Chris are still at the barn. I have to wash the breakfast dishes."

"Can I help you dry them?"

"No, we don't use a towel. We just put them on the rack and when Mom comes in, she pours boiling water over them. It kills the germs that way."

"I see. Well, I'd like to make a couple of phone calls."

"Sure, come on in."

The telephone hung on a wall just inside the door. Pauline reached up and cranked the phone's handle one long ring. She said, "Operator, I would like to call *BHM 6958*."

After talking with Alma Strump, Pauline cranked the phone handle three shorts and one long. When Marian answered, Pauline told her about her call with Mrs. Strump. "We'll have a picnic. Would you like to help me?"

"Sure, and I want to tell Jenny."

"Marian, I'd like to tell Rupert first. Can you tell me how to reach him? I know he and Jenny talk on the telephone."

"Why don't you come over after supper and we can drive down to camp and talk with him?"

"Okay, I'll be there at about six thirty."

At the camp, Pauline parked the truck behind the C's main building. As she and Marian walked around to the front, they saw young men playing baseball. They watched for a few minutes, and then Pauline waved.

Rupert saw them and left the game. Pauline didn't waste any time. "Rupert, I know where your grandmother lives!"

His mouth dropped open in surprise. "Really? How did you find out?"

"I'll tell you all about it."

He led them up to the lodge porch where they sat on chairs made of small logs by some of the C's.

Rupert leaned forward, elbows resting on his knees, and listened to Pauline tell every detail of locating his grandmother.

"And you have two cousins, Phillip and Carol."

"I have cousins? Wow!" He stood up. "How old are they? How old is my gramma?"

"Phillip and Carol are about your age, and your gramma is about sixty. Rupert, you showed me a box of things your father kept for you. There was a wedding picture of a woman and a man we thought might be your grandparents. I think the woman is your grandmother, Olga."

"Yeah, I have the box in my locker, but haven't looked at it since I showed it to you."

"Your great aunt is bringing your grandmother to the dedication. We're planning a picnic so you can meet them."

"Really? She's coming here?" He put his hands in his pockets, looked out toward the water, walked to the end of the porch and back. "I didn't think I'd ever meet my gramma."

"Yes, and your cousins are coming, too."

Marian looked at her watch. "It's getting late, Pauline. We should be going home."

Pauline got up. "Yes, Fred doesn't want me driving in the dark."

Rupert chuckled. "Fred worries about you, but I'm sure you're a good driver."

Marian said, "Of course she is. I taught her."

Rupert put his hand out. "Thank you, Pauline. After all this time, I kind of gave up the idea I'd ever know any of my ma's family."

"I forgot to keep looking, too," said Pauline. "With the fire and all the excitement building the cabin, you and Jenny getting along so…"

Marian interrupted, "Do you love my Jenny, Rupert?"

He put a hand to the back of his neck. Color rose in his cheeks. He looked at Jenny's mother. "Yes, I do. She's wonderful."

"And you want to marry her?"

"I hope to, someday."

Pauline met Marian's glance with a smile. Marian looked back at Rupert and saw that he was smiling. "Well, you'll have to work. Jenny said you'll be out of the C's at the end of August."

"That's right. I'll find work. I know we have to wait a while. Jenny will teach and we'll save until we can have a house and…"

Pauline interrupted, "Of course you will! Come Marian, let's go, it's getting dark." Pauline started down the steps. "It's going to be swell meeting your family, Rupert. Your grandmother is eager to meet you."

He took a step down. "Yeah, I wonder what she looks like. Maybe she has red hair like mine."

Pauline answered, "Come to think of it, her hair was a bit red, but turning gray. Goodnight, now."

Rupert followed them to the truck and opened the door for Marian. She looked at him and smiled. "I just had to make sure, Rupert, that you weren't rushing Jenny into marriage."

"No, we've talked about it, and know we have to wait."

Fred met Pauline at the door. "How'd it go? Any trouble with the truck?"

"No trouble, dear. We told Rupert the good news. He got excited and asked all kinds of questions. Marian gave him the third degree about Jenny. As long as Rupert finds work after leaving the C's, I think everything will be okay." She hung her coat on a hook. "Want some apple pie?"

"Beat you to it, but I left a bit for you. I've been reading about the dedication plans." He sat at the table and bent over the *Farm Bureau News*. "The ceremony will be held at high noon at the center of the longest steel span. Pearl Wanamaker, the state representative who worked to get the money for the bridge, will cut the ribbon. I suppose Governor Martin will come. It's going to be a holiday for everyone in Island and Skagit counties. No one will have to work."

Pauline pulled a chair from the table and sat down with the pie plate. "Alice told Marian that she and Thea are helping the Methodist Church ladies make lunch for the dignitaries. Alice is baking pies."

Fred looked up and watched Pauline scrape the last crumbs from the pie pan. "We'll have to get there early if we want to walk out on the bridge for the ceremony. Hank said they expect maybe three thousand cars. They're going to enlist some of the C's to help with the parking."

"Oh, no. I hope Rupert won't have to help. Gev said

she'll ask Hank to make sure we find his grandmother."

Fred said, "If I know Hank, I'm sure he'll figure it out."

And that's exactly what Hank did after Gev explained how Pauline had found Rupert's grandmother.

When Pauline walked up to get a bucket of milk that evening, he told her, "I figure we have to out-fox hundreds of people coming to the island. They'll line up on the Skagit side and will have to wait until after the ceremony to drive over the bridge. Tell Mrs. Strump to get an early start and come across on the *Cup and Saucer*."

"But how will they know where to go?"

"Tell her to tie a red bandana on her car door handle. I'll have one of my men look for her car, and she can follow him down to the picnic area at Cranberry Lake before the crowd gets there. You can be waiting at one of the picnic shelters."

"But the family wants to go to the dedication."

"Well, which is more important to them? Listening to a bunch of men talk about the bridge or meeting Rupert? It would be hard to find him in the crowd."

"I see what you mean."

"I'll bring Rupert down when he's finished his work. They can drive over the bridge on their way home."

"Thanks, Hank. It seems like a good plan. I'll call Mrs. Strump."

Chapter Sixty-Five... At the Dedication Picnic

Pauline woke early Wednesday morning. She couldn't see past the cabin porch through the heavy fog. She wrapped a towel around the bean pot and put the lemon pie in the picnic basket.

"It might be cold out by the bridge, Pauline, you better wear your coat."

"Oh, the sun will be out by the time we get there."

When they arrived at the park, fog hung in the tall firs. Families had gathered around many of the tables spread about under the trees. An area had been roped off for the VIP cars. The church ladies were busy covering tables in the new open-air kitchen shelter for the dignitaries. Up the slope, not far from the kitchen, a platform had been constructed for the band with chairs arranged in a semi-circle behind a podium for the speakers.

"Bring the basket, Fred. I'll run down and get a table."

Using a rolled-up newspaper, Fred brushed leaves and twigs off a table. Pauline covered it with a cloth and put newspapers on the benches, and then they sat and waited.

Fred said, "The sun's peeking through the fog over the lake. It should warm up later."

Pauline shivered and wrapped her arms around herself. "Well, I'm cold." She looked at Fred.

He said, "I'm not taking off my jacket."

"You would if you loved me."

"Walk around," he said shaking his head. "Wave your arms in the air."

"Let's walk down to the lake and watch the ducks."

Fred took her hand. "You are cold." He helped her into his jacket.

"Thank you, dear." They went down to a narrow plank bridge leading to a small dock. Several rowboats rested on the lake's sandy edge.

Fred jumped up and down making the dock sway and water splash up onto the heavy planks.

"Stop it!" Pauline protested.

"It's fun."

"You're still just a kid."

"Lighten up, Pauline. Why are you so serious?"

"I'm worried they won't find us. What time is it?"

Fred checked his watch. "Only quarter to ten."

Pauline looked over the edge into the water, and then out to a large platform floating about fifty feet from the dock. "How deep is it?"

"Will said the deepest part is about twenty feet. Looks like you can walk out a bit before it gets deep enough to swim. The kids can have fun playing in the shallow water."

"We should go back."

"Will you recognize Mrs. O'Dell?"

"I think so."

"You better go up to the parking area and watch for their car. I'll stay with the table."

"Okay, here, take your jacket, I'm warmer now." She looked up and saw cars filling the parking spaces. A woman wearing black slacks and a bulky red sweater stood beside a car. *She looks about the right age to be Carol. It must be them.* Pauline waved and called, "Hello."

The woman called back, "Hello. Are you Pauline?"

"Yes, and you must be Carol."

"It seems it took forever to get here with Aunt Olga fussing all the way about how we wouldn't be able to find you. Is that Rupert sitting at the table?"

"No, no. That's my husband, Fred. Rupert will be coming soon."

"Aunt Olga is beside herself, she's so excited to meet him."

Pauline walked up to the car and shook Alma's hand. "It's so nice you brought your sister to meet Rupert."

"Once Olga learned about Rupert, there was no way I couldn't bring her." Alma went around to the other side of the car.

"I don't need your help, Alma," said Olga.

Pauline watched Mrs. O'Dell, wearing a rayon print of purple, blue and yellow flowers, climb down out of the Model T. *My goodness, is this the same woman from the store? She's dressed up for Rupert.*

"Olga, this is Pauline Gunther," said Alma.

Pauline took Olga's soft hand. "Mrs. O'Dell, I'm so happy you are here. Do you remember me coming to the

Fabric Shoppe?"

Olga adjusted her glasses. "Now that I see you, yes. I remember you came in often, always looking and wishing, but not buying. Many young women came in to look. They were always short on cash."

Alma said, "You've met my Carol, Pauline. I'm sorry Phillip didn't come, but he felt he should mow hay while we have this dry weather. We'll just have to come again when he's not busy."

"Yes, Rupert is looking forward to meeting him. My husband is waiting at the picnic table."

Alma said, "Bring our picnic basket, Carol, dear."

"I'll bring Aunt Olga's coat, too."

While they waited for Hank to bring Rupert, Olga told Pauline and Fred how she had lost track of Ruby. "When my husband learned Ruby was going to have a baby, he said she wasn't fit to live in his house and made her move out. I was upset, of course, but Butch was a harsh man and I couldn't go against him."

Carol said, "Mom, I'm going over to watch the children's games. Want to come?"

Alma said, "Yes, I'll go with you."

Pauline watched them walk away. *They've probably heard this story too many times.* She turned her attention to Olga digging into her purse. Olga handed a tattered postcard to Pauline. "This is the last I received from my daughter."

Dear Mama, I am very happy. We have a sweet baby boy we call Rupert. My husband is good to me so you don't worry. Love, Ruby.

Pauline turned the card over and studied the faded

postmark, "September 1911. That's the year Rupert was born."

Olga said, "You can see, she didn't put her return address, not even her husband's name." She looked down at her hands and twisted her handkerchief. "My husband Butch lost his job and we moved to Oregon where his family lived. Well, I don't want to bother you with all the details, but after my husband died, I came to the island hoping to find Ruby." She sniffed, took off her silver rimmed glasses and dabbed at her eyes with the white handkerchief. "I bought the little store in Oak Harbor thinking she might come in to buy material or thread, Ruby liked to embroider. I asked the women who came in if they knew her. I met one woman who told me Ruby had died, and that her husband and son had left the island years ago. It broke my heart."

Pauline felt tears coming to her eyes. She put an arm around Olga.

"Alma invited me to come live with her family on the farm, but I didn't feel right about that, and since I had the store, I decided to stay here." She looked over at Fred. "How did you meet Rupert?"

"He came up to our house from the CCC camp. I think he was curious to see his old home. We've had some nice times with him on his days off. He's a good fellow."

Pauline said, "Rupert's other grandmother saved letters his father wrote. I'm sure Rupert will want to share them with you. I could tell you about his early life, but it's better if he tells you. When he came to Whidbey, he hoped to find his mother's family. When I showed him a locket I found in the house, he remembered Ruby wearing it, but didn't know the people in the picture. But now, I'm sure it's you and Ruby's father. I showed it to several people in town, but I never got the chance to ask you. I'm so sorry."

"Yes, I gave the locket to Ruby one Christmas." She patted Pauline's hand. "Dear, I'm just so happy that I'll finally meet my grandson."

Pauline caught sight of Rupert, smiled and excused herself. "I'll be right back." She walked up to the parking area. "Hi. Your grandmother is waiting for you at a table down by the lake."

"Golly, I could hardly sleep last night. What's she like?"

"She's anxious to meet you. Your cousin, Phillip, stayed home to work, but Carol is here."

Rupert took off his cap. "Do I look okay? I should have had my hair cut."

"You look fine. I like your new baseball cap. Come on." She took his arm and they walked down the slope.

Pauline gave him a little push when she saw Olga stand up, take a hesitant step forward, and then open her arms. Rupert put his arms around his grandmother. When she let go, she stood back and studied his face, smiled and put a hand up to his hair. "I'd know you anywhere. It's red like your mother's and you've got her freckles, too. Oh my, I've waited so long for you." She sniffed, took the crumpled handkerchief from her sweater sleeve and dabbed at her eyes. Rupert swiped at his eyes with the back of his hand. Olga reached out to him again and he gave her another hug.

Coming back from the walk with her mother, Carol called, "There you are Rupert." She embraced him and put her hand up to Rupert's hair. "Look at that. His hair matches Phillip's."

Rupert stepped back as if he wasn't used to so much attention.

Olga said, "Rupert, this is my sister, your Great Aunt Alma."

Pauline and Fred sat on a bench, leaned back against the table and watched Rupert and his family getting to know one another. She couldn't stop smiling. Fred took her hand.

She nudged his shoulder. "Isn't this wonderful?"

He put an arm around her and kissed her cheek. "Yeah, it's swell."

"I'm so happy for them."

Fred said, "According to the program printed in the paper, after the ribbon is cut, the dignitaries will walk to the Fidalgo side, get in cars, and drive over the bridge to come here for lunch." He checked his watch. "They should be arriving soon."

"Will you go up to the truck and get the baked beans?"

"Sure, I need to stretch my legs."

Someone yelled, "They're coming!"

"I hear music," said Pauline.

"Sounds like bugles," said Rupert.

People throughout the picnic area stopped what they were doing to watch. The American Legion Bugle Corps came around the bend leading a parade of cars decorated with flags on sticks. The cars brought state dignitaries, the Island County Commissioners, mayors from Oak Harbor, Coupeville, Anacortes, and Mount Vernon, waving and doffing their hats. Mrs. Wanamaker and Governor Martin rode in cars draped with bunting. The cars circled twice and then parked in the roped-off area. From there, the "bigwigs," as

Fred called them, were escorted to the picnic shelter where the Methodist Ladies Aid waited to serve them lunch.

Rupert said, "I helped shake the roof on that building."

His grandmother smiled and said something to him, but Pauline didn't hear because just then she heard Jenny call, "Rupert!"

Everyone turned and watched Jenny bound down the slope. Marian and Will followed behind. Jenny stopped when she reached Rupert and put an arm around his waist.

He put an arm around her shoulder. "Gramma, this is my girl, Jenny."

Jenny gave Olga a hug, and then Rupert introduced Marian and Will to his family.

"I think it's time we eat," said Fred.

"Do I smell fried chicken?" asked Rupert.

Jenny said, "Yep, you do. Mom said this is a special occasion."

Rupert grinned at his grandmother. "Jenny's mom is a great cook."

Marian smiled and took the lid off her Dutch oven.

Picnic baskets were opened and food passed around. Jenny, being her usual fun-loving self, helped make everyone feel at ease. Will and Fred bantered back and forth teasing Jenny and Rupert.

When the band started playing, Alma suggested they walk over that way. "Would you like to come with me, Jenny and Carol?"

Pauline watched them wander towards the make-shift bandstand where the Mount Vernon High School Band entertained the crowd with patriotic music.

Fred said, "Will, shall we go hear what the VIP's have to say?" He looked at Marian and Pauline. "Come along girls. Let's leave Rupert and his grandmother alone for a while." Reluctant to leave, Pauline and Marian went with their husbands. They smiled and said hello to folks as they walked across the grassy picnic area.

Pauline soon tired of listening to Governor Martin expound on how the island population would grow and bring new business. Curious about Rupert and Olga, she inched away and went back to them. She heard Olga laugh as she approached. Olga said, "Rupert's been telling me about Jenny."

Pauline smiled. "I'm sure he has lots to tell."

"Yeah," he said, "We have a lot of fun."

When the others returned after the program, Fred said, "Looks like people are packing up to get in line to cross the bridge."

Rupert checked his watch. "I'm supposed to help count the cars. I better get going Gramma." Olga got up and he put his arms around her and kissed her cheek.

"Can you come to Bellingham? I want you to meet Phillip."

"Maybe I can get one of my friends to drive me."

Jenny said, "Mom, can I drive him in your car?"

With just a little hesitation, Marian nodded okay.

Alma shook Rupert's hand. "Finally meeting you has been wonderful. I can't tell you how happy it's made your grandmother."

"I hope I can see her again real soon."

"Anytime you can get away from your work, come see us. We have extra beds." She looked at her sister. "We should be on our way, Olga, if we want to see the view and get home before dark."

Rupert and Jenny walked them to their car.

Will said, "Well, Fred, are you going to take the drive today?"

Fred shook his head. "I can't see waiting in line when we can come another time."

Pauline said, "I'm exhausted, I don't want to wait in line."

"That's how I feel," said Marian. "Will, let's get Jenny and go home."

They picked up their picnic baskets and walked up the slope to the parking area.

Chapter Sixty-Six... Plenty of News

Fred opened the *Farm Bureau News*. "The paper's full of the dedication. Come see these pictures showing cars lined up waiting."

"I'll be right there." Pauline wiped her hands on the dish towel and joined him at the table.

"Here's the *Heard Around Town* column. *Since the dedication four days ago, 3,114 cars have crossed the bridge. Islanders are bragging they crossed the bridge not once, but several times on opening day. They drove over, turned around at Pass Lake, and came back across to Whidbey.*"

Pauline said, "It must have been quite a job for Rupert and the other fellows to count all those cars, but I suppose everyone drove slowly so they could have a look-see. Don't you think it's time we drive over? I'd like to look down at the whirlpools."

"I'll follow the picnic basket."

She laughed. "Okay, we'll go Saturday and have lunch on that island between the bridges. What is it called?"

"Pass Island."

"And Anacortes is on Fidalgo Island."

"That's right."

"And there are two parks over there."

"Yep, Bowman's Bay and Rosario, and don't forget Pass Lake."

"Deception Pass, Pass Island, Canoe Pass…too many passes."

Two weeks later, Pauline looked up from sweeping the sand off the porch to see Marian's car coming down the dusty road. *It must be Jenny. Marian wouldn't drive that fast.*

The Ford Model T's car horn blared. Jenny parked, jumped out and ran to Pauline. "We have exciting news." She threw her arms around her aunt and gave her a big hug.

Rupert stood with his hands in the pockets of his jeans and a big grin on his face.

Pauline looked from Jenny to Rupert and back to Jenny again. "What is it? You've got something up your sleeve."

Jenny, almost dancing with excitement, said, "Tell her, Rupert."

Pauline looked at Rupert. "Have you been to Bellingham?"

"Yep."

Pauline hung the broom on a hook by the door. "Come in and tell me all."

They sat on the yellow chairs. Pauline rested her arms on the table and looked at the two smiling faces across from her.

Jenny said, "Gramma Olga sat in front with me so she could give me directions. We drove far out into the country to Rupert's Uncle Paul Strump's dairy farm."

"That's where Carol and Phillip live," said Rupert.

Jenny said, "It was so much fun, and Aunt Paulie,"

Jenny's face beamed, "that's not all." Hardly able to contain herself, she leaned back in her chair. "You tell her, Rupert."

"Gramma wants me to have her store."

"No!"

"Yes!" exclaimed Jenny. "He can live in the upstairs apartment and run the store."

Pauline laughed. "Oh, Rupert, I can't imagine you selling material to old ladies."

"I can help him," said Jenny, "I know a lot about fabric and sewing."

"But you'll be teaching."

Rupert said, "I know the store isn't in tip-top shape, but…"

They heard Fred's truck. He came in and hung his hat on a peg in the wall. "Looks like you're having a party."

"Jenny and Rupert have plenty of news to tell you, dear. Sit with them and I'll bring coffee. I made cinnamon rolls this morning."

Fred sat down and looked at Rupert. "Okay, let's hear your news."

Pauline listened from the kitchen as Rupert told Fred about visiting with Olga. "Well, my gramma wants me to have her store. I have money put away from when the railroad bought my land. I figure I have enough to pay the taxes and do repairs on the store. When I get out of the C's I can live in the upstairs like Gramma did."

Fred leaned back in his chair. "Sounds like you'll be staying on the island." He looked over at Pauline. "That fits in with what we've been thinking. We'd like you to have the old home place. Does that interest you?"

"Wow! Are you sure?"

Pauline brought coffee and rolls. "We don't need it. We feel it's really yours. We got it for very little by paying the back taxes."

Rupert said, "I can buy it."

Fred said, "No, we fixed up the house a bit, but now that it's gone, the place isn't worth as much as when we got it. It'll take a lot of work clearing out the trash from the fire and building a new house."

Pauline asked, "When do you get out of the C's?"

"The C's always signed up for six months at a time, and my current six months ends in August. Now that my Pa's family is gone, I don't feel any responsibility to sign up again."

Fred asked, "Do you think you can take care of both the store and the land?"

"He can, Uncle Fred. Can't you, Rupert?" Jenny stood up, her eyes shining, and put her arms around Rupert.

"Yeah, there's no hurry to build a new house. I'll fix up the store first, then I can buy a truck and go out to the property on weekends."

Pauline nodded yes to Fred.

He said, "Well, okay, that's settled then. It's a smart plan. The property is yours."

The men shook hands.

"Just think," Pauline said to Rupert. "It's like you inherited your father's property."

Jenny giggled and gave him a hug. "Oh Rupert, isn't this swell? Let's tell Mom and Dad when we have supper." She looked at Pauline. "Mom said we could take her car into town and look at the store. Oh, I'm so excited. Isn't it wonderful?" She gave Pauline a hug.

Fred stood up. "Don't forget me, young lady." He gave Jenny a big squeeze.

She laughed and said, "Come on, Rupert." She took his hand and started toward the door. "Thank you Aunt Paulie and Uncle Fred. Rupert and I have so many plans."

Rupert said, "Jenny, remember the surprise."

She stopped and dropped his hand. "Oh, will you bring it in?"

"Sure." Rupert returned with a cardboard box and set it on the table.

Jenny said, "It's for you, Aunt Paulie."

Pauline smiled and asked, "For me?"

"Yes," said Rupert, "for finding my grandma."

Pauline opened the lid. "Oh, my goodness! Look, Fred! Oh, my goodness, a kitten!" She took a small gray kitten into her hands and cuddled it against her chest.

Fred felt the kitten's fur. "It certainly has a soft coat."

Jenny asked, "Do you like it?"

"I love it!"

"We brought it from my Uncle Paul's farm," said Rupert. "There were five kittens and we picked this one for you." He watched Pauline stroke the kitten's fur up to the tip of its tail, and told her, "Now you'll have to give it a name."

"Yes, I'll have to think of a good name."

Jenny took Rupert's hand. "We better go so we can see the store and get back home for supper."

As Fred and Pauline watched Marian's car disappear, she said, "Well, this has been quite a day. Those two seem to have their future all planned, and it's going to keep Jenny on the island, just what Marian wants."

They settled in their rocking chairs. Pauline held the gray kitten to look at its face. "It has such bright blue eyes." She let it snuggle into her lap. The kitten started to purr when she stroked it. "I wonder, is this a girl or a boy kitty?"

"Here, let me take a look," said Fred. Pauline handed the kitten to him and after a quick examination, he said, "You've got a little girl."

"Just what I wanted." Pauline took the kitten back. "Her chest and tummy are all white." The cat stretched and yawned. "Look at her, Fred. I think she's a tired kitty. I'll need to make a bed for her."

"Let her sleep in the box tonight and I'll fix a bed tomorrow. Have you thought of a name?"

"I really don't have to do much thinking. I'll call her Snicklefritz."

"Where did you get that?"

"It's a name my dad used to call me. I think I better give this little girl some milk." She took Snicklefritz to the kitchen and poured milk in a saucer. The cat lapped the saucer dry, stuck out her pink tongue and licked her little nose, then stretched and walked away. Pauline decided to let her explore the cabin before putting her in the box for the night.

Pauline sat in her rocker again and thought about the last few weeks. *I have so much to write in my journal.*

Fred picked up his newspaper. "Here's a picture with Berte Olson on the *Cup and Saucer*. Have to give her credit. Now that everyone will use the bridge, she has thought of a way to make a few bucks offering site-seeing rides, fifty cents for a thirty-minute ride."

"When shall we go?"

"You're not afraid of those swirling whirlpools?"

"Not if we go at slack tide. It would be fun. Those jagged cliffs are so beautiful."

"I'll be more interested in looking up at the structure of the bridge," said Fred, turning to a new page.

Pauline closed her eyes. The chair squeaked as she rocked back and forth thinking about the ride on the little *Cup and Saucer* when they first arrived on the island.

Fred glanced at her. "Why so quiet?"

"Oh, I was just thinking how we came from Michigan not knowing what to expect. It took a lot of hard work fixing up the old place. We had so many ups and downs, but look at us now."

"Yep, I have steady work. We have good friends."

"And this wonderful cabin. Oh, Fred, I'm so happy we came to Whidbey. It's truly become our home." She got up and went to the window. "Come, let's go to the beach." Holding hands, they walked out, sat on Pauline's favorite log and watched the beautiful sunset.